Of Might and Magic

We Are Gods
Book Three

Lee Nash

DEDICATION

To Erich

ACKNOWLEDGEMENTS

As always a great many thanks to Erich for your tireless help in making me a better author. Without you, this would not be nearly as good.

PART
FIVE

~ CONSEQUENCE ~

CHAPTER ONE

Lance looked back at the carrier from where he stood next to the broken hut. He kept doing that. Part of him afraid that he'd look back and they'd be gone. He shook his head even as he put his thoughts back to the task at hand.

The trees that had been there, were completely uprooted. Most had been torn to pieces, but a few were on their sides, from root to tip, and it was Lance's job to move those. He'd procrastinated about it for more than a day, but this morning, Harvey had given him a kick in the arse.

He focused his mind on the tree in front of him and tried to imagine the wind picking it up. Nothing stirred or moved. He tried to put more pressure behind it, but was concerned about the balance. He wasn't sure why they wouldn't get Ellis to do this, as her ability to move things with her mind seemed a little more appropriate to the task.

Lance shook himself and redoubled his effort to get that trunk up off the ground without sending it flying. Maybe Harvey wanted him to practice finesse. It was certainly something he was lacking in his powers. He could send a hurricane through and clear the topsoil within a few hours, a day at most. There'd be some question as to whether he could control the direction and shape of that hurricane once it got going, which is why he hadn't. But could he lift this tree?

He wasn't sure how long he was staring at it before the edge lifted from the ground and it started to float in a slight wobble across the ground, in the direction his eyes travelled. He was concentrating so hard on his work, he hadn't noticed anyone come up beside him.

"Nice work," Ellis said.

He jumped, and the moment he did, the tree fell. Lance rounded on her, ready to give it to the woman, but before he could say anything, scarlet bloomed on her cheeks and she muttered a contrite "Sorry," in a very thick Scottish accent, eyes on the ground. All irritation faded in his observation of her honest apology.

Lance took a deep breath and sighed it out. "You want to take it from here?" he asked.

Ellis sucked air in through her teeth. "I really didn't mean to disturb you."

"Did Harvey tell you not to help me?"

She looked to the sky then away, and back again, but refused to make eye contact. "Maybe..."

"Of course." He threw his hands up. "No chance you'll ignore that?"

"Would you?"

Lance grumbled a little, but he didn't push. He probably would, but he knew Harvey.

He settled himself and focused on that same tree. He wasn't sure how far he was supposed to move it, but he assumed away from the debris field. Maybe he *should* throw it. He pondered that for a moment as it started to come off the ground.

"You sure this is what he wanted you to do?"

"He told me to move the tress. Clear out the area."

"Can't you just do a big wind push, like you did at the mountain?"

Lance let the tree fall with a thump as he turned to look at her. "A gale?" He felt at the back of his head where the tattooed eyes were slowly growing back. He was unsure of how that worked, but the others had told him they were faint and growing darker.

Ellis shrugged and looked shyly away. "I guess."

She'd been acting strangely since the turning. Then again, Lance realised, he hadn't really known her before that. Even having spent a good couple of months on the ground with the others, he hadn't bothered to get to know them all.

Harvey had been out every day with a group of soldiers from the carrier. Every day since they landed at the end of the meteor shower. Looking for those they'd left behind. Those who had been lost.

Deidra and Weiz were up on the Docker with that other scientist, making adjustments so everyone could get home. They went up just after the landing, and he hadn't seen them since. Kristin was leading hunting parties and teaching the soldiers about what to expect on the ground in this place.

Zim, Ellis and Bridges took turns patrolling the camp, just in case. Of what, was unclear. In case missing airmen returned. In case the Bahana men came back. In case there were more Giants that they hadn't known about. In case some other unknown enemy showed up.

Gordon had gone off on her own. She'd taken the death of Estard harder than anyone else. Though they'd only known the man for a couple of weeks, he had definitely left an impression on all of them.

Lance still didn't understand *how* those they'd lost had died. They should have been turning up on the field. They were immortal, that was part of the deal. If they weren't, those Giants who forced their lives upon them, could have just waited a couple of days to get what they wanted. The powers of the dead had never transferred, and Lance couldn't bring himself to mourn them. Not yet.

"You still with me, Sinatra?" Ellis waved a hand in front of his face.

Lance let out a growl. Kristin had infected all of them with that name, and he couldn't seem to get away from it. "I'm here."

"So, gale? Give it a push?"

He gave a nod and turned back to his work. Deidra did tell him he didn't need to blow through his mouth in order to make his power work, but he felt like he had more control when he did. He sucked back a large breath and started blowing, bringing more and more pressure until the trees started moving away from the hut.

Dirt and detritus picked up, flew past his area of influence, and landed where the air settled. Pieces of the damaged hut started breaking off and joining the rest of the mess.

From the corner of his eye, he could see Ellis nodding her approval.

"You think this is more in line with what Harvey had in mind?" Lance asked between breaths.

"I can't speak to that, but it is faster, isn't it?" Ellis smiled at him. He couldn't tell if she was flirting, or just being nice. He'd never been great at reading these things.

"I suppose. But all I am doing is moving the mess somewhere else. Not cleaning up."

Ellis shrugged. "Does it matter? I thought we were just clearing the area so we can build. I can't start bringing things over until you're done."

"Oh." He really hadn't thought about that at all. Hadn't really thought about *why* Harvey had wanted him to clear the area. His orders had simply been, 'start with the trees'.

With a sigh, he turned back to his work.

~

Deidra was still wearing a smile she couldn't wipe from her face. A week after such tragic events, and deaths, and she was happier than she'd been in almost a year.

She looked to her left at the man sharing her bed, still sleeping next to her in blue sheets. His close-cropped dark curls, his dimpled chin, hands clasped behind his head, showing off biceps just toned enough they could be seen as strong and capable without being athletic.

Dane, her love, her companion, her intellectual spar partner. The very act of seeing him had brought everything she thought she'd forgotten rushing back to the surface of her mind. She remembered herself more completely now than she had, even before the very first incident on Io.

She didn't take her eyes off him as he rolled onto his side and grabbed at the bedside clock.

"Good morning," she said softly.

With a grunt, Dane turned back over and smiled at her. "It sure is," he replied, and pulled her into a kiss.

When he broke away, she sat up and he threw aside the covers. He got out of bed, stretched, groaned and scrubbed at his face with both hands.

"I still can't believe you're here," she told him.

"You say that every morning," he responded. The smile on his face took out any bite in the words.

It was absurd to her that the scientists aboard this Docker had actually managed to get Io up and running long enough to bring them back here. She had thought for certain that the Station was dust when she sent it back. So certain, that she'd caught a lift with Zim, her protective pilot friend. Ulrich had agreed. It was surprising they were even able to find out where they'd ended up. The marvel was that they not only *made* it work, even after all the direct damage to the core of the project, but they also managed to get the field to extend to the Docker.

They needed her to help put something together here on the Docker, however, which was why she was *supposed* to be up here.

Dane finished dressing and looked down at her. "You plan on getting out of bed today?"

She chuckled at him. "I was thinking of taking a day off," she joked, but threw aside the sheets to reveal her naked form.

Dane immediately held a hand in front of his eye. "No." He put up his other hand in a stop motion. "Not fair. Don't do it." He turned on a heel, removed his hand from his face, and walked out the door with a, "See you at work!"

Deidra just couldn't wipe the smile from her face.

~

Harvey took a look around the cleared zone at the bottom of the mountain. He didn't expect they'd find anyone here. The ones they'd left behind that first time would know they were too late, and either head back toward the camp, or go and find a place to settle down in the belief they would not get home. Or they were dead. Somewhere out there.

With a shake of his head, he took a step and was back at their first landing sight. The mountain seemed to have stopped growing. At least, visibly. The MM ships had all rolled to the bottom facing toward the north.

The plain had been gouged and rent by the meteor shower, leaving dirt runnels and mounds. Some of the trees toward the west were now leaning toward the forest at a forty-five-degree angle, while others were blown to pieces, chunks and stumps littering the edge of the woods.

Some of the soldiers who had come down from the Docker were rooting around in the wrecked ships, pulling out anything they thought might be useful. Harvey wasn't sure why, since they had come prepared with equipment, and most of the ships had already been butchered. But he let them have at it.

Nyugen was on watch and looking straight at him when he appeared. Harvey walked over to him.

"No sign of anyone?" Harvey asked before he stopped in front of the man.

A brief shake of the head. "Not since you asked..." Nyugen lifted his right hand to look at his watch. "Two hours ago," he finished.

Harvey nodded. He hadn't expected there would be. He wasn't expecting to find them anywhere he'd already been. But he couldn't help himself. If there were others alive down here, he wanted to find them. And if they weren't alive, he wanted to find their bodies, so they could grieve their loss.

With a sigh, Harvey gave a final nod to the soldier, took a step, and was on the first deck of the Docker, in the General Briefing Room. The room was empty, but he knew the others would be on their way. They had agreed on briefing times to keep each other appraised of what was happening in their respective areas.

He didn't have to wait long before Colonel Sumner walked in, Weiz, Deidra and Private Miller in tow.

"Colonel, Commander, Doctor, Private," he greeted each in turn. It was strange calling Weiz Commander again, but she didn't seem to mind too much.

They all took a seat at the available table, Sumner at the head, leading the proceedings.

"Who wants to start?" asked the Colonel.

Deidra cleared her throat. "I've made a good start on the frequency generator. Doctor Hans is still trying to find the required materials for a light speed propulsion device. The work is much smoother with my team available, Colonel, so I don't imagine it should take us too long to have it up and running. A month at the outside."

Once it was clear she was finished, Sumner turned to Weiz. "Commander?"

Weiz inclined her head in respect. "I've had my navigators mapping the stars from this position, using the coordinates given to us by Doctor Ward and Hans. My airmen are running hourly patrols, keeping an eye out for the Bahana men. No sign yet."

"And you're mapping the world?" The Colonel prompted.

"Yes," Weiz confirmed. "As well as it can be mapped from space."

The Colonel looked back at Deidra. "Do you think any of the scientists would be able to adapt any of our ships for effective in atmosphere flight?"

Deidra shook her head. "Adapting a fuel source for gravity affected propulsion is not an easy thing to do. And remaking hulls for aerodynamics, inertia compensation, cabin pressure..." The Scientist gave a shrug. "I have Doctor Adamu gathering what he can from the scrapped ships on the ground to make something more suitable for long distance in-atmosphere flight. But truthfully, we should be finished with the frequency generator and light speed propulsion long before that would be done."

"Assuming we decide to establish a colony here, I don't see that as being a problem, Doctor." Sumner turned his attention to Harvey. "Captain?"

"I have yet to find a sign of our people. I am not exactly a tracker, so I couldn't say for sure. I may be missing some signs."

"You've taken some of my ground troops to take a look through the surrounding areas?"

"I have." Harvey stroked at his chin, shaved only yesterday. That was something Weiz had been very happy about. No more beard.

"What else have you managed down there?" Sumner asked after it was clear Harvey didn't intend to elaborate.

"Lance is finally starting to clear out the ground around the hut so we can start building in the area. Greenway's mountain seems to have stopped growing."

Sumner shook his head at the mention of Greenway's name. He

had taken the news in stride, despite what he was being asked to believe, about the man that he knew, about what they were all now capable of. He hadn't disputed their view of events or tried to defend his friend. Harvey had no idea what he even thought about it. But it was clear the man didn't like it.

"I'll send the carriers down on rotation," he told them. "I want all my men to have a chance to spend some time down there. I might take a rotation down there myself."

"Couldn't hurt," Harvey replied.

"We'll see," the Colonel continued. "I am considering leaving a group behind to start surveying the potential build sites. Maybe a limited construction crew."

"Are you sure that Earth Base would want to make a colony here?" Deidra asked. Harvey raised a brow at her, and Weiz suppressed a laugh. Sumner glanced at each of them but addressed the Doctor.

"Finding new places to send the overflow population is one of our mandates. When I tell Earth Base that we found a whole planet, and we won't have to supply long term food, water, or building supplies... Believe me, they'll want to send colonists here A-SAP."

One of the happiest moments he'd had in the last week, was in the realisation that he had a chance to live with his son again. As much as Weiz seemed to have some mixed feelings about it, he no longer felt the tear between home and staying on Eridu. Of course, it did depend on whether or not Deidra was able to stabilize the technology enough to be used multiple times without exploding. But if they could establish a colony here... He wasn't the only one with family that would be grateful for it.

"Any other updates?" Sumner asked, already preparing to leave the table. When all had indicated they were done, the Colonel nodded his head and stood.

Private Miller, who had been standing silently behind the man, moved toward the door and held it open until Sumner walked through, then followed on his heels. Deidra was almost as hasty in her departure, giving them all a muttered goodbye. Harvey completely understood, and it was hard to keep the cheeky grin from his face.

Alone now with Weiz, he gave a smile. "Been a couple of days..." he said suggestively. There was something about being clean and having access to a bed that really helped things flow in that direction.

"John." She put a little exasperation in her tone, but he could tell she was amused. "You have much to do, as do I."

"What? Paperwork and patrolling? It can wait an hour." He was aware he was in the realm of pleading, but he was in a good mood and felt playful.

She waved his suggestion away as she pushed herself up from the table. "We have, unlike most people, an eternity for such things." Weiz blew him a kiss and practically ran out the door.

Harvey breathed a sigh, laughed to himself a little, then took a step into the woods of his new home.

Back to work, however fruitless he felt it may be at times. Maybe Kristin knew something. There was only one way to find out.

~

In a way, it was nice to be around ground troops again. They knew how to travel through terrain without being told. Understood how to be quiet, and when to make noise. They may not have known all the strange animals in this place, but they did understand how such things tended to work.

Kristin currently had her attention on a deer. In the months they'd spent on this world, she'd not seen one. She didn't know if they were rare, or pests, or well-regulated by predators. Either way, she planned on making it dinner for those who were on the ground with her.

They were in the wooded area at the base of the city mountain.

Harvey had taken them there to scout around in the hopes of running into some of the lost airmen.

"I feel like a bow and arrow would be better than a sidearm for this," whispered Duwali beside her.

Kristin gave a nod without taking her eyes off the prize. "I hear you. But we have to use what we got."

The man was more of a purest hunter, and she found she liked him. Quiet unless he had something worth saying, and everything was relevant and considered. A rarity in people.

With a steady breath, Kristin held up her pistol and sighted. Head or heart? The angle she had on it, assuming it didn't shift suddenly from where it was grazing, dictated a heart shot. If she missed the heart, even if she hit it, it might run off and they'd have difficulty keeping up. Then it would take too long to die, and the meat would be tough. Edible, but not great.

Kristin breathed out, held her breath for a second and took her shot.

The sound caused a few unseen birds to scatter into the sky. One of the soldiers behind her muttered, "Very nice, ma'am." The doe fell on its side, gasping for breath.

Kristin brought the gun down and holstered it. She walked over to it and looked down. On closer inspection, there were a few minor differences in face shape and musculature between whatever this was and a doe, but it was close enough that Kristin didn't think it mattered. She just hoped it wasn't in some way poisonous.

Duwali leaned down and checked the pulse of the doe, nodded to himself, then grabbed it by the legs and heaved it over his shoulders. They'd string it up in their small camp two clicks west. Bleed it, gut it, butcher it, and have Harvey take a portion over to the others at the landing site.

Just as they started on their way back to camp, Harvey appeared right in front of Kristin's face, making her take a step back. "Fuck,

Harvey," she growled.

"Too close?"

"You think?" Kristin took a step to the side and moved around him. He turned on his heel and fell in beside her.

"Anything?" Harvey asked after a while.

She pointed with her thumb behind her without looking back. "Deer."

Harvey took a look and nodded. "Not what I meant, but that's good news."

"I know what you meant."

She wasn't mad at him, not really. She just felt the need to put some distance between them. Well, between herself and everyone, really.

After the Firestorm, as she thought of it, she had been the one to go back and find the bodies of Hadley, Estard and Fyord. And while she had not been particularly close to any of them, looking down at these 'Giants', unmoving, missing pieces of themselves, and not disappearing, she felt herself disconnect. She could still function, do her job, be useful. But a part of her was contemplating her own mortality, which was something she had not even done when she was technically mortal.

All Deidra would say, was that it might take time for the bodies to disappear and, possibly recoalesce. She didn't know if they were really dead or just dead for now. Given the shape of the bodies, it was a new situation. But it had been over a week at this point, with no sign of those bodies going anywhere. Harvey took her to check them every day. At some point, though, they would need to bury them. She didn't think they were coming back.

They arrived back at their small camp, where Private Li started covering up their small firepit, Duwali, with help from Henson, strung up the doe and slit its throat, and Forsythe started packing everyone's kits in preparation for the move back to base camp.

Harvey stood by the edge of the clearing scratching at his clean shave. She knew he was waiting for her, pretending not to notice her dissociation.

"I take it there are no updates on your end," she tried as she stopped next to him, kicking a small cloud of dirt into the air.

"Same as always," he breathed.

"How are Weiz and Deidra?"

"I didn't think it was possible for Deidra to be so happy. She was always so serious, and her..." He pointed to his own head, at a loss for words. "But she is. And she seems to be keeping her own mind in there somehow."

Kristin waited. She wasn't about to ask twice concerning the woman who had looked at her as rival rather than an airman. They'd never quite been able to work out their differences and get along. Kristin put that down to age.

"Weiz is fine," Harvey shook his head as if to contradict the statement. "Busy ordering the airmen upstairs around. Organizing patrols, doing paperwork. All the fun stuff we used to do, not too long ago, I think you may recall."

"I might recall." A small smile touched her lips but faded quickly. She'd find her sense of humour again, perhaps quicker than she thought.

After a long and uncomfortable silence, Kristin took a deep breath. "No sign of the Bahana men?" She knew the answer even before Harvey shook his head.

"Nothing." The man turned a full, slow circle, as if a survey of the camp would give him some answers. "No way to track them. Don't know where they went or where they came from."

"Any chance they have cloaking tech?"

"Hmph. Anything is possible."

They descended into another silence as they waited for the soldiers. As soon as the doe was completely drained, Duwali took it down, and gave Kristin a nod. Henson removed the rope from the tree, Li and Forsythe picked up the packs, and they were ready to go.

Harvey moved into an accessible position, and everyone laid a hand on him. Just as Harvey took his step forward, Kristin spied someone at the corner of her eye watching them from the woods. But they were already next to the carrier.

Kristin gripped at Harvey's arm to make sure she had his attention. "Go back, now!" she told him.

He looked askance at her, but he moved without a word. She knew he trusted her completely.

They moved back to exactly the same spot they'd been standing in, and Kristin faced the place where she'd caught a glimpse. And right there, a hint of blue uniform as whoever it was turned their back on them, probably unaware of their return. She pointed for Harvey. "There!"

Harvey took a step, and they were in front of the airman.

A mix of emotions played across the airman's face in quick succession. Shock, relief, scepticism, anger and finally relief again. Kristin knew the face but couldn't pick the name.

"Sir," the man breathed. He looked the worse for wear. Cheeks a little sunken, lips drained of colour, dark rings under the eyes. The smell was less than appealing, though Kristin tried not to let that show.

"Airman," Harvey acknowledged. "Are you alone? Are there others?"

The man nodded slowly. "A few," he said. "Come." As though the short sentences were all he could manage.

Kristin wanted to know more, and she could tell from Harvey's face he felt the same. Where had they been? Why had they not found them before now? Why did he look so close to death?

Despite the desire to know, neither interrogated the man. They simply followed at a respectful distance, while he slowly led the way.

Kristin wracked her brain for the man's name. She knew him. She should remember the name. It was important.

They hadn't gone far before a feeling of danger washed over her. The hair on the back of her neck stood at attention and she found herself looking around, checking the surrounding area for movement or anything out of the ordinary. She tried to shake the feeling off, but it wouldn't budge.

The clearing the airman led them to was empty. Kristin and Harvey shared a glance that didn't go unnoticed by the man. He looked to each of them in turn with something like apology, but still said nothing, simply brought his hand up to his mouth and blew a whistle through thumb and forefinger.

A few moments later, Kristin felt something pushed into the base of her spine. She looked over at Harvey with alarm, but he was halfway through a shift already, the man who had been behind him stretching out a hand for his shoulder.

"One for one," she heard someone say as she turned with the intention of hitting the person behind her. But whatever was pressed into her back clamped down, and she was unable to move.

No more than a few seconds had passed, and she felt a hand on her shoulder that she was sure belonged to Harvey. So, when she was transported, she was not surprised. But when she turned and saw no one, and nothing but walls, Kristin became afraid.

Chapter Two

He was almost halfway done. With Ellis beside him, giving him discreet direction, Lance had made quick work of clearing the area. He was a little concerned with the dirt barrier that was building up around the edges of the site, but he kept going.

It was hard, keeping control in this manner. He felt himself wearing down, like a hole was growing in his middle. It was becoming harder to breathe, and a few times his vision blurred, but he shook it off and persisted.

Since the first day, Lance had barely used his powers. He'd not felt the need to. He had to figure it was like a muscle that needed an occasional workout, but he felt that muscle tightening with the strain.

He stopped after a short sweep and sat down on the bare ground. Ellis looked down at him a moment before joining him.

"I just need a break," he told her, breathing like he'd run a marathon. "Don't suppose you'd help now?" he asked, hopeful.

She smiled at him but shook her head. "My job is making sure you do your job. After you're done, I'll be helping with the building." She looked him up and down. "I might feel like you look at the end."

He grunted at her, then leaned back on his elbows head tilted toward the sky, a step away from falling on his back.

"I just need a moment." The longer he was still, the greater that feeling in his middle grew. It was somewhere between nausea and gas. The pressure was building, a headache forming from the bridge of his nose and radiating along the sides of his head.

He wasn't sure if lying down was better or worse than standing up. If stopping was better than continuing. But he didn't have the strength to get up, so he let himself fall back. He pushed his palms into his eyes and breathed deep.

"Lance," said Ellis with some alarm.

"What?" He croaked.

"You're arching."

He couldn't even manage to ask what that meant. Instead, a steady stream of *something* pushed its way from his stomach, up into the air through his open mouth. He tried to open his eyes to see what was happening, but the best he could manage was to blink. He could hear Ellis talking, but he couldn't make out what she was saying.

As quickly as it had come on, it stopped. When he opened his eyes and looked to the sky directly above him, a dark storm cloud shot through with lightning, arching out in all directions, had formed.

"Well," he breathed. "That happened." He didn't know what else to say. He felt much better.

The dark cloud was still rising. None of the lightning had, as yet, struck the ground. But it was clearly only a matter of time, given the rate at which the thing was growing. He actually started to worry.

"Can you fix that?" Ellis asked.

Lance shook his head, eyes still on the sky. "Wouldn't have the first clue how."

"Could you move it?"

With a shrug, he said, "I could try."

Just as he was about to put all his effort behind a push that would move that cloud away, Harvey appeared directly in front of him. He could only see the man's head, and was about to shoo him away, but stopped at the words, "They have Kristin!" shouted in his face.

Lance got a sinking feeling in the pit of his stomach that made him worry another bout of storm cloud was coming on. He remembered the knives cutting into him. He felt at the back of his head where the eyes were coming back. He grimaced and clenched his hands into fists, storm cloud above completely driven from his thoughts.

"Let's go get her," he said, ready to go. Though he knew, logically, it would not be that simple.

Harvey growled. "I don't know where to go."

"Can't you just use her as the locus of your shift?" Lance asked, confused.

"If I could do that, don't you think we'd have found all our missing people by now?"

Before Lance could respond, Ellis cleared her throat. "Lance."

He snapped his attention to her, and she pointed to the sky with raised eyebrows. It was starting to get very, very dark where they were standing. How intense was this storm going to be? Should he mention it to Harvey right now? Probably not.

"I have to take care of this, Harvey, just a moment." Lance gathered the pressure inside him that he associated with a gale force wind, much as he'd been using on the ground. But this time, he directed it at the sky and willed it in the opposite direction. The clouds started to move quickly, picking up pace as it went along. He hoped it didn't cause too much damage wherever it erupted into a full-blown storm.

When Lance returned his attention to the Captain, the man was pacing and swearing, smacking his fist into his hand. Lance looked to Ellis, and she shrugged at the silent question.

"We found Reeve," he told them, still pacing. "Or Reeve found us, either way." He grumbled something inaudible. "He was going to take us to the others, but instead he led us into an ambush. I tried to get us out quickly. But I wasn't quick enough." He stopped directly in front of Lance and looked him in the eye. There was a plea for understanding in them. "I wasn't quick enough," he repeated.

"You found Reeve?" Ellis and he had been friends, Lance knew.

"He's working with the Bahana men!" Harvey spat.

"Why would he do that?" He didn't actually expect an answer to that. There could be any number of reasons.

"I think the Bahana men have hostages." Harvey finally seemed to have the wind blown from his angry sails. He leaned with his hands on his knees, looking at the ground. "I overheard one of them say, 'one for one'. I think it meant, for every one of us they captured, he'd return someone. Kristin for Reeve. A human for a Giant. That is my assumption, at least."

That was not a happy thought. "We should go up," Lance said, pointing to the sky and holding out a hand. "We'll need some scanners."

Harvey shook his head. "We've spent a week out there looking for these people, don't you think if we could have used scanners, we would have?"

"Kristin is different. She gave herself a degradable tracker when she had her turn in the Docker."

"Bitch never told me that." Harvey looked halfway between amused and angry. But it was the end of the discussion, as the

Captain grabbed his hand, and they were transported to the Docker.

~

Despite the hope that the Docker brought with it, Gordon still couldn't bring herself to stay around people. Not yet. Perhaps never again.

The ability to read minds was not exactly something she had ever wished for. And the fact that everyone knew, now, meant that everyone was on edge around her. They were busy trying to make sure they weren't thinking things they didn't want other people to know. No matter how much she told them that she had to concentrate to read their minds, and that she didn't *want* to know what they were thinking, they still treated her as if she had some kind of plague.

She was unsure of who had told everyone what her power was. She was of half a mind to slap the person. The only one that she had spoken to like a normal person since that day, was Kristin. They were the only ones keeping a watch over the bodies, so they'd shared concerns and thoughts on the situation. No one was sure whether or not they were going to resurrect.

Gordon looked down at the sheets that covered Estard and the airmen. They were not pretty to look at, and dragging them back to this small open space, had been difficult. But she wasn't ready to give up on them. She refused to believe they were actually dead, after everything they went through, and the disappointment of having been chosen by the Giants.

It took a concerted effort to make sure she didn't fall into the trap of self-pity. To remind herself that the Docker was there, and she could go home with the others, and if it turned out she couldn't stay on Earth, her family could join her.

Gordon stood and dusted herself off with a sigh.

"So, you can die," she heard someone say behind her.

She turned quickly, prepared to fight. The man was holding a gun of some kind, pointed directly at her. He wore a grey uniform, and a look of curiosity. She eyed him warily, looking for an opening.

"We'll have to come back for them," he told her, half talking to himself.

It wasn't second nature, not yet, but a part of her mind tried to delve deep into his, to find those thoughts that would give her a clue as to what would happen next. Something that might keep her a step ahead or provide a way out.

"Come back?" she asked, just to keep him talking. She hadn't made a move since her first turn. She wanted to appear as non-threatening as possible.

"Don't worry yourself about it." The man raised his gun with obvious intention to shoot, and panic took over.

She ducked, and at the same time her mind clamped down on his. She hadn't read his mind. Couldn't work out what he was thinking. But in that moment, as she was scared for her life, the man fell dead.

The laser sped through the air above her head, even as he collapsed. In her shock, she wondered how she could possibly have dodged that, but she didn't spend too much time on it.

Gordon breathed out a slow breath and stayed in place a moment before she moved to check on the Bahana man.

He'd collapsed on to his side like a ragdoll. His hand had let go of the gun, and it was now two feet away from him on the ground. She picked it up.

On close inspection, she saw that he was blinking up at the sky. Not dead after all. But not able to move. She wondered what she'd done to him.

Gordon looked around for the first time, checking to see if the man had been alone. It appeared he had been, but if he wasn't, whoever had accompanied him was either hidden well, or gone now.

For the first time in a week, she wished she wasn't so far away from everyone.

She shook herself, remembering her cuff mic would work now. She raised it to her mouth. "Whoever is listening, this is Gordon, I have an incapacitated Bahana man at the clearing. Repeat, I have an incapacitated Bahana man at the clearing. I require assistance."

It felt like forever before she got a reply. "One moment, Ma'am. Commander Weiz is on her way."

Gordon tried not to let her disappointment into her voice. "Copy. I'll be waiting." She hoped that at least one or two of the others came with the Commander.

While the woman did seem to be getting her mojo back now that she was up in the sky, Gordon couldn't forget her lack-lustre leadership throughout their hardships on the ground. It was an open secret that the woman had become obsessed with the deaths suffered on the first day, and instead of getting on with the job, had focused her attention on Harvey.

Now, Harvey was a man she could respect. He didn't pretend to anything he wasn't. He and Kristin had held most of them together that first month. Making sure that people had assignments and things to do. Ways to feel useful in a situation foreign to all of them.

Gordon shook herself, uncertain why her mind was meandering, bringing up thoughts sorted and buried quite some time ago. She didn't hold any animus toward the Commander, or any special love for Harvey.

Just as she was about to seat herself, Harvey, Weiz and Lance appeared in front of her. "Do you always have to be so close when you do that?" she asked.

Harvey shrugged, "It's not deliberate."

"This is your man?" Weiz asked the obvious as she looked down at the man. His eyes were closed now, and she momentarily worried he'd died while she waited, but the Commander found his pulse and nodded.

"Was he alone?" Lance wanted to know. Harvey was actively taking a look around the area, appearing and disappearing.

"As far as I know."

Weiz quickly filled her in on what had happened that morning and what they were trying to do now.

"But you're not picking up a signal?"

The Commander shook her head. "Viatri here assures me that she has a tracker, but it's not showing."

"Is there nothing we can do?" She liked Kristin. One of the only people she felt she could really talk to, aside from Estard, and he was dead.

"Not until you got this guy." The Commander looked down at the man again with a frown. "How *did you* get this guy?" Weiz looked back to her with intense interest.

Gordon gave an uncomfortable shrug. "I don't know."

"Something to do with your power?"

"Something," she agreed. But she didn't know how to explain what had happened. It was an accident. She had no idea if it was repeatable, trainable, or something like a reflex.

Viatri felt at the back of his head. "It doesn't make sense," he said quietly. "Two in a single morning, when we haven't seen them all week, and their ship has disappeared? At the same, time we find Reeve? Did they have him the whole time? Have they been *here* the whole time?" He threw his hands up in the air. "I'm a pilot, not a detective, I wasn't made for this."

Gordon nodded in complete agreement. The man was echoing her own thoughts.

It wasn't long before Harvey was back, eyes still searching the surrounding area. "No sign," he told them. "Either he was alone, or whoever he was with teleported out."

"We should all go back up to the Docker," Weiz advised.

Harvey gave her a nod and went straight for the Bahana man.

Lance put a hand on his shoulder, and a moment later, she was alone with Weiz and the bodies. The bodies that she didn't want to leave.

"I know you don't want to be up there," Weiz started, but Gordon cut her off.

"I get it. I will come. I just don't want to leave them here." She looked around, still not sure he had been alone. "He said they'd come back for them. If they really are dead, and they can work out how, we're all in a lot of trouble."

"I see you're point."

Harvey was back and ready to take them up, but Weiz motioned to the bodies. He sighed, but didn't question, he simply tried to position himself in a way that encompassed all of them. In the end he kind of looked like a crab, so close to the ground, legs wide, arms wide, and an annoyed look on his face. Gordon choked back a laugh and heard Weiz do the same. Harvey muttered something unintelligible as he disappeared.

Having those bodies removed from the area almost felt like the end of something. She wasn't giving up on them. But she was no longer their sentinel, patiently waiting.

A few seconds later, Harvey appeared in front of them again, put a hand on each of their shoulders, and they were on the Docker. Gordon felt a momentary wave of motion sickness that passed quickly.

A look around showed them to be in the gym, almost completely empty. Three airmen were working out in there, in their own little worlds, paying them no mind. They didn't even look their way. At least, not obviously.

"You remember your assigned quarters?" Weiz asked.

Gordon gave a nod. "Bunk 1, 402 deck C."

"We should —" Harvey started, but whatever he'd been about to say was cut off by a very sharp shake of the head from the Commander. There was no doubt in her mind, that in that moment, it was the Commander, and not the woman.

"I guess I'll go find something to occupy myself with," she said to avoid awkwardness. It didn't work.

As she turned to do just that, Harvey put a light hand on her shoulder, and said, "They're in the morgue. I know it's not what you wanted, but we should consider giving them a proper burial."

"You do what you think best," was all she said without turning back, then continued on her way.

She could have tried to read their minds. Could have worked out what they planned, what they wanted, what they thought. But she didn't really want to know. Didn't actually want to be a part of the leadership in this place. She wanted to go home, be with her husband and her children, and forget that any of this had ever happened. There was a hope in her, that in some distant future, she would be able to look back at these months and see them as nothing more than a bad dream.

Gordon had spent a great deal of time on Dockers in her time as an ATF Pilot. More time wandering their halls than she'd spent in the cockpit of an MM ship. At this point, it was almost like a second home. But she'd never been to the morgue. She wasn't sure that was where she wanted to go now.

Caught between the urge to wash her hands of everything and hand in a resignation, and the desire to keep going and not give up on her people, Gordon turned on her heel and pressed the button for the aft elevator.

CHAPTER THREE

Deidra was in the middle of building the base for the tachyon frequency code, when Harvey came and stole Weiz with no more than an apologetic glance. The woman wasn't really necessary to her work anymore, and had no reason to hang around, but Deidra never admonished her for breathing down her neck.

Dane was in the lab next door, with a team of other scientists, building the lightspeed propulsion device from the ground up. It had a new set of schematics, taking into account the damage the original took when Io Station had made its first journey.

Behind her, another team was making the tachyon frequency generator. It was all going much smoother and faster with a team of people who knew what they were doing, and all the instruments with which to do it.

The best thing, she didn't need any of the knowledge that would have to be transferred through the Giant that shared her brain. She could think anything she wanted about the device, and because it was all things she already knew, nothing was removed from her.

With the team she had at hand now, even Heinrich was completely unnecessary. Thankfully. She regretted how things had ended with him, in spite of everything. But things were smoother without him.

She was still busily enthralled with her work when Harvey reappeared. Without Weiz. He waited patiently to the side until she looked to him.

"We have a serious problem," he told her.

"How serious?" Her gut felt tense, preparing for a bowling ball.

"Bahana men," he replied simply.

"Do you need me, or are you informing me?"

He scratched at his chin looking toward the ceiling. "We won't make you come, but we could definitely use your expertise in the area."

This was not what she wanted to hear. He had given her an out, but he also knew that she'd already made the choice to help where she could. "I've told you everything I know about them."

"Probably," Harvey agreed. "But, just in case, we'd like you there when we question this one."

Deidra put her tablet to the side, and she heard more than one set of shuffled feet behind her. Harvey looked to them as if he only just realised, they were there.

"You captured one?"

"Gordon got him. We're not sure how, and neither is she. But he's unconscious in the infirmary. We're hoping that you'll be able to tell us what happened." He adopted a solemn look. "I know it's a lot to ask. But if we can get Gordon to repeat it..." He didn't finish, but she understood.

Deidra stood and motioned with her hand. "Lead the way."

The infirmary wasn't far from the labs, so they walked rather than having Harvey transport them. She was glad, because it was an experience she found unpleasant, despite how many times he'd taken her along for the ride.

In less than a minute they were standing in the med bay with an unconscious Bahana man, Weiz and Lance a few steps away, eyes glued to a work tablet. They looked up and acknowledged her but went straight back to what they'd been doing.

"What am I supposed to do while he's unconscious?" she asked with a frown.

Harvey took a seat on the other side of the bed. "Unless you know how to wake him, we wait."

Deidra stared daggers at the man. "You pulled me away from my work to *wait*?"

"I told you he was unconscious," Harvey reminded her. "And I told you what we wanted. Don't go getting all catty on me now. I don't know how you do what you do, so that part you have to work out on your own."

Slightly embarrassed, she turned to the others, if they had heard a word, they showed not a sign, absorbed as they were in their own work.

Deidra let out a sigh and looked the unconscious man up and down. For all intents and purposes, he could have been one of them. In a hospital gown, dark hair cut short, olive skin, five o'clock shadow, scar running down the outside of his left arm. Though he was lying down, she judged his height at about five-eleven.

She tried to think of questions while she was looking at him, but she was drawing a blank. The only question coming to mind was, 'what do I want to know?', and that was not helpful.

Harvey was respectfully looking at anything but her, while she tried.

A few minutes later, when she was almost ready to admit defeat, there was a voice in her mind. *She's a mind reader and manipulator. If you want to reverse it, you have to ask her to do it. This man won't wake up on his own.* The voice sounded like her own, and yet it didn't. It was a part of her, and yet it wasn't.

Tatiana? she asked it, sure it must be the Giant.

If it makes it easier to digest, sure, Tatiana. Though there are not two separate entities, just one. Let's try this a new way.

I am talking to myself. She didn't think she wanted to go any further down that road, so looked to Harvey and said it straight. "You need Gordon to wake him up, or he won't."

The man made a sound of annoyance and disappeared without standing. Weiz looked in her direction and gave a tight smile. Lance was so busy studying whatever was on that tablet, he didn't seem to notice anything else.

A moment later, Harvey was back with Gordon, who didn't look at all impressed with being dragged there. If anything, she looked ready to tear chunks out of the man. It made Deidra wonder if he'd bothered to ask before stealing her away from whatever she'd been doing. He'd always been courteous with her, but that did not always extend to those he held rank over.

Gordon tore her shoulder from his grip. "What do you want me to do?"

Harvey looked to Deidra to deliver the bad news. "Wake him up."

The woman laughed and shook her head. "You lot can be so useless," she mumbled, but stepped up to the man, looked down with a frown, then delivered a surprising back hand blow across the man's face. That would almost certainly leave a bruise.

Deidra winced in sympathy, though she knew the man probably deserved that and more, given what they'd been doing to Lance and Greenway up on that ship.

"I don't think that's how that works..." Deidra tried. "If it were that easy to wake the man, then —"

The man woke up with a yell, eyes wide, pulling against the restraints. Gordon gave her an, 'as you were saying' look, and Deidra returned a frown. Harvey nodded to himself. Lance and Weiz moved closer to the patient so they could hear what was happening.

"As I was saying," Deidra continued, after the man had settled back. "If it were that easy to wake the man, he'd be awake. Whatever you did in conjunction with that slap, that's what matters. That is what did the job."

Gordon shook her head. "If you say so."

"Don't you want to know how to use your power? How it works? What the consequences are?"

"Not particularly."

Deidra was more than a little taken aback by the Pilot's attitude. She'd always seemed so nice, if somewhat withdrawn at times. She should know what the use of her power would cause. *Paranoia*, the voice in her mind told her. She wasn't sure she liked this new delivery system. Just knowing something tended be a little less creepy.

Just knowing is how you lost yourself. Direct injection. No immunity. That made sense, from what little she knew about biology.

Harvey stepped in. "We may need you here," he told the Pilot softly. "I know you'd rather go feel sorry for yourself somewhere private. But if we can't get anything out of him, maybe you can read his mind."

Gordon gave him a filthy look, but moved to the foot of the bed, arms crossed. It was clear the only reason she was staying was because Harvey was her superior. Given a choice, she'd probably never speak to any of them again. Deidra wasn't sure why she was getting that vibe, but it was strong.

She's projecting her displeasure. The voice again. *And I am about to project mine,* she thought back at it. It was absurd. If the voice was her, and she started talking to it, it might just drive her insane. Was insane better than forgetting herself? Right now, she wasn't sure.

Weiz stepped to the front of the bed and looked down at the

Bahana man's face. His eyes found hers and stayed there in challenge. They were green.

"What is your name?" Weiz asked.

The man stared stubbornly up at her without reply. Weiz asked again, and again, got no reply. Weiz looked to Gordon and inclined her head.

Gordon didn't move or uncross her arms. She just stared daggers at the man who had eyes only for Weiz. "Ensign Brioli Imoisin," she told them matter-of-factly.

The man turned his attention to her, hands once again straining against the bonds that held him. They were strong bonds, and not going anywhere. The bed itself was bolted to the floor.

Once the man had calmed somewhat, though breathing heavy and looking from one person to the next as if memorizing participants in a nightmare, Weiz asked the next question. "Were you alone?"

"Yes," he barked, before Weiz turned to Gordon again.

"Why?" Weiz gave him a chance, and Gordon shrugged.

The man's face expressed frustration as he glanced between Weiz and Gordon. Answer the question, or have the answer torn from you. It was not a choice Deidra would want to make. Though, if he answered freely, he may be lying. But he couldn't know if Gordon was checking to see if he was or not.

"Why?" Weiz repeated.

"Why what? It's a broad question," he spat, clearly unhappy with himself.

"Why were you alone?"

"They were scouting around," Gordon put in before he could respond. "Looking for us. His companion was injured by an animal and returned to their base. He was supposed to go with her but didn't want to give up so early in the day. He should not have confronted me. If he was going to take me, he shouldn't have shown himself. But he wanted to be sure about the bodies."

Weiz nodded. "Where is your base?" But she was watching Gordon. So was the Bahanian.

There was a very long pause before Gordon leaned forward, put her hands on the foot of the bed and stared into Brioli's eyes. The man looked away immediately.

Gordon shook her head. "He's thinking of anything and everything except what we want to know. If I dig deep enough, I might be able to get it. But I also might kill him."

Harvey and Weiz exchanged a glance, but it was Lance who said, "Who cares if it kills him. What they're doing to us is monstrous." He was feeling at the back of his head again.

Deidra could only imagine what it was like to be held by them. The feeling that she'd gotten every time she had tried to remember what had happened to Tatiana, was deep fear. Deep and abiding hatred. Extreme revulsion. And though Lance had only been taken for little more than a day, it was enough for him to share some of those feelings.

"If we kill him now, there may be answers in there that we haven't considered yet," Harvey told him. "Maybe Gordon already knows something, we just don't know if anything is relevant yet."

"None of us has the expertise for this kind of thing," Deidra told them. "But we have ground troops aboard. They may have had some experience with prisoners of war. Perhaps we could ask the Colonel?"

Harvey gave a grunt, but Weiz nodded thoughtfully. "Viatri, you know where he is. See if they can lend us someone more qualified."

While Lance ran off, Weiz turned to Deidra. "Anything so far you can lend your knowledge to?"

Deidra shook her head. "I really need to be specific. And whatever it is in here," she pointed to her head, "has to already have an answer. So, if it's something more recent? It's extremely unlikely I can add anything to it."

"And you still can't remember what happened when the Giant was captured?"

"No."

They stood in a companionable silence while they waited. Though Gordon looked a lot less friendly than she had been only days ago.

It's the paranoia. You should tell her. It might help mitigate some of the symptoms. Deidra wished she could tell herself to shut up, but she knew it wouldn't work. Instead, she looked Gordon up and down, wondering just how unapproachable she might be right now.

"Gordon," she started, getting the woman's attention. "Could we have a word outside please?"

The Pilot took a last look at the man on the table who was trying very hard to pretend that none of them were there and staring at him. Probably hoping he hadn't understood what they'd asked Lance to go get. It really wasn't something that she had the stomach for, herself, but what was inside her, certainly did.

Once they were out in the hall, Deidra checked in both directions. She wanted to deliver this news privately, as a medical doctor would. Allow the patient to deal with it in their own way in private.

"What is it?" Gordon asked tersely.

"Well, straight to it then," Deidra breathed to herself. "Be careful of paranoia. The more you use your ability, the more your brain will seek to fool you with falsities."

The woman's olive face went white. "Then how do I know how much is real? That what I am telling them is accurate?"

Deidra put her hands out in a calming gesture. "It shouldn't come on that quick." She assured. "It will start with feelings of anger, usually against a person or situation. Then a feeling of persecution or being targeted. How you react to that, well, that's generally a personal thing. You're not schizophrenic. Hallucinations are rare, and they'll come very late in the process if at all."

Some of the colour returned to Godon's cheeks and she breathed a sigh of what Deidra took to be relief. "So, I'll just feel like everyone's an arsehole, that their idiots and they're trying to keep me from my children. But they're not?"

"Essentially."

Gordon grunted and looked at the door to the infirmary. "And I should really do this? There is no danger of me getting false information?"

"Do what you feel you can. Remember who you are, and not what the Giant has made of you."

That seemed to catch the Pilot's attention more than anything else she'd said to date. The woman looked into the middle distance, clearly in thought, and giving herself short sharp nods. After a few moments of that, she looked directly at Deidra with a smile. "Thank you, Doctor, you've no idea how much I needed to hear that."

"You're welcome," said Deidra. "Shall we go back in?"

"Yes, of course."

They didn't have to wait too long before Lance was back with a Sergeant Alvarez in tow. Apparently, he had something like a hundred and fifty hours of interrogation time in Earth based wars. Once a person was in the ATF they had to swear off all domestic conflict, due to the nature and makeup of the organization, but old biases were sometimes hard to let go of, and the way he checked out Gordon could have been appreciation or disgust. With that face it was hard to tell.

The man looked around fifty years old, with a severe jaw, dark olive skin, greying black hair, and dark-brown sunken eyes. He was short but imposing none-the-less.

Deidra's guess was he'd fought for the unification — or against, the ATF didn't take sides — of South America. What were once countries, now merely states in a coalition. Peru, Ecuador, Bolivia, Columbia, Chile, Nicaragua, Venezuela and Argentina. Though the countries had spent many years as allies against a Brazilian push, the decision between the respective leaders to make them a more permanent coalition was not as popular among the people as they'd thought it would be. The result had been thirty years of war between the government, and the people who saw it as illegitimate.

Why she was thinking of all that right in this moment, Deidra knew, was because she'd rather think of anything but what may happen next.

Sergeant Alvarez wasn't carrying any tools with him, so Deidra was relatively certain there would not be much in the way of torture any time soon.

"What do you want to know?" The Sergeant asked Weiz. "How I approach this will depend entirely on what you're trying to get out of him."

The captive looked at Alvarez with confusion. Because he'd only been speaking to 'Giants', he'd assumed they all spoke his language.

"We want to know where his base is," Weiz told the man definitively. "If it's on the ground, on the moon, under the ocean, in the sky, or on a ship." She looked down at the man. "Anything at all that will give us a direction to push in."

The Sergeant gave a nod. "Is this something you want to stick around for, or shall I notify you when I am done?"

Deidra cleared her throat. "If it's all the same, Commander, I would very much like to *not* be here."

Weiz gave a nod. "One of us will have to stay and translate. Gordon." Her blue eyes found the woman and held her where she was. "I won't order you do it, but I do think it should be you."

Gordon grumbled something and shook her head, gave Deidra a look, sighed and said, "Fine, I'll do it."

"Good, thank you. The rest of us will take our leave." She got

Harvey and Viatri's attention with a glance and motioned with her head toward the door.

Deidra was the first out. "In this situation, Commander, I doubt I can be of any use. But if you do think of something, you know where I'll be."

"I know where you'll be," she replied.

Harvey took hold of their shoulders and they disappeared.

"I do not have the stomach for this sort of thing," she mumbled to herself as she made her way back to the labs. She still had a lot of work to do. Made much easier by a team who had done it all before. But still, a lot of work.

CHAPTER FOUR

He took them to Hangar One. He knew they should probably fill out the crew with a Navigator and Comms Officer, but it wasn't necessary.

Weiz looked at him with a question in her eyes. They hadn't written up a requisition, and they weren't in the schedule.

Lance clapped his hands together, a large smile on his face. "Where are we going?"

"Dark side of the moon," he told the man.

Weiz groaned. "Why? I could just send a team out. We don't have to be the ones to do this."

"Are you ready to retire?" Harvey teased.

He was already moving toward the closest ship, a few steps behind Lance. A part of him felt as giddy as Lance to have a fully working MM ship at his disposal once again. He felt at the hull as he walked up the short ramp, the smooth metal cool to the touch.

There was a smell that was associated with new things, and this ship did not have it. It smelled sterile, like a hospital. Probably just cleaned out by the previous team.

Sixteen to twenty-four hours of fuel — twelve if they wanted to land on the surface, they'd learned. One thousand small rounds, two-hundred large rounds, four hours or seven-hundred kilowatts of dispersed energy in the shield. It was not perfect, but it was the pinnacle of a pilot's career to take charge of one of these things.

Lance was already in his chair powering it up, while Weiz held the button to close the ramp and compression door.

Harvey took a deep breath, ready to give the order for take-off. Lance didn't need it, but he wanted to say it, and the Pilot looked back at him with a knowing smile. He turned back to the screen, flicked it on, and made the faint outlines of his eye tattoos dance. The Captain couldn't help but shake his head.

For this moment, this one moment, John Harvey was a normal man, with a normal job. The past few months had not happened, were not going to happen, and had no place in his mind.

"Viatri," he said finally. "Take us out."

"Aye, Captain." He lifted them from the ground in a vertical manoeuvre and headed straight for the shielded Hangar exit.

Despite her initial reluctance, when Harvey looked back to Weiz, a broad smile painted her face.

"We can't forget who we are," he told her. "Come down to it, we're all just pilots."

Weiz moved to his side and held him around the waist. "I'm starting to dislike how often you're right," she told him. But there was no bite in the words.

The journey to the dark side of the moon was short and uneventful. Roughly an hour, with nothing to see, but the increasing size of the small moon. It was grey, much like Earth's moon, and tidal locked with only one face ever showing to the planet's surface. But it was probably a good third smaller and a third closer, based on rudimentary measurements.

Harvey didn't expect them to find anything. But if nothing was coming up on the scanners there were only a few explanations, and this could be one. The moon could block the signal.

He held his breath a moment as they poked their nose into the shadow of the moon, then shook himself and sat down at the navigation console. He thumbed through the screens until he found the one he was looking for.

It was almost like sonar, the way it flashed and spun, but it was listening for specific signals, not using echo location. Harvey trusted Lance's eyes, implicitly, without question. If there was a pilot who could man an MM ship without guidance, it was him.

"Anything, yet?" the Pilot asked.

"Nothing," he replied, eyes glued to the screen. "Weiz?"

"Nothing on the mundane eye, but we've barely pierced the shadow, if anyone is here, I think they'd be further in."

"Never be too sure," Harvey said. "If we start being too sure about anything, we may find ourselves missing simple things." It was something they learned early on, in the ATF flight program. Never be too sure that you know what is happening, keep your eyes, ears and mind open. Certainty was a killer.

Weiz grunted at his reminder but didn't respond.

They spent hours behind that rock, moving in a grid formation, surveying by mundane sight, using the scanner. They didn't know what they were looking for, which was half the problem. A spaceship, a satellite, a moon base.

Harvey shot out of his chair. "Do we have something in here that would scan the surface of the moon?" he asked. He could say with some certainty that he'd never used any such instrument.

Weiz looked thoughtful and Lance scratched at his tattoos. "Not here," Weiz said after some time. "But I believe the Docker has a specialised surveyor. They are using something like that to properly map the surface of Eridu."

"We can use that." Harvey rubbed his hands together. "We'll do one last sweep with the scanner and head back."

"I don't think they're out here, sir," Lance told him. "And we don't have much juice left."

"Do we have enough for one more pass?"

"Yes," the Pilot replied with a hiss.

"Then why are we having this conversation." As far as Harvey was concerned, as long as they were looking, honestly, there was no time wasted. Up there, in space, was one place where he couldn't just appear and walk around. With the breadth of it, he wouldn't want to.

The last pass showed the same as all those before. A whole lot of empty space.

Harvey expected Lance to just go straight back to the Docker, but the man waited for his orders. "Take us back, Lance." He couldn't keep the disappointment from his voice.

Those people still had Greenway, and though he could no longer get along with the man, there was no one who deserved what those people were doing to them. Now they had Kristin as well, a woman, who for all her faults, was loyal and always tried to do the right thing.

Harvey hoped that the man they'd borrowed from the Colonel knew what he was doing. That he could extract the information they needed, and not some more useless dross.

It hadn't even been a full twenty-four hours, and he was already getting frustrated with the lack of progress.

They were half-way back to the Docker when Weiz asked, "Do you think it's possible these people are from one of the worlds you can travel to?"

He hadn't considered that before. He knew that a couple of them were populated, though he didn't know the level of technology on those worlds. From what he'd seen so far, none of them were much better than medieval in society. But he had to take into account, that even in his time, on his world, there were tribes who eschewed the use of technology. Mostly the Amish and the Amazonians, that he was aware of. But more, on the African continent and across Oceana.

"It's possible," he responded. "But without some kind of transport, it will take a very long time to find anything."

"So, we'll take a ship." Weiz shrugged as if it was nothing. She clearly didn't understand how difficult it was for him to take more than just himself anywhere.

"Just take the ship," he said, nodding with sarcasm. "Nothing to it."

"No need to be like that," Weiz scolded. "If you can't do it, just say you can't do it."

"Now, I didn't say that." It was a challenge, he knew. She was goading him.

"Then stop whining. We'll take a short break when we land, have some dinner. Then we'll take a ship."

The challenge in her eyes, in here voice. An 'I dare you' tone that he couldn't ignore. Something he both loved and hated about her in turn, depending on the situation.

They stared at each other, but they both knew she'd already won. A smile grew on her face, while a grimace grew on his. Lance, preoccupied with flying the ship, missed the whole thing.

"Fine," Harvey said after a while. "After dinner, I will *try*."

"Couldn't ask for more," Weiz assured.

After a smooth entrance into the Docker, they disembarked. Lance stayed behind to hook it up for refuelling, but Weiz and Harvey went ahead to check on Gordon and Alvarez. If they'd learned anything useful, Harvey wanted to know before he tried to tow a spaceship across the galaxy to god knows where.

The halls of the Docker were more active at this time of the day.

Nightshift up for breakfast, Dayshift winding down, the Swingshifters running busily about. They had to stop and interact with at least a dozen or more airmen. Weiz gave out orders and listened to updates. They'd not been able to contact her while they were searching the moon, so some decisions were made without her, and she'd have to talk to Colonel Sumner.

Weiz took it all in stride. This had been her life before the disaster that was Io. Her element. It had been easy to forget when they were down on the surface for those months. It had been like she'd forgotten who she was supposed to be. But up here, she'd found herself again.

When they reached the infirmary, no one was there except the nurse, changing out some fluids on the sleeping Bahana man.

"Do we know..." Weiz began, and the nurse turned to her.

"I don't know what was learned," the woman said in an irritated tone. "I wasn't privy to it. But the man is fine, just sleeping, exhausted."

That wasn't what Weiz was asking, Harvey knew, but he also understood that Doctors and Nurses were a different breed. They frowned as much on the violence their team did, as the violence visited upon them.

Harvey gave the woman a nod. "Thank you," he mouthed and pulled Weiz away from the infirmary door.

"They should have waited here for us," Weiz growled.

"Oh, should they have," Harvey replied dryly. "We were gone quite a while. If they had something to report, they'd have taken it to Sumner. You already needed to see the man, so let's go see him."

It didn't take them long to get to the Colonel's office. They stopped out front and knocked at the door, waited until they heard someone yell, "Come in," then entered.

There were two desks, both facing the entrance. The one closer to the door was small and had a tablet dock, keyboard and monitor.

Though no one sat behind it, it was usually occupied by whatever Private the Colonel had following him around. The desk at the back of room, surrounded by a data bank, was large, and behind it sat the Colonel, writing something up on a tablet.

Sumner didn't even look up or stop what he was doing when he asked, "What can I do for you Commander?"

"Has Alvarez reported in, Colonel?"

The Colonel did stop then. He looked up with some distaste on his face, even though he'd supplied the man. "He did not provide any details, and he's off duty now. He did tell me that the airman that was with him would be down in the morgue."

"But he didn't tell you what he got out the Bahana man?" Harvey questioned.

"Not a peep, Major."

"Didn't write up a report?" Weiz asked.

Sumner shook his head. "The Sergeant knew he was on loan to you," he replied with a sigh. "He probably didn't think he was supposed to."

Weiz nodded. "I'll make sure he knows you're expecting a report on it. Thank you, Colonel."

"Commander." And he went back to his paperwork.

They walked out of the office and Harvey considered whether to shift them and make it quick, or just walk to the morgue. It was literally at the opposite end. Aft and three stories down, while the Colonel's office was next to the bridge. He looked to Weiz for a clue to what she was thinking.

Her brow was furrowed, and she wore a frown. "Why wouldn't he just report to his superior?"

"We'll ask Gordon," Harvey replied.

He didn't think she'd mind, so he just grabbed her shoulders and moved them to the morgue.

The lights were very dim, and Gordon wasn't facing them. She was sitting, back to the door, in a pose that made her look like *The Thinker*. He silently congratulated himself for not appearing in her face, which was something he often did. It wasn't on purpose, just how it had worked out.

"Pilot Gordon," Weiz said quietly.

The woman didn't turn around. "We would have been on opposite sides of that war."

Harvey and Weiz shared a glance then went in without a word. They stopped just to the right of her, where they could both see her face and she could see theirs. She didn't lift her head or shift position, she only followed them with her eyes.

"Alvarez?" Harvey asked after a moment when it was clear she didn't intend to continue.

"I am Columbian, probably will always think of myself as Columbian. It was the country where I was born. But when I was five, the Alliance merged into a single nation."

"We know the history of the area, Pilot. You're in the ATF now and forswear all allegiance." Weiz looked to the country patch in her fresh uniform and gave a nod. Pride of where one comes from, but loyalty to the world.

"It's hard to push through the paranoia, Commander." The woman did lift her head then, to face them directly. "Whatever it is that makes me read minds, it makes me think bad things about the people around me."

"And Alvarez was a hindrance," Harvey sighed.

Gordon nodded. "I tried to push through and let him know when to change methods. But I couldn't. I just kept getting angry at him. Convinced that he was trying to hurt me."

"Were you actually able to learn anything?"

"Nothing particularly useful," she said with a shake of her head. "Most I could filter out was that they have holding cells in several places on this continent. I don't know where they are, if they're above ground, underground, in a mountain. I can only assume that's where Kristin is, but I don't know for sure."

"It's more than we had this morning, Gordon," Weiz reassured. "Does Alvarez know anything?"

"I doubt he understood a word the man was screaming. He kept looking at me. He never said a word, but he kept looking at me."

Harvey reached out a hand, but let it drop quickly to his side. She was not the kind of woman who liked to be comforted. "Unless we absolutely *need* you, we will leave you be," he told her. It was what she'd wanted since the Giants had forced themselves on the crew.

He grabbed Weiz by the shoulder and shifted them back to the Colonel's office. "Go let him know, Alvarez knows nothing."

Weiz pursed her lips a moment in displeasure but said nothing. She simply entered the room, said whatever she had to say to the man, and came out a moment later.

"So, we'll scan the continent for buildings," Weiz breathed as she exited the room.

"Proverbial needle," Harvey said. "But I don't see what else we can do at the moment."

"We can still take a ship," the Commander offered.

"I don't know how you're so comfortable with that idea when I am not."

"I don't know either."

"I could always take you, and you can *make* a ship," he teased.

"I could. But then we'd probably crash inside a minute, when I forget to consciously maintain it."

"Catherine," Harvey said.

"John," Weiz responded in a warning tone.

"I love you." He could tell she tried to maintain her annoyance, but she couldn't.

Just as he was about to kiss her, Lance came bounding down the hallway, about as fast as he'd ever seen the man move. "We have a problem," he yelled as he ran. He came to an abrupt halt just in front of them. "We have a problem," he repeated.

"Well, what is it?" Weiz was peevish at the interruption.

"Best you come see for yourself."

Harvey sighed. It was another long day, in a week of long days.

Chapter Five

Even after hearing all about what Greenway and Viatri had been subject to, and the cruelty that these people inflicted on their kind, Kristin had a hard time imagining what would happen. Intellectually she understood, but her mind kept shying away from the thoughts and images that randomly popped up.

Her cell was very dimly lit, though she couldn't see where the light came from. It was lined with bevelled grey bricks made from a metal cold to the touch, probably steel. There were no windows, no vents, and if there was a door, it was well hidden.

By her guess, Kristin had been in captivity for at least twelve hours now, and no one had come to torture, interrogate or otherwise check on her. Which was a little insulting. Her powers were benign compared to some of the others. Maybe that made all the difference in how they intended to treat her.

Kristin paced the walls of the cell. Eight by ten strides. It was more than enough to lie down in, stretch out, get some rest. But there was a part of her that needed to keep moving in order to think clearly. If they intended to leave her alone for such long periods of time, then it gave her the opportunity to find some way to escape. Annabelle Kristin was not one to lie on her laurels and wait to be rescued.

If there was a way out from the inside, she was going to find it.

~

From above, it looked so much more innocuous than it actually was. But pilots knew what weather patterns looked like, and this one, was a doozy. He couldn't help but shuffle his feet and feel embarrassed, even though they didn't know it was his fault.

"When did that happen? I didn't see any sign of it this morning," Harvey asked.

"Ahhh, that would be about the time you came and got me," said Lance.

Weiz cocked a brow at him. "How do you figure?"

"Well," he felt at the back of his head. "It kind of just... came out."

"What does that mean?"

"I was working on the area by the hut. I took a rest because I felt sick, and boom." He clicked his fingers to add emphasis. "I was spewing out a storm. I blew it off and hoped it dissipated, then thought no more on it."

He looked down now, on the area where they'd chosen to start their new lives, and saw a roiling storm, with a lightning show taking place inside. It was roughly fifteen clicks across and moving fast. He figured it must have hit some opposing pressure system and bounced back. He might be the Weather Man, but he didn't know much more than what he was looking at. How they were caused, what stopped them, he had no idea.

Harvey shook his head, but it was Weiz who spoke. "I'll order our people up until it passes. That looks like a days long storm, a deadly one."

"I've been thinking about this since this morning," Harvey breathed, "but should I go get Reeve, too? Take a chance, to find out what he knows about the Bahana men."

Lance would say no way, not a chance, don't do it, but he knew it wasn't up to him. He found his eyes boring a hole in the side of Weiz's head as he waited for the answer.

"Might be our best shot," the Commander conceded. "But I cannot say that I like the idea. At all."

"In and out, I promise," Harvey assured.

Weiz grunted at him. "Alert the teams we have down there first. Get them up on the carrier. Then, and only then, can you go find our missing airman." The look on her face, and the way she wagged her finger, told Lance that she was as unhappy about it as he was.

In the end, Reeve was one of them. And so were the airmen that he'd had with him. They deserved to be rescued as much as Kristin, and if Reeve had a clue of where they were... well, maybe Kristin was there too, and they could kill two birds with one stone.

"You," the Commander rounded on him. "Try and do something about that storm from up here. Lessen the blow, so to speak. We don't know how many other villages and towns down there may be hit by this thing."

Lance gave a sloppy salute. "I'll do what I can, but don't expect much. I think Harvey and Greenway are the only two who actually enjoy their powers enough to have mastered them."

Weiz and Harvey shared a look that told Lance nothing about what they were thinking. Then Harvey put a hand on Weiz's shoulder, and they disappeared. As convenient as his power could be at times, he hated the finality when the man left. No way to call him back, ask him to wait. Not that he wanted to. It was always just so... quick.

Lance turned his attention back to the planet below. His eyes traced the mass of dark cloud that had begun to swirl around some invisible circle. A hurricane, enveloped in lightning, with a tail of hail clouds following close behind. It was hard to believe that had come out of him. But he knew it had.

He concentrated on the centre of it. He imagined the vacuum reversing, pulling the air toward the top of the funnel. His first aim was to get that part up off the ground. It would do a damn sight better job of getting all the Io debris out of the ground than he ever could, but it would also pull out most of the surrounding forest, and anything not solidly attached to a foundation.

Nothing was happening. Lance couldn't tell if it was simply slow going, whether he had to combat harder against existing weather, or if nothing at all was actually happening. But he kept at it. He had less than an hour before that thing hit the edge of where they were working.

He pressed himself up against the triple glazed glass and poured all the will he owned into the thought of pulling that monstrosity away. Into gathering it all into himself. He imagined a line connecting it to him and tried to reel it in like a fishing line.

Lance wasn't sure how long he was there with nothing happening when Ellis came to stand beside him.

"You look ridiculous," she told him.

He took his time, but eventually, he pushed himself away from the glass and looked at the woman. "Don't suppose you want to help?" he asked.

"Can't."

"This conversation feels familiar," he said as he turned his attention back toward the planet. He hadn't budged it. Not even a little bit.

"This time, I would if I could. But I literally can't." She moved to stand beside him looking out the window. "It's always strange to see a storm from above. So beautiful up here, so devastating down there."

"Are you my babysitter now?"

"You don't think I might just enjoy your company?" she returned.

Lance took a moment to glance sideways at her. He found it hard to believe that. He was good company, if you enjoyed jokes, hooning and a little lazy flirting. But they had never been friends. He'd not even known who she was until the mountain. And even then, it was brief and in passing.

With a shake he returned his attention to the storm. Now was not the time for whatever this was, and wherever this was going. He had a job to do that he thought might actually be impossible. But he had to try.

He clawed at it, trying to pull it back like a blanket. Sucked at it, as if he were pulling it back into himself. He pushed, and twisted, and wound it up in his mind. But nothing at all seemed to make it budge.

"Maybe you just can't affect what is happening on the ground from up here." Ellis shrugged.

Lance glanced at her without moving his head. "You think I need to go down there to do anything about this?"

"Maybe," she said. "But how would I know?"

"Without Harvey, the time it would take to get down there and do something about it, would make it pointless. It's already on top of our landing site."

"Where is Captain Harvey?"

Lance almost laughed but held it back. He hadn't thought of Harvey as Captain for a good long while now. And he hadn't even noticed. In his mind, they were simply equals now. Maybe he'd quit the ATF at some point without realising he had. Something to think on later.

"He's somewhere down there, I think," he told her, waving his hand in the general direction of the storm.

~

Rain pelted down on him in large droplets. The sky was dark, partly because of the storm, partly from the time. Trees bent and swayed, leaves flying off on the wind, and puddles formed in every small divot. It reminded him of some videos he'd seen of the onset of monsoons.

It was hard to be quick or stealthy in conditions like that. But he needed to find Reeve, to get him up to shelter with everyone else. Even if he did sell them out, Havey was sure there was a reason. Had to believe it.

He moved through the trees below the mountain, toward the area where Kristin had been. A piece of him was completely wary and did not want to be trapped by the Bahana men, and another part of him just wanted to rush and get it over with. He did not enjoy being wet while wearing clothes.

The rain came down so hard it was almost impossible to see more than an arm's length in front of him. Where caution may not have slowed him, that did.

Once he was into the woods, the rain slowed, if only a little, but enough that he was able to see relatively well.

It wasn't long before he came upon a body on the ground, lying in the foetal position, back to him. He rushed over to it, fearing the worst. The airman's uniform was worn thin and torn around the elbows and collar. Harvey pulled the person around, and an arm shot out toward his face, he batted it away and leaned back. It forced him off balance and he fell on his arse.

"Sir," the man said weekly. It wasn't Pilot Reeve, but he knew the face. He racked his brain for the name.

"Abramovich?" He wasn't sure and he hoped that he was pronouncing it correctly. "Navigator Abramovich?"

The man nodded his head weakly, his eyelids halfway to closing. The swipe at the Captain's face might have been as much fight as the man could manage. He certainly didn't seem capable of standing.

"I will take you up to the Docker, airman," Harvey assured. "But tell me, first, is Reeve down here? Are the others?"

Abramovich gave a slow shake of the head that was more like a wobble. "No sir," he breathed. "They have…" his words trailed away and he either passed out or died and Harvey couldn't tell which.

He took a step, and they were in the infirmary, Harvey yelling at the top of his lungs for a doctor. Meanwhile all the water that had lodged itself upon his person and in his clothes, tried to make a pool on the floor.

When Doctor Rowley rushed in a few moments later, he looked harried and annoyed, but he was all business. He indicated a bed to Harvey, "Put him down."

Harvey hadn't even realised he still held the man. He put him down on the bed indicated and stepped back to watch.

Rowley eyed him sideways as he performed a brief examination, but he said nothing about the mess he was making.

"He's alive," the Doctor said, putting his stethoscope back around his neck. "Judging by the paleness in the face, and dark rings under the eyes, I'd hazard a guess and say a combination of exhaustion and malnutrition. Right now, best to let the man rest as much as possible. I'll hook him up to an IV and perform some more tests. Just to make sure."

Havey nodded absently. The man would be safe and dry up here. After he was changed into a hospital gown and moved to a new bed. He could see the Doctor speaking to one of the nurses.

He wasn't sure whether he should go back down to the surface and continue his search for Reeve. Abramovich didn't seem to think anyone else was there, but from the state of him, he simply may not have known. Then again, he had been trying to tell Harvey something before he passed out.

While they certainly had to question the man, it wasn't going to happen right then, and Harvey standing around the infirmary, drenched right down to his pruning skin, helped no one. The Doctor seemed to have things in hand and wasn't asking questions, so he took a step and was in the Locker Room, right in front of his own locker.

Harvey hesitated as he reached a hand out to open it. If he was going to go back down for Reeve, there was no point in getting cleaned up. Another part of him realised he'd already made the decision, and that was why he was standing in front of his locker.

He sighed as he pulled a fresh uniform out, along with a towel and a bar of soap. There were moments where everything felt so surreal it might well have been a dream. It would make more sense than the things that had actually happened. If he woke up one day to find himself in a hospital on Earth, and the doctors told him he'd had some kind of mental break, he thought he might believe them.

The shower water was warm and inviting, but he didn't stay longer than he had to. His skin already felt gross to touch. He soaped up, sloughed off, towelled down and got dressed, all the while berating himself for not going back down for Reeve. No matter how many times he told himself that he couldn't help the man when he didn't know where he was, he couldn't shake the feeling that he should do something.

Dressed and smelling fresh, he went to find Weiz. He may not have Reeve, but they had someone who might know what had happened to the others. He should also check on Lance, it was clear when he'd been on the ground, that he hadn't managed to stop the storm.

He wondered how much of anything would be left down there after the storm. They had been very lucky with the meteors, in the sense that they were small and not explosive, but they had left visible scars on the landscape. And now a violent storm would pass through and collect everything not bolted down. It was just one thing after another.

Harvey didn't phase through space, the way he normally would have. He just walked the corridors much like anyone else, mind and body exhausted by the weeks of non-stop stress. It was time to go on vacation, only the job was not yet done.

He found himself wondering if he would be able to go back to Earth with the Docker even if it was short lived. A chance to say goodbye to those he'd never see again. To explain to his son why he was going to have to pack and move across the Galaxy, even though he had a life and friends of his own. How he was going to manage that, he wasn't sure. He feared very much that his son was going to resent him for what had happened here.

When Harvey reached Lance, he saw the man had his head and hands pressed up against the glass. Ellis stood beside and behind the Pilot, hands clasped at the back, and she turned her attention to Harvey as he got closer.

"He's been at this whole time?" The question felt obligatory and robotic.

Ellis nodded slowly. "Since I got here, at the very least."

"Nothing?"

"He doesn't think he'll actually be able to affect it from up here, but he is trying anyway."

Harvey thought about getting soaked again and made a sour face that Ellis looked at in question. Harvey shook his head at her reaction and moved over to Lance.

"You want to go down?"

Lance pushed himself off the glass and tuned to the Captain. "It might be the only way," he said, but he looked about as happy at the prospect as Harvey.

The landing site was engulfed in night and would be for the next ten hours. They had determined it was in fact summer on the surface, based on orbit and tilt.

"What will happen if we just let it go?" Harvey wanted to know.

"Hard to say," Lance shrugged, then felt at the back of his head. "It looks bad from up here, but maybe it's not so bad down there." His tone said he doubted that.

"Worst case scenario?"

"Everything loose will be picked up and thrown off somewhere. Topsoil, grass, the gutted MM ships, trees, etcetera."

"That's all?"

"That is assuming that it doesn't run into any settlements that we are currently unaware of."

Harvey ran a thumb across his chin. He could feel the stubble. He sighed, "Viatri."

"Harvey?"

"Sometimes, I think I might hate you." He stepped forward and grabbed the man by the arm. He shifted them to the surface, right where the town of Djorik had once been. There were still some people in the area, that he knew of, and he hoped they had shelter. He didn't think they'd fit in too well on the Docker.

Lance yanked his arm away. "Sometimes, *sir*," he screamed over the roar of heavy rain. "I hate you too." The death stare the man gave him indicated that now was one of those times.

"Just do what you can," Harvey yelled against the gale. The wind was so strong, the direction of the rain drops was almost side on. Though it was dark, and difficult to see much of anything, it was easy to tell from which direction the storm was coming.

Why did I bother having a shower? he asked himself. The sense of duty he still felt, not just to his own people, now, but to the people of this world. He hadn't wanted it. Had run from it, as Greenway had said.

He couldn't see what Lance was doing, but he bet it involved standing around and concentrating on the sky. Perhaps the impatience he felt stemmed from the fact that he could move instantaneously anywhere he wanted. Everything felt too slow now. Everything.

Harvey wasn't sure if it was his imagination, moments later, when it felt as though the rain drops slowed and the wind was not quite so forceful. He didn't ask, because the job was not yet done. Though what done was, he wasn't sure.

He scrubbed a hand over his eyes. Why did he feel so tired? He still slept. Still ate. Behaved for all intents and purposes as if he were still human, despite his power. Even up on the Docker just before, he hadn't felt this lethargic.

"Lance," he shouted.

The Pilot turned to him, and he could barely see his face in the dark. "What?"

"We have to go back up." He grabbed him by the shoulder and stepped onto the observation deck of the Docker. Ellis was still there, staring down at the world.

Harvey fell to his knees and breathed in deep. But even up here, he felt as if he could not get enough air in. He was starting to panic. "I can't breathe," he let out in a choked voice.

Lance looked down on him with some concern. "We should go to the infirmary," he said, and helped Harvey to his feet.

It wasn't far, but the trip was a blur in Harvey's mind. It didn't feel real. More like a dream happening around him while he had no control over where to turn his head. He couldn't get enough air in his lungs.

He must have blacked out briefly, because one moment Lance and Ellis were carrying him between them, the next he was in a bed looking up.

"I can't breathe," he tried to tell the doctor who was looking down on him. The person was so blurry, he didn't know who it was.

He closed his eyes and tilted his head back. When it hit the pillow, he gave in, and let the darkness take him.

CHAPTER SIX

She was not accustomed to him looking so weak. Laying there on the bed, face tilted away from her. He had an oxygen mask on and was breathing just fine now. Doctor Rowley said he didn't know what was happening, but he was looking into it. His first assessment had been a panic attack, but now, he didn't think that was a likely cause.

Weiz held his hand and tried not to let her feelings show. Colonel Sumner was on the other side of the bed giving her a rundown of what had happened overnight.

Lance had managed to lessen the impact of the storm, but it had still devastated large swathes of woodlands. As far as they were aware, though, no human inhabitants had been harmed by its passing. It had already petered out, and only rain and less harmful winds were raking the surface now.

There had been no news regarding the Bahana men, Kristin, Reeve or any of the other missing airmen, and Abramovich was still unconscious. They had not questioned Ensign Brioli again, and Sumner didn't think it was worth it to do so.

"We're sending surveyors down in an hour to do a full work up of the proposed site," Sumner said.

Weiz nodded. Her mind was not with the work. She found herself running on autopilot. "You need my pilots?"

"It would be nice to have a couple of MM ships on the ground with gunners," the man told her. "My soldiers have the training for ground work, but those ships have the best weapons."

"Take two teams. Whoever is on the roster for this morning." Her eyes never left Harvey as she spoke. "They'll be happy to get some time on the ground, so you shouldn't have too much trouble with them."

"Supply situation, same as yesterday," he continued. "Five months at full capacity. Easily rationed to ten months, without anyone suffering. Running low on soap, though."

Weiz shook her head. "Some of my people might be hoarding it," she sighed. "After our time down there without the basics... Do a locker check if you have to. But I won't punish them, not this time."

"Very well." The Colonel scrolled through his list of things on the tablet he carried everywhere.

Deidra hadn't joined them for the meeting. Too much to do and not enough to say, she'd told them. Weiz wished that had been her, much as the meetings had helped her find a sense of normalcy. To find herself again. The job had been her for so long, separating her sense of self from it was still a challenge. If she were not the Commander, not part of the ATF, then who was she? Something that Harvey couldn't completely understand, though he tried.

"Well, that's all for this morning," he continued. "If there is anything else I'll let you know."

Weiz looked up at him then. "And I'll do the same, Colonel."

"Very good." He turned toward the door, and Private Miller walked out ahead of him, leading him to his next duty.

Alone with Harvey, Weiz squeezed at his hand, and stared at his still face. Since the day they got their powers, she'd not had to worry about the man. And whatever this was, she shouldn't have to worry, because he was immortal, like the rest of them. But the thought of Fyord, Hadley and Estard made her nervous.

"Don't you dare die, you stupid man," she whispered. "I'll never forgive you." She stretched a hand out to run through his hair but stopped short. He'd always hated that.

A few moments later, Ellis came rushing in, eyes wide. "Where's the doctor?"

Weiz looked around, noting his absence for the first time that morning. "I don't know. Off performing some tests, I imagine, why?"

"It's Lance, he can't breathe." She looked back into the corridor then at the Commander once more.

Weiz got to her feet and made her way toward the door. "Are we talking a storm inside the Docker? Or has he got what Harvey and Abramovich have?"

"Near as I can tell," Ellis said as she moved, "it's the same as Harvey. I saw the way the storm built in him on the ground; it's not the same."

She was practically running through the halls. Weiz followed at a steady pace but kept an eye out for any airmen that might pass by. She wanted to alert the doctors to the contagion. If that's what it was. Did it pass through touch? Through air? Did they all have it now?

When they reached Lance in the mess hall, huddled over a table, he looked like he was in pain. He had a few people surrounding him, all watching on, but non spoke.

Weiz snapped her fingers to get their attention, and yelled orders. "One of you go wake the doctors, all of them. Get them in the infirmary and ready to work. You —" She pointed to the next person, who she didn't know and assumed was a soldier. "Go get

Deidra Ward from the Science Labs, tell her it's an emergency and we require her help. Take her straight to the infirmary."

The man saluted and shouted, "Yes, ma'am!" then was off at a run.

"The rest of you," she said and made a broad sweeping gesture. "Why are you just standing around watching? Two of you help the man up and get him to the infirmary. Everyone else, follow. We could all be infected."

They all looked at each other then, as if it was the fist time they considered that there may be a sickness on board.

Even with all the precautions of space, the one thing they all shared was the air. If it was airborne, the only people who wouldn't catch it would be those who were immune. From time to time, someone who didn't realise they were sick, would board a Docker, and within a week, everyone would have whatever flu they'd brought aboard.

When they returned to the infirmary, it was very crowded. There were only two beds left, and a line of airmen, up against one wall, ready to be tested. The nurses were taking quick blood samples and sending them into the adjoining room to wait for their results.

Weiz couldn't see Deidra or Doctor Rowley. She motioned to an empty bed next to Harvey and the two airmen who carried Lance put him down and removed his boots. When they were done, they entered the back of the line and waited their turn. There were some things that didn't need to be said.

Right next to the door was a palm sized red button inside a sealed box. It would sound the alarm and lock the Docker down into self-sustained sections. Weiz was sure that was only used in the most dire circumstance, and she was not qualified to know if they were in one.

It was a few minutes before the doctors showed up wearing hazmat suits. The only responsible thing they could do given the nature of what they were facing.

"Where is Doctor Rowley?" Weiz asked. He'd been dealing with Harvey and Abramovich thus far. He would be the one who had answers, if there were any.

Doctor Zalenka answered. "We do not know. We sent the airmen who got us to go and find him. If he isn't here yet, they have yet to do so."

Weiz grunted. Some people had a natural way of speaking down to those around them. Zalenka was one of them.

Doctor Namimbi got straight to work on Lance, who had passed out now. He didn't bother to undress him, he simply put on an oxygen mask, took a blood sample, and made sure he was comfortable in the bed. He got an IV bag from the locker on the wall between beds and set it up.

Doctor Horton moved straight to the nurses' station and took over, asking them to join the line.

Weiz felt like she was in some kind of dream. The kind that seemed real but had small differences that made things make less sense than they should. Things that everyone else saw as completely normal.

It wasn't too long before Deidra joined them. She, too, was in a hazmat suit.

Weiz waved her over toward Harvey's bed. A part of her knew she should line up with the rest, get her blood taken and wait in the next room, but she also knew she could get away with one of the doctors doing it where she was seated. Selfishly, she did not want to leave Harvey.

When Deidra reached the foot of the bed she looked down on Harvey with some confusion, then her eyes opened wide, surprised. That was a look that gave Weiz hope.

"Do you know what this is, Deidra?"

The woman looked to her with a straight face. "Hard to tell, but there is a part of me that suspects something."

"Harvey and Lance are both infected," Weiz pushed.

Deidra looked over at Lance in the bed beside Harvey. She frowned and breathed deep, then let it out in a slow sigh. "There has only ever been one thing that has infected the Giants. This may well be it. They won't die, not any time soon, but it does take them out of the equation."

"They're going to attack." Weiz's hands were gripping the edge of the bed.

"That seems the likely scenario." Deidra agreed.

"Is there a cure?" Weiz wanted to know. "Can we wake them up?"

"I am not a medical doctor, Commander, and you know it." Deidra gave her such a disapproving look she actually felt shame. "There wasn't a cure. If there is one, it will be up to these fine doctors to find. I can help them out somewhat, but my rudimentary knowledge of medicine may be more of a hindrance than a help."

"What about..." Weiz pointed to her head, all too aware of what she was asking. If she hadn't felt shame before, she truly felt it now. "Is there anything?"

"If it comes, it comes. It's how I even know what it is. I could learn how to be a doctor, should I so choose, but it would not be helpful in this case, so I don't see a reason to." She shook her head. "I'll assist. I won't leave until it's done."

"Of course," Weiz said.

"I'll be in the pathology lab," Deidra stated, then turned on her heal and exited.

Deidra was a good woman in a bad circumstance. She'd been relied on so heavily for everything since they'd landed in this solar system. Even before she possessed the abilities of the Giant. And she'd received very little in the way of thanks from anyone, only asked to do more and more.

Weiz grabbed hold of Harvey's hand and squeezed. "Our best

person is on it," she told him. Her eyes moved to Lance. "We'll find a cure." She had to have hope.

A doctor came at some point and took a sample of her blood. They left her there, next to Harvey. She wasn't sure for how long. A whole lot of nothing was happening, and she had duties to attend to, but she could not pull herself away.

More people got sick. They gasped for breath around her, and more beds were brought in, until the place was full, and the overflow were directed to a room across the hall. But she only noticed in periphery.

She could not tell how much time passed, but she knew it was more than a day when Private Miller showed up and asked her to join the Colonel in the General Briefing Room. He would not come into the infected area, and truthfully, she should not leave it. But she got up, and moved mechanically, her mind not completely there.

Miller lead the way, glancing back occasionally. Whether to make sure she still followed, or to see if she was displaying any symptoms, she couldn't say. But she suspected the latter. With how many had already gone down, she would be concerned too.

She kept her distance as she followed. She didn't think it was airborne, not at this point. But even if she was immune, she may still be a carrier, and she didn't want to be responsible for more crew going down.

It wasn't long before they were in the briefing room, the Colonel in his usual seat. "Commander," he greeted as she walked in.

"Colonel," she returned. She stayed by the door and didn't sit down. If there was one person on this Docker they could not afford to get sick, it was this man.

"My men and yours have been dropping like flies for the last twenty-four hours," the man started. "It appears to be the same illness that has befallen Harvey. I have no updates on this from the Doctors. Do you?"

Weiz shook her head. "Not for quite some time. But I have faith they're working on it."

"Has anyone died yet?"

"Not that I am aware of."

"Is it likely they might?"

Weiz took a step forward and pulled out a chair. She didn't know exactly how long she had been sitting in one spot, and therefore *should* move. But she was tired. Unreasonably, tired.

"You know as much as I regarding the nature of the illness, Colonel. Assuming the Doctors gave you their original assessment?" He nodded and she continued. "Deidra thinks the Bahana men sent it to us through Abramovich, and when they consider we're at the height of it, they'll attack."

"Yes, she had raised that concern with me."

"Then why am I here?" Weiz wanted to know.

"Because you are the Commander of the ATF Fleet. And while you're aboard the Docker, it *includes* the Docker." He knocked twice on the table in front of him and breathed deep. "I know that with everything that happened down on the ground, things have changed for you. I understand that, so I take on the responsibility. But at the very least, you have to order your airmen. You have to be in charge of the flight crew, because I don't know how to do that part."

Weiz nodded. "Of course," she mumbled. Then she cleared her throat, sat up straight and tried again. "Of course. Please forgive my absence, Colonel, I should know better."

The man leaned back in his chair. "Look, everyone knows about you and Harvey. It's against regulation and all that, but no one cares. We're out on the fringes most of the time, if you don't think there is some impropriety going on, you're not paying attention. But if you let it affect your job, you will lose it."

Everything he said was like a blow to the face. An echo of how she'd been on the ground those months. She'd let everything she was go and poured her whole self into Harvey. It wasn't fair to him, or to her crew, and she knew it. Not at the time, and not now.

"You are right," she agreed.

"Good," he slapped the table with a smile. "So, let's plan what we are going to do about a possible attack. Where will they come from? What are they likely to do? You know, strategy."

Weiz forced out a small chuckle. "Let's do it, Colonel."

~

She was a part *of* and also apart *from* the 'it' crowd, these days. She wasn't sure what to make of it, or how she really felt about it. It just was. Pulled into some things, and then left out in the cold with others.

Gordon hadn't left the morgue since their visit to question her about the Bahana man. She'd stretched, sat, walked, lain down, and done brief exercises. But she had not left the room. Not to eat, and not to sleep. But no one had come.

On the ground, Kristin had come, Harvey dropping her off and picking her up. Kristin had brought her food, and she'd stayed by the bodies when she slept.

Now as she sat, not even looking at the bodies on their tables, she wondered about Kristin. Where she was. How she was holding up, given the kind of torture they knew these technologists were capable of. The woman was a tough bird, but from what Viatri had said, Gordon didn't think anyone would hold up.

She was almost at the point where she was ready to give up on those on the tables. The doctors had done something to prevent the stench from becoming overpowering, but it wasn't enough. They'd suggested she put them in the draws where they belonged, but she didn't want them waking inside a metal tube. Even though she understood that if they woke, it would be in the field, she just couldn't bring herself to put them in.

Much as she was loathe to leave, it was time. She didn't look forward to the looks from the crew, or the snide remarks they thought she wouldn't hear. And she didn't want to run into Alvarez again, she certainly knew what *he* thought of her. If she was being paranoid, she couldn't tell, but was sure any ill effects due to her power should have worn off by now.

The Docker seemed eerily empty. Every hall, every room she passed that had an open door. She had a long way to go to get to the mess, and she'd yet to see a single person. She was starting to become wary.

It wasn't until she reached the observation room on deck C that she finally saw someone. Ellis, standing at the window, looking down on the world they were stuck with. No one else was in sight, and a part of Gordon felt like she was intruding on the woman, only she had to walk through to get to the other side of the ship.

"Where is everyone?" she found herself asking.

Ellis turned to her, startled, then gave a short shake of her head and returned her gaze outside as she answered. "There is some kind of illness aboard."

"We're not in lockdown, though." She thought she would have noticed that.

"It's some kind of sleeping thing, I think," the woman continued as if she hadn't spoken. "We're not immune. It's got Harvey and Viatri. Deidra thinks they are going to attack soon."

It took Godon a moment to comprehend what the woman was saying. What that might mean for them.

She took a breath and leaned against the window next to Ellis, facing inward. "Do we know definitively that they're coming?"

"No," Ellis shook her head. "But I trust Deidra. Do you not?"

"With my life," Gordon returned without thought. "So why aren't we getting ready then?"

"The Commander and the Colonel are working up a plan. But,

could you imagine, we all get into our ships, we start the battle, and midway through we find it so hard to breath we pass out? Not sure we'll be reliable at the moment."

"Probably the point," she conceded.

"Anyway, don't let me keep you." It wasn't the worst kind of dismissal, but it was one.

Gordon inclined her head in goodbye and walked on.

The mess, when she got there, had three people in it, all bowed over their trays in separate corners of the room. It seemed there was some silent agreement to keep their distance from one another. She was fine with that.

Food was mash, peas, sausage and mushroom with a choice of cupcake or ice-cream for dessert. Which gave her a clue as to what time of day it was.

She chose the unoccupied corner to sit down and take her meal. No one so much as looked at her. It felt strange. Alarm bells in her head tried to warn her of something but she couldn't say what.

The meal was over quickly. It had tasted the same as every Docker meal she'd ever eaten, like it had come out of a can or was made with powder and water.

She placed her empty tray on the washing pile next to the food station and left without a backward glance. The people who'd been there when she walked in, still in their respective corners.

Now the decision: risk getting sick by going to find the Commander to tell her what was happening, or just shower and return to the morgue? She probably should have had a wash before she'd gone to the mess, but she'd been focused on food.

Gordon proceeded to the Locker Room and took care of her hygiene needs as if it were any other day. She didn't see anyone on the way there, in there, or on her way out when she was done. She had never seen a Docker appear so empty. Never.

Weiz will know where I am, if she needs me for anything, she told herself as she stood at a cross hall, deciding which way to go. *It's not as if you're hiding.* She knew the lie immediately for what it was but couldn't bring herself to own it.

With a shrug, she made her way back to the morgue. It was as uneventful on the way back as it had been in the opposite direction. This time, though, Ellis was no longer in the observation room.

She was fully prepared now, to do what she had to do. Well, as prepared as it was possible to be. When she got back into the room, she would place the bodies respectfully into their designated cold storage units and let them go.

The only problem was, when she got there, they were gone.

CHAPTER SEVEN

His entire life had flashed before his eyes. That was normal, when one died, he'd heard. But what was not normal, were the changes that happened during that flash. Different choices, leading to different destinations. New people had been introduced to his life, and people he'd considered close, fell by the wayside. It had changed him as a person, during that flash. What lessons he may have learned, had things gone differently, burned deep into his subconscious.

His eyes blinked open slowly to view a night sky. The ground was wet, the air smelled of mud and grass, and he wasn't entirely sure he didn't want to just close his eyes and go back to the dream he'd been having.

Estard rolled over with a groan, and saw beside him Fyord and Hadley, both looking somewhat bewildered, laying on their backs, eyes at the sky. He wondered if they'd experienced the strange parallel timeline with him.

"That," Fyord said, "Was extraordinarily unpleasant."

Hadley was still blinking at the sky. Perhaps taking a moment to reflect on what had happened to her.

"Can't argue with that statement," Estard agreed as he stood and stretched. He felt oddly very stiff. And here he'd thought they were supposed to have good health and vitality on top of their powers.

"Fuck a rainbow," Hadley whispered when she finally decided to get up. "And a sack of dicks."

Estard stared at her a moment. "That's colourful," he said.

"Rather not do that again," she told him, and spat off to the side. "I can still feel myself in pieces."

He didn't remember being in pieces. Perhaps he hadn't been. The last thing he remembered before reliving his life, had been trying hard to keep Kristin alive during the meteor shower. Bullet sized pieces of Io crashing down around them at a velocity he could only guess at. The fact that they had woken at all, told him that the planet had survived the bombardment.

Estard stretched his legs by walking a small circle around where they'd woken. He couldn't see anything. Partly because it was too dark, partly because there didn't seem to be anything to see.

"Are we in the right place?" he asked, finally.

Fyord shook his head. "No idea. I think so."

"Be buggered if I know," Hadley intoned. "Fucking ground all looks the same to me."

The woman kind of sounded like Kristin, but there was a slight difference he couldn't pick. The flag looked very similar, again, but not the same. He felt like he should probably know where she was from, but he didn't. The swearing, though. There was a lot of that.

"Well, should we wait here, or go looking for our people?" he asked. "If they're not here, we'd have to assume they survived."

The other two nodded their agreement, but it was Fyord who led the way. "Pretty sure the river is down this way. If we... you know... in the right place."

Estard understood. What did one even call that. Resurrection?

His brain suddenly went on a tangent wondering about Jesus' resurrection and the possible implications. He was snapped out of it by a tirade of swearing by Hadley as she fell to the ground cradling her slippered foot.

"Motherfucking nut sack," she exclaimed vehemently. She continued, but Estard tried not to listen.

Even Fyord looked at her with some distaste at the sheer amount of invective. "What? What happened?" he asked as he dropped into a squat beside her.

"There's something in me foot," she grated through clenched teeth. "Nail, wood, couldn't tell you, but it's big and it *fucking* hurts."

"Geez, woman, with a mouth like that, I am surprised you're a Comms Officer." Fyord gently took her foot in hand and inspected it, though there wasn't really enough light to see much.

"I can be as well-spoken as anyone else, when I feel like it," she told him.

The man grunted but continued his inspection with fingertips. He seemed to find a point that warranted further investigation, and after a moment, he pulled quickly, resulting in a short scream from Hadley.

"Fuck," she breathed. "Thank you."

Fyord got up and threw whatever it had been far into the distance. "You're welcome. Now let's get going." He held out a hand to help her up and put an arm beneath her shoulders to help her walk.

It took them roughly an hour, Estard guessed, to get to the river. On the other side, a mountain clear to see, even in the darkness. But he saw no fires, no lights, to indicate that anyone was there.

"We're in the right place, aren't we?" He knew the answer was yes, but he wanted to hear it.

"We are," Fyord assured. "They might not be here, though. They could be anywhere. Where were we when we were running? They may have continued in that direction and found somewhere safe to hunker down."

"How likely is that, though?" Hadley wanted to know.

"Not very," Fyord admitted. "But unless you'd like to share some ideas…" He left it hanging there for either one of them to pick up. But silence was all he got, and he let it go on for a good thirty seconds before he grunted and said, "No. Thought not. Let me know if that changes, though, will you?"

He led them across a shallow in the river, and they skirted the bottom of the mountain to the south. Estard could see the glint of wrecked ships in the limited moonlight, but he couldn't work out how many, or what they might have looked like.

Hadley hopped along next to Fyord, every second step a whispered 'shit' or 'fuck'. Estard thought she could match again the amount of times he'd heard those words in his entire life. Including from Kristin.

It was another half hour or so of walking on that side of the river before Fyord stopped, dead still, and scanned the area. He let out a small laugh and shared a look with Hadley. "No fucking way," he said with a huge smile.

Estard moved up beside them to see what they were so happy about and saw a very large rhombus shaped transport of some kind. He raised his brows at Fyord, but the man just looked at him with his silly grin.

"We're happy about this?" Estard nodded toward the transport.

"We're very fucking happy about this, Agent," Hadley said. "That's a carrier. Lights, shelter, and our people. Somewhere."

"I don't want to just walk over there without announcing myself," Fyord explained. "Carriers normally mean soldiers, and soldiers are a different breed to airmen. No telling how they'll take our presence."

"Well, they can't kill us," Estard put forward.

The other man grunted. "I don't know about you, but I am not eager to go through that again any time soon."

Estard had to admit he would avoid it if he could, but he also didn't see much point in hanging back as they were. He'd been a soldier once, he was willing to take the chance.

"Stay here then, I'll go check it out." He moved past and they gave not a word of caution or encouragement, just watched him walk off into the distance.

The lights from the carrier were quite dull, but obvious in the darkness. They didn't illuminate too much of their surrounds, so even close up it was hard to see. But he was able to make out some lumps on the ground. Some equipment over to the side. If those lumps were sleeping people, as he suspected, he did not want to risk waking them. That way lay bedlam. Instead, he sucked once at his teeth, and returned to Fyord and Hadley.

"They're sleeping," he told them.

"No lookouts?" Hadley looked suspicious as Estard shook his head.

"They'll be there," Fyord assured. "There's no way they don't have anyone on lookout." He removed his arm from under Hadley's shoulder and sat on the damp earth.

Estard looked down with distaste, but after a while, followed suit. Despite her foot and already very wet jeans, Hadley remained standing for quite some time before succumbing to the allure of rest.

"You don't think we should get their attention?" Estard wanted to know.

"How sure are you they'd know who we are in the dark, and not shoot before questions?" Estard couldn't answer, and let it drop.

He wasn't sure how long they were waiting, only that the sunrise seemed extremely slow. Probably because he was impatient to meet these new people. A new kind of ship. One that clearly went somewhere other than this forsaken land. His imagination soared to the heights of what it might mean that these people were here, but tried to temper it.

Once they saw two or three bodies stir and get up, Fyord stood, looked directly at them and let out a "Koooooooo-weeeeeeee!"

Immediately eyes and guns were raised in his direction, but he raised his hands above his head and walked slowly toward the camp. Estard and Hadley close behind and in much the same pose.

The leader of the bunch had his gun trained on Fyord, but his eyes wondered between them in question. "Comms Officers, Johannes Fyord and Amara Hadley, reporting in," Fyord said in a strong voice without shouting, once they were close enough.

The man's eyes shifted to him and Estard cleared his throat. "Agent Julian Estard."

Estard breathed a little easier when the man lowered his gun, the man next to him saying, "They're all on the list, sir."

Guns holstered, and men and women going back about their work, the man sat down as he said, "Major Preston Morton." He pointed a finger at the man next to him. "Sergeant Rohelia Singh." Then he indicated they should join him.

They sat down on small camp stools, and the Sergeant lit up a camp stove over which he hung a pot. The Major let the Sergeant finish setting everything up before he spoke again.

"You looking for a lift?" he pointed to the sky.

Fyord and Hadley exchanged smiling glances again. Estard felt very left out, and unsure about what they were supposed to be so happy about.

"That would be... that would be great." Fyord replied. "Who all is up there?"

The Major spat off to the side and muttered an 'excuse me', before clearing his throat and continuing. "Ah, we can't do that. Orders are to stay on the ground until further notice."

"Why?" The obvious question, provided by Hadley.

"Some kind of illness spreading up on the Docker. They want to keep those who are uninfected unaffected."

"Fuck me," Hadley whispered. "Is there anything that won't go wrong in this fucking place. When did you fellas even get here?"

"The Docker? Almost two weeks ago, now. Us, down here on the ground? About two days ago." So they'd been dead at least two weeks, and he could see from their exchanged glances, that Fyord and Hadley were as disturbed by that as he. Even if two weeks was better than forever.

Estard thought the man was a little too open about what he was willing to share with them. Despite whom they said they were, they could have been anyone, and he could be divulging sensitive information to the enemy. He'd asked for and received no proof of who they were. Estard didn't think they were even capable of proving it. But he kept the thought to himself, because he wanted the free flow of information to continue.

"The others," Estard said after a small silence. "Weiz, Harvey, Kristin..." His throat closed over on her name, but he wanted to know. He couldn't finish the list, but the man in front of him was already nodding. It was the Sergeant who answered.

"The Commander is back up there where she belongs. Harvey, Gordon, Ellis, Bridges, Viatri, Zim and Doctor Ward are also up there. Kristin, unfortunately, was captured by the hi-tech aliens a couple days ago."

His heart hammered hard in his chest, 'til he thought it might actually try to break through. He swallowed it down and asked for a full update of everything that had happened since the meteor shower.

For the most part everything seemed to be good with only trivial setbacks. If you could call a mega-storm trivial, he supposed. But a couple of days ago, while performing some routine tasks, Pilot Reeve had been spotted and he'd led Harvey and Kristin into a trap.

They were confident in their ability to get her back, though. Once they found where she was. That was the hard part. But they had captured a Bahana man, and he was up on that Docker, so surely there'd be someone up there who could get what they needed out of him. They'd rescued Lance, and they could rescue her.

Once Estard felt like he'd been fully caught up, he got to his feet, and dusted himself off. "Well," he told them. "Guess I'll try and go back and change it." He braced himself for the world to turn backwards, ready to just go do it, but Major Preston held out a hand.

"Woah, woah, woah there son, hold up some." He made soothing gestures. "What do you mean by that?"

"I'm going to change it," he said.

"And what does that mean?"

"That's my power," he informed. It hadn't occurred to him that the man wouldn't know. "I turn back time and change things."

And he tried. The world slowed, stopped, then ran backwards. It picked up pace and slowed again. But he was stalled at the moment where the Major lowered his gun after hearing their names.

Unsatisifed with the result, he tried again. And again. But for reasons he couldn't begin to imagine, there appeared to be wall to how far back he could go. So he let it play back through to where he had rudely left the Major.

"I turn back time and change things," he repeated, though the man in front of him wouldn't know that.

The Major nodded. "Sure, but what does that mean?" he asked again.

Estard, for the first time in a very long time, felt stupid. He did not enjoy that feeling. "I don't understand the question."

"Sit back down, son, you can do as you wish if I don't convince you, clearly. So, what's the harm in hearing me out?"

Estard looked to Fyord and Hadley for support but they both

just shrugged at him. Likely they didn't see a bother either way. If he went back, they wouldn't remember this moment because it would never have happened.

He sat back down and motioned for the Major to continue. "Please go ahead," he sighed.

"We know the dangers, now, and we've past many with success. We don't have to do them again, because it's already done. But if you go back, and you change things, what is affected? What won't we learn? Do you know? Could it make it worse?"

Estard hadn't considered that and didn't appreciate the thought that was planted in his mind. Make it worse. How would he make it worse? He didn't know, but he knew he could. And easily.

"Now, I am no astrophysicist," the man continued. "I can't tell you all the theory that goes behind it. But as a man who has been interested in the subject for quite some time, I can tell you, that everything you do will have consequences. Every minute you take back and change something. You won't know what that consequence is, until it happens, but there'll be some. Some that you may not be able to change back."

"Strikes me as odd you came prepared with this argument, when I am sure that none of the others even know I could do this," Estard replied.

Preston shook his head. "We were told you all had 'powers'. No one said what. You're the one who mentioned going back and changing things. It just happens to be a subject I've a keen interest in."

"Don't suppose you have any examples?" Estard wanted to know.

"Singh!"

"Sir," said the man next to him.

"Bring me my pack." The Sergeant ran into the ship and back out in seconds with a fully loaded soldiers backpack. He handed it to the Major and resumed his seat.

Major Preston rifled through the backpack and came up with a well-worn book in hand. "Now, don't mistake me, Agent Estard, I've heard all about you and the magical powers you lot now seem to possess. I respect that it is your decision, but this is a subject about which I feel passionately. And I have to tell you, this book may be as old as you are, if you'd travelled here along the same path." He held it out.

The Perils of Time Travel by I.E. Stanley. Estard had never heard of the author. But that wasn't saying much. He did read from time to time, but he wasn't exactly prolific, and it was mostly mystery novels. He did enjoy a good mystery.

Estard took hold of the book in both hands, careful because he understood how brittle old paper could be. But it felt soft to the touch, rather than stiff. He shot the Major a questioning look.

"This edition of the book is only about twenty years old." He smiled and chuckled. "But it was written in twenty-seventy-six."

Estard laughed out loud. "This book is almost a hundred and fifty years my junior, Major."

The man looked surprised, but he gave a chuckle. "Well, closer to you than me, anyway."

That gave some perspective as to how far forward in time he really had come. He suddenly wondered if it would be possible for him to find out what had happened to Bob, and Harris. He hadn't really left much behind, but he knew he'd wonder about them from time to time.

"You want me to read the whole thing?" he asked. It wasn't overly large, but it looked like it might be a slog. He didn't read that fast.

"It is a novel. You might miss a bit if you don't." The Major was starting to sound miffed. Like Estard was rejecting his baby. "Besides, it's not like you're wasting time if you can take it back whenever you like."

Estard had to give him that. Though from the sound of things, Preston Morton was not a fan of the idea of turning back time. He had to decide whether he was going to respect this man's point of view, read the book and find out why, or just do his own thing and see what happened.

In truth, if he couldn't find a way through the barriers he kept finding, it was somewhat a moot point.

The idea of consequence, though. That stalled him. What might he change that would be irrevocable? Was there any way that he could prepare for those things? Get ahead of the potential consequence, or would that, in itself, cause more problems that he could not account for.

Damn you, sir, Estard thought. *All I want to do is make sure Kristin doesn't get captured. Surely that wouldn't change things too much?* But the fact that he was asking only in his mind, and not out loud, let him know that he had already ceded the point.

Fyord and Hadley had an animated conversation with the Major while Estard thought through the obstacle that the man had put before him.

He shook the book, on the verge of an idea. "What if," he asked, and they all went quiet. "What if, I grabbed Kristin just before she was captured, and brought her forward in time to now? That way, you would all still think she'd been kidnapped, nothing else will have changed. But she would be safe."

"That sounds like it might work," the Major agreed. "But let me ask you this, how far back in time can you actually go? From what these two have been saying, you all just resurrected." He shook his head with a frown after that sentence and muttered something unintelligible before continuing. "Can you go further back than the last time you died? Are you sure you can move forward through time? Can you exist in a time where your body is... dead? Is this maybe something you should check you're capable of first?"

Estard let out a half scream, half growl, and was about to throw the book on the ground but refrained before he let it go. He breathed deep and tried to calm himself while everyone had their eyes on him.

"Why?" he asked in a strangled voice. "I understand your point, I will read the book. But, my god man, you are shooting down my hope and it is painful."

The Major shrugged at him. "It often is, son. But truth is always more useful than fancies. I think you might agree."

Estard looked to the sky and tried to control his breathing. To keep his heart rate down. To find his usual, more logical self. He couldn't help what he was feeling, and that feeling was driving him toward stubbornly trying to go back in time, push past the barrier, and get Kristin before she was taken. But he also knew that it would be very difficult to go back that far. During the meteor shower he had only been able to go back a few minutes, and that had been hard going.

"You're right," he said finally. "You are right." And in a way it felt like he had given up before he had even started. So inwardly, he promised himself, and promised Kristin, *I'll work this out. And I will come get you. Whether through time or present, I swear it.*

CHAPTER EIGHT

Deidra frowned at the nanoscope in front of her. She couldn't put her finger on exactly what it was, but it didn't look right. She turned her attention to Weiz and told her as much.

"Well, what's wrong with it?" The woman was very testy, with Harvey down in the sick bay.

Deidra had considered just killing him, so he'd revive down on the planet, but she had no guarantee that that would cure him, or prevent him from reacquiring the illness.

Weiz clicked fingers in front of her eyes, and she knew she'd been drifting. "Hello? Doctor Ward? Are you in there?"

Deidra brushed her hand away and shook her head. "Yes, yes, I am here."

"Good, so tell me what I need to change about this nanoscope."

"There's no magnification setting," she replied. She hadn't consciously realised that was what it was, but after she said it, it was obvious.

Weiz dutifully changed the nanoscope, and Deidra nodded her

thanks before getting to work.

The other Doctors in the lab were actual medical doctors, who knew what they were doing, what they were looking for. At best, Deidra was plucking random knowledge from the trees of Eridu and Earth, so careful that she didn't lose herself in the process that she wasn't sure just how useful she *could* be.

They'd run out of equipment and IV's fairly quickly once people started displaying the symptoms, so they were rushing to find cause and cure. So far, Weiz had been the only one to walk among the infected without going down for the count. Now Deidra was trying to find what it was in her blood that made her immune, or asymptomatic. The problem was going to be separating that from the 'Giant' genes that had flooded their systems.

Not for the first time, Deidra wished they had some kind of virologist on board.

Up on the screen in front of her — another object courtesy of Weiz — was two separate blood slides, on a nanoscopic scale. One side was Weiz, the other Deidra herself. To her eyes, everything seemed normal. Red blood cells, white bloods cells, and platelets, she could barely discern which was which, they were so small. She was sure, if there were any abnormalities, it would be immediately evident. But it seemed so completely normal, it didn't feel right.

Over her should she heard someone clear their throat. She looked back to see Doctor Namimbi staring. "Can I help you?" she asked.

He took a single step forward. "You — uh — you, you really need to turn up the magnification." He managed to get out. He was so soft spoken he was hard to understand at times.

"Thank you, Doctor. Would you care to join us?" She could use him if he knew what he was doing.

The man gave her a respectful half bow and stepped forward again. He indicated the instruments they were using, likely very aware they were all being maintained by Weiz. "Would you mind?"

Deidra took a step back with what she considered to be the universal gesture of 'have at it' and watched on with interest. It wasn't her field, but she was curious, with everything that was going on.

"You had the right idea," he told her, as if she were a student. "You have the wrong instrument. Commander, if you would be so kind." He pointed to the nanoscope.

Weiz let it dissipate, and he gave a bow of the head. "I will require an electron microscope, if you wouldn't mind."

Deidra wasn't sure if she found his over politeness refreshing or annoying, but she could see clear on Weiz's face what she thought.

"And what does an electron microscope do? How does it work? What should it look like?"

Doctor Namimbi blinked a few times at the Commander, then looked to Deidra. She smiled at him. It was not easy for Weiz to make the instruments that Deidra asked for. She could easily make replicas that looked as though they should do what you wanted, but if she didn't know how it worked, then the result might as well be a statue for all the use anyone would get out of it.

"You will need to explain that, in great detail," she told the man.

Deidra tuned out his explanations while Weiz built the thing. Sometimes she made it as it was explained, so things looked like they were coming out of a 3D printer. It was interesting the first or second time, then it was like watching paint dry. Doctor Namimbi was enjoying himself, full of awed wonder.

You in there? she asked the voice in her head. *I am you; you are me. There is no separation here.* Intellectually, she knew that, of course. But it was unnerving. She felt like she needed to get its attention to know things. But in fact it was the same as it had always been, she was just learning differently.

The last time the technologists had tried to use this method on them, Skynar had healed them and remained immune. Richard Zim, who now had that power, was already taking up a bed in the room across from the infirmary. Of the Giants on the Docker, only she and Weiz had not succumb, and Deidra probably only because she was in hazmat.

Weiz had finished building the electron microscope, and Doctor Namimbi was thanking her with small bows as he hooked it up to the other equipment she'd already made.

When he was done, the screen showed blank until Namimbi adjusted the slides, and then it was like looking at a completely different world. It was hard to tell whether it was all in black and white, or it just seemed that way. *Electron beams do not show colour,* the voice informed her. *Even if they did, they would probably look the same, since the objects are smaller than the wavelengths of visible light.* Deidra vaguely remembered learning something like that when she was in university, but had never had cause to use it, and wondered whether that had actually been the voice or herself. *One and the same,* the voice reminded her.

She sighed. She'd get used to it or she wouldn't. But she wasn't going to argue with it.

The inside of her suit was starting to get very warm and uncomfortable. She'd already taken two breaks, to shower and change, though she was least in need of it. Truth was the suit made her feel claustrophobic, and from time to time she wanted to go watch Dane work, to reassure herself the stupid man hadn't left the lab and got himself infected. Without IV's they would have a hard time keeping these people alive. Every moment the clock was running down, and all Deidra thought of was herself.

Not all you think of, just most. Even that felt like she was trying to wriggle out of any responsibility.

Deidra forced her attention back to the science at hand, asking the questions the voice wasn't automatically giving her answers to.

"What are we looking at?" She wanted to know.

Doctor Namimbi didn't look away from the work, just pointed to small things on the screen and named them. There was a long, spiked, almost furry looking caterpillar thing, that had attached itself to one of the white blood cells on Weiz's slide.

"Is that the virus?"

Doctor Namimbi squinted and frowned at it. He scratched his head and grunted. Then he finally turned to Deidra and said, "It shouldn't be, but I think it is."

Doctor Zalenka sidled over to silently observe the screen. He seemed particularly interested in that thing they thought was the virus. "Does it look... dead, to you, Doctor?"

Namimbi eyed the slide sideways, took an extremely fine needle from the draw in the lab desk, and took slow pokes at the slide until the needle showed on the screen. It touched the caterpillar a few times, but there was no reaction.

"We could try a pH solution," Zalenka suggested. "If it's hibernating or inert, perhaps it's looking for food."

Doctor Namimbi nodded and made haste for the fridge at the back of the lab. There was a bunch of chemicals and things in there that Deidra could not begin to name. He found what he was looking for quickly and came back holding a vial of blue liquid and a dropper. Zalenka encouraged him to place it on the slide.

Nothing happened. No obvious spreading of liquid, barely any movement from the cells on the screen, and nothing that would suggest independent movement either from the caterpillar or anything else.

Deidra raised a brow at Namimbi. "I think it's dead," he told her.

"Is that good or bad?"

It was Zalenka who answered. "Depends. If it was Weiz's cells that killed it, great, we can use that information. If it's just dead, for no discernible reason, it's of no use. So." He looked to Weiz hopeful and apologetic.

The Commander shook her head and muttered a string of words in German that no one understood, as she rolled up her sleeve and held out her arm. "Do what you must," she breathed.

Namimbi bowed and thanked her, even as he took a single prick of blood from her fingertip and placed it on a slide. He then put said slide into the electron microscope and removed both of the old ones, the comparison no longer required.

Weiz glared at him with a frown as she rolled her uniform sleeve back down. Deidra could almost hear what the woman was thinking, that face said so much.

Namimbi adjusted and readjusted the slide until he was looking at something akin to the caterpillar, only larger, and fatter in the middle. It was moving, appearing to try in every which way to puncture the white blood cell it was clinging to. It took a few moments, but eventually it achieved its goal. The moment it did, however, it suddenly tried very hard to extract itself. The fatness of it was seeping away, and within moments, it resembled the one of earlier.

"That was interesting," Zalenka said. "In fifty years, I have never seen anything like it. Did we record it?"

Namimbi gave a silent nod and pointed to the network computer.

Deidra breathed a sigh of relief. "So, we can get to work? We know what we're looking at?" If they could direct her in what they needed, she'd feel a lot less useless.

"Assuming that it is something in Weiz's white blood cells that is disabling them, then we can certainly manufacture some kind of antidote." Zalenka informed. "We'll need to see it happen again, examine the white blood cells for what causes the anomaly. If we can manufacture it, fantastic, it not, then we rely heavily on the Commander to be available for extractions."

Weiz looked more than a little annoyed at the notion, but Deidra knew that she would do absolutely anything for Harvey. Even endure the discomforts of being poked and prodded by doctors. She'd probably even let them kill her.

They were on their way with a cure, or antidote, or whatever. *You could know if you really wanted to know, but you keep holding yourself back and you know it. Afraid that you're going to lose yourself again, no matter how the information is delivered.*

The voice was right. She was afraid. And with good reason. Experience had taught her what she would lose. This voice had yet to prove itself.

"Let's get to work," she said, pushing aside the voice in her head and moving toward the desks. "Tell me where you need me and what you need me to do." It was going to be a very long day or two.

~

Kristin had no idea how long it had been since she'd been put in this place. She'd slept a couple of times, but had yet to be given any food or water. And there was nowhere to relieve herself, so that was probably a good thing.

Despite her best efforts, what damage she'd been able to do to the place was minimal, and it was getting her nowhere. Although her strength had not yet diminished, it was not infinite, and it was merely a matter of time.

She'd been hearing something faintly in the distance for a while, but she couldn't make out what it was. It came from what she considered to be the left side of the room, even though, all the panelling being the same, there was no way to tell which way the room was oriented.

From time to time, she slapped a hand down hard on that wall, making a very loud tin roof sound that lasted a few seconds. She wanted to see if that faint sound would respond, but it never did.

Impatient, bored, annoyed. They'd all overtaken the fear that she'd felt in the beginning. She wasn't hungry, but she missed food.

She wasn't overly social, but she missed people. If they were trying to torture her with deprivation, which she had to admit was possible, they were off to a good start. But it wouldn't make her cave. It just made her more and more angry.

She heard another sound, closer than the faint ones had been. More like the reverberation of a pipe. She moved to that left hand wall and whacked it. She squinted against the sound it made, but it didn't last long.

The pipe sound came again, this time, in a definite rhythm, though not one she could define.

Kristin held down her excitement. It could just be the Bahana men playing with her head. She wouldn't put it past them. But she chose to believe that it was something else and responded by hitting the wall in the same pattern.

After a few moments another rhythm played out, and it was one she recognised. Good ole morse code. She doubted that the Bahana men were familiar with that. But they did have Greenway, and there was no telling what the man had given away. So, she contained her excitement. She'd save it for when she was out of this place.

She hit the wall in a pattern that spelled out 'Kristin', and the message she got back was, 'wait'. And so she did. For twenty minutes.

The seam of the door had been hidden behind the panels, she learned as it opened in front of her. It was slow, and she started to bounce from foot to foot as she waited for the space to be large enough to squeeze through. She didn't even look at who had opened it, or what was at the other end, she was just so glad to be out of there.

Once she'd taken a few deep breaths as if she'd not breathed since she was caught, Kristin looked up into the faces of the dishevelled men who had rescued her. Reeve — she had mixed feelings there — Walt, Dames, Ramirez, Garcia, Carson and Deville. As happy as she was to see them all, Walt and Dames were a surprise.

"Thought you two had wandered off on your return trip," she said.

Walt shook his head and Dames frowned. "You thought we'd desert on an alien planet after we put so much effort into getting home?"

Kristin tilted her head. "Well, when you put it that way, it does sound kind of stupid."

"You think?" Dames returned.

Reeve, looking as haunted and gaunt as he had in the woods touched the man's shoulder and said softly, "We may not have much time. We should move."

"They haven't been back in days," Garcia put in. He and the rest all looked as worn and pale as Reeve, and Kristin had to wonder what had been done to them.

"Which way is out?" she asked.

She got a crowd full of shrugs. "We're just making our way through. Stopping at every cell to make sure no one gets left behind," Walt said. "Abramovich is still missing. And we weren't expecting to find you."

She pointed up and down the hall, "We can talk as we move, but I don't know the direction of travel."

Reeve gave a nod and started leading them down the hall to the right. They didn't travel far to the next cell.

"How did you all get out?" She wanted to know. "I could not for the life of me put a dent in those walls. And — I hope you will excuse me for saying so — I'm a lot stronger than you lot."

Walt pointed to Dames, who was standing right next to him. The inseparable duo. "Seems he spent a lot of his free time learning about electronics. Also, you were in solitary, our cells were a little more open."

Dames grunted with a nod, indicating that he agreed with Walt's assessment of the situation.

Reeve was knocking on something, probably a pipe that Kristin couldn't see. There was no response to the sound.

"How many empty cells have you come across?"

"Didn't count, but I'd estimate somewhere in the high twenties, low thirties." Dames shrugged.

"How likely is it we're going to get caught, here?"

Reeve stepped away from the pipe and moved further along down the hall. "They haven't returned in three days. Not sure they're even going to."

Kristin grunted. It was likely she hadn't been in the place any longer than that. Though it was possible.

Now that she was paying attention to what she was looking at, she could differentiate the cells rather easily from this side. They were all painted black and looked like stone, with small rivets. There were keypads next to the doors, lights above them, and alcoves roughly half the width of an average man between them. It was into those alcoves that Reeve reached to make the rhythmic noises.

It didn't take them long to move down the hall. There were only four more cells, and none of them gave any indication that they held a prisoner.

Dames moved to the door at the end. He went about his business without comment. Everyone seemed very quiet and sombre, and Kristin didn't know how to break them away from their inner thoughts. She was not sure she could tear herself away from her own. This whole situation felt absurd.

On the one hand she was glad to see these airmen, most of whom she'd assumed were dead. On the other hand, they seemed to be breaking out with an ease that begged the question, why had they waited? Or, if she were to give them the benefit of the doubt, perhaps it simply took that long for them to have both the means and opportunity.

Things went quickly from that point. There was only one room on the other side of the door, and it housed cameras that looked in on all the cells. No one else was in there. And it gave Kristin an idea of what the more open cells looked like, right next to a guard station. She could see why it might have taken a while, and some of her suspicion faded.

The long hall out wound three times around on an upward ramp and ended in a door that blended into the wall. It took Dames less than five minutes to get it open, and they walked out into a dark room.

Though she could barely make out the entrance, Kristin was certain she knew where they were. She made a beeline for the daylight, and immediately laughed.

The airmen, out in the open now, were looking up to the sky, closing eyes, breathing deep. If they'd been in there as long as they'd been missing, they'd been deprived of sunlight and fresh air for quite some time. They looked wan, ashen, sunken, starving. Kristin was beginning to have some doubts in their ability to keep up if she didn't find them some food and water.

"You know where we are?" Walt asked.

She clapped her hands together. "You know it. About an hour or two from the village. Half a day, maybe less, to the landing site."

Now they were all out, they appeared to lose all the energy that moved them. It was a round of nods, but no one spoke further. While Reeve had led them inside, they were all looking at her, now.

She turned on her heel, looked up to the sky to check her orientation, and took a step forward, only to fall to her knees when a vision flashed in her mind.

CHAPTER NINE

His life over the past couple of weeks had been about as comfortable as it was on the ship beforehand. His powers didn't work, he could barely move while in the company of doctors or scientists. They spoke in hushed tones and low whispers, though never to him.

Greenway, for all that he done on Eridu, now felt that perhaps he deserved this. A little. But not forever.

Face down on a table now, while they took a good look at his exposed spine, Greenway wondered how he had managed to justify the atrocities he'd committed. While he still stood by his earliest statements — they are gods and should not abandon their world — that didn't mean killing entire villages and towns for not worshipping. Why did he need that? His job as a god was to take care of the place, not destroy it.

He felt sharp pressure near his left shoulder, and he supposed they were cutting into the muscle. Though what they imagined they'd find there was beyond him. But he endured, thankful they were at least using an anaesthetic now. The first couple of days they hadn't bothered to. Sometimes, they would even put him to sleep while they worked. He wasn't sure he wanted to know what they were doing then. They certainly didn't tell him.

Every now and then a curious young girl came to see him, but she was as silent as the rest. He had the sense that she wanted to know more about where they were from. How they had become what they were. It had to be obvious to these people that they were not from Eridu.

Greenway sighed inside his mind, impatient to be sewn up and thrown back in his cell where he could sleep and eat. Until he'd come here, he really hadn't bothered with those things. Now, they were comforting. Made him feel better, remain human.

He didn't know how long he was on the table, mind blanking out while they worked. His thoughts went in circles, and sometimes he sang to himself. Played whole albums in his mind, of his favourite bands, some orchestras, and occasionally a very annoying jingle that just would not leave. He did maths, for no good reason, as simple as the times tables, the recitation of pi to the hundredth decimal, or as difficult as the thrust to weight ratio of an effective flight turbine.

Greenway felt disoriented when they rolled him onto his side and a doctor looked directly into his eyes. He blinked a few times, the lights were so bright, and the doctor was wearing one on his forehead. But once his eyes adjusted, he gave as good a death stare as he could muster. The doctor didn't seem to notice. Whatever he was looking for, he didn't find it. He just shook his head and Greenway was back on his stomach facing the floor.

When they were done, he was wheeled back to his cell and placed face down on his bunk with the instruction, "Try not to move too much for a couple of days." Then whoever had taken him left, with the table they'd wheeled him in on.

He wasn't sure how he was supposed to eat or drink while lying in this manner, though he supposed he would figure it out. If they gave him anything to eat or drink.

Just as he sighed at the thought of a day without food, he heard the cell door open. He hadn't heard anyone coming, though. The footsteps in his cell were like a stroke of velvet on fleece, they were so soft. Not at all the thump of boots on concrete he had come to expect. He wondered who it was, but he didn't have to wonder long.

The girl got beneath him, lay on the ground and looked him in the eye. It was almost like they were standing. Her lips were pursed, mouth twisted to one side, in thought or distaste, maybe both. He could only see to her shoulders before the bed got in the way, but she looked comfortable in her black and red uniform.

"This is a tough one," she said, and her voice was like a softly played piano. A little on the high side but, containing lower notes that made it less unpleasant.

Greenway grunted, unsure how he was supposed to respond to a statement like that. His entire time here had been tough. He wasn't sure they saw him as anything other than an aberration that required study. Though what they were trying to ascertain, he couldn't say.

"We're going back," she told him. "Do we take you?"

If he had the capacity to laugh, he would have. But he was in too much pain. "I think I am a little tied up right now," he wheezed out.

She smiled up at him. It was a beautiful smile that lit up her whole face, and suddenly made him uncomfortable wondering how old she was. "Yes, I see that." She looked toward the door and back. The thoughtful lip pursing back on her face.

"What is it?" he asked, not sure he actually wanted an answer.

"I am not supposed to be here," she whispered, to which he grunted in reply. "I don't like what my father and the others do down here. It's one thing to keep you people in stasis until we find a way to reverse what's happened to you, but this is barbaric."

It was like a lightbulb in his mind. *So that is what they're doing!* But it changed nothing. It certainly didn't help his circumstance.

From the sound of things, the woman — or girl? — in front of him might like to help with that.

"So, what are you suggesting?" His voice was getting a little stronger with use.

She looked away and back again. Clearly, she was having her own internal struggle with the situation. "Is it true? What you did to those people?" She looked him dead in the eye on the last word.

It was he who wanted to look away now, but he couldn't turn his head. He let his eyes stay as still. "Yes."

"Why?"

If he could have shrugged, he would have. "I don't really know," he replied honestly. "I started out not wanting to leave, while everyone else did. Everyone was so eager to go home, they weren't thinking of what we were taking away." He tried to shake his head, and screamed as he heard a crack in his neck.

"Careful," the girl whispered to him. "It'll take a few days before you can move properly again."

He waited until the pain calmed, and the flashes of red in his vision stopped. "Maybe I deserve this," he told her.

"No one deserves this," she responded. "Now, tell me more about why you did it." It was a soft demand, but demand it was.

Greenway breathed deep and tried to put himself back there. In the village the first time he got angry. Because they wouldn't do as he said? He couldn't quite remember. Everything was a little blurry after the first few nights of being on the planet. Until he'd come to this hell hole, he didn't think he'd ate, or slept. In what? Three months maybe? He really wasn't sure how much time had passed. But a part of his mind now told him that all living things required some form of sustenance, and it may very well have been this lack that pushed him past that edge.

"I think," he confessed, "I may have gone a little mad."

"A little?"

"A lot?" He wasn't sure what else he was supposed to say. He had done those things. For better or worse, it was done, and he couldn't take it back. Given the way he felt now, if he had them to do over, he would do it differently. But it didn't change anything.

"Look, I gotta go," she'd become so quiet she was hard to hear even that close. She wriggled out from under the bed, but he felt her lean over the bed to whisper in his ear. "I'll be back when I can."

He barely heard her leave, just the faint click of the door closing behind her.

Greenway wasn't sure if he should give in to hope. She was just a girl, or not much older. His first assessment had been early to mid-twenties, but that smile showed so much baby fat in the cheeks, he thought maybe sixteen. Her father worked in this place, but she had access, so he assumed that she still lived with him. It was hard to tell. How much trust should he place in her? How much hope dare he hold onto?

He wasn't going to get himself out of this place. Even if he did, he was no longer on Eridu — though he learned the people here called it Urago — and there was nowhere for him to escape to. Even if he had access to a ship, even if the controls were such that he could fly it without training, he had no idea where this planet was in relation to Eridu. They had him cornered, that was for sure.

And however sincere this girl might be in her desire to get him out, he didn't know what that meant. Maybe she just wanted to take him to stasis with the others. Whatever that would mean. He assumed it was something like the glass canisters he'd seen on the ship.

He was careful not to shake his head again, as he tried to calm his mind. No matter how much he tried to tamp it down and lower his expectations, he couldn't stop the hope from poking through.

~

Estard read, he paced, he ate, and when night came, he slept. The next day, much the same, but a few questions thrown here and there at the man who'd supplied the book.

It was an interesting read. Ana Weights, thrown back in time to just before World War Two — a time he'd personally lived through, so it was strange seeing it as distant past — to kill the leader of the Nazi party, before he could get his invading forces off the ground in 1939.

It had been a deliberate act, the thought experiment long popular: if you could go back in time, what would you change? An overwhelming majority of the public, without prompting or a multichoice questionnaire, responded with kill Hitler. He supposed it was just ingrained in the culture, even in his own time. And it said much about its global and historical impact that it was still widely thought about almost a hundred and fifty years after the event.

Ana did not spend much time in 1939, she simply completed her mission and returned to her own time, 2276. Only to find that things had changed drastically, and not for the better.

There'd been no concentration camps, but there were gulags. National Socialism was defeated before it could get a foothold, but Communism ran rife in Europe, and killed just as many, if not more, in not so straight forward ways. Outnumbered, and outgunned, the West fell in 1949, to a new regime.

The book was all about how she'd go back in time and try to fix little things so it wouldn't turn out that way, but every time she did, the small changes did not return her world to a better place. They might have better tech, or better healthcare, or a myriad of other little things, but often it didn't, and never did they have overall better lives.

Estard understood what the book was trying to say and could find no fault in its logic. But he wished he didn't.

For two and a half days, it kept him occupied, thinking of all the consequences that could arise from something as innocent as trying to save this one woman. He tried to convince himself time and time again that it would be safe, that there was nothing to worry about, what he was reading was just a story, not real life.

He was so engrossed in his thoughts, in his reading, that when Kristin and seven airmen walked out of the woods and into the camp, it took him a moment to comprehend what was happening.

Estard didn't even talk. Couldn't hear anyone else speak. He just ran to Kristin and threw his arms around her, much tighter than she was comfortable with. He could tell, because she hit him twice in the kidneys before he let go.

"Get off," she yelled at him.

He backed away a few steps. "Couldn't help it," he told her. He couldn't take his eyes off her, it was so surreal. His mind was still trying to find a logical way to go rescue her, even while she was standing in front of him. The disconnect was like nothing he had ever felt before in his life. He had no words.

The Major greeted them, and other airmen gathered round. They were given fresh uniforms and food, while happy laughs, claps on the shoulder and firm nods took place all round. In a strange way it reminded him of going to a wake, where all the men would laugh and joke and try not to cry in front of each other.

Estard was on the outside of this. Truly on the outside. They'd all formed a circle and sat down, catching up on what had happened.

With head down, he turned away and walked to the other side of the ship. He would wait until they were done. Much as he'd like to know what had happened to them all, how they managed to get away. He'd wait until he was welcome.

That didn't take long. Less than five minutes, by his estimation, before Kristin came sauntering up. He only looked at her as she approached. She gave him a soft tap on the shoulder as she sat down next to him.

"Glad to see you, Agent man," she said. "Sorry, I... It didn't register to me that it was you. You've been dead a couple weeks, so, I really thought you might actually be *dead* dead, you know?"

Well, he couldn't blame her for that. "I think I might forgive you," he responded. "But I want to know what happened. I was gearing up to go get you, then here you are, depriving me of an opportunity to be the hero."

"You, the hero?" She barked a short laugh. "Yeah, alright. If you say so."

He leaned a shoulder into her and sat back up. "Tell me, what happened? How'd you get here?"

She regaled him with a remarkably short tale of boredom and being rescued by the others, at the end of which she had a vision about a non-specific attack by the Bahana men. All things considered it was really quite underwhelming.

"So, you sat in a box for three or four days. Then someone got you out, the end?"

Kristin shrugged. "You forgot the migraine inducing vision, but essentially. The others' stories are much more interesting. They were there longer, and they actually interacted with the Bahana men."

"And?"

"And what?"

"And aren't you going to tell me?"

She pushed at him as she got up and brushed herself off. He tipped but righted himself before he fell. "Well, get up. It's time for an evening meal and I haven't eaten anything in days. We'll go sit with the others, and you can hear what they have to say first hand. Sound alright to you, Agent man?"

Estard got up and gestured with his arm. "Lead the way," he said, and followed behind.

They made room for them in the circle that had formed. Everyone was sitting to the outside of it, on the inside, it was clear so everyone could see across. To the right of where they entered, a single airman was portioning out some stew and handing the bowls to others who then took them to the ex-prisoners first. When everyone had a bowl, those airmen took a seat, and the Major told their new guests about what had happened since they'd been gone.

When it came their turn to relay information, it was Reeve who spoke. "After everything happened with Greenway, those of us who chose not to follow him just left. We didn't pack anything, just took what we could carry on our backs and started walking in the direction of the mountain in the hope we'd get there before the transport left."

Estard nodded at that. He remembered hearing about those events from Gordon, just from the other side of it.

"We weren't on our way but two days," he continued. "We were all injured from the fight, some of us worse than others. Without a doctor, we lost Oswald and Merriot the first day. They didn't look too bad on the outside, but I'd say they had some bad internal bleeding."

Garcia picked up the story from there. "It was on the second night they came. Just wandered into our camp, sat themselves down and started talking. We couldn't understand a word of it, and between us we speak about twelve languages. So, we tried to communicate. They seemed patient enough with our efforts, but we couldn't seem to find a common tongue. And after a while, they just turned hostile." He shook his head in memory.

Reeve took it back up again. "We lost three more that night. Holston, Abrradi and Ramesh." Everyone took a moment to bow their heads.

Carson was next to elaborate on their tale. "It seemed they didn't want to kill us, because after those three, the man in charge started yelling at the others, and they took out what we thought were guns. Turns out they're some kind of transport device. And we were all transported to the cells."

"We didn't see anyone for at least a day." Reeve again. "But when they came it was with food and blankets. One of them sat outside the cell and showed us photos. He pointed to them and every time he thought he got the answer he wanted, he'd hand over a single portion of food or a blanket. If he thought we were hedging, he would take one away. At that point we didn't understand what they were trying to achieve, so we had no reason to lie. But after about an hour of it, we understood. They were trying to learn English. To understand what we were saying."

Estard had to admit that didn't sound all that bad compared to how Greenway and Lance had been treated by these very same fellows. It was terrible, of course, no question. But it sounded no worse than a regular prison. Not like a P.O.W.

"They did that for four or five days, I think. I lost count." Reeve looked more and more tired as he spoke. Probably between the good hot meal and the feeling of safety, he was ready to sleep for a week. "Then we didn't see them for a day or two, and we didn't get fed. We were left wondering if they'd come back."

"When they did, they separated us," Garcia told them. "Some of us could still see each other, because we were in adjoining cells, but others were taken away. For what purpose, I could not say. Reeve was one of them."

Reeve nodded. It was clear he was not eager to speak about this period of his captivity. But he did, if slowly.

"They wanted to know where the Giants were," he breathed. "We didn't know, we couldn't help them. But they'd learned enough English, even if it was broken, for us to understand what they wanted. So, we were punished, a lash for every refusal to answer. A punch across the face for every 'I don't know'. Well, that's how it was for me, at any rate, and I assume it was no better or worse for the others."

"You eventually told them about the mountain," Kristin put in quietly. "Why else were you there?"

Reeve's voice cracked when he spoke again. "I couldn't do it anymore." The look in his eyes was begging for forgiveness. "I was perpetually hungry, beaten more than ever before in my life. I thought you would all be long gone." And they would have been, had they not returned. "I was surprised to see anyone. But I didn't tell them you were there. I walked away without approaching you."

Kristin took a deep breath and let it out slowly. "That's true. I cannot fault that. I saw you and wanted to come back for you. We'd been looking for you." She gave each of them a significant look. "For all of you. But why did you lead us into that ambush?"

Reeve looked as if he wanted to sink into the ground, but stubbornly, and stiffly replied, "Because once you approached me, I couldn't be sure they hadn't seen you, and I was concerned about what would happen to the others if I simply went with you..." He let it sit there, and Kristin nodded her understanding.

When they were all done with their story, Major Preston gave them spare kit to bed down with, and they took it gratefully. Almost as soon as they had it in their arms, those men walked away and laid themselves down in the middle of the camp.

Estard could imagine. He'd been a P.O.W himself. Very briefly, but even so. Returning to the safety of your own people meant a good night's rest. As much as one might sleep as a prisoner, it was almost never restful.

Kristin looked at them with a mix of emotions running across her face that he could not pick out. He thought at least two of them were pity and concern.

"How do you think things are going up on the Docker?" she asked him.

He was surprised by the question. With her return he'd actually forgotten about their plight up there. "Your guess is as good as mine," he replied. "Best to ask the Major, he's the one getting all the updates. But he won't take us up."

"I know. I just want to know how they are."

CHAPTER TEN

Weiz was ready to hit the man.

They'd worked so hard on this 'cure', and two hours after it was administered, he still hadn't woken up. She didn't know exactly how long it was supposed to take, but she was sure it wasn't this long.

She turned her attention to Doctor Namimbi who was close by, monitoring and taking notes. "How long?" She wanted to know.

"If it hasn't done what we intended by the fourth hour, we may try a different solution," he told her patiently without looking away from his work. "It will take a while for it to penetrate enough infected cells to allow recovery. The longer they've been down, possibly the longer it will take."

"So why did we test Harvey first?"

"Harvey was one of five, you know that. He as a 'Giant'—whatever that means. The others along a timeline of infection. It's only a trial, not a guarantee." He stepped away from the patient he'd been taking notes over and looked at her. "We've been over this three times now, Commander."

"Hmph," she responded, but said no more. It was true. She'd been at him every half hour since they'd given it to him. In truth, she should have been out at the hangar, preparing with the remaining awake and alert airmen, but she needed to know if this worked first. Could they breathe a sigh of relief and move on, or were they going to have to go back to the drawing board and hope they could find another method before some of them started dying? It was already dangerously close for some.

Colonel Sumner had confined the uninfected to the other side of the ship, himself along with them. He was preparing his ground troops for an assault. They didn't know how, or when, or even if. But it seemed likely.

The airmen understood their jobs. It was very straight forward. If the Bahana men came in ships, they should go out and fight them in their regular formations. It was hard to come up with a battle plan when you were on the defensive. You could dig in, give yourself a good barrier. Make the enemy pay in blood for every step they took forward. But in space, the big and empty place that it could be, finding that place to dig in could be almost impossible.

Among the patients in the room, was the Bahana man who'd been brought up what felt like months ago, to Weiz. She had, in fact, forgotten he was still there, unaffected by the illness, until he muttered something that sounded like, "You have no idea what's coming for you."

Weiz's head came up and she stared at the man on the other side of the room. He was still strapped down, and he was looking at the ceiling.

"What is coming for us?" she asked as she got up and moved slowly toward him.

A smug smile grew on the man's face, and she resisted the urge to kill him right there and be done with. Her patience with all of it was wearing very thin.

Weiz slammed a hand down on the side of his bed and leaned over until her face was less than a foot from his. "You will tell me what I want to know, or so help me, I will throw you out the airlock," she whispered through clenched teeth. "What is coming for us?"

Ensign Brioli raised his eyebrows at her and jerked his hands as if to show they were still restrained. "We are," was all he said, then refocused his eyes on the ceiling, smile still on his lips.

If there'd been enough room left in the infirmary, she'd have tipped the bed over and left him there for a while, but as it was, at best it would have tilted, and just annoyed the airman in the bed beside him.

Weiz was frustrated. At the amount of time everything was taking. At everything that was happening. At people's insistence that she lead them. At the lack of information she had access to.

As she breathed and tried to calm herself, she had to remind herself that her heightened emotional and irrational state was a product of her prolonged use of powers. If she didn't use them too often, she'd function normally. But it was one thing to know it, another thing to work through it. The urges were strong.

She turned toward the door, determined to have a shower and calm herself down. To not smell like a sewer when Harvey finally woke.

The moment she took a step outside that door she heard a groan. She spun so quickly to let her eyes find who had made the sound, that she felt momentarily dizzy. She heard the groan again, this time followed by a short movement. It was Abramovich. He seemed to be waking.

Too excited to think, Weiz moved back toward Harvey and resumed her seat at his bedside. If Abramovich was waking, it was only a matter of time, she was sure. He'd been first infected.

Doctor Namimbi was taking readings. Abramovich had yet to

open his eyes, though the groaning and moving was increasing. "He is getting better, isn't he, Doctor?"

The longer Namimbi took to answer, the more anxious Weiz became. "It's hard to say," he replied finally. "His heart rate has elevated, so he's either dreaming or in pain. Both, possibly. But I see no sign of him waking."

"Are we in good or bad territory, here?"

Abramovich's eyes, and Namimbi's mouth shot open at the same time.

None of them had expected any kind of violent reaction, so Abramovich was not strapped down. His entire body shook, and limbs flailed. Namimbi threw himself over the man's shoulders and yelled to Weiz to restrain his legs.

"Airman Abramovich," Namimbi said, "You are in the infirmary aboard Docker C1-2C, in orbit above the planet you know as Eridu. If you understand what I am saying, and are capable, please respond."

Abramovich's entire body calmed. If it was in response to Namimbi, or just happenstance, was hard to tell.

Weiz watched Namimbi do what Doctors did. Light in the eyes, stick in the mouth, listen to the chest. He asked Abramovich questions, and though the man seemed slow and disoriented, he answered.

Every test Weiz felt the man passed, was an indication to her that Harvey was going to be ok. She knew she should care about the lives of everyone aboard, equally, but she couldn't. When it came to that man, she never could.

There appeared to be no order to who woke when. Someone who'd been infected as recently as the day before could wake before someone who'd been infected three days ago, while Abramovich had clearly been the first.

Still, Harvey lay unmoving, and Weiz began to worry. What was taking so long? Why wasn't he awake yet? Did he not want to wake? As if the man had a choice. But these were the thoughts that ran though her mind.

Deidra came in to check on everything. She, among a small group of scientists, had chosen to use the 'cure' as an inoculation, to test its efficacy before infection. If Weiz had to guess, the woman just hated being in hazmat. But it was a valid test, to prevent anything like this from happening again. At least, to this particular group of people.

"How's your work going?" Weiz asked when the woman approached.

"Slow and steady, but we'll get it done soon enough." She looked pointedly at Harvey. "Nothing?"

Weiz shook her head. "He's a stubborn man," she said as if one had anything to do with the other.

Deidra was about to say something when the intercom blared on, "Weiz, to the Briefing Room." It sounded like Private Miller. Deidra pursed her lips and gave a nod, while Weiz got up and sighed.

"Back to work, Doctor," she said as they both moved toward the door.

"What else is there?" the woman asked.

Deidra kept her silent company for a corridor or two before they parted ways.

While they still respected each other, since they'd been aboard the Docker they rarely spoke, and never about personal things. She supposed their experience on the ground had forced them together. Their mutual predicament in becoming Giants, or Gods, or whatever it was they really were. But in the real world, they'd probably never have spoken at all. Though Deidra worked for the ATF, same as Weiz, she didn't work in the Military Division. If it weren't for the incident that began it all, they'd likely never even have crossed paths.

Weiz stopped in front of the briefing room door and gathered herself. She tried to tamp down all the overactive emotions, and unnecessary thoughts so she could focus on the task at hand. Truly, Colonel Sumner had not asked much of her. Just do her job. That's all. That was all she had to do.

Ready, she walked in, nodded to Private Miller, and sat down at the far end of the table from Sumner. "Colonel," she greeted.

"Commander," he said, and gave a tablet to Miller who brought it to her.

She eyed the Colonel askance, but waited for the Private to hand it to her and perused it before she made comment.

For the first time in days, she worried about something other than Harvey. She glanced at the tablet, to the Colonel and back again. "Where was this?" she wanted to know.

"A days hard march from the landing site," he told her. "That was taken less than an hour ago."

Weiz rubbed her eyes. She had no idea what time it was, or even what day. But the photo she was looking at showed dawn or dusk, around a marching army at least a thousand strong.

"What time is it now?"

"Adjusted to the landing site, seven-fifteen A.M." He looked as tired as she felt.

"So, they'll be there tonight, or tomorrow morning?" They did not have a thousand troops to put on the ground. Even with her airmen. "The ground is your arena, Colonel. What's the plan?"

Before he could answer they were interrupted by a knock at the door. It was the Bridge Comms Officer, Graydon.

"Call in from the ground, sir," she said. "Tried to patch it through, but you have it turned off."

The Colonel grimaced and turned his jacket radio on. He pressed down on his cuff mic, "Go ahead."

Satisfied, the Comms Officer backed out of the room and closed the door.

Weiz listened in to the call, as Sumner had it set to intercom rather than personal. She often preferred to do the same.

"Preston here, sir." The line was a little crackly, like they had some interference happening. "We should have called in last night, but I suppose we were just too excited."

"Well, get on with it."

"We have eight survivors," he told them. Weiz sat up in her chair at the words. "Among them, Reeve, Walt, Dames, Garcia, Ramirez, Carson, Deville and Kristin."

Every name on that list was like an arrow in the heart. Both in a good and bad way. It was a feeling she did not think she could adequately explain, but the effort to keep the tears of joy from her eyes caused her to clench her fists and dig nails into her hands.

"While I am ecstatic to hear such news," — though he didn't sound it — "I'm afraid I must rain on your parade."

"I'm listening, sir."

"We've got at least a thousand men bearing down on your position. They'll be there within a day."

"That's a tough one, sir. Are we moving? Or are you sending backup? Do we know what they're fighting with?"

"Even if I could send every soldier aboard, it wouldn't be a fair fight," Sumner told the man. "I want you to pack up, move your ship and your men to somewhere more defensible. Dig in and send me the coordinates."

"Aye, sir."

"Sumner out." And he switched off his jacket radio.

Weiz knew that the Bridge Comms Officer probably got annoyed every time this man got a call. Technically, as the Senior in Charge, he was supposed to *never* have it switched off, even when he was on down time. In case of emergency. But she didn't judge it.

"You pointedly didn't answer his question," Weiz noted.

"Which one?"

"Do we know what they're fighting with?"

Sumner shrugged. "No. We don't."

Weiz was now caught between several warring feelings. Joy at the return of some of her airmen. Concern over the fighting force on the ground. Worry about Harvey and whether or not he would wake, even though there was every indication that the medication they'd developed was working. And a deep, sinking feeling that the Bahana men were going to turn up any moment.

In that moment, she felt like they had been caught with their pants down. Like these people had been one step ahead the entire time, and Weiz was just playing catch up. If they'd not developed the treatment for the sleeping sickness, they would have been in a much worse position. The question was, could they mount a viable defence before these people arrived?

"How are we playing this?" she asked. "You sending all the ground troops to back Major Preston?"

"Depends where he sets up. If it's only defensible from the one position, then how many troops will he be able to comfortably use in his defence? If there are some large outcrops nearby, perhaps we can set up some snipers. But mostly, Commander, I was hoping to send down one or two of you."

She knew what he meant, but she had to ask anyway. "You as in airmen, or as in Giant Killers."

The man spread his hands wide. "From all reports, the things you people are now capable of, are staggering. If we can use you, we should."

"In case you hadn't noticed, almost half the ship is currently unconscious, and that includes 'my people'."

"Miller tells me that the cure was a success."

Weiz furrowed her brows at the Private. How he had known that, when Weiz had only just found out herself, and she'd been in the room... She shook her head. It didn't matter. "We still don't know how long that is going to take. I hope they're all ready by tomorrow. But I am afraid it may take a little longer than that."

"Well, it's a thought, anyway," the Colonel continued. "We're thinking contingencies and strategy here, Commander. Feel free to add your thoughts."

He was losing his patience with her. She needed to clear out the effects of using her powers as quickly as possible. She couldn't help it. Hadn't even known what her weakness was, until they'd started work in the lab a few days ago and Deidra had pulled her aside to question whether she really wanted to do it. It made sense, particularly in regard to how she'd behaved toward Kristin that first month. Not that that excused it completely. Those feelings had to have come from somewhere.

"My apologies, Colonel," she breathed out. And it was hard. "Seems the effects of using my powers for a prolonged period have yet to wear off."

"Perhaps not," he said dismissively, "But we have work to do. Push through it, whatever it is."

"I'm not sure that using any of us is the best idea," she told him. "Aside from Harvey, none of us goes without any kind of consequence. And besides, the Bahana men seem to be here for us, and they have ways of nullifying our powers."

"So I'm told." He made a clicking noise with his tongue then took a deep breath before continuing. "I wonder what makes Harvey so special."

Weiz shook her head slowly. "The only one that had the answer to that question, died the day Harvey got his power. Even Deidra doesn't know."

"Give me a firsthand accounting," he demanded. "Tell me what all of you can do, and what the consequences are. Then, perhaps, we can decide best disposition."

~

Greenway's recovery was shorter than he ever could have imagined, but much longer than he'd have liked. By the end of that first day, he was able to move his head. By the next morning, he could almost sit up. When the girl came again in the afternoon, he had his legs dangling over the edge of the bed, but he couldn't walk more than a few steps. She'd brought him his food.

She watched him warily from where she stood next to the door. He supposed it was one thing to speak to a dangerous murderer while he was strapped face down on a bed, quite another to meet him face to face in a small room. He couldn't blame her.

He sat very still on the edge of that bed, and said, "Can't walk yet."

She gave a slow nod, raised her brows, pocketed the keys in her hand, and moved forward. She placed his meal on the end of his bed and then stepped away.

Greenway thanked her and placed the tray in his lap. He couldn't tell what the food was supposed to be. There were four sections on the tray and three of them were full of mashed substances: one white, one pink and one orange. The final was some kind of red meat, well cooked, and cut into very small pieces. He supposed they wanted to give him no reason for anything beyond the spoon they provided.

The silence between them as the girl watched him shovel food into his mouth was more uncomfortable for her than it was for him. He was accustomed to it. Even liked it most of the time.

He was halfway through the orange mash, that he thought might be pumpkin, when she finally spoke.

"Two days. We have two days to decide," she told him.

He swallowed before he responded. "Before who decides what?"

"My group," she whispered and glanced at the door as if it might suddenly open at any moment. "Reform Faction. And whether we take you back."

Greenway stopped eating for a moment and stared at the girl, trying to gauge her sincerity. Since her visit the day before, he had not been able to tamp down that hope, but he had also tempered it with a good deal of cynicism.

"You would do that?" he asked finally. "Take me back? Even after everything I've done?"

She moved a little closer to the bed so she could lower her voice further. "Reform Faction believes that we are interfering in things that we don't understand, and that we should not be involved."

Greenway shook his head. Seemed that the galaxy over had its fair share of such conflicts. There had been many such on Earth, over hundreds of years. So many, he couldn't name them all. Some people in a country wanted to get involved in a war, usually the ones in power, and others thought it was a bad idea, and sometimes tried to do something about it. Rarely, but sometimes.

He took another bite of mush before asking, "What's your name?"

Her face flushed, whether in embarrassment or anger, he couldn't tell. He'd never been great at reading people like that. "Rochelle," she replied.

"Well, Rochelle, tell me, why are you all involved in the first place?" He had so many questions at this point, if she could answer even half, he might be satisfied.

She looked toward the door again. He had to figure she was once again not meant to be in there. She seemed to settle herself, and said, "Alright, a little history lesson, and then I have to go.

"This world is Bahana. But our people came here across the stars millennia ago. So long ago, that it was almost completely forgotten during a dark age for us, where we had no technology, and no knowledge of how to build it."

Greenway almost choked when he let out a, "Hmph," while his mouth was still full.

She ignored him and continued. "They found the old ships about a thousand years ago, now. It had everything, about where we'd come from, how we'd got here. *Why* we came. And who the Shadowmen were.

"These destructive beings who had been created near the same time that we'd taken our maiden voyage into the stars. The Captain of one of those ships knew at least six of the Shadowmen personally, before they had turned, and he saw nothing but a monster in their place. He was determined to drive that monster from them, if he could catch them. But he didn't have the technology yet."

Rochelle sighed and looked at the door again. Greenway shook his head.

"So, based on the logs of a single Captain, in a ship that you couldn't make or fly, your people decided to what? Make it your mission to finish what that one man started?" He put the tray down. It was almost finished. "We're a different group of people now."

"That's half the problem," she let him know with a frown. "The others, the ones we had yet to catch, they had become dormant. We didn't have to worry too much about them becoming violent and disturbing the natives. It made hunting them a lot harder, but we managed."

Rochelle stopped there and seemed to listen to something outside. "I have to leave it there. I must go. I'll try to bring you dinner." She grabbed the tray off the end of the bed and left without saying goodbye.

Greenway wasn't sure what to think of the situation. It seemed to him they inherited a task that didn't matter to them. If that Captain had known the people infected, he could understand why he would have wanted to 'drive the demons out', so to speak. He'd been personally invested. But these people? They didn't know them. They had no reason to get involved. Perhaps that was the point of view of the Reform Faction that Rochelle spoke of. He would have to wait until she came again.

When dinner did come it was delivered and overseen by a very large, well-muscled man, who stood in the exact opposite corner of the room while he ate with his very dangerous spoon. Greenway didn't take his eyes from the man, and the man refused to look at him. He just stared directly ahead into nothingness. When he'd finished eating, the man took the tray and left without a word.

Greenway tried every once and while to walk. To the door and back. The first few times he failed, but by the time night rolled around — or what he assumed was night — he could manage three laps of bed to door and back. He wasn't going to be winning any races, but he was definitely on the mend.

He slept fitfully that night, dreaming of things that had never happened, but he could have all too easily done, had he desired. It was like a life of worst-case scenarios, and he couldn't stop himself. He woke up sweating and breathing hard well before breakfast and spent his time doing his laps from bed to door and back.

Breakfast passed without a meal being brought to him. When lunch rolled around, it was the burly man who refused to look at him. The closer it got to dinner, the more Greenway began to lose hope. Just a little. He had one more day, he reminded himself.

Dinner came, and it was the same guard. He ate the mush mechanically and handed the tray back without a word. Perhaps his cooperation would earn him some outside time, though he doubted it. He wasn't sure how long he'd been in there already, but he hadn't seen outside since the first day.

Convinced that he would not see Rochelle that day, he lay himself down to sleep. He would need the rest. He was healing very quickly, but he couldn't take it for granted. If he got into an altercation of any kind, it wasn't likely he'd win. Especially since his powers had been nullified. Another question he had for Rochelle. How were they doing that?

For the first time he wondered how many people on this planet even knew about them. He knew that on Earth, the ATF military wing kept a lot from the general public, and when things were released, it was done in such a way that though the information was out there, very few people paid attention to it. If he were to escape this place, and he was stuck on this world, would he be safe due to the ignorance of the public? Would he be able to use his powers?

Greenway was close to drifting into sleep, so deep into his thoughts was he, that he didn't hear Rochelle come in.

"Put these on," she whispered so close to his ear that he jumped, even as she lay clothes on top of him.

He didn't question her, he just put the brown pants, dark blue sweater and brown beanie on. It was a guard uniform, he realised.

She looked him up and down with a nod. Clearly satisfied, she instructed him. "Whatever you do, don't speak. Your accent is a dead giveaway. And follow me, one step behind and to the right. I'll fill you in on everything once we get to where we need to be. Then we'll have plenty of time."

He gave a sharp nod. He was accustomed to taking orders. As a member of the military, it was essentially his life, taking orders and not questioning them. Even when it had taken him away from his wife, who had begged him to stay. Just following orders. He'd bucked orders somewhat, after that, he realised now. Reckless, but effective, he'd been called. So, no one had pulled him up on it. Well, he was going to get back in the habit of listening to them, starting with this young girl.

The compound they were in was large, but not the biggest he'd been in. They were four stories underground, and above ground were fifteen large hangars that he could count, five to either side, and five, way down the back. He had to assume that they all could hold space ships such as the one that had brought him there.

They continued on silently over snowy ground that crunched

underfoot. It was very cold, and his breath misted in front of his face. In a small way, it reminded him of home. He didn't see anyone, though he was sure people were watching.

When they reached the third hangar on the right, Rochelle turned into a small open door and stopped. Dutifully, Greenway stopped one foot away and to the right.

There was a guard inside, sitting in a small booth, an array of electronic equipment in front of him that Greenway could not guess the use for. He seemed tired and disinterested until he saw who was in front of him.

"Rochelle," the man said with a smile. "Your father going out tonight, is he?"

"Yeah, he's with the hunting party."

"You know," the guard said and leaned forward conspiratorially to continue in a low voice. "We had contact from our people there. Those new ones, they got some guns. Won't be like finding and fighting them others. Word is, we have five ships out tonight." He leaned back in his chair and looked side to side as if he'd shared some sensitive information.

Greenway tried to mimic the burly guard who'd brought him food. Extreme disinterest, eyes ahead. No words.

Rochelle shuffled closer to the window and whispered to the guard on the other side, as if she wanted to know more about this secret. But what she said was, "I know. That's why we're getting on this one."

The man blinked at her for a moment, then burst out in a laugh. "Of course you are." He shook his head. "I should have known. Your father will never let you stray too far until you're married, will he?"

Rochelle pursed her lips in clear distaste. "No. Probably not."

The guard chuckled deep and low. "Well, go on round then, I'll open her up."

"Thanks Tilden." He gave her a nod as they turned and left back out into the cold.

Greenway wanted to ask the obvious question — why was the door not in that room? But he kept his mouth shut as instructed, and followed her around the side of the hangar, and into an elevator.

Inside, there were no buttons, she just waved at the camera above the doors. They closed, and the elevator went up, Greenway guessed, eight stories. All the way to the top of the hangar.

Once they were out, Greenway got his first look at the outer hull of the Bahana ship. It was ugly. Parts were red with rust, some of what he thought to be the front was covered in black he assumed was soot. There were knobs and protrusions all over it, square, round or an occasional octagon. There were no portals or windows to be seen, though he knew there was at least one somewhere on the ship. It's how Lance and he had known they were in space.

Rochelle pulled at the cuff of his sweater. She didn't say anything, but the look was telling. He followed until they reached a hatch, and she got in. He waited for the way to be clear and got in after her.

The ladder went down three floors and ended in what appeared to be a very full cargo bay. Just like the ones on Earth, everything was strapped down with some kind of webbing.

Rochelle led them through the space until they reached an ordinary looking wall that she put her palm to. It opened immediately, a very small door that she crawled through. Greenway had some doubts that he would fit, but managed to wriggle his way through.

The room they ended up in was at best three metres by three metres. And it was empty. It was not a bad sized room to be trapped in.

"Alright, we're safe," she told him.

"I have a lot of questions," he responded, relieved to be able to talk again.

"We have five days," she sighed. "And the passage is not going to be fun for us without a stasis pod. So, ask away, maybe it will keep us occupied enough we won't spend the entire time puking our guts up. I won't answer anything I think will put my people in jeopardy, though. Freeing you, does not mean I'm on your side. I just disagree with your treatment."

"You could have just put me in stasis with the rest, like you said before," he countered.

"Perhaps I should have."

"So why didn't you?"

She shook her head and looked to the ceiling. Deciding, he guessed, whether to tell him the truth of it.

"They are from before," she said finally. "You should be able to just go back to where you came from. You have nothing to do with any of this."

"We do now, though."

"Maybe."

He wondered if he should tell her that they actually couldn't go home. That they were trapped on that world for the rest of their lives. He decided not to, however. If her benevolence was based on that assumption, then he would let her assume. At least until they were well under way. He wanted no chance that she would change her mind.

After a short while of silence, Rochelle moved to the wall on their left and pushed an unseen button. Four beds slid out of the walls. Two on the left wall, two on the right, in bunk fashion.

"Strap yourself into one, it's going to get very bumpy, very quickly."

He did as bid, choosing the wall opposite her so he could see her face while they talked. "Are we on our way then?"

"Soon enough." She didn't seem too keen on it.

"You travelled like this before?"

"Just once," she said. "It's not something I'd make a habit of if I can help it."

Greenway nodded. "Five days."

"Five days," she repeated.

They settled in for the long flight.

CHAPTER ELEVEN

Harvey was home.

He stood before the broad doors of his Calzona home, staring through the small side window which had the privacy curtains pushed aside. The not so little face that stared at him had a cheeky grin, and Harvey was not sure he planned to open the door.

"Jason," he said in a playful, but warning tone. "Open the door."

"Who are you to demand such a thing?" The grin took all the bite out of his words. It was only a game.

"Well, I am your father," he replied. Simple, direct.

"You don't look like my father," Jason rejected his assertion with a shake of his head.

"What does he look like then?"

"Purple head. Green eyes. Yellow spots. Got him a few tentacles too." The boy raised his eyebrows.

Harvey turned away from the door and donned the mask he had been hiding behind his back. It was basically just a purple octopus that he put on his head, but with eye slits, and breathing holes. He turned back to the door.

"You mean like this?"

The door opened and Jason came out, barrelling into him with a hug. "I missed you," he said, arms wrapped tight around Harvey's chest. The boy was getting much too big.

"I missed you too," he replied, putting an arm around his shoulders.

In that moment, he noticed a very bright white light in the sky that looked like a firework suspended at its apex. It seemed odd, but not overly noteworthy.

When Jason let him go, they walked inside. He greeted Myrta and Henry, his in-laws who had been looking after the boy while he'd been away. They were good people, and he'd always gotten along with them.

It was near time to have dinner, and the table had already been set. The table seemed too elegant, and too large. The wood a dark mahogany, the chairs carved into patterns of scenes that made very little sense to his mind's eye. Yet despite the oddity, he accepted that it was his, and had always been his, and it was odder that he'd noticed it.

He sat down at the head of the table, Jason to his right, Myrta to his left. They spoke of how his son had been doing at school, of his achievements in rowing and soccer. How the boy was on track to become an engineer in the aerospace division, and he was very excited about that.

Harvey told them what he could of his short trip out to Jupiter. He went there, he fought some scary aliens and won, then he came home. And he was handing in his resignation.

At some point during the dinner, a very bright white light appeared above the table, like a firework frozen at its apex. He squinted and held his arm above his eyes. The others didn't seem to see it. The odd thought, *no, not yet,* flashed through his mind.

After dinner was finished, they went out the back and played soccer for a while. It had never been Harvey's game, he'd been more football, or basketball. But it was the boy's favourite sport, and as his father, he'd oblige a game or two.

When they were done, and Harvey tried to catch his breath, hands on knees, that damnable light appeared once again. He simply ignored it this time and walked inside.

After they'd cleaned themselves up and prepared for night, they sat in the parlour and talked. Harvey let them know that he was going to hand in his resignation to the ATF and get a more Earth based position with the USAF so he could be home more often. Everyone seemed to appreciate the news. Even Henry gave him a pat on the shoulder and told him it was a great idea, that he and Myrta had paid their dues, and they were getting too old to be looking after such an energetic young man.

Just as he was about to get up and go to bed, exhausted from his day, the light appeared so close to his face he had to put an arm up. His eyes closed and head jerked back in reflex. He heard someone say his name, at first softly, and then loudly.

"Harvey!" It was Lance, but what was the Pilot doing in his home. "Harvey! Get your arse out of bed!"

Harvey tried to open his eyes against the bright light to find that it had dimmed considerably. His vision was blurry, but he could make out Viatri leaning over him. He felt confusion and dismay at being displaced before the rush of memory told him where he really was.

A groan escaped his lips. "Fuck," was all he said.

Lance grunted and poked him. "You are one of the last, you lazy fuck. It's not so bad once you're up and moving."

Harvey closed his eyes. He wanted to go back. But even as he did, he felt that dream slipping away. He'd never remember it the same as he did in that moment just before waking. But he'd remember that feeling.

"Fine, fine," he said and pushed himself into a sitting position. "If I have to."

While he mentally prepared himself to be awake and useful, Lance filled him in on what had been happening and what their current position was. It didn't sound good. But it would have been a lot worse if Doctor Namimbi and Zalenka, with the help of Weiz and Deidra, had not been able to manufacture a cure.

For all that it had been designed to disable their enemies in such a way they'd be too preoccupied to notice an incoming force, Harvey had enjoyed the down time. As strange as that might have sounded had he said it out loud.

"How'd you know you could wake me?" Harvey asked after a while, confused. "From the sound of things, the rest of you woke naturally."

"You've been in and out of consciousness all day. You've just been too stubborn to actually get up."

Well, he had been having a good dream.

He felt at his chin and raised his brows. A few days indeed. "I suppose, shower, shave and get back to work."

"We have a lot to do," Lance agreed. "Weiz will fill you in on the plans when you're ready. She's in the Briefing Room with the Colonel and the usual suspects. Good news as well as bad, but I'll let them give you that."

"Kind of you," he said drily.

Lance backed away from the bed. "Just go get yourself in working order. Weiz is pissed that she couldn't be here to get you up herself, so you'll want to make it quick, or she might think you're trying to avoid her."

That was definitely not something he wanted to deal with. "Thanks."

Lance gave him a wink, then turned and made the tattooed eyes dance. "See you on the flip, sir. I'm headed out to the bays." He practically ran out of the room, probably because he knew how much Harvey hated those tattoos. Though they looked whole again, and he couldn't forget what had been done to make them so faint.

With a shake, Harvey forced himself out of the bed. At first, he felt a little dizzy, but as he moved, things righted themselves. After a few steady steps, he shifted to his locker and went about his business.

It didn't take him long until he was smelling fresh, had a clean shave, and felt like nothing had ever happened to him.

Weiz and the Colonel were indeed in the Briefing Room, along with Private Miller, Doctor Namimbi, Deidra, Gordon, Bridges, and Zim. The usual suspects and then some. He had a feeling he knew what was going to be asked of them. It made sense. To some degree, at least.

They were all happy to see him, of course, but Weiz launched herself from the other side of the room into his arms. He was quite taken aback at the display, and it took him a moment before he wrapped his arms around her. Normally she'd be careful not to be so public in her displays of affection, but clearly the cat was out of the bag.

Everyone in the room was suddenly very interested in anything other than them.

"Never do that to me again," Weiz whispered into his ear. "Or I'll make your life hell."

She pulled away and resumed her place at the head of the table next to Colonel Sumner. Her cheeks were quite flushed, and he knew that she felt embarrassed. He could play on that if he wanted to, but he decided the situation required his full attention.

"So, what's the plan?" he asked.

~

After Lance left Harvey in the infirmary, he moved straight to the hangar. The carriers were getting ready to deploy troops onto the ground, and Weiz wanted him down there to confuse things with his weather magic.

He thought it was a pity that it didn't work from space. How much damage could he have done if he didn't have to worry?

But they also didn't know what they were up against. The technology of the Bahana men, or the ploughs and swords of the native Eridu people. He had to admit he would feel bad if it was the latter. They were kind of invading them, even if the land was not currently in use.

There were three soldiers in front of him strapping their kits into the webbing of the aft section, and he was waiting his turn.

Carriers were like cargo planes; plenty of room, not much in the way of seating. He'd been in a few in his time. Usually on the way up rather than the way down, but he was fairly certain he knew what to expect.

Lance moved forward once the last soldier was done and clipped his bag into the webbing. It was odd to have one, as a space pilot. His kit was generally whatever he had on him, and except for the one scenario they'd lived through, the likelihood that a space pilot was ever going to be in a position to need a kit, was extraordinarily low.

He shook himself from the thought. He knew that he was just putting off preparing for what work needed to be done on the ground. He turned away from the aft, moved to the back of the row of soldiers, pulled the straps down from the low ceiling and buckled himself in. He shoved his booted feet into the depressions in the deck until he heard a click. Then a neck and shoulder guard descended from above to cradle his upper back and shoulders, neck and head. It was far more comfortable than it looked or sounded.

The soldiers moved quickly. They had practiced this thousands of times. Had made hundreds of drops. They knew what they were doing the way Lance knew what he was doing in a pilot's seat. The prep was done quickly, and the carrier was ready to go.

The side doors slid shut with an ominous hiss. The cabin was pressurised. The first shifting move felt like hitting a pothole in a car doing sixty.

Lance held onto his chest straps and forced himself to breathe. The carrier could barely be called a ship. It was less piloted, more coerced. It was a road train, where he drove a Mercedes.

Once they were out in the open space, the ride was much less bumpy. They also didn't have gravity. Which, for Lance, was not fun. But they didn't bother to put the tech in these things. It was a waste of the limited element.

All said and done, the ride to the ground took all of twenty minutes. But it was twenty minutes that Lance would prefer to forget and never repeat. He'd never been motion sick before, but he was close to emptying his stomach on this one.

The soldier next to him clapped him on the shoulder as the braces retracted into the ceiling. "First time down on one of these?" Lance swallowed and nodded. "No shame. We all felt it the first few times. Takes some getting used to."

While Lance appreciated the words, he could not imagine having to do that ever again. The upward trip was definitely a much smoother experience, and his expectation that the landing would be similar was thoroughly disabused.

When he walked out into the open air, Lance breathed deep. He threw his almost empty bag over his shoulder and looked to the sky. Although a little overcast, it was mostly fine. He had plenty to work with, but he'd have been lying to himself if he didn't admit his concern that what happened the week prior might happen again. An accidental superstorm, stopped in the nick of time before it could do any major damage. It had only been five or six days, yet it felt like forever. Even after a full day of sleep thanks to the Bahana plague.

Lance breathed a sigh and looked back toward the ship. Seemed they were to move to the other side of it, and he'd gone out the wrong way like a moron.

Just as he turned around, he saw a flash from his left that he couldn't quite follow. There was a tap on his arm, and a voice in his ear. "Got you this time, Sinatra."

He spun again, this time with the odd thought that he might look like a ballerina. It was Kristin. He'd known it from the voice and the nickname, but he wanted to see her.

"Solid C minus," he told her. "It was lazy, no effort, felt like a bug bite."

This time when she hit him, it really hurt. "How bout now?" she asked.

He was rubbing at the spot that she'd hit. "Ahhh. A. fucking A." He blinked at her, not sure whether he was going to say it after that hit. But he had to. "Good to see you out, Belle." He braced himself for another hit, but it didn't come. He guessed she'd paid it forward.

She indicated a direction with her head and started walking with the clear expectation that he'd follow. He did.

"They fill you in on everything up there?" she asked as they walked.

"I'd assume on everything important. But *everything*? I doubt it."

"Then tell me what you do know, and I'll fill in the gaps."

She was taking him toward the woods, which in this particular area looked massacred. Whether from the meteor shower, or his impromptu storm, or perhaps both, he couldn't tell. But the trees were shattered here and there, some had fallen over, roots and all, and the ones left standing looked as if they'd taken a lick from a wood chipper. Some of the ground nearby looked charred and pitted, and that gave it away. Meteor shower.

Lance filled Kristin in on what Weiz had told him. By the time they reached the small clearing where three people sat around a fire, he was done.

"That would be about it," Kristin nodded.

Because he couldn't make out their faces through the heat haze, Lance gave a general wave in their direction without comment. He didn't want to be rude.

"Fyord, Hadley and Estard," Kristin told him softly. The surprise must have been clear on his face. "Guess she left that out."

"Guess so."

Lance threw his kit down and took a seat next to Estard, and Kristin sat beside him. Estard looked momentarily annoyed but said nothing.

"Good to see you up, Agent man," Lance nodded. "Fyord, Hadley. Wasn't sure you lot were planning on rejoining us."

"Fucking weren't goin' down like that," said Hadley.

Kristin mumbled under her breath, barely audible even to Lance, "Fucking Kiwi."

Lance raised his eyebrows at that but refrained from question. It was clearly not meant to be heard.

Fyord just shrugged and shook his head, while Estard looked thoughtful. Seemed they didn't have much to say.

"So, fill me in," Lance said.

Kristin gave him the story of her capture and rescue. He was glad to hear that most of the airmen had made it back, though he didn't know any of them personally. He had some sympathy for what they might have been through.

He felt at the back of his head, as had become his habit after his short capture. Kristin patted him companionably on the shoulder, as though he was the one who'd just been released.

Estard told of his down time, and asked them, "Is it just me? The whole life thing?"

They all looked at each other in consultation and curiosity. Lance shook his head and shrugged. The other three all agreed it was strange and hadn't happened to them, which made Estard withdraw into thoughtfulness.

Lance took a deep breath and tapped the log next to him with bare knuckles. Aside from the day they'd killed the Giants, he hadn't died. And even then, it may have just been a close thing, because he hadn't woken in the field. Though he did wonder if being pulled across the galaxy on a ray of light counted, as had happened when they were trying to make their escape from Estard's people.

"Now to why we're here," Lance said to get their attention. "They might just have worked out how to use us right." He looked directly at Fyord and Hadley. "I don't imagine either of you has had time to really work out your powers, but if we can manage what Commander Weiz and Colonel Sumner have asked, then it could really make a difference in how this all plays out."

"Ten minutes ago, you thought they were dead," Kristin said with a frown. "How could they possibly be in the plan you had coming down?"

Lance gave her one of his best smiles, the kind that drove her crazy and almost always got him hit. But she didn't hit him. "Because they left the *how* up to me, and I see their usefulness."

Kristin rolled her eyes toward the sky. "We're screwed."

CHAPTER TWELVE

The flight was like going on a rollercoaster through Hell's most famous attractions. He'd found it hard to imagine when she'd told him, but going through it... He hoped after the trip was done, he'd never have to do it again.

There were periods of weightlessness, followed by extreme inertia, followed by the sensation of tremors through the body. Things got searing hot, then freezing cold. There was the feeling of disconnecting from the body, only to be jolted by the sensation of sinking into the bed. Ups and downs, highs and lows, and absolutely no way to predict when which was going to happen.

While they were both awake, he asked questions in an attempt to keep his mind from what was happening. He believed she answered for the same reason.

"Why did your people restart this war?" he wanted to know.

It took a little while for Rochelle to answer, and he wondered if she'd passed out. He wouldn't have blamed her. But perhaps she'd just been thinking.

"I guess our ancestors wanted a safe way home," she replied finally. "I don't know why we keep going now, though, unless the Corps and Govs think there might be something there the rest of us don't know about."

Greenway grunted at that. It was very human. He didn't know why he kept being surprised by the similarities when there were some things that were just inherent. "What have the old ones taught you?"

"The old ones, as in, the Shadowmen?"

He nodded before he realised she had her eyes shut. "Yes, the Shadowmen."

"I couldn't tell you," she responded. "I know that we got a lot of our tech from them. After we'd lost our knowledge and were stealing from our ancestors' graves. We got our understanding of it from the old ones. A lot of them were scientists before they were changed. At least, that is what the logs said. They were caught by the original captain and kept in stasis that whole time."

It was hard to keep track of the conversation at times as the trip seemed to mess with how sound played across the room. From time to time, he had to repeat himself, or ask Rochelle to say something again. There were times when they both passed out. Whether because they were both exhausted or they were just going through some kind of rough patch, he could not tell.

"What's Earth like?" she asked him at one point.

He wasn't sure how to answer that. Not because there was a lot to say about it and he needed to pick and choose, but because he didn't spend much time there. And what time he did spend there was mostly either underground, or in some secluded cabin.

"Like most worlds, I would think," he replied eventually. "Big cities with lots of people, doing unfathomable things. Farmlands stretching miles, with all kinds of produce to keep the world fed. Woodlands, rainforests, tundras, deserts, icebergs and lands full of snow. Ancient wonders from those who came before us, and ancient mistakes that plague us in the modern day." At some point he forgot that he was answering a question and just became introspective about Earth, and how he saw it.

"That does sound a lot like Bahana," Rochelle agreed.

"Not Eridu, though."

"No, not them."

"Do you know why? Why they don't have tech, I mean?" He was suddenly curious, even though in that moment his stomach was trying to rise to the ceiling while the rest of his body was being pushed into the bed.

"It was forbidden, after the incident." She took a moment to swallow and breathe before she continued. "That much was written in the captain's log. It had caused such widespread chaos. So many people had died, and so much had been destroyed, it was deemed only the most necessary tools for survival would be made thereafter. The cities were either buried or cannibalised for building materials. The people there now don't even remember how advanced their people had been."

During a short lull in the ride, Rochelle unstrapped herself from the bed and made a trip into the adjoining room. She came back with some food and suggested to him that if he had to use the bathroom, then was the time, and gave him instruction on the where and how.

They shared a meal in silence, then they strapped themselves back in, and Rochelle slept while he wondered when the next loop of the rollercoaster would start.

It was only five days. But it felt like months. Somehow, Rochelle knew when to use the facilities, and when to eat. Even if the break was a mere five to ten minutes long. It was always during a period of weightlessness.

"Why did you rescue me?" he asked again at some point, though he couldn't have said what day it was.

"I already told you," she said, her tone exasperated.

"But even after all I did, is that really your answer?" The guilt he felt about the situation was greater than he could ever have believed. Some of the memories that flashed into his mind at times, made little sense. But he knew them for what they were. It was a kind of madness.

"What else would you have me say?" she asked in turn. "We're aware that being what you are does strange things to the mind. Many of the old ones suffered consequences for use of their 'powers'." She put so much derision into the word that he wondered at the prejudice.

"And that is why you see it as 'curing' us? With all that torture?"

Her face flushed a deep red, and her brows drew down as she looked at him and said, between clenched teeth, "*I* do not see it that way. That is why you are here."

"I didn't mean to imply it was you, specifically. I meant the people who had me, before you got me out."

She grunted at him and returned her eyes to the bunk above her while she calmed. "Yes, I suppose they see it that way. At least, that is what they say. And I have to believe it, because how else could they possibly justify to themselves what they do?"

That was not something he could answer for her. He suspected that she was concerned about her father, and his reasons for doing the things he did.

Another time, as the tremors shook through his body, he wondered aloud, "Why are we going to Eridu now?" It was strange that it had not occurred to him at any point before then, to wonder why they would want to take ships back, when they'd run away two weeks ago.

"Partly to scare off your people," she admitted, teeth knocking together on every other word. "The Council discussed it after we brought you back, and they didn't want to leave it too long before we made a move. A full show of strength, including the Uragoan, and we're hoping you will all just go, and leave us to ours. Obviously there are others who believe we should capture you all — the Shadowmen, that is. The Council will allow it, so long as it doesn't interfere with getting rid of the others. Ideally, they'd prefer no others have technology to rival ours."

"It's not going to be that simple," he sighed. "My people won't leave without a fight. They're military. If they think they're about to be attacked, they'll dig in."

"We made sure they wouldn't have the manpower." She sounded almost guilty with the words. "Besides, you were all so eager to leave before. We watched you trying, that's why we left you all alone for so long. Why would that have changed? We couldn't understand why you'd come back."

Did he tell her then? That the 'Shadowmen', the 'Giants', the 'Gods', couldn't leave? That they were as stuck as a tree? He wondered if it would change her belief about whether or not he belonged on their world. Even if it was just in stasis, rather than being tortured. He didn't want to risk it. Not until he was well off the ship.

"They came back because they got it wrong, the first time," he told her. "Not so nefarious."

"And the giant ship they brought with them? An accident too?" She sounded bitter and angry.

"What big ship?" The last thing he remembered before he'd been transported to Bahana, was Harvey trying to rescue him with a small group of soldiers. He supposed those soldiers had to have come from somewhere, but he really hadn't considered it.

"We may have caught you before it arrived. I wasn't with them on that trip, I am unclear of the exact timeline."

"But there is a big ship?"

"Of that I am certain."

For another undefinable period of time, they remained silent. Greenway tried to sleep, as he found the constant motion gave him a headache. But he had trouble with it and found himself puking into a bag more than once. He was not alone, as he saw Rochelle raise a bag to her own face on more than a few occasions, and the sounds were almost as bad as the ride.

"How much longer?" he asked.

"Three days," she responded.

He truly had no sense of time, and he wondered aloud how she managed to, with the windowless room, on a ship in the middle of space.

She raised her hand and pointed to her wrist. For the first time he realised she was wearing a watch. Or, what he thought of as a watch. "Day, time, date," she said simply, with a swallow on the last word.

Still, three more days. He couldn't believe it had only been two. It felt like a lot longer. The remaining time would feel like just as much and half again. He wished the halfway point had already been reached. He was not enjoying this flight.

They spent much more time not talking, than talking. The level of misery he felt for the most part, was not conducive to conversation, and he had to assume she felt the same. For all that she'd told him they'd have plenty of time to talk, he didn't think they'd had more than an accumulated three hours in three days.

They ate, they slept, they moved from time to time, and they talked in brief patches.

When the rollercoaster stopped, it took his body a moment to register it, but when it did, he was ready to be up and out of there. He didn't consider stealth. He didn't consider anything. His only thought was fresh air and an end to the tumult.

Rochelle rushed to his side and pulled him back from the door. "We can't leave yet," she hissed.

He turned on her, ready to fight his way out. But when he saw her face, he calmed. "I don't know how much longer I can take this," he told her.

"We're not there yet," she said. "If you leave now, you'd be walking into space."

Another thing that had not occurred to him. "Will this ship land?"

She shook her head as she made her way back to her own bunk in slow steps. "Strap yourself back in, it's not over. We've just started deceleration." She pointed him toward his own bunk.

He took a deep breath and did as she bid. "This has to be the worst space flight I've ever endured."

"I did tell you it would be bumpy," she grumbled, "And you won't have to make the return trip!"

"Perhaps not," he conceded, and was more than a little thankful for that. The thought alone made his stomach flip. "But I ask again, will the ship land?"

"No. We'll have to use the transporters." She pulled a gun from her bag and showed it to him side on.

It took him a moment to realise it was of the same design as the one the man on the ground had used on him, when he'd tried to take that village. He shook his head. Not at the gun, but at the memory of himself as a monster, who would kill and maim in order to get what he wanted. And what he'd wanted didn't even make sense to him now. Worshippers. What for? What possible use could they be?

If there was only one thing to be thankful to these people for, it was the clearing of his mind. Bringing him back from what he'd become, to the man he had once been. He just had to make sure he didn't let that happen again. Though he wasn't sure how much of a choice he had in the matter.

"How much longer?" he wanted to know.

"Half a day."

He settled back, hoping against hope that it wouldn't return to the rollercoaster.

~

They could see the ships coming from the port observation window. Tiny specks in the distance, magnified by eight hundred percent.

"And we're certain that's them?" Colonel Sumner asked.

Weiz raised a brow at him. "Who else? If there's another dog in this fight, I don't know them."

"This place has been full of surprises, Commander. Would it really be a stretch to think there's another faction out there somewhere?"

"Probably not, but still, I think we can safely assume it's them."

Harvey shrugged uncomfortably beside her, and she looked to him with a small smile. They had yet to have a proper reacquaintance after his awakening, and she looked forward to that. But his mind was somewhere else entirely. She wished she knew what had been going on in there, but it would have to wait.

"We can't face an Armada," Harvey breathed at last, his eyes on the ships in the distance. "Even if I can get groups of men on board. It was the meteors that sent them packing last time, not us."

Sumner shook his head. "Last time doesn't matter," he told him. "That was a search and rescue. This is drop and go. My men are trained for infiltration, I don't need you to do more than get them in there for me."

"And get them out," Havery mumbled.

Sumner did not respond to that and Weiz shared a glance with Harvey. It felt like the first time he'd looked at her since the briefing room.

"Lance is in position on the ground," Weiz told Sumner. "Between him, Fyord and Hadley, they should have a pretty effective defence."

"And how many teams do you have to fly the MM ships?"

"More men than ships, ironically." She breathed deep at the sudden intrusive memory of the men and women who had rushed to die at the hand of the Giants. It was a memory she had tried to stay away from, in her quest to be a better leader.

"Which is how many?" The man wanted specifics.

"One hundred and twenty-seven ships, one hundred and thirty-six teams."

"Does that include... you?" He waved his hand to either side, indicating both her and Harvey. She assumed he meant any of the Giant Killers.

"No," she said sharply. "I do realise we have other obligations." Much as she occasionally resented that.

The Colonel nodded as if he'd expected no less. "How close do you need to be before you can board them?"

Harvey shrugged. "I could do it now. I only ever need to know where something is. If I can see it, I can move there."

"Even that far out?"

"I don't see why not."

"Show me."

Harvey looked at Weiz. Captain to Commander. She gave him a small incline of the head to indicate permission, and he shifted.

Moments later he returned with something in his hand. It was small, round, and had a single switch on it.

"Souvenir?" Weiz asked as he handed it to her. When she was done looking at it, she handed it to the Colonel.

"Something like that," Harvey replied. "Just proof that I was on their ship. Nothing more."

"What does it do?" Sumner asked. It was small enough that it rested comfortably on the edge of two fingers. Sumner had his thumb above the switch.

"No idea."

The Colonel made to press it, but Weiz stayed his hand. "That could be bad for us," she insisted. "It could be for anything."

"It could be for a door," the Colonel responded. But he didn't push it.

"It could be for a weapon," Harvey said. "I didn't get much context from where I landed. I just picked it up from the table beside me and got out of there. There were people in the room."

"Did they see you?" Weiz wanted to know.

"I don't think so, their backs were turned. But if there were some behind me, maybe. I didn't check."

"That was reckless," the Colonel mumbled, but more as an observation than disappointment. "If they saw you, the element of surprise will be lost." He turned away from the window and looked directly at Harvey. "Start moving our people across. If we can capture one or two of those ships, it'll turn the tide."

Harvey nodded and ran off to where the troops were waiting in the hangar. Weiz looked after him for a moment before she became conscious of Sumner's eyes on her.

"When they're close enough, you know what to do." He held eye contact with her for longer than she would normally consider comfortable, but she didn't look away.

"I know my job, Colonel."

"I know you do, Commander." His words were soft, and he reached out a hand to her shoulder. "I wouldn't say this to anyone else," he continued, "but I wasn't expecting that many ships. Are you *sure* you can manage this?"

"No," she said just as softly. "But we're about to find out."

He squeezed her shoulder and let go. "To war." It was the way an ATF soldier said goodbye when they didn't think they'd come back.

"To war," she returned, and watched him as he left her alone on the observation deck. It was time for her to get started.

PART
SIX

~ MAGIC ~

Chapter Thirteen

From where they stood on the ridge line, Kristin could watch the natives strike camp and get ready to move, while she was covered by large rocks and trees. Even if they were to chance a glance upon her position, it would be hard for them to see.

Kristin turned back toward the others and reported on what she'd been seeing.

All Kristin knew of the natives was what she'd been told, and what she'd seen in the village that they used to steal food from. She hadn't expected them to raise a force so large, or so orderly.

Their weapons were swords, pikes, bows and arrows, axes and quarterstaves. Nothing that could do much damage to those from Earth. She almost felt bad for them, and definitely wondered why they were even there.

"This doesn't make much sense," she told Lance. "They have no hope against us, not with what they're using. There has to be something more, something we're not seeing."

Lance shrugged uncomfortably. "I'd be lying if I said this didn't make me less inclined to use my power on them."

"If we let them go, and there is something more behind the march, when they hit our lines, it could be disastrous." Estard sat on a rock close by and continued his thought as he absently pulled bark from a stick. "I would personally assume that they are under direction from our friends in the sky."

Kristin had to agree and said so. "It makes no sense otherwise. How would they even know we're here?"

Lance squinted down on the natives folding their tents and packing their gear. They were almost ready to march on, so if they were going to do something, it would have to be soon.

"All it would've taken was one person to get away from Greenway," he breathed after a while. "He did so much damage I would not be at all surprised if this was a reaction to him. It need not have anything to do with the Bahana men."

Kristin weighed it in her mind. Both scenarios had merit, and either way it went, they were holding tools for war that were so far outdated in her mind, it didn't really matter. They would be slaughtered.

"We could go down and talk to them," Fyord offered. "If there are any techies down there, it should draw them out."

"You volunteering?" Hadley wanted to know.

Kristin shook her head. She had not had a vision since she'd walked out of the underground cells. She was in no rush to have another one. But she had to admit, that from time to time, they could be useful in helping to make some decisions. But this time, it wasn't up to her. Weiz had given Sinatra the lead.

"It's up to you, Viatri," Kristin sighed. "I can't help you with this one. Either turn them around or go down and talk to them."

Lance felt at the back of his head and the look on his face betrayed his every thought. This was one pilot who would never get a Captaincy. He was far too obvious.

"Let's just do it," he said. "Turn them around. Fyord?"

Fyord gave a nod and stepped out so that he could see the people on the ground.

They'd agreed that Fyord would make them see the Giants in their path. Given they should be familiar with the figures, it was hoped their reaction would be immediate and decisive. Though they couldn't figure out how they could personally become those Shadowmen, Fyord assured them the image of them was so burned into his mind, he'd know their every detail 'til the day he died.

Hadley stepped forward to stand beside him. As soon as Fyord tapped her elbow, she got to work. Her ability appeared to be directed emotion. She would try to instil those below them with a sense of fear and urgency. The hope was that the extra push would cause a chaotic retreat.

After a few minutes, the columns of natives had formed up and they were ready to move. Fyord wore clear concentration on his face. Hadley wore frustration and determination.

The first column took their first step and Fyord growled. "Why can't you see it?"

When all the columns resumed their march toward where the soldiers had moved, it was clear that what they'd intended was not working.

Lance took a step forward and placed himself between Fyord and Hadley. Unlike them, he had a tendency to direct his power through gestures. No matter how often he was told he didn't need to. He took a deep breath, probably to blow a gale, and it started off well. But before it hit the ground in front of the marching men, it petered out and stopped completely.

All three turned around after that, with a simultaneous realisation. "They've got Bahana men with them," Fyord and Lance said at the same time.

"There is no other explanation," Hadley agreed.

Kristin swore a diatribe that Hadley seemed impressed with, while Estard's eyebrows climbed. "I thought they could only do that with the cages."

Lance shook his head. "Why would that be the case?"

"I don't know," she admitted. "I just assumed, I guess. I mean, what could they be using that prevents us from using our powers? And how did it differentiate between your powers, and a regular gale force wind?"

That was something they hadn't considered. That the Bahana tech would be able to tell the difference.

Estard threw up his hands and said, "I've gone back three times now, and the results are always the same."

Kristin looked to him. "Your time travel powers are intact?"

"We're far enough away," he dismissed. "Lance's power works until it gets close to that army. That's not the point."

"What is the point?" Fyord asked.

"What did you change?" Hadley wanted to know.

"The first time, I told Hadley and Fyord that it wasn't going to work, and Lance tried and failed." He listed off his failures on his hand. "The second time I tried to get down there and find what was causing the issue, but I couldn't get close enough. This time, well, I did nothing."

"So why tell us?" Kristin was curious.

"Get some ideas of what I can do the next time I go back and try to figure this out." He sucked at is teeth and looked into the middle distance. "If we don't turn them back here, things could get ugly."

"Have you been further into the future than this moment?" Lance asked.

Estard shook his head. "I can't go very far back. At least, not yet. I don't know if there is a hard limit or if I just need practice. I've never tried to go forward. But I have to admit," he continued, looking uncomfortable, "Major Preston got to me with the book he lent me."

Kristin shook her head and sighed. While she could appreciate the point of view, she had to say it, "We took you from five hundred years in the past, brought you to a different planet, and stopped you from doing whatever it was you might have done otherwise. The world didn't end."

"But we'll never know what the unintended consequences were," he returned. "Perhaps nothing, because I didn't have much of a life. I had no friends outside of my work, and not many within. I could have just as easily died in your escape."

"Which would never have happened if we hadn't gone back in time in the first place." Lance put in.

Kristin cut them off before the conversation got too animated. "We're here for those people down there. If you think there is something else we can do to try and turn them around, say your piece. If Estard can't go back too far, then we should get this done sooner rather than later."

The columns were already halfway through the small pass. They were only half a day away from where Major Preston and his men had set up their defensive position.

Everyone shook their heads one after another. "I got nothing," Hadley said. Fyord echoed the sentiment shortly thereafter.

"I wish I could offer something more helpful," Lance sighed. "But if we can't use our powers against them, it's going to have to be conventional weapons. I feel bad for them, being used by the Techies like this. But it is all I can think of. I'm not a strategist."

Kristin snorted. "No, you're a Pilot. And I am a Comms Officer. As are Hadley and Fyord." She shook her head. "We'll report back to the Major and see what he has to say. If we can pinpoint what they're using to prevent us from using our powers, then I am all for a raid to do something about it. But without it... It's soldiers' work, and we'll be better off putting ourselves to use elsewhere."

They all looked crestfallen. Their first real opportunity to use their powers to do something useful had come to nothing, and their specialties in the ATF weren't conducive to ground warfare.

They descended the ridge and started back toward the Major at a jog.

"Harvey would have been useful here," Lance's tone was mournful. "By the time we get back to the Major, he'll be able to see our failure with his own eyes."

"Harvey would be useful everywhere," Kristin shot through grit teeth. She was accustomed to Harvey turning up and flitting her about, even when she didn't want him to. It was actually good, to her mind, to be without him for a while.

"Not a runner, Viatri?" Fyord wanted to know.

Lance just shook his head as he huffed along. It wasn't that he was completely unfit, he just didn't run much. It looked as though he spent his fair share of time in the gym on the Docker, though.

"Who's our fastest?" Kristin asked.

Fyord put up his hand and said, "I'll run ahead, I'll see you lot when you catch up." Then he took off through shrub and tree.

Kristin beathed a heavy sigh. She'd been doing that quite a lot since landing on Eridu. Nothing ever seemed simple anymore. There was always something happening that they had to deal with. But this one, she didn't know how. It was the first time they'd be up against high tech aliens face to face, and they were outmatched.

A thought occurred to her. "They're still aliens, even if they're human, right?"

Hadley snorted a laugh. "It took you that fucking long to ask the shitting question?"

Kristin shook her head but decided not to engage. "Well? Are they?"

"Of course they are," Estard said. "Everyone who isn't an aboriginal is an alien."

They all fell back into a walk for a while. "But we're all human."

"From the outside, maybe," Estard said, "And that is something I would like an answer to — how? How are they all human too?"

"The one person who might have had all the answers died the day we met you, Agent," Hadley put in. "Unless one of them other scientists found his work, or understood what he was trying to do, I doubt very much we'll ever know."

"Deidra doesn't know?"

Lance shook his head. "If she does, it's buried deep. But no, whatever the connection to Earth is, it was probably lost along with all the tech in this world. That's assuming there ever was a connection."

They fell into silence again once they started jogging. They were making good time, but they all had one thing on their minds. How were they going to fight the Bahana men?

~

Deidra held Dane close, her head on his chest, listening to the calm beating of his heart. She was very afraid that once she started, she was not going to remember who he was. That strange voice in her head or no, that sensation of losing herself was too recent a memory to let it go.

"I'll be here the whole time," he told her soothingly. "I promise I won't let you forget me."

She pulled away from him slowly but held onto his lab jacket by the waist as she looked up into his brown eyes. "You'd better not," she told him seriously, then changed the topic. "You've finished the frequency generator? And Doctor Hans is finishing the code for it?"

Dane gave a nod. "Everything we need is almost in place, and we can head home. Take a vacation. Get married with your parents in attendance."

Deidra shot a laugh. They had not discussed any of that, but she knew he was just trying to make her smile. "All of that?"

"All of that," he assured.

She pushed him away and took a step back. She knew it wasn't fair to be so abrupt but, she had to steel herself. Get ready for the task.

The Colonel had asked her to come up with a way to prevent the Bahanians from using their tech on them. To use every resource at her disposal, and yes, he knew what that meant. The other scientists were busy with the work of fitting and testing the light speed propulsion and frequency generator. But even if she had them to help, only she was aware of what the Bahanians would bring to bear.

She was going to have to deep dive, as she had done before. Push past that barrier and truly see. Get the being that was Tatiana to let go and realise that Deidra was not her. That she could separate herself from the event. Zim would have been helpful in this endeavour if he'd known how to use his power better. He was currently studying with the Doctors and nurses aboard to get an understanding of the things he might be able to achieve.

Deidra sighed and stopped herself from going down long tangents in her mind. It was her way of avoiding things she did not want to do. And she was prone to overthinking.

It was like Dane could sense the turmoil in her mind. He usually could. "Don't do it," he told her. "If you don't want to do it, don't do it."

"This could be the only method for me to find the answers I need, to create the tech we all need, to fight these people." She was trying to convince herself as much as him, she realised. "I'd gladly give it away to another if I could. But that would mean death. Final and immediate."

He reached out for her hands, but she held them up in the universal stop gesture, and he let his arms fall to his side.

"Best to just get it done," she told him. And it sounded cold, almost as if she were already gone, though that wasn't how she'd meant it.

Dane nodded. His eyes watered, but his tears didn't fall. "You could still come out of this fine," he reminded them both. "You might not forget this time."

She gave him a sad smile and sat down on the cushioned bench against the wall in her office. She closed her eyes and tried to remember what she had learned the last time she'd dived deep and found Tatiana's name. How the Giant had bid her go, and told her there was nothing to find. But physiologically, that was wrong. Deidra was a different person. Her neural pathways had not been closed off against the memory of a terrible event. Nothing should be closed to her. Nothing off limits.

This is not the best way, the voice told her. *I can just give voice to what happened, spare the detail.*

Deidra mentally shook off the voice. It made her feel insane and she didn't understand how to use it. Despite its insistence that they were one and the same, she could only think of it as a separate entity.

She pushed herself deep into the core of the memory that had cut her off the first time.

She needed to get out of this place. The easiest way out, since she did not know where she was, was death. If she could find some way to kill herself, she'd wake in the field, and it would be over.

A light surrounded her cell, so bright she couldn't see anything.

She was strapped down again.

This was where she'd been thrown out, but she stubbornly held on. Even if the memory did not move forward. She dug her metaphorical nails in, determined that she would not move.

"You shouldn't be here," Tatiana told her, a ghost like image of her appearing next to the bed where she'd been strapped down, almost blind from the light directed at her face. "There is nothing beyond this point," the apparition reminded her.

"Except what broke you," Deidra hit back callously. "If you can't tell me what that was, I need to see it."

Tatiana grabbed her by the shoulder and shoved her back effortlessly into a memory of being alone in the virgin woods. "You need not see anything."

"I need to know the enemy to fight the enemy," Deidra told her. "If you won't get out of my way, I will remove you."

The apparition laughed heartily and smiled. "I *am* you," Tatiana said. "That's the thing that you seem to keep forgetting. We are not separate, in heart and mind. Though to a point, we led separate lives, we are now together."

"You're the voice," Deidra said flatly.

"I am the voice that tries to teach so you will not forget. That gives you wisdom unearned and knowledge unhindered. I am the piece of you that was a Giant long before your birth, but also knows you better than any other. And I am telling you now, there is nothing beyond that point that you need to see."

Deidra was frustrated. "I am you, you are me."

"Yes," Tatiana returned.

"So why is there conflict here?"

"Subconscious versus conscious. You are the conscious level of our existence. You present to the world, all the surface thoughts and imaginings. I am the subconscious, the representation of everything that came before that makes you who you are on the surface. Including your childhood memories and moments, though I wear a different face."

"And there is no way you will allow me past that point?"

"No, you don't need to be there," Tatiana said firmly. "It is the breaking. All that we are, would break again."

"How do you know that?"

"How do I know anything?" Tatiana gave her a moment to reason it out. "It's not necessary."

"But you will tell me what I need to know?" It was starting to make sense. In a way.

"If it helps you, I can remain and communicate as Tatiana," the apparition said.

"That might be best for my sanity," Deidra replied.

"Then you should go, and we should start work," the apparition put a hand on her shoulder and shoved.

When she opened her eyes to see Dane watching, worry painting his features, she felt more disgruntled at the outcome than thankful for having her memories. Her eyes shot to him, and he let out a breath he'd clearly been holding. "Still me," she told him.

"Oh, thank god," he breathed and made to move toward her, but she stopped him with a wave of a hand.

"Turns out the voice in my head will be a permanent addition." She wasn't entirely sure how she felt about that, but now that it was clear who — or what — it was, it was less daunting.

"We'll work it out," Dane assured her. It was clear that he wanted to come closer, though he was only three steps away.

"I'll work it out, Dane. Me. Alone. Because it's in my head." She saw the sadness spread across his face and wanted to wipe it away. But she didn't know how, so she just got up, and gave him the embrace he wanted.

"I wish there was more I could do," he said into her shoulder, and she felt a wetness on her cheek that she assumed came from his tears. She hadn't noticed.

"You're here," she said reassuringly. "That helps more than you can imagine. You keep me grounded. You keep me here."

He pulled away a little to hold her face in his hands and stare into her eyes. "That month, when we worked on Io, all I thought about was you. I couldn't believe that you were dead. We'd found other bodies, but not yours.

"I promised you that with the ring, though you've made me wait such long years for the wedding, in my mind, we're already married.

And it will take a lot more than moving over five hundred light years through space, to get rid of me."

Deidra leaned forward into a kiss, because she had no words to respond to that. How could she? The man had literally followed her across the galaxy into dangers unknown.

When she pulled back, she patted him on the cheek and gave him a sad smile. "Much as I would love to continue," she told him, "we still have work to do."

He pulled away immediately. "Right. It's easy for me to forget, sometimes. It's all military stuff, and we don't usually get involved in that."

"Not usually, no."

"So do you have any ideas?"

Deidra took a deep breath and reached out wordlessly in her mind for Tatiana. She could feel the smile of the apparition, though she couldn't see it. Couldn't hear it. She understood it was in the surface of her mind, where she had her everyday thoughts.

You'll get the hang of it, Tatiana told her.

Do I even need to tell you what it is we need?

She had the impression of a head shake and pout, even as the representative of her subconscious said, *No.*

Then let's get started.

Chapter Fourteen

Harvey stood in a side corridor, three soldiers behind him, trying desperately to be as still and soundless as humanly possible. There were four guards in the chamber beyond, and they were all facing in Harvey's direction. No matter how this went down, those men were going to see them coming.

With a deep breath, Harvey made a few motions with his hand and gave a nod. The second he moved, the men behind him did too.

Harvey shifted behind the men in the chamber and screamed loudly, like a child playing a game, "Boo!"

All enemy combatants turned to him with their guns raised, surprise on their faces. Surprise that turned to confusion when he disappeared.

Before they could work out what had happened, his men were in the room and subduing them.

"Put their tech gadgets in the bag," he reminded them. "We don't want them calling for help."

It had occurred to him early on that they might have jacket

radios, such as the ATF used. It was an innovation started more than a hundred years before he was born, that prevented airman and soldiers from being separated from communications. That wasn't to say that the enemy couldn't just take your jacket away if you were captured. It was just that most didn't consider the need to. It had prevented a lot of long imprisonments over the years.

Each of them now had an enemy, bound, gagged and hooded, over a shoulder. They waited for Harvey.

He sighed. They were the soldiers, not him. If they expected him to have all the good ideas, they were going to find themselves in some fairly dangerous situations. He was the only airman on this mission, and the rest of them were trained for this sort of thing, so why they were looking at him, he didn't know. Well, he did know, he just didn't like it.

They moved back the way they'd come, and in a small room off the main corridor, they dumped their catch with the others they'd already subdued. Then they continued on as they had been.

The ship was much larger than it looked from the outside, and they'd already taken twelve enemy combatants out of commission. Though, for the most part, the ship was eerily empty.

He wondered where their crew were. Who was running the ship? It seemed like it was more like a Docker than anything else, in Harvey's eyes. Though they didn't appear to have any hangars for smaller ships. At least, not that he'd seen.

"This is creepy as fuck, sir," one of the soldiers next to him whispered. He had to agree.

As they moved on down the main corridor, that hopefully led to the bridge, Harvey started hearing mechanical sounds, and urged caution in his men with a hand gesture. He swayed from one side of the corridor to the other, trying to pinpoint where it was coming from. He found it in a room to his right that had the door slightly ajar. He peeked in.

Inside were two men in green, standing at consoles talking to each other and pushing buttons. There was a hissing sound, a bang and clack, and then a mechanical whirring.

"Five hours from orbit," one of the men said to someone Harvey couldn't see.

He was caught between his need to capture the ship as quickly as possible, and his caution that they should subdue as many of the passengers and crew as possible before they did in order to prevent an uprising once they had. There were six other groups of four soldiers on the ship with them. It would have been much too great a task with the one team.

"We should go in, sir," the man next to him said so softly it was almost completely inaudible.

He gave a nod of his head, then moved into the room slow and silent. He needed to get a better look at what was happening to judge how he might take them. But as soon as he saw it, he urged them to back out.

They retreated a short distance down the hall to confer. "This is a tricky one," he said, thoughtful. "They're waking them up from in there. Lance had mentioned something about stasis, but I didn't think much on it."

"So, what's the problem?" asked the one who had whispered to him earlier.

"Problem is, it's the two guys at the consoles, looking into a separate room, and they can look right back. On top of that, there are four people sitting by a door that connects to that room." Harvey shook his head. "The room is large and some of it was in darkness, there is no telling how many are in there already."

"But if we take these ones out, there'll be less to deal with, yes?" This from the only one who'd remained silent so far. Harvey felt bad, but he didn't remember any of their names.

"Sure," Harvey agreed. "But how do you propose we do that?"

The oldest of the men, with full grey hair and lines on his face, held up his hand. "Run and play."

The other two seemed to approve of the suggestion with emphatic nods. Harvey had no idea what they were talking about, and the man filled him in.

"One of us goes in, pretends to be surprised when we get caught, run out. Two by the door will grab the ones that run out. After they're subdued, disguise yourself as them, and subdue the rest."

It sounded both simple and difficult to pull off. It would depend on if they could pull off that second part.

Harvey shrugged. "You're the experts, I'll follow your lead on this one."

Harvey used himself as bait. He walked in, and when no one looked directly at him, he made a sound and swung back on a heel as if he were surprised to run into people. They all turned at that. Perhaps it was an effect of how they travelled, but they were slow to react, even in the face of such obvious threat.

He waited a full three seconds before he took off running down the hall. He heard some footsteps behind him, and he looked back. Four had come out the door. None of them noticed his men, and they were all being swiftly delt with. He stopped running and walked back toward the room.

"That was almost too easy," he said in a soft voice.

"Don't jinx us, Captain." That from the young one tying up the last soldier with flexicuffs.

When they were all done, they stood two a side in the doorway, and Harvey gave the wall a loud tap to get the attention of those left within.

He heard one of the techs mumble, and someone screamed, "What? I'm busy."

They took that as a good sign to enter and were not disappointed in being able to take down both the techs as well as two others who were just coming out of the other room.

Satisfied that no more would be waking up, Harvey looked to the other room and back to the hallway.

"Do we keep going as we are, or do we check the other side of this thing?" He asked.

The three soldiers conferred, and once they'd come to a conclusion, it was the older one who spoke. "We go on. We have to stick to our route and have faith that our counterparts on that side will take care of what needs taking care of."

Harvey knew that it was tempting fate to think that something was too easy. To wonder if there was something coming to bar the way and concentrate too much on what it might be. In some circles that might be considered manifesting the worst. And although he didn't really believe in such nonsense, he couldn't shake the feeling that something was about to happen, and the easy run they were having, was almost over.

~

Gordon stood with her back to the wall, and eyes looking down on the one Bahanian they had in custody. She wasn't trying to read his mind. At least, not in that moment. She was just staring at him to make him uncomfortable.

Weiz had asked her to stay with the man and keep an eye on his movements. If she thought at any time that he might know something they didn't, she was to make a deep dive.

Every fifteen minutes, like clockwork, Private Nyugen would come in with an update of what was happening on the ground and how far away the enemy fleet was. Then he would give a lazy salute and leave.

Gordon wasn't sure exactly what Weiz had hoped to illicit with these updates. So far, the most she'd been able to read from the man was an overwhelming sense of confidence that his people knew what they were doing, and they would win. By virtue of them winning, he would be free, and therefore only had to hold on for so long through any torture he may need to endure.

She felt bored, and annoyed. She'd spent so much time over the bodies of Estard, Fyord and Hadley, keeping her vigil, she should have been accustomed to the feeling. She'd contracted the stupid sleeping sickness, and those were a few nice moments of oblivion that she didn't remember at all. Then, when she'd woken and told Deidra about the bodies, the woman had all but accused her of being the reason they hadn't just disappeared in the first place.

Gordon couldn't remember the exact words the scientist had used, but it was something along the lines of the observation of an atom was akin to the saying, 'a watched pot never boils.' At least, that was what Gordon had taken from it, though she'd probably mangled the meaning of it. And it made no sense, anyway, as she'd left them for an extended period when Weiz asked her to, and they'd still been there when she'd returned. If anything, it seemed to her they'd been waiting for the field to be fully cleared of meteor debris. Which Lance's accidental storm had taken care of.

She breathed a sigh and kicked at the legs of the bed that held the Bahanian. She didn't think she was going to get anything out of him, even if they brought Alvarez back in. But she'd follow her Commander's orders.

Private Nyugen came in to give his update, saluted and sauntered off. It was a whole lot of nothing. And it would probably continue to be a whole lot of nothing for the next few hours.

"Want to play a game?" Ensign Brioli looked taken aback at the sudden question. He'd been strapped to the bed for five days. He'd had guarded trips to the bathroom, but otherwise he'd stayed in those cuffs. His food was spoon fed to him, water given through a straw. Why they didn't just put the man in the brig was something she didn't understand. Why leave him in the infirmary?

"No," he responded after a moment.

Gordon shrugged. "Well, your loss," she told him. Even though she was certain it was she who would go mad before this man broke.

Hours passed and updates came and went, explaining the nothing that was happening at that time. Doctor Rowley came in once to check on the Bahanian, then left without saying anything at all.

Gordon couldn't help but wonder why she'd been given this task. Beyond her obvious ability to read minds. What did they think this man knew that could possibly help them in the fight to come?

With a frustrated growl, Gordon began pacing the length of the infirmary feeling like a caged animal. Brioli's eyes followed her as she moved, a look of slight amusement on his face.

Maybe the Commander was trying to torture her. She pushed that thought down and stepped on it. She didn't want to start down that road. Deidra had made her acutely aware of the possibility it was something that could take over.

She was starting to get a headache.

Private Nyugen came in for his update, and she almost dismissed him before he could speak, but he started without waiting for permission.

"The ships are almost on us," was all he said. No update from the ground, no indication of what the statement might mean.

He gave his lazy salute and left, and Gordon was left to interpret the words as she will.

From the corner of her eye, she could see Brioli smiling smugly, as if he might know something she did not.

"You won't get away," he told her. It was the first sentence he'd volunteered since she'd walked in the room.

"Getting away is not the point," she replied dismissively as she dove into his mind.

He was angry, frustrated, stiff from being held in a single position for so long. But he was also confident, and hopeful that his friends and coworkers would come to his rescue. If they knew he was there. That was a little niggle at the back of his surface thoughts that he shoved down and repressed.

"They'll get you all this time," he insisted.

"Or I can get them like I got you," Gordon returned.

"Pfft. Please. You getting me was nothing more than a happy accident, having to do more with my stupidity than your intelligence."

That was something she could agree with, and she found herself nodding as he spoke. "True. But I could get lucky."

"Not if they brought the ships." He was so smug, and so sure, that she tried desperately to find the link that formed the surface thought. It was tenuous. Almost like he was speaking as soon as he thought, so there was nothing different, no lag time.

She could delve deeper. At least, she believed she could, she just didn't want to if she could help it. Mostly because she didn't want to end up knocking him out again. Then she wondered if she could read the mind of an unconscious person, because she'd never tried that before.

"You're so certain, aren't you?" she asked, mostly just to keep him thinking and talking. The more she did, the more likely she was to get something useful out of him.

"The ships are death." He smiled broadly. "There's no getting around that."

Again, his surface thoughts were flooded with the hope that he would be rescued. That he would, in some manner, find a way out and get back to his people.

Absurdly, she wondered if letting him loose of the bonds would help to get something different. She doubted it.

"Why are they death?"

He looked right at her and the thought that came from his mind was at once potent and childish. *I ain't telling.* It told her that he was aware of what she was trying to do, and deliberately preventing her effectiveness, somehow.

Yes, you are, she shot back loudly inside his mind.

Something happened then that was unexpected. His mind opened. Completely, nothing barred, everything available. And it was a lot. But it wasn't anything particularly useful. He was almost disgustingly uninformed. His rank was nothing more than the equivalent of a Private.

But it was this small moment, as she rifled through his thoughts that she understood what it was she'd done. She'd forced her way in. Forced the compliance. She didn't need permission; she could create it. And that, could be a terrifying power. She didn't think she wanted to tell anyone about it. If it was bad now, when they just thought she would read their minds, how bad might it be if they knew she could force them to it?

Ensign Brioli was looking at her with an adoring and dopy smile. She hoped she hadn't maimed him.

"You still alive in there?" she asked worriedly, even as she continued her search for useful information.

"Yes, I am still alive." He seemed perfectly cogent, if a little dim-witted.

"Tell me, what should I know that I don't know?"

"The ships can target your people."

"Explain that."

He smiled as he spoke, but he was no longer confident of escape. His thoughts were actually of pleasing her. Which felt wrong, but at the same time, very useful.

"Our transporters require us to aim and shoot," he said. "So, we need to see you to use them, obviously. The ships have broad scanners. They can pick out an infected person quite quickly, and they can be taken without us needing to see them. We have never actually used them before, because we've never seen one of you in space and we don't usually land the ships."

"So they won't reach the ground?"

"No."

"Thank you, Brioli. You've been quite helpful." She gave him a pat on the arm, then left the room.

His gaze followed her out, and it was somewhat disquieting. Now that she'd somehow enthralled him, she'd need to figure out how to undo it.

But for right then, in that moment, she just had to find Weiz and let her know what the man had told her.

CHAPTER FIFTEEN

They'd made it back to Major Preston three hours before the natives showed up on the horizon, marching in lockstep, and singing some kind of war song that none of them could understand the lyrics to. If lyrics they were. Estard thought it sounded an awful lot like a tribal tonal song from northern Europe.

Between them, they had yet to figure out a way around the nullification problem. He was prepared to have to go back and prevent certain things from happening. Though his mind was now aware of the problems that might cause, he really didn't think a few minutes here and there would be too big of an issue.

If something is meant to be, it'll be very difficult to change without drastic interference, he told himself. Mostly just so he wouldn't be paralysed into inaction.

"You done it yet, Agent man?" Lance asked beside him.

Estard looked at him. He liked the Pilot. He was a good man, and funny. Sometimes. But since they'd got back to camp, he'd asked that same question more times than Estard wanted to count.

"Not yet," he replied testily. "I'll let you know if it changes."

The Pilot held up both hands and backed away slowly. Seemed he had finally got the message.

Fyord and Hadley were still out by the road, following the incoming army. They'd decided they would keep trying to make something happen. Estard thought they would run out of energy before they actually got the army to turn and run, but he mentally applauded them for the continued effort. He could certainly understand it.

He'd stopped thinking too much on past and present, though it was, of course, his preeminent course of action if anything drastic happened. But he had decided to focus some of his time to the riddle of how to become a Giant. It was something they were all supposed to be able to do, but no one had yet done. He suspected it was because no one knew how, and they had no desire to find out. But if they couldn't provide the illusion, then perhaps the real things would do the trick.

"You're looking very thoughtful, there, Julian," Kristin said beside him, and he jumped.

"You scared me," he breathed, hand to chest.

"Only a little," she replied. "What you thinking, Agent man?"

"How do we become Giants?"

Kristin shrugged. "No idea. Why?"

"That was what I was thinking," he explained simply. "How do we do it? We're all supposed to be able to become these Giants, or Shadowmen or whatever anyone else wants to call them. And if Hadley and Fyord can't make the illusion, then maybe the real thing would do just as well in chasing them away."

Kristin shook her head. "If they have a Techie with them, I doubt we'll be able to do much of anything. But if you do figure it out, let me know. I wouldn't mind giving the form a test run."

"Well, what is it, then, that they do to stop us from using our powers?"

"The billion-dollar question," she sighed. "If anyone would know, I'd imagine it's Deidra. But she's aware of the problem and has said nothing."

"That doesn't mean she doesn't know. Maybe she just can't do anything about it."

"But that's what I meant, though. She hasn't said anything, ergo, she can't do anything. She might just be too busy."

"We're not going to have much longer to work this out," he said. "They're going to attack at some point, and they have the upper hand."

Kristin shook her head. "We still have guns, or have you forgotten? I'm fair certain that gives us a leg up here on the ground."

He *had* actually forgotten, but he also hadn't thought they'd use them. It would be a slaughter. And he had to assume that guns had become more efficient in the future. That place that he kept forgetting he was in.

Perhaps he was dead, and this was some kind of long goodbye that his brain was giving him. A way in which to explore the worlds he had dreamed of while working for ISAC. He doubted it, but it was a nice thought, for that moment.

"I'm trying to think of answers before I know the questions," he told Kristin.

Kristin sat, her eyes staring in the direction the army would be coming from. Aside from the odd dense group of trees that might hide them, it was a clear line of sight.

"Sit down, Agent." She patted the ground beside her aggressively, kicking up dirt and dead things.

With a sigh, he sat. "I don't want to kill them." Until it was out of his mouth, he hadn't realised that was what had been bothering him.

"None of us do," Kristin empathised. "I think that's partly why the Bahanians are using them. Because they know we have no interest in starting a war with these people."

"Why are they fighting for them?" Estard wanted to know. "That's the part that makes the least sense. Unless they have some kind of long-standing agreement with each other. Even Greenway couldn't get many people to follow him, as I understand it."

"Who told you about Greenway?"

"Who else? Lance."

Kristin started to draw absently in the dirt beside her as she spoke. "Galsin did tell us that they had a different kind of relationship with the people here. That they didn't much care about the powers, and we'd find out. Maybe the Bahanians are why. Deidra did say they had been very aware of them."

"I suppose. Though none of this is going to help me become a Giant."

"Oh, you were serious about that?" Kristin seemed surprised.

"Yes," he replied. "Serious enough. I can't do much with time until I know what happens, and even then, how much would be enough? As a Giant I would be able to do something in the now, even if it is minimal."

"Alright then," Kristin said as she clapped her hands together. "Let's figure this out."

Estard shot a laugh. "You're always surprising me."

"Well, my power isn't much use in a fight, either. So, I wouldn't mind being the thing that chased us through the woods on the first day we landed here."

"So, what is it then?" Estard asked. "A matter of will? Do we just decide that is what we want to be?"

Kristin shrugged. "It may well be that simple. I don't think anyone has tried. Too much trauma attached to it."

Estard hadn't thought of that. They had been through something horrendous with the Shadowmen that greeted them. He hadn't seen any of that.

"Maybe that's why I needed to come," he said softly. "An outside pair of eyes, on your side."

"I don't believe in fate, Agent."

"Even after everything?"

Kristin raised a quizzical brow. "You see fate in this? I see a hot mess that just keeps getting hotter and messier."

Instead of answering, Estard just stood up and took a deep breath. "I am going to try now, and you, are going to tell me if it's working."

She craned he neck to look up at him. "Go ahead, then."

He concentrated on the form he'd seen that day in the woods. Dark, mist like, red eyes, no mouth. He tried to impose himself on that image. To imagine that he was one with the Shadowform. That his body would grow to accommodate the mass.

"Something's happening," Kristin said.

He was so excited, that he lost his momentum. Annoyed with himself, he asked, "What? What happened?"

"You were just getting very faint. Like… misty, I guess." She shook her head, out of words.

Estard gave it another go, but when she informed him that it was happening again, he put some colour into himself. Then she told him he was growing and changing colour. And he kept going, until he felt he was inside the form that he believed was right.

Kristin's head had tilted all the way back to look up at his face. "That's it," she told him. "I can't believe you actually did it. I wasn't expecting it to be that easy."

He tried to talk but he had no mouth. He imagined one, and concentrated until it was there. Then he said, "Easy? I would not call it easy. Simple maybe. But not easy."

"My turn," she said. "Tell me what to do."

Estard instructed her, and though she wasn't as quick, she did eventually manage.

They stood there looking at one another, admiring their new forms, when Lance interrupted them with a fake cough to get their attention.

Estard glanced down at the Pilot who was looking rather pale. "What is it?" he asked.

"Ah, uhm." He was blinking rapidly and whatever he'd come to say seemed to be locked inside.

"You want to try this?" Kristin wanted to know.

Lance just shook his head and swallowed, but the question seemed to help him find his voice. "Less than an hour away, as the crow flies."

"We're going to go try and scare them off," Estard told him. "Want to come?"

Lance shook his head again. "I'll ah, I'll.... Be.... At the camp." He shook his head again and backed away. The man actually took off at a full run once he thought they couldn't see him.

Estard looked askance at Kristin. "He had a particularly bad experience with them, though he never talks about it," she said. "But being like this is liberating. I can see the appeal."

While he wouldn't have called it liberating, he certainly liked the feeling of being so tall that he could look over most things. If not the canopy of a forest.

"Shall we go see if this works on the incoming army?"

"I think we should."

"They might just kill us, you know?" He was all too acutely aware of what that might mean for him, but he wasn't sure she'd even considered it.

"I know," she replied.

And with that agreement they were off at a run.

There was an unspoken race between them, their heavy feet landing on solid earth and causing small, localised tremors. The army would have to hear them coming and wonder at what was headed their way.

Kristin lifted her head to the sky and let out a screech like that of a massive bird. Though he didn't hear her laugh, he got the impression that inwardly, she was. He lifted his own head to join her in chorus.

The army came into view ahead of them very quickly. But they didn't slow. They kept their forward momentum with silent agreement it may be the best way to get them all to scatter. And that was all they really wanted to do.

Instead, in one stride, they went from terrifying Giant, to underwhelming human, and fell on their faces in the dirt.

They looked at each other, too stunned to be able to move quickly. While they'd known it was a possibility, they had not expected it to be so abrupt. And they'd had no effect on the marching army at all. It was as if they never even saw them. Never heard their cries or their giant footsteps.

Estard forced himself to his feet and helped Kristin to hers. Even now, with his eyes straight on the army, it appeared as if they could not see them. They could not have been more than a hundred yards away, but there was no indication that anything strange was happening.

"You are seeing this, right?" He wanted to know that he wasn't losing his mind.

"Yes, I'm seeing it. But it doesn't mean I want to stay here and wait for them to walk over me." She grabbed him by the sleeve and pulled him over to the side of the marching column.

He was still a little shaken from the fall. "Is it them or us?" he asked.

Kristin gave it some thought before she answered. "I have no idea. But I tell you what, I hadn't realised how much I relied on Deidra for answers to everything until now."

The army moved past them at a good clip, and not a one of them even looked their way. They were so close that Estard could have reached out and touched one as they moved by, but he didn't want to chance it. Whether they were in some kind of trance, or being a Giant had done something to them, these people were blind to all but the path before them.

Estard shook himself vigorously, like he was trying to get a bug off. Then turned his back on the marching strangeness. "At least we know how to do that, now," he said to be conciliatory.

Kristin shook her head. "The Techies have to know that we'd use guns on them. They'd have to know they were sending these people to their deaths."

"They seem pretty well protected to me," Estard mumbled.

"I think they've made sure the natives can't see us coming."

Estard frowned at the assertion. "That doesn't make sense. Why bother nullifying our powers, if their only job is to die for them? I think there has to be more to it."

"Are they real?" Kristin moved with a sudden burst, so quickly that Estard could not stop her as she moved out to touch one of the passing 'soldiers.'

Every fibre of his being screamed out to prevent her from making them aware that they were there. But nothing happened. Her hand grazed along the shoulders of five men before she pulled it away and looked at it. What she was inspecting it for, he wasn't sure, but it was facing some intense scrutiny.

He took a step toward her, still feeling a nervous concern. The end of the column was nearing, and he had a bad feeling. He grabbed her by the arm and pulled her away. She allowed it, though she didn't stop the examination of her own hand.

"What are you looking for?"

There was a look of confusion on her face. "I don't even know," she replied as she glanced between him and her hand. "They felt real.

There is dust on my hand from their clothes. I suppose, I was wondering if the dust was real."

"Then they're real," he returned. "That's one mystery solved. But we should go. Now."

"What's the rush? They clearly have no interest in us."

"It's got to be a trap," he stressed as he pulled her further from them.

That seemed to get her attention and he no longer had to pull at her arm to get her moving.

But it was in vain, because rather than taking them away from danger, he had been walking them into it. From behind a tree, not too far away, stepped a man in a grey uniform, who made them halt in their tracks. He said nothing as he held up his gun and took his shot.

Estard held tight to Kristin, unsure what to expect once the beam hit him. He heard her groan into his ear, "Not again," before they were transported to a dark room.

~

Greenway was so eager to be off the ship he could barely think of anything else. His days of captivity had been few, and the trip back to Eridu short, but it felt like lifetimes since he'd seen earth and sky.

"We'll be coming into range shortly," Rochelle assured him. She was looking at a screen on one of the many devices she carried in her bag. "As soon as this lights up blue, we'll be able to transport to the ground. I just need to calibrate the gun to the right coordinates."

Greenway nodded along, but he wasn't really listening. He was tense. He was excited and he was terrified. He wanted out of this place, but he also wondered if he should be down there. He wasn't sure he yet forgave himself for his actions and did not believe that Weiz and Harvey would. As much as he longed to be back with his people, he was preparing himself for a possible, righteous rejection. If they told him to leave, he would.

There was a beep, the light Rochelle had indicated turned blue, and she started inputting coordinates to the gun.

It was about to happen. He watched Rochelle finish her work, stick the screen in her bag, and turn the gun on him. "You first, obviously." At such close range he didn't even see her shoot before he was on the ground in the middle of the woods, close to a stony outcrop that seemed vaguely familiar. Moments later, Rochelle was with him.

"Your people are that way," she told him. "Maybe half a day, less if you put some effort in." She put the gun away and shouldered the pack.

He was stuck for a moment. What was he supposed to say? Thank you? It didn't feel like enough. At the same time, the look on her face did not invite any kind of emotional farewell.

"So, that's it then, hey," he said. "How do I thank you?"

She raised her brows at him and shook her head with a slight hitch of the shoulders. "Go home. Stop this war before it starts. I will try to do the same, but fighting a thousand years of history will take more than just me yelling at a few generals to stop their stupidity."

Greenway smiled. "I'll do what I can," he promised, though he too doubted that anyone would listen to him. As a murderer. As the person who had tried to get them all to stay in the first place. Who had chased them down with a small army at his own back in an attempt to prevent them from leaving. Would he suffer anything less than a jail cell when he got back?

It was a moment before he realised he was staring into the distance behind her, while she patiently waited for him to turn and leave. He reddened a little, gave her a one finger salute, a nod, then turned on his heel with an arm in the air and said, "Fairwell, my friend."

"Goodbye Greenway." He imagined she left after that, but he

didn't hear her go.

He felt free, and lucky. That there was one among the Bahanians who believed he had the right to be free, even after all he had done. When he could easily have been put to death in many cultures, without remorse or regret.

As he looked around, taking slow steps in the direction Rochelle had indicated, he realised he knew where he was. Not far from the village. The village he had terrorised, and eventually sunk into the ground. Men, women and children, snuffed out because he had a tantrum.

Greenway didn't feel that anger now. That pure rage that could not be contained inside himself. He still didn't know what had caused it, specifically. But he knew it had something to do with his power. So he swore to himself, that he would never use it again. Not just in anger, but at all. If he lived as a man, then perhaps, he could in some small way atone.

The walk was long, and he had too much time to think. He tried to think of good things. The fresh air, the dampness of the leaves underfoot, the sound of a gentle breeze. The blue of a midday sky.

If there was a Docker in orbit, there'd be men on the ground. And he was looking forward to seeing some people who had not been there when he'd gone mad. Who hadn't seen the mess that caused it all. He was glad he'd found his mind again, because if he hadn't, he was sure he probably would have tried to kill them all rather than let them leave. Now, he hoped they were able to get home.

Some time later, going at a good jog, Greenway broke forest and found himself facing a rail gun, mounted over a man-made trench. He immediately came to a halt and put both his hands up high in the air.

He couldn't be certain that anyone would recognise him, so he said loudly, "I'm Captain Aiden Greenway, and I have information for Commander Weiz."

~

Weiz had been in the observation room making her Docker vessels as convincing as possible, when Gordon rushed in. They were difficult to maintain, from their sheer size, and they would not have been functional in any meaningful way. But they had lights and looked menacing enough. She was quite proud of her work.

"Commander!" Gordon shouted. "Commander!"

"What?" Weiz turned from the window where she was tracking the progress of the fifteen ships headed their way.

"We cannot be aboard when they get in range," the woman breathed.

Weiz shook her head. "Don't be absurd. We *have to* be aboard. The plan doesn't work without this."

Gordon took a deep breath and seemed to centre herself before explaining the urgency. "So, if they get a scan going on us, we're as good as gone," she finished.

Weiz was irritated by the news. If she had access to such things, and their roles were reversed, she'd do the same thing.

"Get everyone who is left into an MM ship, and I'll meet you in the hangar," she instructed.

"Everyone?"

"You know who I mean."

With a nod Gordon ran off to find the others.

Weiz turned back toward the window and frowned at her work. It would remain, if she let it. But it would morph and change before settling into something completely different. She couldn't say what, only that they wouldn't remain Dockers. So, she either had to undo it, or leave them and hope they didn't turn into something that would become a problem for them later.

There were only two of them. She actually thought it amazing she was able to do that much, given the depth of knowledge required for her to make anything functional.

She put a hand on the window. In sadness, in frustration, in resignation. She'd let them go, and hope, she decided. They were far enough away from their own Docker, that it would take a mighty good push to get them close enough to do any damage. Whatever they ended up turning into would likely be rendered harmless by the void of space. Whatever they ended up turning into, their sheer presence should deter any immediate engagement. She hoped.

With a final sigh, she turned away and moved at a brisk pace toward the hangar.

When she got there, she saw Bridges, Ellis, Zim, Gordon and Deidra, all standing by a single ship talking amongst themselves. Deidra looked ready to tear strips off the hide of anyone who dared speak to her, though. The others didn't look too concerned.

"Well, get in, what are you waiting for?" she ordered them. Between them they had a full crew, so the going would be smooth enough. But she felt such regret at having to leave the Docker behind.

Once they were all in, the doors sealed, the cabin pressurised, there was some argument over who was flying. Gordon was halfway to sitting in the pilot chair, Zim on the other side, attempting to do the same. Weiz had to raise her voice to be heard over them.

"Rock, paper, scissors, go!" she said. They understood what it meant.

They both stood on opposite sides of the chair and shook their fists to the sound of Bridges saying, "Rock, paper, scissors, now!" Zim was paper, Gordon was scissors, the duel decided.

"Now let's get off the Docker shall we," Weiz said brusquely. "Apparently we're in a bit of danger here."

Gordon had the good sense to blush at that, but she said nothing as she prepared them for take-off.

The hangar exit was facing the planet, so there was no danger of the enemy ships spotting them departing. Well, less of a chance.

There was no way for them to know if the Bahanians used the scanner. If they truly had the capabilities that Gordon suggested. Weiz had to give her the benefit of the doubt, though, given how the woman had obtained the information.

The trip down didn't take long and wasn't at all eventful. Which was exactly how one would wish a flight to go.

They landed near to one of the carriers, next to Greenway's mountain. The soldiers hadn't moved very far to get a defensible position. They simply moved up the mountain a way, onto a ledge for good line of sight, and set up some barricades and trenches. Simple but effective.

It wasn't until they were all out of the ship and on the ground, that Weiz realised Deidra was missing.

"Did you see her get on the ship?" Weiz wanted to know of everyone there. They all looked at each other and one by one shook their heads slowly.

"No," Gordon said. "She was there, in the hangar. But I do not recall her getting on the ship."

Bridges shook his head. "I could have sworn she was behind me, but I didn't check. I just assumed."

"*Sheiße!*" Weiz swore.

"Just radio her," Zim suggested.

"Scientists don't use radio jackets," Weiz breathed. "There is no one left up there to talk to, is there?" She honestly didn't know. Most of the MM ships had been taken out to hide behind one of her fake Dockers. As far as she was aware, all of the soldiers were on the ground. The only people left on the Docker were scientists and Doctors.

Ellis cleared her throat and waited before she spoke. "The bridge crew will be there. They never leave their post. It's what they do."

Mollified by the information, that she should have already

known had she not panicked, Weiz put the call in.

"This is a page for Doctor Deidra Ward," she told the bridge Comms Officer. "She needs to get off that Docker, and down to the surface. Now!"

Weiz was aware that she technically had no authority over the scientists, and that Deidra could ignore her if she wished. But she felt there was enough of a recent history between them that the woman would respect her urgency as founded.

"Would you like me to have her respond in person, ma'am?" the Officer asked.

"Yes, please."

"A moment while I go find her."

They all stood around by the ramp of the MM ship while they waited. Weiz noticed Major Preston moving toward them and greeted him with a nod of the head.

"Commander," he said, coming up beside her. He nodded to the rest of them. "I'll brief you in short."

Weiz was annoyed it was taking so long for the Bridge Comms Officer to call back, so she made a quick motion with her hand. "So long as it is *brief*," she said.

"Fyord and Hadley are following the army as they move. Viatri just came to tell me that Estard and Kristin have gone out to try something, in a hope to slow them down or break them up. We've dug in, we're set up and ready to receive them here if we must."

She heard and understood what the man told her, and she nodded to let him know she was listening, but all her mind could think was, *come on Deidra, where are you?* Because she was getting the sinking feeling that maybe, just maybe, the Bahanians did get a scan off, and somehow, she'd been caught in it.

"Very good, Major —" She was interrupted by the Bridge Comms Officer.

"Commander, we could not find the Doctor. We looked over the hangar footage, and it appears that she got on the ship with you."

"Thank you," Weiz sighed, and ended the call.

The others all looked at each other and had an animated conversation that she did not hear, as a shout that came from the direction of the woods held her attention.

"I'm Captain Aiden Greenway, and I have information for Commander Weiz."

CHAPTER SIXTEEN

Lance picked up dead leaves, crumbled them, and tossed them aside absently as he listened to Greenway tell his tale of what had happened since they'd lost him two weeks ago. It was strangely uneventful, for the most part, though Lance was interested to learn that not everyone was on the side of the hunters.

"And the one who let you out, brought you here," Weiz was saying. "Would she help if we asked?"

Greenway shook his head, slow but steady. "I don't think so. She made a statement of it. She'd let me go, because she believed what her father was doing was wrong, but she wouldn't tell me anything that would harm her people. Helping me did not mean hurting them."

Weiz gave a nod. "We could have used the help, these lot bring a few too many surprises."

The Commander was stretching her neck and making faces like it was an effort to concentrate on what she was doing. Several emotions flitted across her face before it settled again in calm repose.

"What about Deidra?" Gordon asked. "Are we just going to ignore the fact that she's disappeared?"

Weiz looked like she wanted to turn and smack the other woman in the face, but she restrained herself. "One thing at a time," she said through clenched teeth. "Major Preston! You have the bridge!" The way she turned, and left, was so abrupt it left them all with furrowed brows and open mouths.

Major Preston stepped in like the professional he was and gave them all a nod. "Greenway, why don't you go clean up? Sergeant Singh will find you a kit."

Greenway gave a grudging nod but moved off after the Sergeant without further word.

"You doubt his word?" The Major addressed Lance directly, so he stopped his leaf crunching and stood.

"I don't," the Pilot replied. "I think he's telling the truth."

"Man's a murderer," Bridges said with more venom than Lance expected. "He should be locked up."

"Are we not concerned that he will turn on us? The way he turned on you all when you were trying to leave this place?" said a private Lance did not know the name of.

While Lance shook his head, he saw Bridges and Gordon both wide eyed and nodding. They saw more of it than he had. Gordon had even marched with the man, so she probably knew better than anyone.

"Gordon," he said. "Tell us."

She took a deep breath and blew it out. "I do not know that he was as insane, even then, as he became later. He spoke to me a few times, though I don't know why. Some of what he said actually made sense, if you looked at it from a certain point of view. Though I had to disagree, of course." She took another deep breath before continuing. "Until I got my own power, I didn't understand the struggle, inside, of what it was like to keep your mind the way it should be. And if Greenway faces that, I am not sure he'll be able to help himself, any more than you were able to control that storm, Viatri."

Lance gave a tight smile at the reminder. "That seems to only happen if I overdo it, though. You don't think, perhaps, just maybe, it might be.... A possibility that he'd overdone it?" How he came to be the one who would defend a man who sank a village and half a city, he didn't know. "That perhaps, if he limits his use of his powers, he might be useful to us, rather than a threat?"

They all looked at each other, except Preston and his Private. Judging by their faces, he was winning this particular argument, but they were going to allow Gordon to speak for them all. So, if she agreed, they all would.

Before anything else could be said, Lance heard an eruption of angry voices close to one of the carriers, that grabbed all their attention.

Greenway was backed against the outer hull while several of the airmen who had escaped captivity surrounded him. They were yelling and screeching over the top of one another, so loud, that Lance couldn't make out what anyone was trying to say. But when Reeve moved in on him, and Carson and Garcia each grabbed at a shoulder of his blue sweater, Major Preston arched a brow.

"Should we do something about this?" he asked.

"We probably should," Gordon said begrudgingly after a few moments. "But one sign that he is losing his temper, and I believe we should lock him up. Or have Harvey take him somewhere he can't hurt anyone. What he did, is not so easily forgotten. And you can't blame them."

Lance and Gordon moved toward them with a purpose, even as those who surrounded Greenway started laying into him with abandon. Fists, feet, knees and elbows. All the while held up by Carson and Garcia. And Greenway didn't fight. Didn't try to break away, or even protect himself from the blows. He just let them.

As they got closer, Lance could pick out what was being said. "...died," yelled Ramirez, as he landed a blow to the kidneys, then moved aside for Deville.

"You're the reason we got stuck in this forsaken place," the man gave a solid cross to the jaw, that sprayed blood from Greenway's mouth.

There were others he didn't know the name of, adding their grievances to those who had been held prisoner. Friends of those who had died. Family.

While there was a part of him that could understand their anger, he knew that he had to put an end to it, before the man decided to fight back.

Lance looked to Gordon who shrugged. "Up to me then, I guess," he mumbled.

"I don't think anyone else wants to defend him," Bridges put in with a smug smile.

"It's not about defending him," Lance said, even as he moved forward and yelled into the crowd, "All of you, stop it right now!"

The force of the gale he put behind the words knocked them all into the side of the carrier, and suddenly, all the anger that had been directed at Greenway was now facing him.

"Let him go," Lance said more calmly. "There will be a reckoning, but this is not how it's done."

There were mumbles and loud objections, but Lance just held up his hand for quiet.

"It's time to go," Gordon said quietly beside him.

The others looked to her as if she were some kind of abomination in need of cleansing. But they didn't try to argue. They looked to Viatri and seemed to measure the likelihood that he would try to stop them again. Apparently the believed he would.

Reeve moved away first, and as he passed Gordon, he spat at her feet. The others followed suit, without comment or reprimand.

When they were all gone, Greenway glanced at them, and without so much as a thank you, turned and left.

Lance turned his attention to Gordon. "You alright?"

"I'll live," she said with sadness. "Truth, I deserve it."

Lance nodded, but it was Major Preston who spoke. "All settled then." His eyes were following something in the distance.

Lance turned to see what the Major was looking at and saw Fyord and Hadley running full tilt toward them. If the looks on their faces were anything to go by, the news was not good.

They arrived huffing and puffing, hands on knees, heads drooping and rising as they tried to get sufficient air into their lungs. Everyone waited patiently for one of them to speak.

It was Hadley. "Motherfucking trap," she breathed. "The army is a fucking trap for us." She fell on her arse and looked up to the sky. "I think we were meant to see them and go investigate. They got Kristin and Estard."

It took a moment for that last sentence to register to Lance, but when it did, he was ready to go into action mode. "They got them, how?"

"The usual," Fyord said, still winded. He mimicked a gun and made a pop sound to indicate they'd disappeared.

"Permission to leave the camp, sir." He didn't think he really needed it. He wasn't even sure he was technically still in the ATF, the way that things were going. But old habits died hard.

"Not if you're going straight to that army, boy," Preston returned. "I don't see any sense in that."

Lance shook his head. "Not the army. The cells. Where they all came out from."

"You know where that is?"

"From what Kristin said, it's the same place we sheltered in our first night here when we were hiding from the Giants. Half a day at a walk, much faster at a run." Lance gave him a look that would convey his intention to go with or without permission.

To his surprise, before Major Preston could answer, the others stepped forward. Gordon first, then Ellis and Zim. Fyord and Hadley looked at each other, shrugged and stepped forward. Only Bridges muttered to himself before he joined them. He didn't bother to justify his reluctance with any words, he just stared defiantly at the Major.

Preston smiled and gave a chuckle. "I can see you're all determined. But might I point out one simple thing?"

Lance gave a nod. "Go ahead."

"They may not be there."

"That is a possibility, but just in case. We should check it out."

"And you know that they can stop you from using your powers. So having the super squad go in is not likely to make a greater chance of success."

"You won't talk us out of it," Lance insisted. "I won't allow them to do to anyone else, the things they did to me. To Greenway. To I don't even know how many others before us."

Preston spread his hands wide in surrender. "I have no authority over you," he told them. "I don't think it's the most responsible thing to do, but I wish you well."

Lance took a few steps, then a thought had him turn back around. "What if the army doesn't come here?"

"Then we let them do whatever it is they want to do," the man answered. "If they're not threatening us, I see no reason to go after them."

Lance gave a final nod, and moved off, the others following close behind.

~

After she left the others, Weiz went to hide behind one of the carriers and take a few deep breaths. Knowing that her power was the cause of her overemotional state did not always help her to rein it in and get it under control. It affected her ability to think clearly and lead effectively. But she had to find some way to push through, because too much was going on to leave it all in the hands of a ground force Major.

Briefly, she wondered where Colonel Sumner had gone. She knew that he had a plan to deal with the army headed toward them, but she had been so wrapped up in her own part, that she hadn't really paid much attention to what it was. If he'd even explained it. She wasn't sure he had.

Harvey was capturing one of the ships with the help of forty ground troops. She didn't know if it was enough, given the size of the things. She could only hope. Those men knew what they were doing. And Harvey could get away from anyone. He'd be fine. Though she knew it, intellectually, she had to keep reminding herself. He'd be fine.

Her mind skipped and dodged and ran all over the place until it landed on Deidra. What had happened to her? Had she deliberately gone off somewhere without informing anyone? Weiz didn't think it likely, and that left only one answer that she didn't want to admit to. They'd taken her. Gordon had been too late to warn them about the scans, and somehow, Deidra was taken. Though that didn't make a lot of sense either, if the rest of them had been left. Unless Deidra had only just been in range, while the rest of them had not been. Unlikely, but possible.

That woman was a headache for her. She'd spent so much time with her, at times she felt like a sister, and other times like an over-tasking boss.

"I see you struggling."

Weiz jumped at the sound of Greenway's voice. Hand to pounding heart she turned toward him with the intent of shredding him to pieces. But when she saw the sorrow on his face, and the blood, words died, and she fell back against the hull of the carrier.

"What do you want?"

"I can't face them," he replied. He took up position a few feet away and slid down with his back against the hull until he was in a seated position.

"And you think there is something I can do about that?" She wanted to know. She also wanted him to go away so she could face her own difficulties and get through them well enough that she could be a functioning Commander.

"I need you to forgive me," he told her.

Weiz scoffed at that and couldn't help but stare. "You can't be serious."

His eyes were pleading as he looked at her. "I don't know how I can be back here with you all if you don't. And I need to be here."

"You killed hundreds of people! You tried to kill *us*."

He didn't deny it. How could he have? "It doesn't make sense to me now. Not most of it. And certainly not the rage." He shook his head. "It's hard to explain it. But I see you here, struggling with your own inner problems. So I have to believe, it wasn't just me. Please, Commander. I will forswear all use of my powers if I could have the forgiveness of you. Only you."

"Well, I can't very well make everyone forgive you," she snapped. "I'm not sure I *can* forgive you for *myself*. You caused us all a lot of trouble, and you're responsible for some truly despicable acts, Greenway. Killing people for not following you? Who does that?"

He shuffled uncomfortably in his seat. "There is not really much excuse for it," he admitted. "And the guilt of it will follow me to the grave, though the memory is foggy. I know what I did. That madness can only excuse so much. But I ask it of you, my Commander, because I have no one else to ask."

Weiz closed her eyes and tried to imagine the man before the day of the Giants. He had been a sad man, but a good Captain. He took care of his people, performed his duties, often went above and beyond. Fearlessly, he had been the first to land on Eridu. In the before, he had been a regular man, doing the best he could.

Did that mean she could forgive him for what he'd become? Perhaps. If she remembered that man, it might be possible. He wasn't wrong about her having to struggle with her own *demons* as it were. Caused by overuse of her power. On top of it all, he hadn't eaten or slept during that time, either, and Galsin had warned that doing that would come with its own set of drawbacks.

She let out a long breath and looked up toward the sky. "You have to behave like a human being, Greenway," she said. "We're not Gods. We're an accident. Behave like a human, give me your word that you will do that. And I will try to find it in me to forgive you. That will have to be enough."

Weiz looked at him then, to see tears flowing freely down his face. He nodded and swallowed, but it was a few moments before he got the words out. "Thank you."

She gave him a short while to have his emotions and compose himself before she asked the next question. "What do they want from us?"

He wiped tears from his face with the back of a hand, but his voice was still tremulous. "Us?" He pointed between himself and her with a finger. "Or *us*?" He made a circle motion indicating the whole camp.

"All of us," Weiz clarified. "All the Earthlings."

Greenway shook his head. "Nothing. They're just trying to chase them off, mostly. They want us. You, me, the others with powers. Apparently, they think they can 'cure' us. That what we have is some kind of disease that in cases like mine, can effect the human population. So, they must, in their eyes, remove us."

Weiz shot a grunt of disbelief. A disease? "And how far along have they come with the cure?"

"Far as I can tell, they got diddly. In some ways their tech might seem more advanced than ours, but it's not. They found much of it, buried. The ships, they didn't even build them."

She looked at Greenway with a raised brow. "Then who did?"

"Their ancestors. Thousands of years ago." He scratched at the top of his head. "Apparently, they had some kind of dark age where they didn't remember where they came from, or the technology they had. Just a vague memory that they'd had it. And one day, they found a ship, and deciphered the Captains logs. He had some of us in stasis, and his mission had been to collect us, to find the 'cure'. The Bahanians have taken that mission very seriously ever since."

It was preposterous, but here they were.

Weiz was going to ask more questions when she heard a bang from inside the carrier, and Major Preston announced loudly, "If you've a moment, Commander."

"Back to work," she said to Greenway, and he got up. "I'm coming, Major!" She responded just as loudly.

Once she was beside him and walking out toward camp, the Major told her of the decision made between the other Giant Killers. He recommended that she try to stop them, because a rescue mission without recon was as dangerous as parachuting without a chute. Death was almost always certain, and those who lived sometimes wished they hadn't.

Weiz could not help the annoyance that flooded through her, not just at the thought that her people would do something so stupid, but because she was expected to stop them. As if she could. Viatri had become a decisive young buck through their whole ordeal, even if at times she wondered how he ever got by without orders. If others had chosen to follow him, she didn't see herself tearing them away. Not in her current state.

"How long have they been gone?" She wanted to know.

"Not more than five minutes."

"I'll —" She was cut off by a very loud bang coming from the forward trenches. Either they'd fired a round, or something had exploded.

Weiz and Preston gave each other a look before sprinting toward the commotion. There was another bang before the trenches were in sight.

Immediately she noticed the enemy bearing down on their position. They hadn't reached the line, yet, and the gunners were giving warning shots with the shard cannon. While Preston may have known what that sound had been, Weiz had never heard anything like it.

It was clear that no one in the camp wanted to engage with the natives. More and more warning shots were going off, in other directions, but no one was aiming at them. No one had yet drawn blood.

The natives were either unafraid of what might happen, unaware of their capabilities, or all too aware of their reluctance to fight against people with swords and sticks. It wasn't a fair fight, and everyone knew it. Once first blood was drawn it would be a massacre, and no one wanted to be that person.

A part of her was drawn back to the memory of Greenway leading those locals to the mountain, in a misguided attempt to stop them from leaving. But at least then, it was closer to a fair fight.

Weiz watched the opposing army come to a full stop in a half-moon formation, at least a hundred metres from their trench position. They had plenty more positions to back up into, if it was necessary, but given what the natives were fighting with, she doubted they'd need to.

"They might have Bahanians among them." The words came out as she thought them. "They might be using them as shields!"

Preston shot her a look of pure disgust. But quickly returned his attention to the enemy.

There was movement within the enemy ranks, though she couldn't make out what was going on. Everyone in the earthling camp might well have been holding their breaths, for how quiet they'd become.

Moments later, five Bahana men were standing at the front of the native line. One, tall and broad, was a few steps closer. He raised his hand and shouted.

"Go home!" The words were slow and deliberate.

Major Preston turned to her with some confusion on his features. "I thought they couldn't speak English?"

Weiz grunted. She hadn't realised they were. She hadn't worked out how to tell the difference, the way that her mind worked now. "Reeve did mention they'd been learning," was all she said.

No one in the earthling camp made a move or a sound. The Bahanians took so long to continue, she wondered if they were waiting for a response.

"We have more on the way." The man seemed to struggle with what he was trying to say. Perhaps he'd forgotten the words. "We confine you to this place, until you leave."

Weiz nodded. Blockade. They wanted to make sure they didn't go out into the world and wreak havoc the way they'd been doing. But he didn't realise that they weren't all here. Or he didn't care.

"Understand?" the man questioned.

Weiz walked forward, painfully aware of the exposure. But she continued on until she was standing just behind the shard canon that had been firing. She could see the man clearly, and he could see her. Both knew the damage the other could do, though she wasn't sure he knew she was a Giant Killer.

She hoped that what came out of her mouth was English, because she didn't want to give herself away. "Understood," she said. "But you must understand, we'll not be chased off by the likes of you. You can come at us, or you can piss off. But we're not leaving."

Weiz made sure she was staring the man who spoke in the eyes. So, when he started to squint in confusion, she wondered if he'd understood. If he'd learnt English, he couldn't have known it for long, and was probably just translating in his own head.

It took a few moments, then he repeated what she'd said in what she assumed was their own language. Their lines did not move, though the Bahanians looked concerned. Apparently, they hadn't predicted this outcome. Which Weiz found strange.

One of the gunners in the trench in front of her turned and asked, "Do you think they understood what 'piss off' meant?" His accent was middle eastern, though she wasn't familiar with the flag on his patch. "I say, as one who spent years studying the language. I would not have known, had I not spent some time in the UK."

Weiz shook her head with a sigh. She'd figured they would have taken her meaning, but just in case she repeated her message with an amendment. "You can attack, or go away." It didn't have the same oomph or feel to her mind, but it would get the message across.

The man in the trench seemed to be right. The change of wording had their attention and the same man responded.

"You have two days to change your mind, or we will drop a bomb on you." He didn't wait for an answer that time, they all just turned around and walked back into the mass of natives, who were holding preternaturally still. Their eyes were forward, their pikes and sticks and whatever else, held very precisely. There was something not right in this image.

"I think two days is plenty of time to disabuse them of the notion we'll run along like good little children," Preston said beside her.

"I think in this corner of the universe they may just be accustomed to getting their own way."

"Whatever their might," Preston said turning full toward her. "They'll learn that we're an adaptable bunch. Always have been.

Besides, we can't leave. Even if we wanted to. Not until the scientists up there finish the equipment, programming and whatever else."

"Not wrong," she sighed.

"So, if it comes to it, it comes to it. It cannot be helped. We can't be squeamish in squashing the natives to get to the Bahanians. They can show their might, and we'll show them our magic."

Weiz raised a brow at him. "Did you forget they have some kind of nullification that prevents us from using our 'magic?'"

Preston shook his head. "Not that kind of magic," he said. But he didn't explain.

Soldiers and airmen might, from time-to-time, work together, but they were different breeds, Weiz thought. The way they thought, the way they moved. Everything about them, was different.

"Either way it goes," she responded. "I don't see them winning this. If they want us to leave, they're not going to attack the Docker."

"I hate to butt in here, but they did say they'd drop a bomb on us," Greenway said.

"The dome is up, so unless they know about it to sabotage it, it won't matter," Preston assured them. "We have defences. Possibly more than you in the Air Force know about. But you're about to learn, if they come down here en masse."

Weiz wasn't sure she *wanted* to learn. She didn't like this kind of warfare. Of all the other battles she'd fought, she'd known nothing of the enemy they were fighting. Generals may have, but she didn't. She just fought based on what she was seeing. In *this*, she could see the people. And they were *people*. Not a nameless race, from a nameless place, that was trying to invade *their* space. They were human, and the earthlings were the ones who didn't belong. It left a sour taste in her mouth.

"Why don't you fill me in, Major," Weiz said. "Tell me what we're working with."

CHAPTER SEVENTEEN

"You have got to be fucking shitting me," Harvey exclaimed as he reached for the bridge controls.

Ahead, between them and the Docker, were two very misshapen, very large, spacecraft that had taken on minds of their own. His first reaction was to reduce the forward momentum of the ship he was in, lest he crash into the abominations.

The soldiers with him were looking on in horror as one of the lumps started firing *something* at them. It looked like giant piles of black and silver goo, but Harvey doubted it would be that benign.

"Can we pull up?" the oldest of the soldiers asked.

Harvey shook his head. "This thing is a barge, not a darter. What can be done I am doing." And one of the things he was desperately looking for on the console was the reverse thrusters. Turned out, just because he could understand them when they spoke, didn't mean he could read and understand their language. It was all gibberish to him. So, he pushed buttons and pulled at levers until he found what he was looking for. When it came to flying, it was a dangerous thing to do — the button mashing — but he was desperate.

The thrusters came on with such force they were almost instantly stopped and within seconds, moving back.

A comm came on, and someone from another ship spoke. "Admiral Thwait, what are you doing?"

Harvey supposed he was meant to be Admiral Thwait. He ignored the call, and the man spoke again.

"Why are you backing up? Admiral? Can you hear me? Are you there?" A short silence. "Admiral? If you do not respond, protocol dictates that I fire on your ship. As you know."

"Ahhh shit," Harvey sighed and looked at the soldiers who wouldn't understand a word coming out of that console. He couldn't get them to answer it.

They'd avoided the goo, but he couldn't be sure that something else wasn't headed their way.

Harvey turned off the reverse thrusters, and resumed forward engines, before he found the comms console to respond. The man on the other end had not stopped talking. Harvey was beginning to feel sorry for anyone who had to work with him.

In what he hoped was a convincing voice, Harvey said. "I was avoiding some fire. Come in cautious." He had no idea what the Admiral was supposed to sound like, so merely speaking could be enough to get the other ships firing on them.

There was a brief silence in which he could hear his own heart hammering. He was prepared to move himself and the men with him back to the Docker, but he wasn't sure how many of the others he'd be able to get to before the ship was damaged beyond ability for survival.

"Call in the others and get ready for a quick departure," he told the men with him.

"Admiral, you do not sound yourself." The voice now sounded less concerned and more stern. "I think that Matricuesse should take over."

Harvey wasn't sure how to play this one, but he knew he wouldn't have long to make up his mind. He hoped that the others would be at the bridge shortly. But it seemed odd to him that someone should be so willing to shoot down a ship full of his own people.

Just as Harvey opened his mouth to respond he was saved by another voice. "Don't be an idiot, Mendel. He's back on course and he's *our boss*. We all know what you think, but we're all sick of hearing it. So shut up."

Harvey was more than a little relieved. He wished that he could thank the man, but without knowing his name or rank, or how he should sound, it was just too dangerous.

Besides, they might have dodged that small bullet, but they now had Weiz's monstrosities to take care of. He had no idea what she had been thinking, as he knew the plan. She was just supposed to make Dockers to go along side theirs to confuse things a little. Make it hard for the Bahanians to get at them. Whatever these were, they weren't that.

He pressed down in his cuff. "Weiz, you reading me?"

It wasn't Weiz who answered. "The Commander has moved to channel 897, if you like I can patch you through, or you can manually change it."

"Just patch me through." He waited a few moments, eyes staring out at the misshapen lumps. If they started shooting again, he wanted to be on it real quick.

"Harvey, you made it to the bridge," said Weiz.

"But honey, you left us a present." He was trying to be funny, but it came out serious.

"Excuse me?"

"Your Dockers? What are you doing?" A string of German he didn't understand came through the comms and he waited patiently.

"What happened to them?" she asked eventually.

"What happened to them? What... That is what I was asking you." He felt at his chin, brow drawn in confusion. "I don't know what these are supposed to be, but one of them shot at me."

"Fuck. I am sorry Harvey. I am on the ground. I left them and I thought they'd probably be fine. I gave them almost perfect shape."

"Well, not anymore," he returned sourly. "Why are you on the ground?"

Weiz laid out the short story for him and ended with, "If they do have Deidra, I suspect she's on one of those ships. I think you should probably go looking."

Harvey clamped the bridge of his nose between thumb and forefinger. "There are fifteen ships," he reminded her. "And they are not small." Not to mention that they all probably had everyone out of stasis at this point, and he would have to fight through a lot more crew than he'd had to on this ship.

"Do what you can," Weiz pleaded.

"Of course, of course," Harvey assured. "But I'm just one man, Catherine, there's only so much I can do."

"I know. Now get back to work." The radio clicked off. He would have been offended, but he'd heard the smile in her voice. And she wasn't wrong.

Harvey looked to the men with him. "I know you all heard that. Suggestions?"

The younger one took a step forward. "Well, sir, with your ability to move around from place to place the way you do, and now that we know where the bridge of a ship is located, we could just go along and take one bridge at a time. If nothing else, it might slow them down."

"To what end?" the older soldier asked. "We don't want to slow them down; we want to turn them away. And we don't want to give up this ship. It's a good get, and I think our scientists back home would be thrilled to have an alien vessel so large. That has stasis." Harvey inwardly agreed. Stasis and faster than light travel were things that they hadn't worked out yet. Well, except for Deidra's experiment, but he wasn't sure how well understood that tech was.

The middle guy put a hand on the older guy's shoulder, and opened his mouth, but Harvey had to interrupt him before he said anything. "I'm sorry, truly I am. But, what are your names?" He just could not keep going thinking of them as older, younger and middle man.

While middle man looked offended, and the younger, thoughtful, it was the older who smiled with amusement.
"Hamond, Sleiman, Adrigal," he said, pointing to each of them in turn, starting with himself.

"Thank you," Harvey nodded. "Please continue what you were going to say, Sleiman."

The man blinked at him then looked to Hamond and back. "You know, I can't remember."

Hamond laughed and pushed the man away from him. "You useless sack of turd," he said jokingly, then turned to Harvey. "Look, Captain. We can do as the youngster said, capture bridges, slow 'em down. Give ourselves some time to work out what we want to do. But seems to me, you want to rescue the lass, and, well, that will take some searching and doing. In that case, I would have to ask these questions: where were Greenway and Lance held while aboard one of these things? Would the Doctor be in a similar position? Where are the regular cells? Find those places on this ship, and then maybe you can pop in on the other ships, take a quick look and pop out."

Harvey nodded his approval more and more emphatically as he went on. It made sense, it would take less time and energy, and with only one person to worry about, it would be a lot easier for him.

"Sounds like I've got a plan, then." He turned on his heel to get started with it.

"Ah, sir," Adrigal pulled him up.

"What is it?"

"You can just send the other teams to find the places you're looking for, then just go to them after."

He had become so accustomed to doing everything himself since they'd landed on Eridu, he hadn't considered all the other soldiers under his command while they were aboard this ship.

"Alright, then. Give the order, Hamond." And Harvey sat back to twiddle his thumbs and wait while someone else did the work for him. He knew that it was the right thing to do, but he couldn't say he liked it. The thought of resigning when he got back... That thought brought him up short. When he got back. Surrounded by all the familiar things, for a moment, he'd forgotten that he couldn't. And his heart lurched a step before settling back where it was meant to be.

Would he be able to bring Jason to this place if the Bahanians were going to be a constant threat? Would Earth Base actually want to send more ships out this way if it just meant another prolonged war? To that he thought the answer might be yes, if only because of the potential for resources on Eridu. But if they didn't send civilians? If he couldn't see his son again?

He was pulled back to the situation at hand by Hamond speaking into his radio.

"They're on it, sir. They'll let us know when they find what you're looking for."

"Are you sure they know what to look for?" Harvey wanted to know.

"A science lab or infirmary, a brig and any place that might be used as a cell," Hamond confirmed.

"I'm not good at this part," Harvey confessed. "Waiting has never been my strong suit."

"I can tell you that waiting is a great deal of what we do with ground work," the old man said. "Waiting for intel, waiting for the right time, waiting for your soldiers to catch up with you. Waiting on orders, waiting on supplies. Waiting, waiting, waiting." He chuckled.

Harvey made a face that he thought might show his disgust. "Sounds like hell to me."

"You spend six months on a Docker to fly in space for a day or two, and then spend another six months to get home, and you think waiting is hell?" His amusement grew.

Harvey had never considered it that way, though he supposed it was true. They spent a lot of time on a Docker doing nothing much but training in the immersion pods or doing paperwork. It was like roaming around on Earth Base, you just couldn't go outside.

They didn't have to wait long, thankfully. "Boss," Harvey heard come through on Hamond's radio. "We got us a brig, aft grid section three."

"Copy," Hamond returned. He directed the next comment at Harvey. "Off you go, then. We got the bridge."

Harvey gave him a nod and shifted. He wasn't exactly where the other soldiers were. He just aimed for aft section three. It was a small enough section that it would not take him long to find them.

He moved at a fast pace, glancing around corners and opening doors until he found the men he was looking for. They were standing in front of a narrow corridor, looking out in his direction. The first man to see him gave a nod.

"There are four cells down that way," he informed Harvey. "I can't rightly tell if there is anyone in them, 'cause I can't figure how to open it. But I am sure it's the brig."

Harvey moved forward without comment and shifted into the first cell as soon as he saw it. It was empty and he moved to the next. It held a man strapped down to a bed attached to the wall. He was unconscious, but alive. Harvey didn't want to accidentally let loose someone dangerous, so he left the man there. The other two cells were empty.

When he came back out, he shook his head. "Not here."

"Harvey," he heard through his radio. It was Hamond. "Harvey, someone is talking on the comms. No idea what they're saying, you best come now."

Harvey let out a frustrated hiss. "I'm coming, relax!" But even before he could shift, the ship shook. He took that moment to shoot a wide-eyed look at the men beside him and said, "Get everyone up to the bridge." He didn't wait for an answer.

"...warning. Admiral, respond." Was all he heard as he appeared back on the bridge.

Harvey smashed a hand down on the console and shouted into the mic. "What do you think you're doing, Mendel?" He hoped that his voice held enough authority, and that he remembered the man's name correctly.

"You are not the Admiral. Where is the Admiral?" That from another voice.

Fuck, fuck, fuck. He wasn't sure how he was going to get them to stop firing. He had heard the word warning, and he hoped it meant that had just been a warning shot. He genuinely wished that Hamond had understood what they'd been saying before he'd come back.

What was he going to say. "He's in the brig," Harvey said. There was quiet for a long moment, in which a dozen different scenarios, all bad, ran through Harvey's mind.

"What did he do this time?" That from the voice that had saved him the first time.

"It doesn't matter what he did," from Mendel. "He should not be in charge."

"Shut up, Mendel. You are close to being stripped. Now tell me, who am I speaking to? And what did the Admiral do?"

Harvey looked around the bridge for some kind of inspiration. He had no idea what the Admiral might have done in the past that would lend weight to anything he said. And as for who he was supposed to be...

"This is Reichs," he told them, and hoped that it was the kind of name that these people might have. "The Admiral had an episode."

"I told you," Mendel started, but the other guy shut him up quickly.

"Stripped, Mendel. Reichs, I have not heard the name before. What's your position?"

Harvey panicked and channelled British navy, because Admiral was for seafarers. "Lieutenant," he said.

There was a silence over the line that told him he'd messed up. Guessed wrong. They would want to make sure that he believed he'd gotten away with it, but he knew.

"We're sending over Rear Admiral Eposius to take command. Stand her down and await instruction."

"Aye, sir," Harvey replied, but as soon as he got off the comms, he turned his attention to the bridge door. He heard shuffling feet and could only hope it was his men.

He wasn't sure whether the man was sending over a more senior officer to take charge from a friendly crew, because he bought the story Harvey was selling. Or if he was sending in a crack team to retake the ship. Either way, one look at Harvey and their empty ship would be enough to tell them something had gone down.

Hamond perked his head up and asked, "What's happening, sir?"

Harvey had forgotten that none of them would be able to understand. "I don't think they bought it," he told them. "They're sending someone over. Not sure if they'll be hostile or expecting to walk into a friendly situation. Either way, once the others get in here, we're out. We'll go to the next ship up and take the bridge. Proceed from there."

The bridge doors opened and several soldiers in ATF garb filed in, wary and ready. Harvey counted them as they came, wanting to make sure everyone was there.

"Missing a team," he said, addressing the first in line. "Where are they at?"

"They're coming, sir." The man assured him. "Had to take the long way around. Minute or two."

"Alright. I'll start with you lot and come back for the others." He set himself and stretched out his arms to give the soldiers as much spaces as possible to get a hand on him. "We'll be going straight to the next bridge, so guns up," he warned. Once the were all in place, he shifted.

CHAPTER EIGHTEEN

Lance and his little cadre of superheroes ran through the woods at a pace that few could have matched unaided. They were unconcerned about the native army, despite their knowledge of the Bahanians among them. They were almost halfway to the structure near to where the village had been, after only an hour.

Ellis slowed down beside him, and noticing, he did the same, until they were all going at a brisk walk.

"I am not fit," she heaved, "enough — to continue." She took a very deep breath and stopped for a moment. "At this pace." She finished, starting to walk again.

Lance hadn't considered anything about those who had come with him, he had to admit. Not whether they were fit to the task, or fit in general. Or that they could be unfit, with their newfound power. He had just been incensed that once again, the Bahanians had taken some of their people, while they had yet to be able to do much damage of any kind in return.

A few rescued prisoners, who had realistically, rescued

themselves. One captured soldier, who had made the mistake of confronting Gordon. The meteor shower was what had scared them away the first time, though he wasn't entirely sure they realised that. And now they had an army of natives, nullification fields, fifteen giant ships that carried who knew how many soldiers, airmen, aircraft, weapons or whatever else might be thought of.

And what did they have? A Docker that carried a few MM ships, a bunch of soldiers, some airmen and scientists. And twelve absolutely useless, Giants. Lance hadn't really considered how bitter he felt about the fact that the Bahanians could take his powers away. Even temporarily. It suggested that they knew more about them, understood them better, than he possibly could.

"Drifting Sinatra?" Ellis asked, still catching her breath. They were moving swiftly, but it would take them twice again as much time as it had already taken at their current pace, and Lance felt impatient.

"They have all the advantages," he complained. He kept it on the quiet side, but not quite in a whisper. "I am trying to think of a way out, or around, that would get the least amount of people caught or killed."

Ellis took a few deep breaths before responding. "That's not really our job," she said.

Lance dismissed that with a gesture. "It shouldn't matter whose job it is. Anyone should be able to come up with an answer."

The others had pulled ahead of them but were staying close. Lance wasn't sure any of them knew where the opening was, so they couldn't get too far without him.

"What's the question, then?" Ellis wanted to know.

Lance shook his head slowly, looking for inspiration. "I don't know. How do we win?"

"Win what?"

"This war?"

Ellis took a couple of breaths and picked up her pace again to bring them level with the others. At the first step, she said, "That's the wrong question."

"Then what is the right one?" He wasn't sure he was the one to give the answers to all their problems, but he at least wanted a crack at it. He felt at the back of his head where the tattooed eyes were. They might have grown back, somehow, but there was a time when they'd been taken away, not very long ago.

"If I knew that, Viatri, maybe I would be in charge." She smiled at him, but he couldn't find the levity.

It didn't take them too long to get where they were going. The cave. It did appear man made, now that he really looked at it, though without knowing what he knew, he doubted he would have noticed.

They all stopped just outside, unsure how they wanted to proceed. It was Zim who asked the question. "We're probably not going to be able to use our gifts in there." He spat off to the side as if merely saying it, was distasteful. "So, what are we going to do?"

Fyord and Hadley seemed to communicate without words for a moment, then Hadley spoke up. "If Reeve and the rest gave a good accounting of how they got out, I don't imagine it would be too difficult to pull this off. If there are no guards, and no defence systems, what do we need to be wary of? We go in, one at a time, a little space between in case there are some of the enemy inside. Leave someone out here to keep watch."

"Who's got the skills to get the doors open?" Lance asked. "I'll go first and scout the way, but whoever can get them open should be first behind me."

Zim nodded. "I'll get that part. It shouldn't be too hard."

Ellis slapped a hand down on the rocks of the cave. "I'll stay here and keep watch."

"I think I'll join you," Gordon said. "We can be backup in case anything goes wrong in there. Protection, if something goes wrong out here."

Roles worked out, they moved into the cave, until they were in near total darkness. Bridges moved to the front with fire in his palm to illuminate the situation.

Lance ran his hand along a smooth wall, that appeared to have no seams in it. Though it was flat like worked rock, anyone could be mistaken for thinking it was a natural cave wall, simply smoothed out.

He took a step back to look at the wall in the firelight. Weiz would have been great help here, with her tiny ball of sunshine, but Lance knew how to work with what he had.

"It won't be too obvious, but it should stand out," he mumbled to himself as much as to the others. "Step on it, push it, key it in, something..." And then he saw it, on the ground, two steps away from the wall. It would probably need a good amount of weight on it to trigger, and it would need to be there for a good amount of time, or they would have accidentally triggered it the first time they found the place, what felt like an age ago.

With a nod, he stepped onto it and waited. After a few moments, when nothing happened, he stepped off, and was narrowly missed by some kind of arrow or dart that came from one of the side walls. It moved so quickly he could barely follow it with his eyes, until it embedded itself just under Hadley's throat.

She looked at Lance with a wide-eyed surprise before mouthing the words, 'oh get fucked,' and falling forward onto her face. Lance rushed to her side, but Fyord was there first. He turned her face up, and though her eyes moved, the rest of her didn't. It was hard to tell if the placement of the short arrow cut off her airway, or if she'd been poisoned. Either way, Hadley would not be coming inside.

It was a quick death, for which Lance was grateful, but he also shuddered. He was suddenly very thankful that he'd stepped backward and not forward, or that arrow would have got him.

Which, he supposed, it was designed to do.

Solemnly, and carefully, they moved Hadley's body back toward the entrance, and returned to their scrutiny of the cave wall. Unlike other people, death didn't worry them too much, because they knew they'd be resurrected in the field. Fyord kept glancing back, though, and Lance supposed he just wanted to make sure the woman wasn't dead for another two weeks. When he nodded to himself, Lance took it to mean the body had disappeared, and chanced a glance himself to confirm the fact. She was gone.

"They've hidden it masterfully," Zim said, tracing the wall with a finger. "How sure are we that they'll be in here?"

"It's the only one of their strongholds on this planet that we're aware of," Lance returned. "Sure? No. But it's all we have."

Zim grunted at the response. The others just looked determined.

"They could be on one of the incoming ships," Bridges offered.

Lance shook his head. "They were taken before those ships were in range. I'm sure of it. They have to be down here."

He had an idea. He gestured for them all to step away from the back wall while he took a deep breath. Perhaps, like the mountain, if it was an old enough wall, he could just make it collapse with a good gust.

It came out of him like water through a pressure hose and hit the wall with a snap. He stopped immediately, concerned he'd accidentally hit a load bearing section of wall, and the roof might collapse.

The snap sound came again, followed by a whirring and click. The door to the cells swung open.

For a brief moment, Lance was very pleased with himself. Then he became concerned. He hadn't broken the wall, he'd triggered something. His eyes searched for movement in the side walls, wary of another dart, or some other defense mechanism.

Once the door was open, revealing three Bahanians within, his concern became surprise, then fear, then self-preservation, very quickly. He didn't know if the Bahanians were there to stop them, or if they'd even been aware of their presence. His first instinct was to launch himself forward like a cannon ball, and hope he got them all to the ground, and in so close that weapons couldn't be used.

After the first moment of surprise, he was glad to see Zim, Bridges and Fyord join the fight. It gave them the upper hand on numbers, and it was over with quickly.

Lance slammed the head of the one he'd landed on into the concrete of the floor, and his eyes rolled backward into his head. Passed out or dead, Lance didn't care either way. These people deserved whatever they got, as far as he was concerned.

Zim and Bridges worked together to restrain one, until Bridges got in a good blow and the man simply crumbled. And Fyord seemed to be performing wrestling moves on the man beneath him, who was trying every which way to squirm out from under, or buck Fyord off. Zim walked over and brought his heel down on the man's forehead. There was a loud crack, and blood started flowing, but the man remained conscious. Zim raised his boot again, and the man looked terrified, but Zim didn't let that stop him.

"Piece of shit," said the Frenchman in a strong accent. He then went on to mumble a few more choice things in French, which Lance only partially understood.

Heart hammering in a way it hadn't while he'd been running, Lance stood and looked around. They were in a dimly lit, long corridor that lead slowly downward. There didn't appear to be any other Bahanians in sight, but that didn't mean there weren't any around the first corner.

Lance looked at Zim, who nodded. Bridges and Fyord followed up behind, and Lance lead them inward.

He hadn't expected there to be any Bahanians in this place after the way Kristin had described it. He figured they had abandoned the post. But perhaps they had simply been understaffed.

Lance rushed down the long sections of corridor as quick as he dared, while making as little noise as he possibly could. Which was hard, because every breath and every step echoed off the bare concrete walls.

When they reached the bottom, his heart resumed its heavy rhythm as he looked into a small room that held two Bahanians watching screens. The only surprise was that they were paying no attention to Lance and his fellow airmen. Instead, their eyes were diverted to one particular screen, though from where they were, Lance couldn't tell what was on it.

Lance looked back at the others and waited for their mute approval before pushing in the guard door. He made it quick, like a squeaky gate, hoping if it did have a usual sound, the rapid move would shorten it. No sound came.

In a crouch, Lance moved up slowly and deliberately behind one of the guards, while Zim restrained the other. He put the man in a headlock and pressed down on his vagus nerve until he stopped struggling and his head drooped forward. Zim did something similar with his man.

He looked around for something to tie the men up with but saw nothing useful. As a general rule, he hesitated to kill people. He had no problem killing in a space fight, not knowing the aliens or what they looked like. And it struck him then, that if there were humans on two other planets in the universe, perhaps there were more, and he may have fought them. He didn't like that idea. Though why he should feel any different about it, he wasn't sure. He just did.

Zim was perusing the monitors and controls trying to find them a way in, and locate Kristin and Estard. But the more empty cells he flicked through, the more scared Lance became that they weren't there. That they'd been shifted off to some other site, where Lance wouldn't be able to get to them.

The door to the cells opened, and they all filed through, Zim in the lead. He walked at a brisk pace toward a single cell with intent.

Without a word, Lance, Fyord and Bridges took up positions around Zim as he worked on trying to get the cell door open. They faced outward, eyes scanning for any threat, though Lance was sure they'd got them all.

It took longer than Lance was expecting, and he started to get nervous. He looked back at Zim with frequency, his boots shuffling on the concrete. The moment the door started to open, Zim walked in, and Lance followed so close on his heels, the man swore at him until he backed up.

But it was not who he expected in the cell. It was an airman, in a tattered uniform, passed out on the floor. She was pale, cheeks sunken, dark rings beneath her eyes. Drool was forming in a puddle beneath her cheek, or Lance might have thought her dead.

Zim moved forward on light feet, crouched before the woman and picked her up as if she weighed nothing. Lance stared, not just because this women was unexpected, but because Zim had a tear running down a cheek, and lips pursed so tight, they almost completely disappeared into his stern face.

Lance let the man take the lead as they walked out of the cells and back up toward the entrance. He wanted to ask about the woman, who she was, if he knew her, but his expression did not invite questions. And as for where Kristin and Estard were, he had to believe that if they'd been in those cells, Zim would have gotten them out before shutting down in this way.

Once they were up on the surface, out in the sunlight, which was fast fading now, Zim placed the woman carefully on the ground. He brushed matted hair from her face with a tender hand, and frowned when some of it came away with his hand. His tears were raining down on her face, and they caused her to stir a little. She looked as though she was struggling to breath.

Gordon and Ellis rejoined them, both looking curious, but obviously not wanting to ask the questions. They both stayed to the back and spoke quietly amongst themselves.

"Are you sure she doesn't have the sleeping sickness?" Lance asked indelicately, and Zim looked up with anger. "I don't mean to be that guy, but Harvey brought in Abramovich in a very similar state. Just saying."

Zim didn't seem capable of speech at that moment. Not a grunt, not a shout. He just picked the woman back up and resumed his walk back toward camp.

Lance let himself lag behind a little until he was beside Fyord. The man was looking thoughtfully toward Zim's back, but otherwise seemed at ease.

"Do you know who that is?" Lance asked in a whisper.

Fyord nodded slowly as they picked up their pace. "That's his wife. They thought she'd died at the mountain when Greenway came. Anaise, I believe her name is."

"She was at the mountain with us?" Lance didn't remember the face, but he supposed it was possible.

"She was. But she never made it onto the ship. Zim was devastated that he'd made it out without her."

Lance couldn't imagine what that must have been like. In truth, he hadn't paid a lot of attention to anyone who had not been on his ship when they'd first landed. He felt bad about that sometimes, but other times he realised that he simply wasn't built to deal with so many people.

"I thought there was a no fraternisation rule between airmen?" In fact, he was certain of it, because he'd been reminded several times when trying to flirt. "How are they married?"

Fyord shrugged. "Not sure on the logistics, but I think they were married before they joined the ATF, and they had some kind of understanding that at any time during their advance of rank, they could not serve in the same squad. Or something to that effect. I know there are provisions in the rules for people like them."

Lance nodded, though he couldn't really understand. As much as he felt for the man, his thoughts kept turning back to Kristin and Estard. They were the reason they'd gone to that place. And they hadn't been there. So where were they? Was it close or far? Were they being treated as poorly as he had been? Or were the Bahanians too busy with other things?

Perhaps it was only because of his personal experience that he felt a dread for them, while the others seemed to take their failure in stride. He worried, and his experience and imagination took care of the rest. So, he racked his mind for ways in which to search for them, much as he had a few days ago.

There had to be a way. These Bahanians could not be so far ahead of them that there was nothing they could do.

~

The biggest problem Estard found with the darkness, was that he could not tell what time it was, or how long they'd been there. He'd attempted to take them back to before the Bahanian had popped out in front of them, but his power wasn't working. Which meant there was something in the cell that prevented it.

He couldn't exactly look around, so he felt at the walls with his fingertips, and slid along at a snail's pace as he noted several things. The first, the walls were made of rock, not concrete or metal. The second, the gaps between the stones were uneven, and the stones themselves were not uniform in shape. And there was only one place that could have been a door. There was no way for them to disguise it.

Estard pounded on it while Kristin sat with her back to a wall and listened to him shout. He could imagine her shaking her head at him. He *heard* her sigh more than once. But he had no idea what she was actually thinking. After her last capture, perhaps she was just settling in for a long wait.

"You could help," he breathed after a while.

"With what?" she asked.

"Moving the door?"

"How sure are you that you know where it is?"

Estard rubbed at his face with both hands and sucked at his teeth. He would have given anything for a cigarette in that moment. "It's the only place it could be, based on the seams in the walls. Also, it's indented, as compared to the rest. If it's not the door, it sure is a strange architectural choice."

"Damn, Agent man. No need to get so snippy." He heard her get up, though he wasn't sure how close she was until she bumped into him from his left. He grunted and she shot a laugh. She ran a hand from his back and down the length of his arm until she had a hold of his hand. Then she spoke so close to his ear he could feel her breath on cheek and neck. "Show me."

His body had such an automatic response to the stimulus, that it took him a moment before he could do anything but breath without giving himself away. Then slowly, he guided her hand toward the door and let it go. "Feel the indent," he instructed as he took a painful step away from her. It was not the time, and certainly not the place, for such things. And he tried to remind his body of that, though it didn't want to cooperate.

"Alright, I feel it," she said after a few moments. "What do you want to do about it? It feels pretty solid to me."

"Push, shove, kick, hit... Whatever you can think of, really." He didn't have a plan. He didn't know how the door worked. It might push, it might slide. If it slid, they likely had no hope.

"And you expect any of that to work?"

He shook his head, even though he knew she couldn't see him. "No, not really. But I'd rather try and fail then sit on my arse and feel sorry for myself."

Kristin made an indignant sound, then said, "Is that what you think I was doing?"

"Wasn't it?"

She seemed to think about her response for a while. He let her. "Maybe," she agreed finally. "Second time I've been caught by these fuckers in a week. The first time, that cell was just a box. I assumed this one would be too. And I tried for at least half the time I was in that one."

He couldn't really fault that train of thought, even if their circumstance was different. And they were clearly in a different place.

"Well, you got lucky last time," he said, moving back to the door and pressing his palms against it. "I would be extraordinarily surprised to find there are others in this prison who have the know-how to break us out."

"I know, I know," she sighed.

"Now, I am going to push as hard as I possibly can, on the count of three, just to see if there is a budge in it," he told her. "No budge, and I am like to assume that the door slides. That would be more difficult, but not impossible."

"Not impossible." She sounded like she was trying to convince herself of that.

"Nothing is impossible," he returned. "Are you ready?"

"I'm ready."

"Three, two, one!" He pushed as hard as he could. His shoes slid on the floor, and he had to readjust, but he put his full weight into it. He strained until he could feel the veins in the side of his head throb. Sounds of the strain escaped his mouth, and he heard Kristin doing the same.

It took a few minutes, but he felt the tiniest shift in the stone. The grating sound was like balm to his failing hope. He redoubled his efforts to get the door moving in that direction, only semi aware of Kristin doing the same. There was another hitch and shift, but it was so minute that Estard had to wonder whether they were actually achieving anything.

He heard Kristin fall to the floor beside him. "Give me a minute," she said. "I never knew pushing an immovable object could be so exhausting."

Estard barked a laugh, even as he slid to the floor beside her. He reached out to find her hand in the dark as he replied, "It's not immovable, just very set in its ways."

He thought she chuckled a little. When he found her hand on the ground, he didn't squeeze, or make any sudden movements. He just left it there, so he could be aware of her presence, and she of his, and they would know they were not alone.

"What do you think they plan to do to us in here?" Kristin asked. It was the first time he had ever heard the woman genuinely scared.

Estard wanted to comfort her. To take her in his arms. But she was a jumpy sort, and slow movements were best. "At best, I'd say they're just trying to remove us from the fight. Get us out of the way so we're not a great danger to them."

"And at worst?" She put her hand on top of his and squeezed a little.

"I imagine we'd be in for something similar to Viatri." He didn't know how he was supposed to sugarcoat that.

He felt Kristin's hand move and tighten, until they were holding hands in earnest.

"I don't want to go down like that," she told him. She let go of his hand and felt up his arm until she found his face. He could hear her shuffled movement but didn't know what she was doing until he felt her other hand on the other side of his face, cupping a stubbled cheek.

"What are you doing?" he choked out, his excitement rising as he felt her straddle his legs.

"It's what you want," she whispered, and pressed her lips down against his.

His hands came up automatically to her waist. He didn't need to be able to respond to this situation. And for a moment, he kissed her back. But then he pulled away and faced a cheek toward her as he bit at his lip.

He swallowed before asking. "Is this really what you want?"

It felt like she was silent for so long he didn't think he wanted the answer. A dozen scenarios on what she might be thinking flashed through his mind, while she tried to form her own answer.

"I think so, sometimes," she said. "I think about it, which is more than I have done with anyone else." She stayed where she was, though she leaned back a little and he could feel her arse on his thighs.

Estard wasn't sure what to make of her confession, but he knew that he had to be delicate. She had just given him something precious to hold onto. He just wasn't sure it was the right time or place for it. Much as his body responded to her, he didn't really fancy getting it on in a dark stone cell. It meant more to him than that.

"I tell you what," he breathed, finally. "I'll wait. We have time. Until *you* are sure, I can't be comfortable with this. And that will plague me." He tried to lighten his words with a smile that she couldn't see.

Her hands dropped away from his face, and he felt their loss. She breathed deep and loud, and he had to imagine she was either frustrated or angry, but didn't know how to articulate it. That fire was a part of what drew him to her.

He let her move off him slowly, without comment, without judgement. It was hard, because he did want her. In every way. And until she'd done that, he hadn't realised quite how much. A part of him had held in reserve that perhaps he only wanted her because she was the unobtainable, and at some point, he'd find someone more willing to set his sights on. But not now. Now he knew it was for real.

Estard waited for her to gather herself and let her speak first. He felt if he tried to regain control of the situation, she might start getting skittish. She certainly had a propensity for it.

It took longer than he would have liked before he heard her voice again. "Alright," she said, "let's get this done."

He rose to his feet and felt the wall until both his hands were on the door. "Ready when you are," he told her.

The way it was going, he didn't think they were going to get the door moving. But it gave them hope, and something to do, until help arrived. He just had to hope that was soon.

CHAPTER NINETEEN

As they approached the camp, the native army was easy to see. The columns had broken up, and they were moving amongst each other, talking in sombre tones. It was near dark enough now that they had a few fires going, over which they cooked various meals.

There was something disquieting about the scene, Gordon thought, as she tried not to be seen coming in. She couldn't quite put her finger on what it was, but she was sure it would come to her if she stopped thinking about it.

Behind her, Lance had taken the burden from Zim, while the man took a moment to rest and catch his breath.

They had all figured they would need to go the long way around to get back to the camp, but they had yet to agree on which way that was. Gordon was ambivalent. They could go either way. They would end up in the same place so, to her mind, it didn't really matter. But the argument was really between Fyord and Ellis, who for some reason no one knew, had a kind of rivalry going on.

Gordon sighed. Having listened to them whispering heatedly at each other for at least fifteen minutes she was more than a little bit over it. She wanted to yell at them, as one would at unruly children, and the only thing that kept her from it was the army she was currently observing. If she could see that army, then they could see them.

Lance shuffled up beside her. "Do you want to just go and leave them here?" he asked in a faint whisper. He sounded serious, though he could have just been playing it deadpan. With Viatri, it could be hard to tell.

She searched his face for some clue before she answered. "Yes, let's, shall we?"

He gave a single nod, then motioned with his head to Bridges who helped Zim to his feet, and they started moving. It wasn't too long before Ellis and Fyord caught up with them. Fyord was gloating, which made Gordon assume he had thought this direction was best. They didn't understand that no one else cared.

It wouldn't take them long to get around, they would just have to be vigilant and quiet. Two things Gordon felt Ellis and Fyord were not.

Hesitantly she let her mind power wander out into the minds of the opposing army. It wasn't until she found a few minds to rifle through that it occurred to her. "My power is working," she said.

Lance almost tripped beside her, and the woman he carried in his arms tilted as if she might fall, but he held tight. "What?" he managed to get out in a choked whisper.

"Either the Bahanians are not close, or my power is immune." That last was something she hadn't even considered until she said it out loud. Until that moment, they all knew that *only* Harvey's power was immune. But what if hers was too? There was only one way to find out. "One of you, try and use your power. Nothing too grandiose, just, you know, use it."

She couldn't tell who was doing what until they spoke up, one after the other, starting with Ellis. "I got nothing," she said with a shrug.

Fyord just shook his head, while Lance swore and rebalanced his load. "Not me," he breathed.

Bridges took longer, thrusting out his hands as if he somehow needed the action for his power to work. But after a minute or two, he shook his head and said, "I really tried."

Gordon looked to Zim. He had barely done anything with his ability, at any time. Either because he did not know how, was afraid to, or didn't feel the need, was hard to say. He mostly acted as if he were still a regular man, with no power.

"Zim, how 'bout you?" She asked when it was clear he would not try without prompting.

He shook his head emphatically. "No. I will not try until we get back to the carriers. If I wake her up, I want her in a safe place surrounded by people she can trust, not out in the open where she is still in danger. No." The glare he shot at each and every one of them told her there would be no argument.

Gordon raised both her hands in supplication. She had not thought he would feel so strongly on the subject. But it had diverted everyone from the original purpose of it. Gordon was immune. And *that* would be helpful, in many ways. Not for her sanity, as she found the struggle against paranoia intense when she dived too deep. But she thought it could be worth it, if the Commander could direct her successfully.

She withdrew her searching tendrils to keep herself free of consequence until she had a better idea of how best to use it. Meanwhile, she wondered what it was that made the difference.

Harvey was the one they all knew was unaffected and could get away from them. Even the Bahanians were aware of it, and for the most part, worked around it. But none knew that she could. Would that make any difference in what they were doing?

Her mind went back to when Ensign Brioli had come out of the woods and disrupted her vigil of Estard, Fyord and Hadley. How she had managed to knock him out with an unconscious thought. It was unlikely that he had walked into the situation without whatever it was that could prevent them from using their powers. But at the time, no one had even thought of it. They'd all just assumed he didn't have one. Though if that were the case, if he *did* have one, then it would be on the Docker somewhere, and surely someone would have noticed? Or perhaps it required more than just simply being there. It was something to think on.

Gordon shook her head and let the thought go. She'd only have herself going in circles until she had the means to search for the answers. And there was no sense in that.

Absorbed as she'd been in her own thoughts, it was a surprise to see the carriers so close after they breasted a small hill. They were almost there, and no one stood in their way.

Weiz saw them coming and sent out two soldiers to help carry the woman from the cells. She still thought it was strange that the others had never even mentioned her. If she had been with them, at any time, they should have known she was there. Mentioned her as a loss, at the very least. So, there was either something very fishy going on there, or she'd been moved from another place. She wasn't sure which would be more plausible.

"No Kristin or Estard?" Weiz asked, her eyes focused on the distance.

Gordon shook her head. "If there was, they'd be here," she told the woman. "But I do have something that could give us an edge, if we can figure out how to use it."

"Do tell."

Gordon gave a short rundown of her thoughts on the fact that she could use her power, even though the others couldn't. She also gave her thoughts on how the Bahanians may need to consciously use whatever instrument it was that caused the nullification. That it might have a limited battery life, or require a lot of power. Weiz looked thoughtful for some time before she replied.

"I will think on how best to put this information to use, but I will definitely find something, I can assure you." She looked around as if she'd misplaced something, then waved and said, "I've got to go do something, but if you come up with anything else, let me know."

She could never quite get in with the Originals, as she was beginning to think of them, now that she shared their predicament. It wasn't that they were trying to keep her out of things, simply that they had, for the most part, been a crew before everything, and so were naturally closer. Then again, she was possibly just being paranoid about it.

She took a step forward and tripped over the leg of a sitting soldier. She heard the man bark a laugh, even as she twisted to look at him.

"Watch where you're going," he said with a broad smile.

Gordon refrained from reply as she got up and dusted herself off. She gave a look of disapproval to the man, and he laughed again. She growled and moved away.

There was nothing for her to do in this place, and she felt it. No ship to fly, no enemy to shoot at. No battle to engage in. So her mind went to the same thing it went to every time she had too little to do. Her children.

Her heart lurched inside her chest and tears welled in the corners of he eyes. She went to the side of the camp and faced away from everyone so they wouldn't see.

Before she could fall into self-pity, Greenway stood beside her, hands in pockets, looking up into the fading light of the evening. He didn't say anything at first, as the now familiar stars began to appear, and Gordon thought about leaving. She had nothing to say to the man. But he'd clearly come for something.

"I'm sorry," he said after a while, and it seemed a genuinely difficult thing for him to say. "I don't really remember it all very well, but I remember you. Being there on the march, keeping the others in check."

Gordon shuffled her feet, uncomfortable at being reminded of her choice to go with him, whatever her motive had been at the time. He just stayed beside her, looking up like he was waiting for something.

"Are you apologising? Or making excuses?" she burst out after a few moments of inner turmoil.

He looked at her then and took a step back. "Ah, both, I suppose." He frowned at himself and really seemed to think on what he would say next. "I'm sorry for what I put you all through. For asking you to trash the camp, and your chance of going home. That I asked you to follow and fight, for nothing more than my own hubris."

Gordon stared at him for a long moment, unsure how she felt about it. In her own way, with everything that had happened since, she'd simply moved on from it. But he couldn't. He'd been caught up in his own madness and was then taken by the Bahanians. Left to deal with what he'd done, and who he'd become. Alone. Which was no less than he deserved, in her mind.

Even as she opened her mouth to say something, she had to close it again, words unsaid. Because she didn't know what to say to him. It's fine? It's nothing? Don't worry about it? None of those things were true. She'd gone with him in the thought that perhaps she'd be able to stop him, but she'd never found an opportunity. And he'd made her see his point of view, skewed as it was. He was apologising. But was he asking for forgiveness?

"What's done is done," she said finally. "It's time to move on." Words as much for herself as for him.

He seemed to take it well, as if it were more than he expected. But he didn't leave, so Gordon waited for him to say something. When she felt enough time had passed and he remained quiet, she simply walked away. She didn't plan on becoming that man's friend.

She looked around at the camp. It was night now, and the lights of fires and electric lamps lit up the space so well it would be easy to get night blind. As she walked toward the carriers, she looked over to the enemy camp, and while they, too, had fires, they lacked the lamps. It was an eerie kind of contrast.

The natives seemed more sombre than even those who had followed Greenway to the mountain. She had to wonder at the natives, and how they felt about what was happening. Two warring factions that had nothing to do with them, fighting on their land, conscripting their people. And though she'd never spoken more than a word or two to any of them, language being a large barrier, she got the impression that they were not that much different from the humans of Earth.

She sent out a tendril of her power. She wanted to test it, to see how far it would go. If she could actually read thoughts at a distance, or just sense the minds beneath. If they would sense that their minds were being rifled through.

It hit a man at the very edge of their camp, closest to them, and though she couldn't understand clear thought, she could easily infer from the images and feelings, that the man was tired and didn't want to be there. His feet were sore, because his boots were wearing unevenly, and he wanted to go home.

She moved on to the next closest man.

~

Weiz got distracted by a private call from the Docker that she had not been expecting. She held up her hand and said something absently to Gordon as she moved off toward the back of the carrier. The one place she had decided was hers. No one else went back there.

"Go ahead," she said. "I've got some privacy."

"Patching through the Colonel," the Bridge Comms Officer told her.

She waited impatiently, foot tapping, until she heard his voice in her ear. "Commander," he greeted.

"Colonel," she returned.

"We've taken up position and are ready to close in on the enemy position from behind. I need you to create a distraction while we come close. Something loud. I was thinking fireworks, maybe? Can you do that?"

Weiz took a deep breath and tried not to sound as annoyed as she felt. She'd become a convenient magic trick. "It depends how close the Bahanian tech is. I can do it, but I may need to walk away from camp. *May.*"

"That's all I can ask," he said.

"Colonel," she didn't want him to just end the call like he normally would. "What were you going to do if I wasn't down here? I wasn't supposed to be. And what comes after that? What's the expectation? Do we rush them from this direction? You know it's going to be a slaughter, don't you? If we use our tech."

"Major Preston knows what to do," was all he said, and the comms clicked off.

Weiz closed her eyes and took a deep breath, then looked toward the sky. She saw some flashing lights that she assumed were the Docker and the Bahanian ships. But of course, they were all too far away to see more than that.

As she prepared herself to make fake fireworks, she found herself somewhat reluctant to get them bursting in the air when she didn't know the plan. The slaughter of her people to the giants their first night kept playing through her mind, and she knew that the natives of this world would be similarly defenceless. That if that happened, they might join in her nightmares.

Angry with herself, she let out a soft growl and went to find the Major. If they were just going to massacre that army, she didn't think she wanted to play a part in it. Wasn't sure she could, in good conscience. Even if that played right into the plans of the Bahanians.

The Major was talking to his Sergeant when she approached. He noticed her straight away and broke off his conversation to wait for her. "What can I do for you, Commander?" he asked when she was close enough.

"Colonel tells me you know what's going to happen as soon as I make my distraction."

"I do," he smiled. "And I think I know what you're worried about, but you needn't be." He looked slightly amused.

"Look, we've never tried this before, and it may not work. But, we're not interested in committing war crimes. So, we're planning to rush in with barricades."

Weiz cocked a brow at him. The idea was absurd. "You want to rush in with barricades and... what? Hit them over the heads with them?"

"No no," he assured. "We'll rush in, shooting at the ground, digging holes with blasters. Not too deep, but deep enough. It'll keep them all back from that line, too, we hope. Then we'll place the barricades, shutting them in. An open-air prison."

"Where they still have all their weapons. They'll break through a barricade like butter. You can't be serious."

It was the Sergeant who spoke next. "The barricades will not be so easily breached. And the intention is to start erecting a more permanent fence on our side of it, if we have to. Though they may get though the makeshift one, I doubt they'll break through the second any time soon."

Weiz shook her head. However clever the man thought he was being, she didn't think it was going to work. And she got a sinking feeling that, as much as the native army might be easily slaughtered, the Bahanians with them probably had something up their sleeves that could turn the tide. Else why bring them here? She still couldn't work that out. Unless the Bahanians knew that the Earthlings would be reluctant to fight people of such primitive means, in which case they would make an effective barricade themselves. Or they might simply be a distraction. Whatever the motivations of the Bahanians, the Earthlings were marching to their tune.

"I'd like it stated for the record, that I think this is a bad idea," she told the Major. "I have a bad, bad feeling about it." And she couldn't shake it.

Major Preston gave a single nod, "Duly noted. But unless you have something better in mind, I think we're going to have to go ahead with this."

"Unfortunately, I do not."

"Then our way it is. Do you have a rough estimate of when your distraction may be ready? We're still forming up, but we don't want to be too obvious about."

She concentrated and made a small torch appear in her hand, then made it disappear. Whatever they used to nullify her power, wasn't close enough to do so. "About three seconds after you tell me when," she responded.

Her nerves frayed the longer it took for them to get in position. What she wouldn't have given to be in a C90 TS plane, or an MM ship. To go back to being a simple pilot on rotation between Earth and Mars.

It felt like an age before Major Preston turned to her, and with a nod said, "Ready when you are."

She looked up to the sky, then down at the ground. She knew only the most rudimentary things about fireworks, but she was sure it was enough to make it convincing. She made the shell, then the innards. The first was a test to see how right or wrong she was. When it left the ground with a whistle and burst in the air with a shower of green sparkles, she was confident that she would be able to do a whole show.

She lined them up, twenty at a time and set them off only a second or two behind each other. It was consuming for her to make sure every one had the correct composition to do what it was meant to do. So, when the soldiers ran into place, she didn't see them. What the enemy was doing, she didn't know.

But when a bright light flashed all along the dome, as bright as a sun at noon, she noticed. It blinded her, and she couldn't continue with her distraction. She could only hope that it had gone on long enough for the soldiers to do what needed to be done.

Just as she was blinking her eyes clear and vision was slowly, through blurred lens, coming back, another blinding white light flashed. This time she put a hand up to protect her sensitive eyes.

She didn't know what was causing it. Where it was coming from. But anyone else inside the dome would be having the same issue as her, unless they were under cover. She couldn't see to move. To get one foot in front of the other without tripping on something.

The sounds of the soldiers yelling and running, some gunfire and clanging metal. It was the only thing that reminded her of where she was. Though she couldn't tell what was happening. If they were winning or losing.

While she was trying to think of what to do, she removed her hand from her face the tiniest bit to peer out. She didn't want to see that bright light again, because she felt it might take a while to recover from. But though her eyes hurt, she could see the dark blue of the sky, even if she couldn't make out any stars. And there was a rainbow patch, shifting around on the surface of the dome, as if a search light with the wrong colour were looking for something. If that blinding flash were a function of the dome itself, she considered it a dangerous flaw.

She squinted off in the direction of the natives. From where she stood, she should have had a good view, but it was obstructed by the panelling Major Preston had told her about. It wasn't sturdy. She could see it being rocked from the inside, each swing loosening its grip in the ground. The sound of metal hitting metal — loud, clanging, more like a factory than a battle field.

Major Preston's men were rushing to fill their side with dirt and start shoring up their position. But the fences were too far askew, and the enemy was getting out. The natives with their primitive weapons were stepping out from between sheets of fencing and shoving sharpened blades into the closest soldiers. Until they saw what was happening.

Weiz didn't know who gave the order, or if it was an organic movement, but once those who came out were noticed, they died. She saw one man get his face blown clear off, others lost limbs and were left to lay where they were, screaming and shaking. Blood and body parts littered the ground, and almost none of it belonged to the Earthlings.

Another bright flash had Weiz bringing her hands up to her eyes with a string of swear words that would have impressed even Hadley had she understood them.

She hoped there was someone who could work out where that was coming from and put a stop to it. She'd never been inside a dome under attack before, so for all she knew, this kind of thing might be normal. Her thought had been that the dome would be a shield much as an MM ship used, and if that were the case, it would be down fairly quickly at the rate it was being hit. But it was possible it was a technology she was unfamiliar with, and the bright flashes a side effect. If that were the case, they should have warned her.

Once her eyes were working sufficiently, she made herself ignore what was happening near the failed fencing and looked for Major Preston. He had been at her side when they started, but after the first blinding, she hadn't seen him.

Over near the carriers, she could see her people peering out, faces curious and scared. She made her way to them. From where she'd been standing, there was nothing she could do.

Once she was there, hands ushered her in, but stopped her before she could step on the injured woman they'd rescued. She was ashamed to say she didn't know who it was, though the face was familiar.

"Just keep your eyes looking toward the storage crates at the back," Lance told her. "After a flash, you can look about for a while. But not too long. Those flashes do not appear to be following a pattern, as far as I can tell."

Her eyes readjusting to the interior lights of the carrier, Weiz glanced about to get a gauge of who else was there. Zim had his hands on the injured woman's head, leaning over her. Trying to heal her, Weiz supposed. Fyord was toward the other side door, looking out onto nothing.

"Hadley, Gordon, Ellis?" she asked with a frown.

"Hadley got shafted when we were looking for a way into the cells," Fyord said without turning around. "I suppose she should have been here by now, but she might have decided to take her time in the field. Or simply be stuck on the other side of the dome, now it's at full strength."

"Gordon was with you, last I saw," Lance added. "And Ellis went off somewhere to 'throw rocks', she said." He shrugged and raised his hands to indicate he didn't know what that meant.

Another flash lit up the interior of the carrier, but it didn't blind her. "Do any of you know what that is?"

"Bombs, I think," Zim mumbled. He didn't look up at all and didn't remove his touch from the woman's face. Though now Weiz looked closer, it appeared the woman might not be breathing.

Weiz turned her attention to what was going on in the distance. It was harder to make out individuals in the muck of it, but it was very clear the fencing had completely failed. And she was not at all surprised. She didn't know how the Colonel had thought that would be a good idea. It simply provided cover for the enemy.

From somewhere further toward the back of the camp, Weiz saw projectiles shoot past, headed oddly slowly in the direction of the barricades. They were large enough that she could see them for a good part of their journey toward the enemy, but they did hit a point where they became too small to observe. She imagined they were probably fist sized.

It took her a moment to realise it was probably Ellis doing that. 'Throwing rocks', as Viatri had said.

Things were already starting to calm down behind the barricade, as they learned they could use it as cover. There was no native who survived stepping outside of it. But at the same token, it was not capable of keeping them in. Skewed, bent, upended, twisted. She didn't see a single fence that had gone in as planned.

The ATF soldiers were backing away. Any who got close enough to one of those fences was struck down by a pike or a scythe or a sword, by someone hidden close behind it. And though those soldiers would survive, if properly tended to, she still thought it was quite humbling that the natives were capable of doing any damage at all.

Then, just as she was about to look away in anticipation of another blinding flash, the fencing seemed to rise, as if guided by remote. Like drones, moving in sync. But it was also so quick, it would have been easy to miss, as the fencing lined up, interlocked, then dropped.

Weiz blinked at the suddenly almost silent scene.

CHAPTER TWENTY

Deidra sat patiently in her metal cell. She'd been in there perhaps half a day, as far as she could tell. She wasn't afraid, though a part of her thought she should be. Tatiana was assuring her that if she stayed calm and collected, she might find some chance to escape their situation. But the longer she was in there, without anything happening, the more annoyed she became.

She had to assume they planned to take them all back to their home planet. Though she couldn't understand why. If she didn't find a way to escape, she supposed she'd find out.

There was a loud bang, and she felt a tremor. Her mind flashed back to the corridor of Io Station, and the look on Alex's face as he started running back toward her. Her heart skipped a beat, and she breathed deep. So much had happened since that moment, she was taken aback by the memory. The intensity of it. Unprepared for the sudden anxiety it made her feel.

It's in the past and cannot hurt you, Tatiana told her soothingly. *You'll have to deal with it all eventually, but now is not the time. Just breathe and concentrate.*

Deidra shook her head at the voice but did as she was bid. She closed her eyes and thought about how she might go about disarming these technologists. A simple EMP might do the trick, depending on what kind of shielding they used for their equipment.

It would work, they don't use shielding. Don't even understand the concept of it.

Her train of thought was once again disturbed by a tremor in the ship. She didn't have a flashback to go with it, that time, but she did have to wonder what was happening. Were the MM ships attacking? Was it the Docker? Or whatever it was Weiz had been working on before they all got on the MM ship bound for Eridu?

Deidra breathed a sigh through her nose. She'd been in the far back of that ship. But they hadn't quite left the hangar yet when she'd been transported. She couldn't be sure that anyone had even noticed. And it was likely she was going to have to find her own way out of this.

"Do I know which panel is connected to the door?" she wondered aloud. She didn't like constantly talking inside her own head. It helped having Tatiana present as separate, but the constant inner chatter made it feel there was just too much going on up there. But if the trade-off for the information dumping was losing her memory, then she had to at least try it this way.

No, I've never been in a room like this. My experience was quite a bit less pleasant.

Like Viatri and Greenway, the entity that had been Tatiana had probably been taken to a lab straight away. And her memories of that time, having been stripped, were not helping now.

"Well, I can't just sit around," she whispered to herself.

She'd been trying to appear compliant, in case anyone was watching. But if she was going to get out, she had to move.

She studied the walls until she found the seam that marked the door. Then she felt along the sides of it, looking for anything that might give her access to the electronics.

"It's probably a sensor," she mumbled.

There was nothing obvious in the place. The panelling was uniform grey metal, that could have been steel or aluminium, or titanium. She wasn't so well versed in such things that she could tell by the way the light shone on it.

It's Tungsten. To use a term you're familiar with.

Deidra couldn't say how much that information even helped, but it might. Her mind travelled back to grade nine science class to inform her that it was a nine on the mohs scale of hardness, it had a very high melting point, and could only be a good conductor at temperatures over sixty-eight fahrenheit. None of that was something she could use.

After a long breath, she sat back down on the floor of her empty cell, as she pondered how she could possibly get herself out. It wasn't looking good so far.

"They've made sure all the panelling is on the outside," she mumbled over the hand she was leaning on. "So, no access to electronics. At least, not in any easily accessible way." She made a sound in her throat as she thought and looked around for inspiration.

Maybe something in the ceiling, Tatiana suggested.

"That would be fine if I was tall enough to touch it," she invested some scorn into that, feeling that the voice in her head should have known better.

I have faith you'll find a way.

"Fine, fine," she breathed as she got up and took off her lab coat. She let it drop to the floor as she grabbed hold of the highest gap she could reach. It wasn't even deep enough for her to slide her fingers in to the bed of a nail, much less get a good firm grip, but she was determined to try.

With great effort, she hauled herself up, placing feet in the lower gaps, and hoping they held long enough to get a hand up on the next panel.

You probably should have taken your shoes off, Tatiana said.

Do you want to do this? Deidra asked in her mind.

I could, but you wouldn't like the result. It's why we are like this now.

Deidra growled at her in dismissal as she tried to get a firm hold and lever herself up.

It took her seven tries before she got high enough to touch the ceiling without sliding back down the wall. It took a further thirteen attempts before she managed to move a piece of ceiling panelling. It made such a loud sound when it hit the floor, that she lost concentration and fell right on top of it. She took a break then. She'd never been a particularly physical person, and she was beginning to wear out. She didn't want to pause too long, though, because the Bahanians could come for her at any moment. And it seemed likely that she was being watched, even if she couldn't see any cameras.

Deidra studied the wiring she had exposed. She was a little disappointed, as she'd hoped to find a crawlspace, so she could climb up and search for a better exit. To mess about with the wiring... It was going to take a while.

With a final breath, she forced herself off the floor and back to work. It took three goes before she got up high enough to transfer her weight to the ceiling crossbeam. It left her hanging by an arm, while she worked with the other, which she could not maintain for long, and she needed decent breaks between. But she kept going.

She had no tools to speak of, and she had no idea where the wiring led, if it even had anything to do with the mechanisms in the room where she was being held. So, she was using nails and teeth for stripping, and a great deal of trial and error.

By the time she dropped off the crossbeam for what she thought was the eleventh time, she felt she'd been hard at work for a full day. She was exhausted. Though she may not technically require sleep, it didn't mean she didn't feel tired from time to time. As much as she was in a rush to get it done — whatever it was — she also thought it may be best to get a little rest in.

Do you really think that's a good idea? Tatiana queried.

"I was not made for this kind of thing," she informed the voice. As ludicrous as the whole situation was, she was becoming accustomed to it.

Maybe the old you, the human you, but what you've become is more adaptable. Be the giant.

"The nullification field..." Deidra started.

Isn't working, or we'd not be talking.

"And you didn't think to mention this before?"

Deidra was both irritated by the exchange, and elated at the news, but also down on herself for not realising it sooner. Not that she would have thought to become the giant. She'd never done it. But somehow, that knowledge was there, innate. She frowned at the thought that Tatiana had left it so long before suggesting it, but then had a thought.

"As a Giant, you all seemed to be able to travel like Harvey, in some kind of mist..." She wasn't sure how to finish.

Not like Harvey, Tati sighed inside her mind. *Faster, perhaps. But not like Harvey. You still have to travel the distance, it won't open a portal or fold space.*

Though she was somewhat disappointed by the answer, she shook it off and concentrated on the task at hand.

She imagined a dark fog, and she filled herself into the mist until she felt the very top of her head hit the ceiling. She gave a brief moment to considering whether she should just tear a hole in the wall, before deciding that would probably be a bad idea. If the nullification field was not working, that would be fine, she could rampage, and no one would be able to stop her unless she was caught by surprise. But if it simply wasn't turned on, and they spotted her... She'd be back in a cell, and at square one in a heartbeat. So, drawing that kind of attention with the noise it would make, wasn't the best idea.

She reached up with her giant hands and examined each of the wires carefully. Some were tied together in ways that suggested they belonged to the same functions. But she could not begin to guess at where they led or what they would do, so as before, she was left to experiment and hope. Though, this time, instead of nails and teeth, she used the sharp talon at the end of an elongated finger.

As hard as she tried to concentrate only on what she was doing, she had to marvel at how being a giant made her feel. Powerful, energetic, predatory. There were senses she could not describe with her human knowledge of how senses worked. A certain awareness of her surroundings, of what was behind the door and beyond. She could actually in some way 'feel' the presence of people close by. Though she couldn't tell much more than that they were there.

It was an effort to keep going with the electronics and not just let her curious mind find the limits of what it meant to be a Giant.

Stay on task. Once we're back on Urago, you can run free.

The scientist side of her was completely content with that. The Giant side of her wanted to growl and be petulant about it. Another duality to her existence. Dane would not be thrilled. But he would stick around. That, she thought, he had made clear.

After a short while of fussing about, she finally found a combination that opened the door. She doubted she would be able to easily repeat it if she were to find herself in such circumstances again, but it was done.

Deidra allowed herself to return to human form and picked up her coat from the floor. She donned it, and walked out as if she owned the place. She had no idea how she was going to get back to the Docker, or to the camp, but she had to imagine they had a transport system, given the way they transported them to cells without a thought.

She was around two bends and down a long corridor when she saw someone walking in the opposite direction. He was wearing a uniform that looked a lot like those worn on the Docker. She tried to remain calm, and not stare. Just as she was walking by the person, she heard, "Doctor Ward? What are you doing here."

She spun on her heel so fast she almost fell. "Ahhh," she didn't know where to start or what to say.

"I'll let Harvey know we've found you. We were just going to check the brig. Wasn't expecting you, out here in the open like this." The man clicked on his radio and did just that.

"Well, get her up here, I don't think we should stay much longer." Harvey replied.

"Yes, sir," he responded, then with his head indicated the direction they'd take.

It was clear he assumed she'd just follow while he took the lead, and she did. But now knowing the place was under control of her own people, she felt herself relaxing. Her sense of time was off, and she wasn't sure how long she'd been there, but she was grateful that she'd come out to find a friendly figure. Even if it meant her efforts to break out had proved unnecessary.

It wasn't a long walk to the bridge, though it was winding and confusing. She thought if it were a straight walk it would have been no more than a few minutes.

Harvey was at a set of controls she couldn't begin to guess the use for. A man on the Comms was screaming about Harvey giving up control of the ship, and that he would send troops. Harvey seemed be ignoring that and watching the forward screens intently.

Deidra moved her own attention to them and took a step back. On the screen were two extraordinarily large amorphous blobs, a black chrome in colour, and light shining from some sections. She couldn't guess at what they were, but they were shooting some kind of goo, and Harvey was trying to counter the attack.

"What is that?" she asked in disgust.

"Just a present left behind by the boss," Harvey told her. "I'm of half a mind to take us all down to the surface and let these idiots deal with it. But those things won't shoot unless they're close enough to them or threatening them. She's going to have to do something about those."

Deidra gave the objects a look of disgust, but told Harvey, "I don't think there's anything she can do, once she's let go of her work. It's its own thing. That's why she carefully unmakes everything after she's done with it."

Harvey grunted at her, his face a mask of concentration. The man on the radio had yet to stop talking, though he didn't appear to be saying anything different.

"Well, then," he breathed after a while. "How are we supposed to get rid of these things?"

A tremor rocked the ship and she had to assume one of the goo shots had landed. "I don't know." She looked at what she assumed was the comms console. "Does that guy ever shut up?"

"Not so far," said one of the six soldiers at the back of the room.

Now that she was really paying attention, she thought that the bridge seemed fairly small for a ship the size of those she'd seen on approach. She said that to Harvey.

"What do you really need a bridge for?" he asked in return. "You can do most of the jobs elsewhere, it's simply a central hub. An easy way for the crew to communicate face to face. But it isn't necessary."

Deidra had never thought about it. Would probably never think about it again. But as a comparative size, the bridge on the Docker would be ten times that of what they currently stood in.

"I hate to be that person," Deidra said after a while. "But could I possibly get a lift back to the Docker? If they've already done their sweep, and got me, I doubt I am in danger of another one."

The tirade from the man on the comms stopped, and there was an odd silence, where everyone except Harvey stared at the comms console, then looked to each other. She wasn't sure if the cessation was cause for alarm, or simply a break to catch his breath.

"I'm a little bit busy right now, trying to get those blobs to aim at the ships behind us. But, once I'm done."

She wanted to ask him so many questions, like how had he come to be on this particular ship? How long had they been there? Why was that man shouting at him, and what did he mean when he shrieked about leadership? But Harvey did look like he was concentrating hard on what he was doing, so she moved toward the older soldier who had spoken earlier and directed her questions at him.

His eyes flitted between the screen where the blobs were, Harvey and her. But he answered courteously. "We were assigned another ship," he told her. "We cleared it, all went well, we kept most of them in stasis, so we didn't really need to fight at all." He stopped abruptly and flinched just before another tremor hit but continued on as if nothing had happened.

"Some fella started shouting at Harvey through the comms, couldn't rightly tell you about what, don't understand a word of it myself. But as he breaks it down, we had to move ship, because some young buck thought we were some insane Admiral, and he had it on his mind to take over or something. Some other man tried to deescalate the situation, but the hothead can't help himself. I'm of the opinion that everyone is simply ignoring him. I don't know what he is saying, like I said, but were I his commanding officer, he'd be stripped right quick, and in the brig for insubordination. A month of mandatory on the heels. Man like that should not be in charge of anything.

"Anyway, we're on ship three now, and they've figured we've been moving along. They might not know exactly who we are, but easy enough to figure where we come from. Harvey has been shuffling their crew around to other ships, and things are getting quite mixed and messed. No one is happy, and that fella keeps yelling. Harvey says it's because no one will shoot at this ship, and he's livid about it." The man finally took a breath.

Deidra had to admit that was as decent a rundown of events as she'd ever had. "So, you shuffled the whole crew from this ship to another ship?"

"I had to put them somewhere," Harvey defended himself. "If I let them stick around here there'd be too much danger of them finding a way to take the ship back. Battle and bloodshed, the nasty stuff I'd rather avoid."

She couldn't argue with that. "So, what's the plan long term, then?"

Just as the soldier was about to answer, the screaming man started up again. The soldier paused momentarily, then simply spoke loudly over the top. "Mostly we're just trying to keep them all busy up here. As long as their worried about us and what we're doing, they won't be aiming at that Docker and what might be our only way home."

"How many of you are up here?" She had been at the briefing, but she had not really paid a lot of attention to the ins and outs of the strategy the Colonel had laid out for everyone.

"About forty of us, give or take. We're spread across two ships. Though I think we should probably get ourselves some of those transport guns these guys use. Poor Harvey is being used as a shuttle bus."

Deidra almost laughed at the thought of it but caught herself and swallowed it. She had to agree, the man was very useful in these circumstances.

"These are their ships, with their supplies," she said after a moment. "They should have some of those transporters aboard somewhere. If you can find them and fetch them to me, I can see if I might work out how they function and get some working in our favour."

A few of the soldiers mumbled things to each other that she couldn't make out, and shuffled around like something exciting was about to happen. The older man in front of her, whom she'd been speaking to, was more restrained. He simply bowed his head with a slight smile, and said, "Harvey, permission to do as this woman says?"

"Go ahead, Hamond, take whoever you want."

Deidra watched Hamond and at least half of the other soldiers leave, with the sense that maybe she could finally get something helpful done.

CHAPTER TWENTY-ONE

Morning was appearing over a dome that swarmed with colours. Major Preston had informed her that those moving colours were nothing to worry about and were completely normal after a bombardment. Each of the blinding flashes had been a disintegrated bomb that could have dropped on them, and the colour of the flash was due to the composition of that bomb. So, it was obvious the Bahanians had gotten a message out to someone close by.

Weiz scrubbed at a tired face, her eyes still drawn to the barricaded area. Behind it, she could hear the natives doing something, but she couldn't imagine what. The fencing was only twice the height of an average man, so she didn't imagine it would hold them for very long. But soldiers were erecting something a little more permanent a metre or so away from it.

"I just don't get it," Weiz said. "They still have radios, and weapons. The nullification field is still active if we're too close. All you've achieved, and I'm surprised you managed that, is to stop them from moving anywhere for a while."

She'd expressed these things to Major Preston a few times, and he'd simply smiled and shrugged and told her he followed orders. Now she was looking at Colonel Sumner, his demeanour far more serious. "Do you know what we usually use that fencing for?" he asked.

She was surprised by the question. "No. I didn't even know it was a thing until I saw you use it."

He gave a slow nod but kept his eyes on the soldiers at work. "We would usually take four or five of those, to surround an unruly mob. Or trap in a dangerous animal we don't want to get too close to, but don't want to kill. They're a temporary tool. They're not meant to hold up. But they are useful. I will say I have never used *twenty-two* at once, before." It was the closest thing she had ever seen to a smile on that man's face. "I wasn't sure it would charge. Thought there'd be too much interference for the interlocking mechanisms to magnetise, because we had to use four modules to make it work. But we managed."

"We did that," Weiz agreed. Though she wasn't even sure any more what the point of it all was. Now that the natives were closed up behind that barricade, it all seemed rather silly. All the Bahanians, and she supposed the natives, had asked of them, was to go home. That was something that they had planned to do anyway, until they'd learned they couldn't.

She supposed that having the Docker show up made all the difference. She no longer felt she was forced to stay on Eridu. Though she had no more choice than she had before, the fact that Earth Base would make a colony on this world made her feel less isolated from the life she once had. She had to remind herself that she couldn't leave. Couldn't visit Earth on a whim if she wanted. Marvellous as Deidra's transport tech turned out to be.

"Why don't we just leave?" she asked of no one in particular.

The Colonel looked at her then, both brows raised. "You've been a military woman for the better part of your life, Commander. You know the answer to that."

She did, though for reasons she could not explain, she could no longer see the sense in it. Perhaps becoming a Giant had changed her more than she was aware of. Perhaps she was simply feeling the emotional after effects of using her power too much.

Her private channel came on, the Bridge Comms Officer offering to have Harvey patched through. She felt that she should probably learn the woman's name, since she heard from her so frequently, but she simply said, "Go ahead."

Colonel Sumner eyed her sideways a moment, and after seeing she didn't move, stayed as he was and waited patiently.

"We got Deidra." Short, sweet, and to the point.

"Is she alright? What's the damage?" She switched from private to public so the Colonel could listen in through her lapel speaker.

"Looks as though they hadn't got to her yet. And she escaped on her own before we could even go and check." He sounded proud. Weiz supposed she was as well.

"Give us a report of what is happening up there. We're as clear as it gets down here for the moment."

Weiz could almost see the Colonel's ears prick up in anticipation of new information. He did have a good many men up there with Harvey.

"It's been wild," he said. Then gave a quick rundown of the situation up on the ships, and finishing with, "I'm afraid the next bridge I jump to, they'll be waiting, so I am hesitant to move to another ship. This man who is squawking at me, is driving me mad, anyway."

"Are you saying that you want to come down to the surface?" Sumner asked loudly to be heard through her cuff mic.

"Is that Sumner? Yes, I want to come back down to the surface. Your men are very good at their jobs, Colonel, but they need rest.

And they know we're here now. They've already managed to repopulate one of the ships we had originally taken over. If they come onto this one in force, it might not end well." He took a pause, and Weiz thought he was done, but when she opened her mouth, he spoke again. "Sorry, had to dodge a blob. Where was I?"

"You are concerned about the Bahanians taking back their ships," Weiz offered.

"Right," Harvey breathed. "So, got some of them off looking for the transporter guns these guys use, and Deidra is going to see if we can maybe get some working in our favour. But once they're back here on the bridge, I'd like permission to bring us all to the surface."

Weiz clicked off her mic and shared a look with the Colonel. There was a part of her that absolutely wanted that man on the surface with her. A part that argued that he should not be in such danger, and it was idiotic to stay up there if at any moment the Bahanians could raid the ship. But then the other side of her, the side that was the Commander and should know better, was whispering in her ear that maybe keeping him up there was the better choice. That so long as he was keeping them occupied, they would not be aiming to the surface with whatever weapons they had at their disposal.

She couldn't read the Colonels face, but she felt that he was thinking some similar things.

"Well?" she asked him after a moment.

"Weiz, you still there?" Harvey wanted to know.

She pressed her mic. "Just a moment," she told him.

Colonel Sumner shrugged. "There's benefits to both. I'd rather keep him up there as long as possible, but he is your man." He looked her up and down, and she took the double meaning in the statement. "It's your call."

Weiz closed her eyes a moment and took a deep breath. She'd take the Colonel's lead on it. "Harvey,"

"Still here," he assured her.

"We'd like you to stay up there for as long as you can. Cause chaos. Break things. Do whatever you can." She pursed her lips and took another deep breath through her nose. "If you feel you'd be better off with a smaller force, or fresh troops, then bring down some of the soldiers. But stay, as long as you can."

He wouldn't say exactly how he felt about that, not over a public channel. But she knew he would be feeling disappointed. "So, mission statement change, is it?" He sounded disappointed. "We're not trying to capture one of these ships?"

"We're trying to keep them busy, so they don't aim down here, or at the Docker. The size of their force, and their tech..." Weiz felt Harvey should know this.

There was a long pause, and she couldn't help but wonder what he was thinking. "Alright," he said. "I'll bring Deidra and some of the men down once they're back with the transport guns. But I'll stay up here with a small crew." He didn't sound too pleased with the idea. But he would do what he had to do. He always did.

"I'll see you when you do," Weiz told him. "Weiz out."

"Harvey out."

The silence when the comm shut off was stark. It set off a ringing in her ears and a hammer in her heart.

Beside her, the Colonel nodded his head slowly and said, "You made the right choice. It may not feel like it right now but, trust me. You did."

"You don't need to convince me of it, I know." Though she didn't feel good about it. "But I think me and my people might go up there with him. Not sure if or how well our powers might work up there, but sitting around, doing nothing... I don't think any of us were made for that."

The Colonel gave her a shrug. "That's up to you, Commander. I won't stop you. Just keep me apprised."

She gave him a nod before doing a quick turn on her heel and marching back toward the carriers. All her people had stayed in there.

Lance's head popped out at the sound of her approach. "What's the news?" he asked.

She told him in as few words as she could manage. Then told him she thought they should go up. His reaction to it was more emphatic than she had anticipated.

"No," he said with a vigorous shake of the head. "No, we do not want to go up there. No, our powers will not work. No, we cannot do what soldiers can, we have different training for a reason. Why don't we just take the MM ship, get up there and do what we know how?"

Weiz scoffed. "And fight who? Did you see any smaller fighters? Those ships aren't as big as Dockers, but they're at least as big as Freighters. We're not going to be able to do much damage with a few MM's. I don't know what they have on board, or how many people, but I would rather keep them busy up there, than have them landing down here. And if we have enough pilots between us, perhaps we can steal a few of those ships."

Lance was looking at her as if she'd grown a new head. "Well, what are the other MM ships supposed to be doing? I know you sent them out."

"They were out, hiding behind the Docker, just in case we ended up having to fight smaller craft, they wouldn't get caught coming out," she told him. "Given it's been almost a day and a half now, I suppose they've probably re-docked. If they haven't, they will soon."

"And that's it for us in this fight, then?" Hadley wanted to know.

"Unless we try and take over a few of those ships." Weiz felt like she was repeating herself, but maybe that was just in her own mind.

"No." Lance was firm this time. "It's not a great idea, Weiz. Much as I would love to stick it to them."

Zim was still hovering over the woman they'd rescued. She was awake but weak and smiling up at him tiredly. Weiz couldn't see the man's face, but it was clear to her he had no intention of joining the conversation. Hadley seemed to want to fight but was taking Lance's lead. Fyord was thoughtful behind both of them. Ellis had eyes only for Viatri. Greenway and Gordon were M.I.A, though probably not together. Weiz was not sure she had much of a chance in turning this crew to her side of things. Despite working hard to find the woman in her that had been the well-respected Commander, these people had seen her withdraw from her duties and sink into self-pity.

Anyone else, and she could have just given the order. But not with this lot. And a part of her needed it to be them who did it. Needed the affirmation of people who had been affected as she had.

But those faces told her they weren't going. Not without a very good reason. And she couldn't give it to them, other than the pure desperation she felt to *do* something other than stand around and feel useless.

"What are we even fighting for?" she felt herself ask, though she didn't mean to say it out loud.

The others all shared look between them, but it was Lance who answered, shrugging uncomfortably. "They kidnap us, they attack us, perform experiments on us," he said, feeling the back of his head. "They have ships bearing down on our position. If we let them have their way, we'll all be imprisoned and tortured for the rest of our extraordinary long lives. What else are we supposed to do?"

"We could just leave." She knew, in a way, that her words were defeatist. That anything worth having, had to be fought for.

"I don't know if you remember this," Lance said in the most condescending sarcastic tone she'd ever heard out of him. "But we cannot go home. We tried that. It didn't really work out for us."

"I didn't mean home. At least not for us." She let herself drop into a squat and breathe a heavy sigh.

"You want to us to give up our connection to Earth?" Hadley asked with some scorn. "You want them to go home, and us to go... where? Are you shitting me?"

"I can think of a few people who would have a big problem with that, and Harvey is one of them," Ellis put in. "That Docker coming was the best thing any of us could have hoped for after the Giants chose us. You might have nothing to go back to. But most of us do."

Hadley, Fyord and Lance were all nodding along. "That's what we're fighting for. Don't forget it." Lance told her.

"Maybe we can just go to a less populated world," she tried. "One of the ones Harvey has access to. With Deidra's tech, I don't suppose it would be too difficult to get the Docker to follow along. And I don't think the Bahanians know about the other worlds."

"Maybe," Lance said after a while. "Maybe that is something we can do, if we can get a good enough navigator to map the stars quick enough and work out where that planet is. But that could take months, and these guys are here now."

They were right, she knew. She really didn't have anything at home that mattered so much to her that she felt the need to fight for it. All that mattered to her was on Eridu. Harvey. The man she'd wanted for more than twenty years and could never have. And now she had him, and she didn't want to let go even a little bit.

"We should be more concerned about finding Kristin and Estard, no?" Zim asked from where he now sat beside the woman, holding her hand.

Weiz felt guilty at the fact that she had not thought of them all night. Not once. There was a part of her that was simply content the woman had been anywhere but near her. But that wasn't fair, and she knew it.

"Any suggestions on where to look?" she asked.

They all looked to each other, and slowly, they all shook their heads. But Zim had successfully refocused their attention on a different goal, and they started to throw some ideas around.

~

After so long in the dark, the bright light that filtered in from the suddenly open doorway, was blinding. Estard's eyes stung and watered, his vision blurred. He put a hand up to reduce the glare and see what was happening.

In the doorway stood a shadowy figure. He couldn't make out any clear features, but it looked like a woman from the shape.

"Come out," she said. "We don't have too long if you want to make it out without incident."

Estard exchanged a look with Kristin, shrugged, and then took a step toward the door. The woman in the doorway was actually on the other side of the hallway, and they had plenty of room to squeeze through and get out.

He eyed her warily. She looked young, maybe eighteen. Dark hair, dark eyes, a serious cast to her features. Her lips were pursed, and she was tapping her middle finger into her thumb, which he thought might be a stress tick.

When Kristin came up beside him, she put her hand in his, and he gave it a squeeze. He expected her to take it away as soon as he did, but she left it, and he held on.

"We have to go, follow me," the young woman said. She closed the cell door with a remote, turned and started leading them down the hall. "Transporters don't work inside the cells, for obvious reasons. We can get you in, clearly, but the tech is nulled in here," she continued as she walked. "So, we have to get to the surface first."

Estard shared a look with Kristin, who asked the obvious question. "Why are you helping us?"

"Suffice to say, there are those of us who disagree with what is happening." The young woman stopped abruptly and put an arm up to prevent them from going forward. After a few moments, she opened a door that had not been visible, into which they turned.

"So, you know who we are?" Estard asked, surprised.

To this, the girl actually turned and gave him a confused look. "No, no idea who you are. I am just clearing out all the cells. It's likely that there will be some who get captured and left in the cells I already went through or be moved and have the same happen. But I am going through methodically."

The path she lead them down was long and confusing. So many of the doors were hidden in the architecture, that had they managed to break free of the cell themselves, Estard doubted they would have been able to find their way out. He said as much to the girl, who gave a tiny smile as she responded.

"Our ancestors were very good at such things, yes. Though I doubt very much the use to which we put them now, was the use for which they were originally intended."

It took them a good ten or fifteen minutes to get to the surface. The last part was up a very long and winding ramp, much like a set of stairs in an apartment building. Outside, it was morning, and when Estard looked back at the door from which they'd emerged, he could barely see it. It, and its surrounds, blended so seamlessly into the landscape, one would have to know exactly what they were looking for.

Kristin squeezed his hand and let it go. She was breathing deep and had her hands at the side of her head. Estard couldn't tell if she was about to have a vision or, preparing for the possibility. He didn't take his eyes off her, and when she fell forward with a scream, he caught her before she could hit the ground.

The girl who had led them out, looked down at her with some surprise and moved forward as if she wanted to help, but stopped short at a look from Estard. When the fit was over, Kristin took a few deep breaths and bounced back to her feet with a grimace.

Estard was slower to rise, while asking, "Anything we can use?"

Kristin shook her head. "I'd love a painkiller."

The girl was adjusting something on her transport gun, and when she was done, she looked up at them seriously. "Tell Greenway, Rochelle said, one more day. If it's not done in one more day, bad things are coming. I don't want my people hurt any more than I want yours hurt for no reason. So, I am only telling you so you can run. Just go." Then she lifted the gun and pulled the trigger.

It wasn't exactly like getting moved around by Harvey, but it was very similar. They had been deposited in the middle of nowhere, to his mind. He couldn't tell tree from shrub when it came to one part of the landscape or another. He was a man who needed road signs and landmarks.

"Where'd she dump us?" he wanted to know.

Kristin just pointed a finger behind him. He turned and found himself looking up until his neck was at a ninety-degree angle. "Greenway's mountain," she said. "At a good walk, we can be back in camp in less than ten minutes."

"Just out of curiosity," he responded. "How can you tell one mountain from another? I mean, it's not like that is the only mountain here. I've seen quite a few others around. In the distance, but even so."

Kristin shook her head then stood so close beside him that their shoulders touched. As she looked up, she raised the arm touching his, and pointed. "Look exactly where I am pointing," she instructed.

He did, but he didn't know what she was pointing at. It was both too close, and too far. But as he squinted and looked a little to either side of her finger, he saw the glinting of metal. Of glass. Fragments of blue and white. "The ships," he breathed.

"The ships," she agreed.

It seemed she was ready to get going. No questions, no discussion. But Estard was confused and curious. "What do you think will happen in one more day?"

"I'd be buggered if I know," Kristin responded tiredly. "But I have to assume it isn't good."

Estard followed a step behind as Kristin led the way back to the camp. "You don't think it's the least bit strange that we were rescued by one of them? That they just let us go like that? Aren't you suspicious that maybe we are some kind of walking trap?"

Kristin stopped dead in her tracks and turned to him. "After my second stint in a cage in less than a week, I'm not all that inclined to look this gift horse in the mouth," she told him. "But I doubt we're any kind of trojan, because they didn't work on us. No experiment, no medical procedure, no torture. Hell, they didn't even come and talk to us. I think they're probably a little preoccupied right now, and they would have got to us *after* this stupid little 'war'." She put her hands up for air quotes on the last word.

It made sense, the way she put it. But it struck him as odd, the way she said war. "What do you mean, 'war'?" He imitated her exact movement.

"You can be so thick sometimes it is both endearing and irritating." While he was momentarily happy to hear her use the word endearing in connection to him, it was soured by the irritating part.

"Just tell me," he insisted.

"I don't think they're serious about this," she said. "I think they're probably just trying to chase us off and didn't count on the fact that we are a fighting force that doesn't tend to back down. I think they want us, the Giants, the abominations. But I think they want the rest of them to just leave."

"They sent an illness to butter us up," Estard replied. "That doesn't exactly scream 'please leave'."

"An illness that was fairly easy to cure with the tech at our disposal." She shook her head as if there were more to the thought, but she didn't share. After a moment she just looked up and said,

"None of it means a damn thing if we're just going to stand in the woods and argue about it," and with that, turned on her heel and continued walking.

Estard, as usual, stayed a step behind and to the right. "You don't think that we pose a danger to the people in the camp? Which was my initial point, by the way."

"No." Her succinct reply invited no further talk on the subject, and Estard remained quiet for a few minutes.

Eventually, he asked, "What happened back in the cell..." He sucked at his teeth a little self-conscious at the forwardness of it. "Is it —" he didn't get to finish.

Kristin turned on him again. Only this time, despite the look of annoyance on her face, she reached up and grabbed his cheeks and pulled him down into a kiss. He was so utterly shocked by it, he simply let himself melt into it. When she pulled away, they were both a little breathless.

"We'd do better without your obsessive need to talk about everything," she told him, and swung back around as suddenly as she had faced him.

"Noted," he replied with a swallow and slight smile. Every other thought, about the Bahanians, and their precarious situation on this world, left his mind in favour of a dream in which Kristin played the star, and he her leading man. Wherever she led, he would follow, and right then, that was back to camp.

Chapter Twenty-Two

Harvey couldn't hide his disappointment when the call cut out. It had been hard work to get as much done as he had in the past day and a half, and he hadn't had a chance to rest or sleep. Neither had the soldiers with him. He didn't know whether Weiz had even taken that into account. He'd mention it while he was on the ground.

More goo shot from the thing that Weiz left behind, and Harvey lazily manoeuvred the ship out of the way to the sounds of yelling from Mendel. He'd blocked the man out for the most part, he never seemed to say anything important. There had also been a long period of silence where Harvey had to assume there had been a shift change, for which he'd been grateful. But for at least an hour, the man had been back, yelling nonsense and threats, but doing nothing.

They knew they weren't Bahanians now, and Matricuesse had been silent since he'd sent that Rear Admiral to a ship without an enemy aboard. They had given it up and moved to the next, and again to the next, trying to find the best method of slowing them down, and tying them up. Harvey had thought they'd done a fairly good job, but if Weiz and the Colonel wanted more, then more they could have. After they'd all rested.

Deidra popping herself out of the brig had been a boon, because he'd not had a chance to go check on it after they'd taken the bridge. He'd sent the soldiers to go clean out the crew that was awake, and if they could manage it, shove them back into stasis. But he had been at the bridge, the whole time, playing chicken with the blobs.

He was tired, and he wanted nothing more than to shoot the man who kept yelling and take a long deep sleep. What he was doing was not a long-term solution. Sooner or later, the Bahanians were going to send more to the ship he was on, and they wouldn't announce it. Not like they had the last two times. Harvey had to wonder if Matricuesse was allowing Mendel to yell into comms so much because he was aware of how intensely irritating it was. It could serve as sufficient distraction, if he let it. He was of half a mind to just blow the whole console, and perhaps should have done so earlier, but he'd been hoping to hear from Matricuesse again.

Harvey turned to the soldiers still on the bridge. "Someone, please, for the love all that is holy, shut that man up."

It was like one man in particular had been waiting for that exact order, as one of the soldiers stepped forward to turn it off, another shot the console with an electro dart round. It seemed to do the job, and silence returned. He should have done it hours ago.

Harvey looked to Deidra who was propped up against the hull, in what he assumed was the navigators chair. Her head leaned back, eyes closed, arms crossed. He didn't know if she was actually asleep, but he found himself jealous of just being able to sit and rest.

"This is ridiculous," he said to himself. "We have to get out of here." He looked to the soldiers surrounding him. "Who's first? I know I have to wait for the other lot to get back, but I can start now."

They all looked to each other, nearly all appearing as tired as he felt. They seemed reluctant to put themselves ahead of one another and were instead uttering phrases like, "You've been awake longer, you should go." Though Harvey didn't pay attention to where those voices were coming from.

Just as he put his arms out to encompass those nearest him, the door to the bridge opened and he prepared for the worst. But it was just Hamond and the men he'd taken with him, returning with armfuls of transporter guns and what looked like other tools.

"Is this everyone?" Harvey asked.

Hamond got a quick grasp of what was happening. "We're ready to go," he replied.

Harvey stretched out his arms and made his first deposit on the ground without stopping to look or say a word. Within a second, he was back up on the ship, spreading his arms out for the next lot. They were in the middle of redistributing the load, so Harvey allowed for it, trying not to tap a foot with impatience. As soon as they were done Harvey was off again.

It took him six trips to get them all down, and then he was up in the ship alone with Deidra. She was still seated against the wall, but her eyes were open, and she was looking at him sadly.

"What's that look for?" He wanted to know.

"We're not done yet," she told him. "I have something in mind, but I don't know how well it might work."

He reached out a hand and placed it softly on her shoulder. "If it's from you," he said, "I'm sure it will work just fine." He tried to give her a smile, then shifted them to the ground.

They were just inside the camp, the carriers off to their left, the bulk of the soldiers in front of them in small groups. To the right, a short distance away, several groups were working on constructing something, though Harvey couldn't have said what. Deidra was already walking off in the direction of the carriers, and Harvey thought he probably should to. Or he could go up to the Docker and get a good rest in a bed, and a shower.

He spotted Weiz coming toward him seconds after the thought entered into his mind, and he thought it best to discard it. She was probably mad enough that he had ignored her, if he ran away without her as well, she might actually do something about it.

"What are you doing down here?" she asked him sternly, though the look on her face expressed happiness to see him. So, she was being the Commander in this moment.

"I resign," he said and let himself fall to the ground cross legged. She looked down on him with a frown, and he slowly leaned back until his head touched the ground and he closed his eyes.

"John," she said softly. "What are you doing?"

"No," he responded. "I resigned."

He felt the warmth of her body slide down beside him, and her breath pricked at the hairs on the side of his neck as she whispered to him. "Not yet. Take us up to the Docker. We can't just lie down in the middle of the camp."

Harvey breathed a heavy sigh of annoyance, but rolled onto his side, making the shift as he did so, straight into the bed they often shared. "I'm too tired for more," he told her honestly.

She didn't respond. Or, if she did, he didn't hear it. He felt himself falling down into sleep quickly, now that he was lying down on something soft. He couldn't even be bothered to remove his boots.

His dreams took him back to the world he had to leave behind. To his house. To his son. They had conversations about the world, and Harvey tried to teach him all he could about what limited things he knew. Often, as in the manner of dreams, the timeline would jump around, the faces and scenery changed, and he found himself in strange scenarios with different people.

When he finally awoke, his eyes felt glued together by what he called morning gunk. Drool had formed a pool on the pillow, which now felt unpleasant against his cheek. He breathed deep and sat up fast, head clearing.

Since he'd been on Eridu, he had never felt as tired as he had before he fell asleep. Often, in fact, he'd had to force himself to sleep despite not feeling the need to. Though his mind was just waking, it was his very first thoughts.

He looked down beside him to see Weiz, fast asleep. She looked quite peaceful, lying on her back, one arm across her stomach, the other cradling a cheek that leaned off to the side. He contemplated waking her but decided against it. She'd probably wake on her own soon enough.

Instead, he went and had a shower. Completed what would have been a regular morning routine, had they been anywhere else. It was somewhat eerie, being on a nearly empty Docker. He was usually one of the last in and first to leave. But he saw only one person as he moved back and forth between Locker Room, sleeping pod, and gym. It was almost like being in an abandoned bunker.

By the time he was done with everything, he was still a little tired, but more awake. And Weiz was blinking her eyes open. He smiled down at her from where he stood as he ran a towel over his damp hair.

"Nice close shave," she told him through a yawn.

He sat down on the bed beside her as she sat up. "I don't think I have ever been that tired in my life," he said. "I'm considering going to the Doc and getting a checkup. See if that sleeping sickness left some kind of nasty in me."

The look of concern that Catherine sent his way made him reach out a reassuringly to pat her hand. "If you think you should," she said.

"How long were we asleep, do you think?" He knew the time, looking at the bedside clock, but he didn't know the day.

Weiz's eyes flashed to that same clock. "Twelve hours, maybe."

"At least?"

Weiz shrugged and nodded. "I hadn't considered it, but we needed it. Do you really think it's cause for alarm?"

Truthfully, he wasn't sure, but he had a suspicion that something wasn't right. At least, not inside him. He'd been the first after Abramovich to go down, and one of the last to wake up. Lance had said he'd been coming in and out of consciousness for the better part of a day, but what if he simply needed more time to recover?

"I don't know," he breathed. "But better safe than sorry. I can take you down before or after. Up to you."

"I should check in with the crews up here, anyway," she said without even thinking about it. "I can get cleaned up and take care of that while you do what you have to do."

He leaned in to give her a brief peck on the lips, then got up, still holding her hand. "See you soon," he said, and let go.

Doctor Rowley was in the infirmary checking on their resident Bahanian, who, in that moment, was sleeping. He looked up in surprise when Harvey entered.

"Captain," Rowley greeted.

"Doctor." Harvey explained the issue and his suspicion that he might have some lingering effects, while the Doctor nodded and listened intently.

"Sit down on a bed. I'll run some tests." He left the room momentarily and came back with some equipment.

Harvey did as instructed as the tests were performed. The Doctor asked questions, pricked his finger, listened to his heart, did a brief scan of heart and brain. And after some twenty minutes, the man put down the equipment and asked, "Until now, have you slept regularly?"

Harvey thought about it. "I suppose it depends what you mean by regularly," he responded slowly. "But if you mean, did I sleep every night for a reasonable amount of time, then I would say yes."

"And the other 'Giants'," Rowley scoffed around the word as if he thought it silly. "They've all expressed, to some degree or another, a weakness, or a 'price', I suppose, for want of a better term. For the use of their abilities, I mean. Emotional dysregulation, paranoia, megalomania... I'd say an exhausted sleep is an incredibly mild exchange for the gift you've been given."

"I guess so," he wasn't entirely sure of that, but it made sense. "You think I just over did it?"

"Given that I can find nothing out of the ordinary with your tests so far, it is a likely scenario." He looked Harvey up and down and gave a nod. "Whatever else you might be able to do now, you're still human, at the core."

Harvey slid off the side of the bed to stand in front of the Doctor. "Thanks, Doctor," he said, and moved past him with a pat on the shoulder.

He was still human. That was the thought that he now pondered and clung to. He had never considered that he wasn't. Greenway certainly had, but that had not gone well for him. And he wondered what the Giants of before had thought of themselves. Gods? Humans? Something in between?

His thoughts on the subject lasted only as long as it took him to get to Weiz, who was looking fresh and ready to go in their quarters.

"Should we get back to it?" he asked.

"You know what, John, after twenty odd years of this, I'd kind of like a break," she replied.

"But we're not going to." He phrased it as a statement, though she answered it as a question.

"No, but I do have a proposition. We'd need the others to agree, and some work would have to be done. But I think it would be for the best."

"What is it, tell me."

She outlined what she had in mind in a few short sentences, that had him nodding. It would avoid conflict and take them out of the danger zone. Convincing Colonel Sumner would be another matter altogether, though, and Harvey was sure they would have their work cut out for them. He'd only have to transport the other Giants, and those who would absolutely stay with them.

"So, what do you think?" she asked, looking suddenly very tired and self-conscious.

"I think it's the best idea I've heard since this whole nonsense started," he told her.

"You don't think I'm a coward?"

He stepped forward and embraced her, pressing his nose into her freshly washed hair and breathing deep. He kissed the top of her head and breathed. "If you are, then so am I," he said. "But the bigger question is, why fight if you don't have to?"

Her arms were tight around his waist and her head was pressed hard to his chest. "I hope the others see it the same. I did mention the idea to them yesterday. They didn't seem particularly keen. I think they were mostly concerned about being able to keep in contact with Earth. I felt sure you would feel the same."

He shook his head. "I do. But a few months is not never. Perhaps it's simply that I can travel so easily that it had not occurred to me. If it makes them feel better, I can shuttle them back and forth, until they find a way to get to us on the new world."

"That will leave the problem of the Docker still being under threat. And therefore, anyone who is on it."

"If Deidra is finished with what she needs to do, they can go home and wait it out there. We can give them a time line and be ready to come back for them."

"You make it sound so simple."

"Isn't it? Can't it be?" He leaned back to look at her face, as she looked up at him.

"There is always that hope," she said softly, "but it rarely ever is."

She sighed and pushed herself away.

"Time to go?" he asked.

"I think so," she responded, though she didn't seem too happy about it.

A moment later, they were back in the camp, looking around at the soldiers preparing their fires for a night meal. He was momentarily disoriented by the fact he'd expected daylight but got the artificial kind.

Weiz still clung to him, though she would have normally let go as soon as they moved. He looked down at her to find her eyes closed. She was pretending she hadn't noticed, at least for a moment.

It didn't take long before Colonel Sumner noticed them and started striding over with a purpose, Private Miller a few steps behind. Harvey gave Weiz a warning tap, and she shot away from him in a flash.

"What if he says no?" Harvey asked out of the side of his mouth as he watched the man get closer.

"Then we continue on as we are. These are his men, if he doesn't get them to leave, there's nothing we can do."

Harvey felt at his now clean-shaven jaw and looked the Colonel up and down in a measuring manner. He wasn't sure how he was going to convince him.

"Deidra has a plan," the man announced as he stopped in front of them. "I'm inclined to go along with it, pending your thoughts." The words were directed at Weiz, and all Harvey could do was shrug.

"What is it? I'm listening," Weiz said slowly, almost as if she could feel the hope of just leaving it all behind drain away with his words.

"The way she puts it, she'll need you lot and a couple of scientists to stay down here." There was no question what the man meant when he said, 'you lot'. "She figures it's best we go back to Earth space, or at the very least, deeper into the system. I haven't decided on that part yet."

This was starting to sound very like Weiz's plan, only with scientists, for some reason.

"And then what?" Harvey wanted to know.

"As she tells it, she wants Greenway to do something that will temporarily prevent the use of all tech on the entire planet. She doesn't know how long temporary is, but assumes less than a month." He turned to look at his Private as the man grumbled something under his breath. Whatever it was, neither acknowledged it. Summer just turned back to Weiz and Harvey to continue. "Once that is done, she and some of the scientists are going to strip your powers, and remove your connection to this world, and therefore, your threat to the Bahanians."

"Strip our powers?" Weiz scoffed. "Does she even know how? Where to start?"

Colonel Sumner shrugged and raised his hands. "How should I know? I'll take her at her word, though. The other scientists aboard seemed to know what she was asking for."

"What if it doesn't work?" Weiz asked. "Are we not concerned they'll just come back? And how would they know that we are trying to, or have succeeded in, removing the Giants from us?"

"Look, the finer details belong to the scientists. If all we had to deal with on this planet were the natives, then I would happily just pick a different patch of land and get out of their way. But what these Bahanians are capable of bringing to bear could cause us some serious problems."

"So, a month. Just a month?"

The Colonel breathed a heavy sigh and looked around the camp. "When we came to get you *a month* ago, do you think we expected to find anything like this? I'll tell you true, Commander, we were expecting bodies. Much can change in an instant, much less a month."

He looked ready to turn and walk away, but Harvey stopped him with a partially outstretched hand. "Where can we find Deidra?"

"Out behind the left hand carrier with Greenway, Kristin and Estard."

"You found them? Where were they?"

It was Private Miller who answered this time, while the Colonel continued to walk away. "They just walked into camp this morning." Then he turned and ran to catch up with his boss.

Harvey shared a look with Weiz. He knew the question, even as their eyes met. How had Deidra convinced everyone to back off, where Weiz couldn't? In the same breath, Harvey had the answer. "Because she's a scientist," he told Weiz, as much for himself as for her.

"I suppose," Weiz breathed. "Shall we go join them and find out what the plan is, specifically?"

"I think we probably should," he agreed. And they started off toward the carrier.

~

Deidra hadn't been in the camp long before Kristin and Estard walked in, looking annoyed but none the worse for wear. They seemed to be searching with their eyes for someone or something, and Deidra was surprised to find that when Kristin's eyes alighted on her, they zeroed in on her direction.

The scientist stood still and awaited them. She noted that others were eyeing them sideways, curious but unwilling to say anything. So many had behaved in that manner since they'd arrived. After finding out what had happened to them, of course.

"We need to talk," Kristin announced before she stopped in front of her. "Is there somewhere a little more private? I think this is important for you, but I am not sure how other people might take it."

Deidra pursed her lips and looked at Estard who was making

puppy dog eyes at the woman and following a half step behind. She didn't know that he would ever get what he wanted from Kristin, but she wished him luck.

"I think there may be a small level of privacy on the other side of the carriers," she told them. "Otherwise, we may need to go off a ways beyond the dome."

"Carriers are fine," Kristin said, and started moving in that direction without waiting for anyone.

Deidra couldn't help but look to Estard for some clue as to what might be going on, but it was clear the man had no idea. Kristin seemed determined and focused. Her mind was set on something, and whatever it was, it was important. That much, she could tell.

As soon as they were in the relative privacy of a carrier, Kristin looked around to insure they were alone, but it seemed she found someone Deidra couldn't see. She just grunted, then said, "You can stay."

Deidra's eyes widened a little when she saw it was Greenway Kristin had spoken to. While she had heard it mentioned, she hadn't fully understood that the man was back with them. He looked different. More troubled, less angry. And he moved slowly, as if afraid he might scare them off with sudden movements.

Kristin waited until the man joined them in their small circle, then began. "I had a vision," she said. "I can't say of when exactly, but the feeling is soon. Greenway, Deidra is going to ask you to do something, I can't say what, but I think she knows. Whatever it is, there are going to be some ships falling right out of the sky."

Greenway shook his head. "I promised I wouldn't use my powers again. I wouldn't do it." He shook his head so emphatically Deidra was slightly concerned he might give himself whiplash.

"You might," Deidra told him in a near whisper. "If I told you why. Kristin, please continue."

The woman gave her a nod. "It wasn't directly after, but the timing felt very close. You erected some structures, here, and on other worlds, that we might use as portals. I don't know how you would get them to work, that's on your side."

Deidra nodded. There had been some things she had been playing around with in her mind since the soldiers had brought her the transport guns. Some designs that might help her with getting people around without having to know the star charts. If they stayed, of course. But she'd also been playing around with another idea. One that she was not certain the others would appreciate.

"Is there anything else?" She wanted to know.

Kristin shrugged uncomfortable and looked at Estard. "Well, this man might do a few rewinds until you get the timing right on whatever it is you ask Greenway to do. I know I saw at least three iterations before you seemed satisfied with what happened after."

"Might simply knowing that help to get it right the first time?"

Kristin shrugged. "You're the scientist, I am just telling you what I saw."

Deidra's thoughts flicked furiously over how she might go about getting Greenway to make an EMP wave directed from the core of the planet. Low enough level that it didn't affect the migration of animals or the strength of the magnetic poles. But high enough that it would prevent the use of circuitry for a time.

You're assuming an iron core, Tatiana put in. *You are correct, but you should try not to assume.*

She grimaced at the voice in her head. Much as she was trying to get used to it, and work with it, to better herself, she would have been much happier without it.

The others were looking at her intensely, awaiting an answer to the vision. But the plan wasn't fully formed.

"I only have half the plan at the moment," she told them. "Until I have ironed it out, I don't know what to tell you."

Kristin gave a sharp nod and turned to Greenway. "I almost

forgot. Some girl released us from our little prison cell. Said to tell you, 'Rochelle said, one more day. If it's not done in one more day, bad things are coming.'"

Greenway stood stock still, eyes wide. Deidra would never have called the man afraid before, but she saw it in him now. He swallowed and nodded. "I was supposed to give that message," he said.

"What message?" Estard asked.

"They don't really want to fight us. They want *us*" — he pointed to each of them with a circular motion of his hand — "but they don't care about them." He gestured in the general direction of the soldiers. "So, they're just trying to scare us off. Lots of ships, big army, mobilise the natives, all that. But they do have the weaponry, should they chose to use it. And if all we have is one more day, whatever your plan, Doctor Ward, we'd best do it as soon as is practically possible."

"If the carriers go up, and the Docker leaves, will they assume that we have gone with it?" She doubted it. They had to know that in some way the Giants were connected to this world.

Greenway shook his head and shrugged with a frown. "I don't know. Maybe? If they take it at face value, and don't do a scan of the ground, I suppose it's possible. But how likely do you really think that is?"

"Why did you think we wouldn't be able to defend against whatever they have?" from Estard.

Kristin nodded and added, "Do you not think we could win against them?"

"It's not about winning or losing, it's about life," he replied, tears welling in his eyes, though they didn't fall. "We might be able to win. We certainly have the technology, but how many soldiers will we lose? How many of them will we kill? Is it worth it?"

A little rich coming from this murderer, she thought, but didn't say it. People were entitled to a change of heart, and who was she to judge the consequence of his power? There was a part of her, that she supposed Tatiana leaked through without words, that understood Greenway would always struggle with delusions of grandeur if he used his power too much.

The day passed relatively quickly. They remained behind the carriers, out of sight of the soldiers, as Deidra performed rough calculations based on the land level diameter of the planet. Kristin and Estard walked away by themselves for a while, and Deidra barely noticed. About an hour before the sun set, she felt she had enough to get started with.

She stood and dusted herself off, then left the others to go find Colonel Sumner. She felt no particular like or dislike for the man, but he did listen, and wasn't inclined to waste the lives of his men where it could be helped.

The man was not too far away, in front of a carrier three down the row, giving directions to Major Preston. His hand was moving around and pointing at things, and every now and then Preston would do the same. Deidra tried to wait a respectful distance away while they discussed whatever they were discussing. But she made sure they could see her and knew that she wanted their attention.

When Sumner gave her the chin raise with raised brows, she stepped forward and presented her idea. She tried not to get too bogged down in the math of it, but did explain that it may not work, depending on a variety of factors. And, if they were terribly unlucky, the Docker would not be able to come back, but that would be a one percent scenario. He seemed to understand the science of it better than she would have thought, given the questions he was asking as he nodded along, thoughtful.

"Once I've had a chance to speak to the Commander, assuming she'll approve, you have my blessing," he told her. His arms were crossed, his brow drawn in thought, and seemed to be nodding along to something in his head, but he didn't tell her he was done.

She looked for confirmation that she could leave from Preston who gave her a knowing look and nod.

Deidra returned to her place behind the carrier, updated those there, and got to work on a list of people she was going to need to stay behind. She didn't know how she would convince them, and truly hoped she wouldn't have to. Dane would follow her right into the arms of death if she asked. Ulrich though, had been left alone in that mountain for two weeks, and she didn't think he wanted to set foot on Eridu again. He was very happy to be up on the Docker doing all the things he would have been doing if nothing had happened to Io Station. She suspected that he had some kind of trauma and had actually blocked a lot of it out.

All the Giants would obviously have to stay, if she was to redirect their power. She didn't know if she would get any resistance from them. Estard had been the only one of them who had been able to choose, and he seemed fine with the idea.

You're letting it become too personal, Tatiana told her. *Don't worry too much if they'll like it or not, just concentrate on the how and who and at what time.*

Oddly, that reminded her of Kristin's premonition. Timing. She didn't know how far into the orbit of the planet would be affected by what she had in mind, because she wasn't sure how far out the magnetosphere stretched. But the timing would mean the Docker had to be far enough outside the influence of it, that the waves or pulses, didn't hit it, or none of them would be able to go home.

Deidra closed her eyes and breathed. She wanted to go home. She wanted to be rid of the powers that Fields had bestowed upon her what felt like an age ago. Though she had come to some kind of peace with Tatiana, she definitely would be happy with only herself in her brain.

You wouldn't miss me? She chuckled to herself at it.

Before she could get back into what she was doing, Weiz and Harvey arrived. It was just after dark, and they were both looking well rested. She wasn't surprised, given how tired Harvey had appeared on the ship. They all had to find rest when and where they could.

Weiz looked at her with a smile. "The Colonel tells me you have a plan."

CHAPTER TWENTY-THREE

Harvey had collected them one by one, and they'd all gathered in just after dark to hear what Doctor Ward had to say. All of the Giants were there, behind the carriers, waiting while the Doctor decided what she would to say.

Behind them, the soldiers were packing and getting ready to go up to the Docker, which would leave those who remained with a lone MM ship. Unless she counted the broken ones on the mountain beside them.

Gordon pressed her fingers down on the ridge of her brow as she tried to cut out the chatter that surrounded her. Everyone was excited. The native army was trapped behind the barricades, which they would let fall after they had taken off. Gordon suspected they'd get out soon, anyway, from the delving she'd done around the edges of that camp.

Maybe she should not have done it. But she had been testing the theory, thinking that somehow, she might be able to help them. And she could. But, if Deidra had some plan to make her powers unnecessary, all the better.

She waited as patiently as she could manage, trying to keep her foot still, and her mind on task.

"While these fine men are returning to the Docker, Harvey will be gathering some scientists from up there and bringing them to the ground. They are not like any of you, and I suppose me now, and I would hope you are sensitive to that." She cleared her throat and continued. "They are not accustomed to living rough, and we're going to have to for a little while, regardless of whether or not this will go in our favour."

Gordon did not like the sound of it already. She hadn't spent as much time on the Docker as the rest of them, but she was going to miss being able to take a shower. Her eyes searched the others for clues, though most were only hearing it now, and accidentally locked eyes with Greenway. She gave an involuntary grimace, then ironed it out. He returned a knowing sad smile.

"The plan is a simple one. Weiz, as soon as the carriers are gone, is going to announce to the Bahanians behind the barricade, that they have to leave orbit if they want their ships to remain intact and functioning."

The look that Kristin gave the woman suggested she knew something of what might happen. Though she had not had a chance to speak to her, Gordon was glad that she had once again walked away from the jaws of danger unscathed. As far as she was concerned, Annabelle Kristin had nine lives.

"Once we have confirmation that the message is understood, we will go somewhere and get started on our work. I'd like to spend a little more time with the calculations, but essentially Greenway is going to create an electric pulse that will spread out through the magnetosphere, starting at the iron core of the world."

Deidra shuffled her feet and seemed uncomfortable at the thought of that. Gordon resisted the urge to delve in and find out what was making her squirm. For the most part, she trusted the woman, though she couldn't say exactly why.

"According to my rough calculations, that should give us three or four months of intermittent protection from any technological threats. Despite what you all may think, I don't know everything, but I hope that doesn't damage your trust in me. And that is why we will have the help of three other scientists."

"Why?" Hadley asked. "What are we doing *after* you mess with the magnetic field? Which might well be a pretty bad idea, don't you think?"

"I'm sure she knows that," Fyord said with a calming hand on her shoulder.

"I do," Deidra assured. "I am aware of the potential risks, but I believe it to be our best chance of removing the Bahanian threat."

"But what about our ships? Our people?" Viatri asked. "I'm more in favour of this than simply slinking away." He gave Weiz a meaningful look, but continued without addressing her. "But obviously there is more to it, or you wouldn't need other scientists with you."

Deidra was beginning to look annoyed. "An astute observation, Viatri. Yes, once that is done, and we have a limited window of freedom, the other scientists and I will be working on a way to redistribute our 'powers' back into this world. My hope is, we rid ourselves of the 'Giant' we each possess, and when the Docker returns, we can all just go home. And I don't know about the rest of you, but that is all I have wanted since we got here."

There were looks and grumbles all round, and it sounded to Gordon like agreement. She certainly would prefer to go home to her children, if not her husband. Much as she loved him, she had to admit to herself that she really didn't miss him. Not anything close to the way she missed the kids. As much as she usually liked her job as a pilot, the whole experience on Eridu definitely made her want to quit. She didn't think she was alone in that.

Deidra gave them all the silence they needed to let it sink in. They might not understand how she planned to do what she said, but they wanted her to do it. There was no argument there. If they could go home, if there was a possibility after having it so ruthlessly ripped from them by the Giants, then every one of them would take it.

Except Estard, who took a step forward. "Will I have to go back to my old life?"

It was clear from the look on her face that she had not even considered it. "I have to be honest, I do not know how I did that the first time," she told him. "I can try, if that's what you want. I am sure the answer is in here somewhere." She tapped lightly at her head with a finger.

He shook his head. "No, no. I would much rather…" He didn't finish the sentence as he looked with some angst toward Kristin, who avoided his glance by looking to the ground. Estard looked back at Deidra and asked, "Would I have to stay here, by myself? Or could I come back to Earth with you?"

The scientist shrugged. "I see no issue in you returning with us. Had it been the other way around, well, you know we could never have stayed there."

That seemed to be all he wanted to know as he took a step back and turned his attention fully toward Kristin, who was now looking up at him. Gordon would never have thought of Kristin as shy or timid, but she looked it in that moment. It was obvious there was something going on between the two of them, and now it made sense why Kristin had stood with her over the bodies.

Deidra looked around at everyone, though her eyes stopped on no one in particular, it felt like she was connecting with them all. "I can't promise what will happen, after we disperse. I don't know the consequence of it, or if it will work. We may be greatly changed, we may remain largely the same. This may not even work. You all have time to make your decisions on this one. Don't feel rushed into it. I just don't want to lie to you. There will be some risk."

After a little more murmured discussion, everyone seemed to agree to the proposition. No one else stepped forward or expressed concern. Certainly, no one was opposed. Even Greenway, who had believed with such fervour that they now belonged to this world and could not abandon it, looked hopeful and anxious.

They spent some time at the back of the carrier, milling about, speaking to one another about home, and the possibility of actually getting back there. She saw more than one tear shed at the possibility.

Estard approached her, Kristin right beside. "You must be thrilled at the news," he said with a smile.

"More than I can say," she replied, her voice on the verge of cracking.

To her surprise, Kristin didn't say a word, she just lunged forward and caught her in a strong embrace. For a moment, she felt she might tip backward, but Kristin held her straight. Gordon looked at Estard who looked halfway between mortified and amused.

Gordon returned the hug, just as fiercely. She hadn't realised just how deprived of affection she had been these months. Within seconds she was crying into Kristin's shoulder, wordless but thankful. The woman didn't move, just held on until Gordon pulled away.

"It's home time," Kristin's smile was full of stifled hope and mischief.

Gordon wiped the tears from her face with the back of a hand and breathed a short laugh.

Before Gordon could even think of an appropriate response, Major Preston was amongst them, urging them all to move elsewhere. "Let's go, let's go." He clapped his hands above his head to make sure he got their attention. "You're all airmen, you should know better than to stand so close to airborne vehicles in pre-flight. Let's move!" He ushered them further back away from the carriers, and once he was certain they would keep going to a good distance, he let out a "Woop woop!" and laughed as he headed into the closest carrier and the large side closed.

Gordon had been so intent on Deidra and her plans that she hadn't even noticed that the carriers were ready to go. That the pilots had switched them on, even though the whining sound they made could be quite irritating, and in some cases cause nosebleeds.

They all stood well back and watched as the carriers slowly got off the ground, then shot up into the air, with a terrifying sonic boom. Gordon, if no one else, could safely say that she had never witnessed that before. She'd been on them, and she'd seen them descend, but she'd never seen them take off. It was quite interesting, watching the streaks they left behind fade into the night sky. And the sound of Major Preston yelling *woop woop*, echoed in her mind as they disappeared.

She looked back down at the now evacuated camp to see an almost barren ground. Where they'd had their fires, and their kits. The paths they walked that flattened what grass was left after the meteor shower. There was a near silence that came, broken only by the sounds of nature, and a few natives knocking steadily on the walls of their enclosure.

Weiz stepped forward and took a deep breath. "I guess I should start," she murmured to them. It was clear she was feeling the nerves of it, but she stepped forward, and kept moving until she was close enough to be heard.

"May I address the men who came in ships?" she asked loudly. The bang and clack of methodical effort continued, and Weiz looked back to the group for encouragement, which she got from most. She created something with her power, and when she held it up, Gordon could see it was a simple megaphone.

"I wish to speak with the Bahana men!" she stated, and this time the bang and clack stopped. It was a moment before they could hear a faint yell, though Gordon could not make out what was said.

It seemed that Weiz could, as she turned back to them with some consternation.

Gordon stretched out a tendril of her own power to ascertain what might have happened. She felt about with it, until it reached a mind that was clear enough to give her an impression of what had been said. *The Bahana men are not here.*

She withdrew quickly with a shake of her head. The others were all looking confused. No one seemed to know what was going on. But, of course, the Bahana men would have had their transport devices. They could have used them on themselves, even if they didn't free the natives. Why none of them had thought that likely, she did not know.

Weiz moved back to join them, the megaphone gone, brows drawn and eyes darting in thought.

Deidra just clicked her tongue and sighed. "I had not considered they would not be there," she told them.

"Oh? Well, you don't look worried," Bridges said. "I assume that you can think of another way to get in touch with them."

The look that the Scientist shot the man spoke volumes on what she thought of his manners, but she just replied, "I have many, though none of them are the safest of ideas. Considering that we cannot die, I suppose we'd be the best ones to carry them out. Just in case."

"We die just fine," Hadley put in sourly. "Did it not long ago. Wasn't fun."

And Lance looked green, as he and Greenway shared a knowing look. "And in case you forgot, we are the very reason these people are even here. They might not be able to kill us permanently, but they've demonstrated numerous ways in which they are capable of preventing our continued freedom."

"I suppose it's on me then," Harvey sighed. "I'll go grab some random grunt from one of their ships."

He was just about to shift when Gordon yelled at him to stop. Everyone looked to her with some surprise and annoyance. They all wanted to get it over with, but none of them had considered the obvious, to her mind at least.

"Ensign Brioli," she said. "He's in the infirmary. Just go get him, and we can leave him near the prison entrance or something. A lot less likely to run into trouble that way."

Harvey grunted at her with an assessing look, and said, "Good call."

The others were all nodding amongst themselves, but whatever they thought about it, they said nothing, as Harvey disappeared, then reappeared moments later with a rather stupid looking Ensign Brioli.

Deidra looked at the man with some horror, then at Harvey and back to the man's face. "What happened?" she wanted to know.

Harvey gave a shrug as he held onto the man. "I don't know, he came like this."

Gordon felt her cheeks heat as she cleared her throat. "I uh... I did that. Accidentally." She wanted that to be clear. Everyone was already wary enough around her, she didn't want them flat out avoiding her.

The scientist shook her head and breathed a sigh. "Well, is his brain still intact?"

"He's fine," she told them. "He just feels compelled to do as I say."

Deidra's lips pursed in thought. "That could be useful, but I don't know how seriously he'll be taken, looking like this. Is there any way you can undo it?"

She didn't think there was, because she wasn't sure how she'd done it in the first place. But she said, "I can try," and stepped forward to look the man in the eye.

Brioli gave her a large smile and reached out a hand. "How can I serve?" he asked happily.

"Just stand still and let me do this," she replied.

A tendril of her power reached out and delved deep into the man's brain. She wasn't sure what she was looking for, only that it would be something out of the ordinary. Though she didn't know how she was supposed to tell what was normal and what wasn't.

She felt herself becoming irritated, flustered and a little bit paranoid, the longer she held on, and the deeper she delved. But she pushed through, made herself do it. She didn't know how long she was in there, just rifling around, until she found something that seemed like it didn't belong. She anguished over what to do about it, afraid that she might be wrong, and that the connection might be important, before she cut it and withdrew her probe to stand back and look at his face.

Anger writhed across the surface, and Gordon took another hasty step back, even though Harvey had a good hold of him. He looked like he was ready to spring into violence in a heartbeat, and it was all directed at her.

"How dare you," he spat at her in a raspy whisper. "How dare you mess with my mind like that!"

Gordon took a few further steps away. "I didn't mean to," she almost whispered, and looked to Deidra for help. She'd done her part, but she wasn't sure how to make the man comply like this.

Deidra put up her hand and shoed Gordon off to the side as she stepped forward to fully take up the man's field of view. He tried to maintain a little distance from her by pushing his body back into Harvey.

"Ensign Brioli," Deidra addressed him, which seemed to get his attention through the anger.

"What do you want?"

"We want you to deliver a message to your people," she told him. "We're going. Leaving this world behind. But, before we do, we are going to make sure you can't come back. You have one full day to remove yourself from orbit, or face losing every ship you leave behind."

The man twisted violently in Harvey's grip, then growled and said, "You can't stop us from coming back! This is our world. Who do you think you are?"

Deidra shook her head firmly. "It may have been once, millennia ago, but it's not your world now. And you don't need to be here. This strange obsession you have with the Giants of this world, is going to end, because I am going to end your ability to hunt them."

He scoffed at her, but it was clear he had nothing to say to that. Having a conversation while one was being held tight from behind must be in some way undignified, Gordon thought.

Deidra looked to Harvey, "You know where to take him?" Harvey gave a nod, disappeared, then reappeared a moment later minus the burden that was Ensign Brioli.

"Do you think that will be enough to actually make them leave?" Kristin asked.

Everyone looked to one another, as if it were a question for the group, rather than just the Scientist, but it was Weiz who answered. "We can only hope and move on as planned. If they're caught up in the pulse, then so be it. We've warned them."

Deidra gave a singular brisk nod. "Yes, we've warned them. Let us hope they heed it. Harvey?" She waited until he acknowledged her before she continued. "I think you should go up and get the scientists on that list before the Docker takes off. It may be harder for you to transport once it is further away from the influence of this planet."

"Maybe," he agreed. Then he turned to Weiz, gave her a kiss on the forehead and said, "See you soon."

Left with only themselves in the dark, the natives behind the barricade, and no other technology to be seen beyond the MM ship they'd come down in, the weight of what they were about to do hit Gordon in the gut like a bat. If the pulse really did prevent the tech of the Bahanians from working, then how were they supposed to create something that would allow them to put their powers back 'into' the world? Had Deidra lied to them? Were they going to be stuck here, after all?

An icy feeling crept down her throat and into her stomach as panic almost took hold of her thoughts.

She felt a grip around her arm, it was soft, but she wrenched her arm away before it could clamp down. She turned to face the person responsible and saw Kristin.

"It will pass," the woman told her. "Don't panic. Just breathe and concentrate on that."

She spoke as one who understood what was happening in her mind. Perhaps she did, perhaps she didn't. But she was the one person on Eridu next to Estard that she trusted. She should have been able to say that about every person there, but she couldn't, and she didn't know why.

Gordon felt herself calming, and Kristin held a firm hand on her back. "It will pass," she told her again and again like a mantra.

No one else was paying attention to them. Even Estard was off, talking to some of the other airmen. For all that he was from another place and time, he fit in strangely well with them.

"You and Estard, then," Gordon said to distract herself. "That a thing? Or am I misreading it?"

Kristin didn't look at her, she just made a face and kept her eyes on the others. "Early days. I figured, give it a shot. I like him well enough, but we'll see how she lands."

Despite her dispassionate response, Gordon could hear in her voice the desperation that it would work out, that she did want it. Even if she would never be able to admit it with words.

It wasn't long before Harvey returned trailing three scientists, one of whom she recognised as Dane, Deidra's other half. So, regardless of how it all shook out, Deidra would have *her* one and only. She felt so much bitterness at the thought she almost sent herself back into panic mode, but Kristin hit her on the back lightly to get her attention.

"I don't know where you went, there," the woman said, "but just remember to breathe."

Gordon took a few more deep calming breaths, shook herself, and stood erect.

They were going to go home. She had to hold onto that thought, and not let it turn into something it wasn't. No one was out to get her. No one was going to sabotage their own chances of going home, just to make her miserable. None of them, as far as she could tell, was inclined to sadism, except perhaps Greenway.

She didn't know how long she stood like that, with Kristin's hand on her back while the woman chewed over her own thoughts. When she twisted around, put her own hand on Kristin's shoulder and looked the woman in the face, it seemed she was anxious about something.

Gordon searched her face. "What's going on in there?"

"I really don't think this is going to work," she said. "And I am not sure if I want it to. I have a brother back home. I worry about him. Less so, since we got here. I get to think about me, here. Not where I came from. Not my responsibilities. Just me."

That was more than she expected. She sucked in a deep breath and tried to comfort her. "Here or there, you can still look after you. I don't know your situation, but I assume your brother is old enough to look after himself. So, let him. It's how they learn."

It was enough to make the woman give her a brief smile and nod. "We should probably get in on the action. See where and how we can help this thing along."

Gordon nodded her agreement and turned back to view the small gathering. Together, they walked the few steps to join in, then turned their attention to who was talking. It was the blonde-haired scientist they'd left in the mountain.

"...how dangerous it might be," he was saying. "Have you considered that you may not be able to reverse it?"

The other two scientists that Harvey had brought down were nodding along, while Deidra frowned at them. "I hate to say it, Deidra, but the man has a point," Dane put in.

"By my calculations, the field should fully dissipate within a few months," Deidra told them in a calming tone, pushing her hands in a downward motion. "Four at the outside."

"You don't know that. No one has ever done it before. We do not know the total mass of the core, or how much iron is in the ground, or other magnetic substances that could be triggered by what you're proposing." The older Doctor that Gordon had no name for looked mortified at the idea this was something they would do. With or without their blessing, because it was not what they were there for.

"What effect will it have on life?" the blonde one asked. "Do you even know that much?"

Deidra breathed a sigh and rubbed at her temples as if she were getting a headache. She left her eyes closed as she answered. "I had you brought here for the second part, not so you could get worked up about the first."

All three of the scientists scoffed and looked offended. Even Dane. If they were going to be involved in a world changing event, they clearly wanted to have a say in it.

"I think it's a mistake, Deidra," Dane told her in no uncertain terms. "I don't believe you've truly thought it through. You haven't had the time for more than a few back of the napkin calculations, and now you're working on the assumption that it's settled and doable."

"I am not looking to magnetise the world," she replied in a tone that dripped with condescension. "Merely partially electrify the core and send pulse waves out. That's all. From time to time, suns and planets give out such pulses, it's not unheard of."

"That is not even remotely close to the same thing, and you know it." The blonde man was as close to irate as she had ever seen. From what she remembered he was a timid little thing. What a difference the Docker made.

Harvey stepped in between the three scientists and Deidra, arms spread as if he were expecting some kind of violence. They all looked at him with frowns, Dane the largest of the lot.

"That's enough," Harvey told them. "We're doing this part with or without your blessing. If you believe strongly that you cannot participate, then I will take you back up to the Docker while it is still in orbit."

Almost immediately, the old one and the blonde one opted out. Dane, on the other hand, looked pained. He looked to the other scientists, then he looked to Deidra, and the way he held his eyes on her, Gordon almost looked away.

"For right or wrong, dear heart, I'll follow you. But know that I feel I must protest what you're about to do."

Harvey took the other two scientists by the elbows and disappeared. Deidra looked disappointed, but not surprised.

Dane reached out a hand to her, and she reached back. The way they looked into each other's eyes, was as if no one were there to see them. They didn't speak, or do anything more intimate, but Gordon about blushed in witnessing it. She turned her face away to see Kristin watching them thoughtfully.

Harvey returned moments later with two more scientists.

Another old man with pepper grey hair, close trimmed beard and unruly brows. The younger one with dark brown hair and eyes in a pasty pale face.

"Did you tell them first?" Deidra asked without letting go of Dane.

Harvey gave a sharp nod. "They don't like it, but they agreed. It may be our best shot."

"It's time, then," she breathed. "Weiz, you can release the natives. I don't think they pose much threat by themselves. We can move elsewhere, for the time being, while we get this done."

No one said another word, of argument or agreement. When Deidra turned and began walking, everyone simply followed. It felt like the march to the mountain with Greenway. Full of purpose, yet silent and waiting. Though that had turned out to be utterly anticlimactic and disappointing on Greenway's end, the feeling had been the same. She wondered now, if he felt it to.

They were coming to the end of something. The possibility that everything that had happened on Eridu could be undone, and at some time forgotten, if they let themselves. There was hope and desire, warring with dread of the unknown. An anxious excitement building in the core of her. And not just her. She could see it in the faces around her. Hear it in the occasional accidental overheard conversation. They'd been somewhat aimless, listless. It was all well and good to help the people of Earth who had shown up on their doorstep, but for themselves, knowing they could never go back? It was like holding on to air. But now they had a real plan.

And of course, as such things went, it was never going to be that easy. Not far into their walk, they were suddenly surrounded by at least ten dour-faced Bahanians with electric staves.

CHAPTER TWENTY-FOUR

Harvey's eyes darted quickly around as he saw them shoot seemingly out of nowhere. Weiz's hand gripped him hard and let go. He knew the others would likely not be able to do anything. There was no way one of the Bahanians would get that close without the nullification field.

He leaned slightly to the left, then launched himself unexpectedly at three of them. While he tackled the one in the middle, he allowed his fingers to touch the two to either side and shifted. Not to some random place in the world, but another world. Maybe theirs, he had no way of knowing. Either way, he was certain they would not be able to come back.

As quickly as he had taken them away, he returned, aiming for a spot behind the one in the lead, ready to take him to another place entirely. He had had enough of these people and their self-righteous crusade. But when he got there, all of the Bahanians were sprawled on the ground, unconscious.

Harvey looked up and around, confused, until he remembered

what Gordon had done to Ensign Brioli.

"Is everyone here? Is everyone okay?" he asked.

He saw Weiz nod slowly, wide-eyed as if stunned. "We're all here. They took no one."

"What happened?" He wasn't questioning anyone in particular, they all looked as stunned as he felt. "Gordon?"

The woman looked up at him like a skittish rabbit. "I didn't mean it," she said, her face pale. She looked as if she were about to be sick, and Kristin had a hand on her back, whispering something close to her ear.

He turned his attention to Kristin. "What happened?" he asked again.

"She knocked them out," the woman replied, as if the answer were self evident. "Best we get them tied up and sorted out, or she'll have damaged herself for nothing."

"What do you mean damaged herself?"

Kristin gave him the most long suffering look he had ever seen out of her, and he took a step back, hands raised. Clearly there had been some kind of repercussion for rendering the Bahanians unconscious, but damage? He took a breath, shook his head, and turned to get on with restraining them before they woke. He wasn't alone.

Once they were done, Harvey looked to Deidra. "Do you think Brioli sent them? Or is this a coincidence?"

Deidra gave a shrug. "Hard to say, since we can't question any of them. Unless you wanted to bring back one of the ones you whisked away? No?"

He thought about it. Truly did. But he didn't want to bring one back and have to worry about them using their transport guns or communicating in some way. He could simply go to them and ask them questions there, but he felt if he didn't move quickly, it could be just as dangerous for him alone. They might not be able to permanently lock him up, or transport him as they could the others, but they could definitely hurt him. He wasn't immune to being hit in the head, shot or shocked, and they had weapons with them.

"I will if you think I should, but otherwise, best to leave it, I think." She didn't question it.

"Are we just going to leave them here?" Fyord asked.

"What else are we going to do with them?" Lance asked in turn. "We sent our message. What they choose to do with it is up to them, don't you think?"

"You're assuming they got the message!" Hadley yelled.

"So what if they didn't?" Greenway put in. Everyone went quiet at his words and looked to him as if gauging whether or not he was about to lose his mind again. While the man had a point, and a personal grudge about it, he probably wasn't the best person to be saying it. Despite their willingness to work with him, more than a few might have been just as happy to put a knife in him, regardless of the consequence.

Harvey was about to say something, just to alleviate the tension that was building, but Lance seconded Greenway, and the tension died on its own. "They didn't exactly give us warning when they started going after us," he told the others. "If they get stuck here, so be it. We all know how that feels. It sucks, but it's not the end of the world. Their gadgets won't work, and they shouldn't be able to do much damage to us, unless we are careless. But they will live. Which is more than they gave us."

There were nods all round, and Harvey felt oddly proud of his pilot, though he couldn't say exactly why.

"How did they even know we'd be out this way?" Weiz asked. "I don't think anyone knew. I think Deidra just picked a direction and stated walking."

Harvey heard sighs and grunts, and feet shuffling uncomfortably. He saw Greenway look at the mountain and away, several times, before he forced himself to look at it, breathing deeply. This monument he had created was at least half a kilometre per side at the base, and maybe eight-hundred metres high. The burial grounds they had set up, the monument for Fields, were right at the foot on the hut side of the mountain, closer to the river. They had landed the carriers closer to the woods, when they'd evacuated due to the sickness.

With a shrug and a shake, Harvey started moving. "I'll drop them all off near their friends," he said. "In good conscious, I cannot bring myself to leave them here." And three at a time, he moved them, quicker than the ones awake on the other side would be able to react.

When he was done, he didn't look to the rest of them, he just started walking in the direction Deidra had been going. It didn't take long before he heard the others following behind. There was a lot of murmuring, though he couldn't make out what was being said. He wasn't sure he wanted to know. The only thing that mattered to him, was that Deidra thought she knew a way that would allow them all to get home.

Deidra turned to Kristin and asked, "What time?"

"Midmorning, is my guess from the look of the sky," she replied. "But Estard will watch. If the Docker is affected, he'll take us back and radio in."

Estard's head snapped around at that. Clearly, she had neglected to tell him some things. "Radio in? Where am I supposed to be?"

"Up with Viatri in the MM ship. You won't be able to tell from here if the field is working. It would take too long for the ships to reach entry point and fall." Kristin shrugged by way of apology. "We need someone up there to see if the systems are shutting down, or if the ships are leaving. Either would be good enough. But if you see the Docker shut down, obviously we need to wait until it's out of range."

Lance cleared his throat. "You didn't think that perhaps I might want to have some choice in whether or not I go up there?"

"You were in my vision," Kristin answered simply. "I had to figure it's either because you wanted to go up there, one last flight or whatever. Or, maybe, it's just because you are the only pilot here who can guarantee a soft enough landing you won't have to die to get down."

The smirk that crossed the Pilot's face told Harvey that Kristin had hit the sweet spot. Just a touch of ego stroking while claiming it could be for any number of reasons.

Harvey had watched what was left of his crew grow and change over the few months they'd spent on Eridu. Even Walt and Dames, though they didn't share the Giant dilemma. Kristin had hit the ground running, and for a while, in the void of leadership, she occasionally took the reins. Viatri had not coped well the first month, and they'd all had to keep an eye on him, concerned that he might do something he might not come back from, as yet unaware of their immortality. But he'd taken hold of himself and become a useful contributor to everything they had attempted to do thereafter, particularly when they'd been on Earth in 1957. Walt and Dames had meandered, for the most part, but after they'd helped themselves out of the cells with the others, they'd kept the group together and kept things light, despite how dark the capture had become for them.

Xavier, of course, had gone home with those who had been left after the Giants had made their choices. Harvey hoped that worked out well. The man was a very good navigator and found himself hoping the man didn't quit after the experience.

Catherine. She wasn't part of his crew, but the changes he saw in her were a combination of what being a Giant had done to her, and the relationship they had begun. He didn't believe it had much to do with anything else, because that woman was far too stuck in her ways to really change. But he thought he made her happy, most of the time, and when she wasn't being painfully jealous, she made him happy. He wondered how much he had changed in the minds of the others.

He felt a soft touch on his left arm and realised that his mind had been wandering. He had not paid any attention at all to what had been discussed, but he could see now that everyone was preparing to get some sleep before they attempted the plan in the morning. Given that he and Weiz had already slept for the better part of the day, he really didn't feel the need to do so, but he might give it a try.

"We could go for a walk," Weiz said softly beside him, as if she had read his mind.

"Where would you like to go, my love?" Every time he said those words her face lit up and then she blushed like a schoolgirl.

She grabbed hold of his arm and leaned into it as she would his torso. "Anywhere but here," she told him. "I would love to see one of the other worlds."

"As you wish," he said, and gave the top of her head a kiss as he shifted them to a world where they stood next to an oasis in a red desert. The sky held three moons, all smaller than Earths Moon, and quite close to one another. The largest was tinted green and yellow, while the other two were white and grey, much like the Moon. The stars drifted by lazily, in patterns that were unfamiliar. Until he looked down at the horizon, and he could see the nebula in the centre of the Milky Way. It was smaller, and slightly askew, but he knew it immediately.

Excitement ran through his veins, and he forgot for a moment that Weiz had wanted to do something with him. But she pulled him around and planted a kiss on this lips so firm, every other thought fell from his mind.

When she pulled back, she looked around, grabbed hold of his hand and led him to the very small pool surrounded by small plants. She was about to strip and lead him in when he stopped her.

"Would love to," he said as diplomatically as he could manage. "But, uh, have you considered what might be in that pool? I mean in terms of wildlife you don't want to contend with?"

She slapped his arm and breathed a growl of annoyance. "Get your kit off," she commanded.

The rest of the night was spent divesting themselves of the cares of the moment, and simply taking pleasure in each other. They spent a great deal of time talking about a future they now saw as possible, if they made it home. Who would move with who, and whether or not they would continue with the ATF. Harvey admitted that he might take Earthside only assignments, but was emphatic that if it were not possible, then he would absolutely quit, because with his mother gone, Jason needed him as he grew into adulthood. And the longer he spent away, the more often he thought about the boy, and feared that some of the bonding required might already be too late.

Weiz let him talk for a long time on the subject, but eventually brought it back around to lovemaking. She didn't seem to have much going on in her life on Earth, and she told him she was happy to move in with him, and she might take some Earthside assignments for a while, but she hoped to eventually come back out to space. Even back to Eridu.

When dawn began to show on the horizon, they washed themselves off, taking handfuls of water from the small pool. Then dressed and prepared themselves for the shift back to reality.

"I wish we could stay here, just a few more days," she whispered into his shoulder as he shifted them.

"Sounds to me like we'll be doing a whole lot of waiting around while Deidra and her team get their plan together. Maybe we can slip away for a week or two while they do that." He thought, as he said it, that they would have no real use for him at all. But Weiz burst his bubble.

"Much as I would love to," she told him. "I have a sneaking suspicion that our beloved scientist is going to want me to make instruments for her to use. And if it gets us all home, the way we wanted from the beginning, how can I possibly refuse?"

"And if she doesn't need you?" he asked.

"Then it's a date," she assured, and leaned in to give him a peck on the lips before pulling away and looking around.

The light of dawn had yet to reach where they stood, and most, if not all, were still asleep on their foldable, land conforming, camp mattresses. If nothing else, after sleeping rough for a couple of months, those mattresses would feel like sleeping on a cloud. He was thankful for his ability to move back and forth at will, but he forgot sometimes that the others did not share it, and they'd had things a little rougher.

His eyes drifted to Kristin and Estard, and he smiled. They were asleep side by side, but not so close they might accidentally touch, though they faced each other. Harvey had suspected that something might develop there, Estard certainly hadn't been too stealthy about his chase. But he'd not been sure that Kristin would allow it, for whatever her reasons might be.

It wasn't long before the full light of morning was upon them, and the others began to rise in varying degrees of annoyance. Though not all relationships were romantic in nature, Harvey did notice a kind of pairing off. He with Weiz, and Deidra with Dane were the obvious, but there was also Lance with Ellis, Fyord with Hadley, Zim with Bridges and Greenway with Gordon. The last two surprised him most, if only because the day before, Gordon looked like she'd rather punch him in the face than share a meal. He couldn't help but wonder what had happened between them since. Or perhaps he'd read it wrong, and despite their close proximity, they were not in fact pairing, and it was just his mind trying to put people together because he was in that mindset.

With a shake of the head, he turned his back on the waking crew. He started to feel a little voyeuristic.

A moment later, he shifted back to the camp on the other side of the mountain. He could have walked it, but he was only there to see what was left in the light of day.

The natives were gone, which surprised him. He'd thought they'd stay the night at least, before they ran off. The Barricade had fallen outward and had been heavily trampled over and battered from the inner side. They would prove somewhat useful in erecting a semi-permanent structure, if they were to stay for a few more months without the Docker close by. While that was not a welcome thought, the thought of what came at the end of it, was. Jason and home. He kept reminding himself of that. That it was finally going to happen.

Through the scraps of the old camp, Harvey noted or snatched up anything they could use for the next few months. It wasn't until he turned back toward the shadow of the mountain that he noticed a whole row of bags, almost bursting at the seams. He walked over to them and found a note sitting on the one furthest to the right.

I KNOW YOU LOT AREN'T USED TO CARRYING ANYTHING WITH YOU, BUT TRY NOT TO FORGET YOUR KITS. YOU'LL FIND A CHANGE OF CLOTHES, A GOOD BOOK, A SMALL MED KIT AND SOME RATIONS IN EVERY BAG. IT'S NOT MUCH, BUT IT GOES A LONG WAY ON THE GROUND.

BE SAFE,
M. PRESTON.

Harvey hadn't really had much interaction with the man, but he'd seemed a happy sort. And he thought the others would appreciate the gesture as much as he did.

With a heavy sigh, Harvey began to shift the bags over.

~

Deidra woke to the light of the morning and a hand on her shoulder. She knew it had to be Dane, because no one else would dare be that familiar with her.

He still disagreed, but he would stay. There was some part of her that felt bad about that, like what was between them was slightly out of balance.

She sat up, leaned in for a brief kiss, then levered herself from the ground and stretched. The camp mattress had been a welcome gift from the scientists who'd come down for her, but as she looked at it now, she wasn't sure how she was supposed to repack it into the pocket-sized vacuum seal bag, so she just glared at it.

"You don't have to worry about that," Dane said with a laugh in his voice.

She looked at him. "Still waking up."

"I see that."

"What time is it?"

Dane did laugh at that. "It's all rough estimates when it comes to the time of this world. It's not exactly the same as Earth, so it does put the clocks out. But, at a guess, I'd say seven A.M."

It was about what she'd expected. She thought she'd have Greenway give his first shot around ten A.M. It would give Estard and Lance enough time to get to the upper atmosphere and see what was happening. She looked around until she spotted them, both already awake, though doing their own things.

Harvey popped in with a couple of bags and popped out again. If she'd blinked, she might have missed him and thought the bags had appeared on their own. But she kept her eyes on them and saw Harvey make the trip and increase the pile quickly. When he was done, he kept hold of the bags he had in hand and walked over to Weiz, while he announced loudly that Major Preston had left everyone a present.

People spun to see what he was talking about, and Estard asked to clarify. Yes, they should each have a bag.

Everyone, despite not being organised by any leader, lined up and took their bag in an orderly manner. When Deidra got hers, like everyone else, she rifled through it to see what was there. A change of clothes, a sci-fi novel, a med kit, and a sealed bag full of rations. The front pockets held a foldable shovel, a Leatherman, foldable knife, spoon and fork. A small length of rope, eight carabiners, a spool of twine, a compass, six needles of varying size and a reel of black thread. There was also a fresh notebook inside a Ziplock bag, with a pen. She hadn't used a pen and paper in a long time, and it made her smile.

"Do you think this is what all the soldiers have in their packs?" Dane asked.

"Probably a lot more than this," she responded, as she put everything back.

That small distraction over, her eyes darted around and found Lance. He wasn't looking in her direction, so she moved over to him.

"You about ready to get going, Pilot Viatri?" she asked as she approached.

The look on his face when he turned said enough. "If I must, I must," he said in resignation.

There was a part of her that wished she could just give the job to someone more willing, but they all knew he was the one for it. "Grab Estard and get up there. Radio down to Weiz when you're in position. If all goes well, when you make the fall, you won't be able to tell us where you're aiming, so pick a spot before we start, and let us know so Harvey can go and wait for you there."

The Pilot nodded at her, but said under his breath, "Am I the only one who thinks wasting our only shop this way, is a bad idea?"

She could tell the thought of dying bothered him. Whether there was some belief behind that, she couldn't say, but given their current situation, she didn't see anything to be particularly afraid of. Maybe it was the simple thought that death should be final.

"Is there anything else?" he asked, and she realised that she had been staring.

She shook her head. "No, just thinking," she told him.

"Do I want to know?"

"Probably not." He grunted at her, finished repacking his kit, and moved off toward Estard. She watched as Estard said his awkward goodbyes with Kristin, and then took off with Lance toward the last working MM ship.

For the next hour or so she was not going to have much to do. And even after, it was really all up to Greenway. She could guide him, but he would be the one to actually do it.

Doubt grabbed hold of her guts and squeezed. Everything Ulrich and Doctor Levenson had said was true, and now, the closer she got to actually doing it, the more she wondered how wrong she might be. What if they did this, and the field never dissipated? The Docker would never be able to come close enough to pick them up, and if they did drift into the field, they'd lose power and die in space. Not an ideal outcome.

Dane seemed to intuitively know what was on her mind, as he came over and wrapped an arm around her. "Whatever happens," he said softly, "you are doing what you believe is right. Let that be your guiding star."

She looked up at him and searched his face for any sign of doubt but found none. He might have initially disagreed with her, but he would back her to the grave, and she knew it. When she felt she might falter, he would hold her up and keep her facing the direction she needed to go in, because he believed in her.

"I love you," she said.

He smiled at her and gave her a kiss on the forehead. "I love you too," he replied. "But I think we should prepare ourselves for what comes next."

That was harder to do than he made it sound, and she thought he knew it.

There was a slight edge to everyone as they repacked their kits after a small breakfast. Kristin stood with Gordon, talking softly, and Weiz with Harvey, but everyone else seemed to be in some kind of silent contemplation. Greenway had walked off by himself, and Deidra could see his chest rise and fall slowly, which indicated to her that he was trying to keep himself calm.

Deidra gave Dane a small sad smile and indicated the man she was watching. "I should go to him."

Dane nodded and let her move off by herself. He was very good at that. Knowing when his company was welcome, and when he should just stay back. It was one of the many qualities she loved about him. That instinctive social awareness.

She was careful to make a lot of noise as she approached Greenway. The last thing she wanted was to cause him any kind of distress in thinking someone was sneaking up on him.

He turned to face her when she was still a few arm lengths away. "Is it time already?" he asked.

She shook her head. "Not yet, but I wanted to prepare with you."

He let out a guffaw and she frowned at him. "I'm sorry, Doctor, but I do not see how you can possibly prepare for something *I* have to do."

"More about the how," she breathed.

"I understand the concept," he defended.

"Humour me, for my sake." She closed her eyes and breathed deep. "We won't have to do anything until after we get a radio in from Lance. And once we do, it might take an hour, or a day, before you are able to achieve what we're aiming for."

"Based on Kristin's vision, I would tend to doubt that,"

Greenway said. "But I am readying myself. I haven't used my power since I was captured. I'm afraid of what I might become."

"But you *will* do this?" She was suddenly apprehensive about it. "You won't just pretend and say we can't do it?"

The look on his face first expressed anger and disbelief, then acceptance and sadness. "I will do it, you have my word," he replied. "Can't say I am happy about it, but I will do my very best."

"Do you need me to explain what to do?"

"Not this time. I know how."

Deidra refrained from asking how he might know already. "What do you want to be done with you if you show symptoms? We don't have a nullification device, and I'm not sure if one would work after this."

He shot a laugh. "Well, I thank you for considering it, Doctor. I really don't want to put myself in that position again. I can't say I know what to do about it, just that the thing that is in me, is always in me. Even when the Giant's gone, it will be inside me. But as I am now, I know it for what it is, and I know better. Which is something I haven't had for ten years or more. Maybe that will make the difference." He gave her a weak smile.

She didn't know what to make of that. Always in him even without the Giant implied that he had ego issues, or perhaps an idolisation of godhood. Either was disturbing, and she was questioning whether she had actually wanted to know that.

"For my sake, Captain, talk me through what you plan to do, because this is not a simple task."

Greenway sat on the ground and waited until she joined him before he answered, a hand hovering over the ground.

"I am not going to engage the core," he told her. She was about to protest, but he held up a hand. "Your colleagues will agree with me, I think. It would hold too much of what I give it with nowhere to go."

"It will pulse out," Deidra said, "that's the point."

Greenway shook his head, then stopped midway at a tilt and raised a brow. "Maybe. And maybe that excess energy causes earthquakes, and volcanic eruptions, and tidal waves. And probably a dozen other phenomena I haven't thought of yet. But you have, and you should know better."

She had thought of those things, and decided that the risk was low to none, given the type and amount of power, and the fact there was an existing magnetic field. But perhaps Greenway saw it differently in the *how* he could create it. Did she address the how or the what? Let him do his own thing? Could it be better? She had to hear him out, and so invited him to explain.

"We want consistent, far-reaching pulses that move along the magnetosphere, yes?" He waited until she gave a nod. "And rather than charging the magnetosphere, as you suggest, I propose giving the charge to ground particles, and creating an ionospheric pressure."

"Which would cause a lightning storm," Deidra said dryly. "For how long? How many people might get caught in it? Can you control it? Have you done the math?" She didn't mean to run rough shod over his idea, but to her mind, it was as idiotic as it got.

He looked more amused than offended. "Well, it's that, or Viatri can do it from where he is, since he is better equipped to create both the magnitude and the charge. I don't understand why you want me to do it."

"The core," she started, but he cut her off.

"Doesn't mean anything," he said, shaking his head. "I can do it, and I will if you are absolutely certain this is the only way. I do mean, the *only* way. But you're messing with a whole planet. Asking *me* to mess with it. When all you really want is a build up of opposing charges in the upper ionosphere that clashes with the outer magnetosphere. Have I got that right?" He suddenly looked as if he doubted himself.

She thought about it in earnest. And he was right. If they did it his way, it would cause outer atmospheric disturbances, but leave the world itself largely untouched. It had the potential to mess with the atmospheric makeup somewhat, but without testing, she couldn't tell how much. She didn't know why it had never occurred to her. The thought of the consequences that might occur began to give her doubts and she looked around.

"I need to find to Kristin," she told Greenway absently as she took off in the woman's direction. She wasn't far, and she made a beeline for her.

"What is it?" Kristin said with a worried look. "You look like you ate something bad."

"Will what we do have any ill effects on this world? Do you know? Can you see that far?"

Kristin's head shot back at the tirade, and she put her hands up. "You know it doesn't work like that," she said.

Deidra felt like she was on the verge of panic. The breadth of what was about to happen weighed heavily on her. She felt like it was hard to breathe, and her heart was pounding in her chest. She tried to calm herself down. Closed her eyes, took a few deep breaths, and when she felt she could speak, opened her eyes again.

"You can," she told the Comms Officer. *Just repeat everything I say to you, once she's ready to hear it,* Tatiana said in her mind.

"Can what?" Kristin asked with some confusion.

"You can see, if you want to. You can make it happen on purpose."

Kristin looked horrified at the thought. "Headaches on demand then, hey? Not sure I want that, thank you."

"It's important," Deidra insisted. "The rest of us have had to learn to live with what we do, it's your turn." She hadn't intended to get angry with the woman, but she looked suitably chastised at the words, even though they annoyed her.

She grumbled something that Deidra couldn't quite make out, then gave an angry growl and said, "Fine. I'll do it then. Tell me how."

Her short sharp demands made it very clear how she felt about it, but Deidra knew they had limited time to deal with her feelings. She pulled the woman off to the side of the others and sat her down.

"Close your eyes and concentrate," Deidra told her. "Concentrate on a point of time that you want to examine. Maybe five minutes from now, or an hour."

Kristin took a deep breath and did as was bid, though it was obvious she had some trouble with the concentration part, as various parts of her face and body twitched. Deidra did not believe it to be deliberate, but the woman was uncomfortable.

Tell her to imagine what she would be looking at if her eyes were open and faced toward the sky. Deidra did as bid. *Now quietly, softly, as calmly as you can, ask her what that looks like at night.*

They stayed that way, Deidra vocalising what Tatiana said, for longer than Deidra would have liked. But it probably wasn't much longer than any other conversation she'd had with the woman. Nothing was happening, that Deidra could see, at least, and she was beginning to wonder if Tatiana truly knew what she was talking about in this case. Or if Kristin was incapable of doing it because she had some personal mental block.

In reality, it only took about five minutes before Kristin leaned forward with her head in her hands, a muffled scream escaping her. Deidra waited until the woman stopped and looked up at her with hatred in her eyes. It faded quickly, though. Thankfully.

"There was nothing to see, what am I looking for?" She took a deep breath. "That just felt like a lot of unnecessary pain, Doctor." Her teeth were clenched on the last words.

Deidra tried not to let the way she felt get to her. Any other time, she might have been a bleeding heart about it, but not this time. She had to close herself off, and let it happen. "How far ahead did you look?"

"Two days? I think."

"And what did they sky look like?"

"Same as normal," she replied tersely. "How is it supposed to look?"

Deidra shook her head. "Never mind that. Try two months for me. Sky and ground right here where you're sitting. Picture it and picture the time."

Kristin gave her a sour look, but she did as was bid. She closed her eyes, took a deep breath, and let Tatiana, through Deidra, guide her in it. It didn't take as long that time, and Deidra heard a few very distinct swear words aimed directly at her, before the woman looked up from her hands, spit flying.

"It's fine. Nothing unusual." It seemed that she was going to say something else, but before she could, she leaned forward with another painful vision.

Deidra wanted to reach out and comfort her for this one but felt she had probably made herself enemy number one. Her eyes searched around for Estard, before she remembered the man was up in the MM ship with Viatri. She looked at the others until her eyes landed on Gordon, and she gestured with her head for the woman to come and join them.

She got up and let Gordon sit, suggesting to her in a whisper that she coax whatever it was slowly from the woman because Deidra had put her in a bad mood. Gordon gave her a look of pity and shrug before she sat, then leaned forward and spoke softly.

Deidra stayed off to the side where Kristin would not see her when she opened her eyes. She wanted to know what she'd seen, but she wanted the woman to calm down, too.

"Lightning in the sky," she was telling Gordon. "Brief, without clouds. Then the ships fall, breaking up in the atmosphere."

"How many ships?" Gordon asked her, with a meaningful look at Deidra.

"Two enemy ships."

"And ours?"

Kristin shook her head. "I didn't see them."

"And that's what's going to happen today?"

"It's changed, a little, but yes, I think so."

Deidra breathed such a heavy sigh of relief that Kristin turned to look at her with an angry frown. Gordon caught her attention and held it before the woman could say or do anything, then gave Deidra a look indicating it was time for her to leave.

So, Greenway was right. Upper atmospheric might be the way to go. She hoped that Lance would be up for it. Though, if Kristin's vision were true, then regardless of how much it took, Deidra could to convince him.

She couldn't help but feel stupid for not thinking of it herself. She'd run all the calculations for the use of the core but had never even considered charging the upper ionosphere. She didn't like that she was not the smartest person in the room anymore. And that was a thought that startled her into a full stop.

Does that really bother you? That someone else had the idea? Tatiana asked. *You've had plenty of your own, but if you're going to be honest with yourself, you have to admit most ideas you've worked on weren't your own. Even Io belonged to Heinrich. Always did. It's okay. It doesn't diminish your intellect. You're just not as imaginative, that's all.* If Tatiana thought she was being soothing, clearly that part of them was not connected.

She'd never really thought of it before, and she didn't know why it had suddenly occurred to her now. She'd simply worked on things. She was never the one to create it. And right up until that very moment, she had been fine with it. So what had changed?

Dane was at her side, though she didn't remember him

approaching. "What's wrong?" he questioned.

"I don't know if we should do this," she answered.

He took her into his arms and breathed into her hair. "What's changed?" he asked. She explained her exchange with Greenway and the conclusion she'd drawn. "How sure are you that he wasn't trying to get out of doing it?"

"His reticence is expected," she returned, but she didn't know if she was trying to defend him or herself. She broke the embrace to lean back and look up at his face, but they still held each other by the arms. "What if it's a bad idea? What if, we do this, and the consequences are so big, so far reaching, there's no way to take it back?"

"That is the point, isn't it?"

"The thing that concerns me, is I did the calculations based on an iron core of rough approximation with Earth. Every centimetre either way, changes the duration, the magnitude, and strength of charge."

"I know all this," Dane said. "What's the problem? What's wrong?"

"I think I am going to let Viatri do it, like Greenway said. Less ramifications down here, where it matters most." She let herself fall back into his chest momentarily and then pushed off before he cold fold her into another embrace. She didn't have time.

"That's up to you, Deidra. But you didn't do the calculations for the second case, only the first."

"Do you not agree that Greenway's method might be safer?" She wanted to know his honest opinion, and the look on his face as soon as she asked, said enough, but she waited it out.

"Safer, I think yes," he replied with a pained face. It was clear to her eyes he felt like his words might come as a betrayal, though she didn't feel that way. So she leaned into to give him a kiss on the cheek for assurance.

"Whatever you feel about my work, it's how you feel about me that counts," she told him just before she started to walk away. "I have to go to the Commander, so I can speak to Lance about what needs doing."

And hope Viatri understands the scope, Tatiana put in.

"He'll do it," she whispered to herself as much as the voice in her head. "He'll do it, then we can move on from this."

CHAPTER TWENTY-FIVE

The call cut out with a thump as he landed his fist on the button. His grip on the control stick was firm, and he was in danger of jerking them off course if he didn't release.

"Hell of a thing," Estard said behind him.

"You heard that," Lance replied in a strangled tone. "She's lost her god damned mind."

"Or maybe she found it." The Agent was good at being reasonable in unreasonable situations. Lance wondered if it took a special kind of insanity to deal with the world in that manner.

"You don't really think I should do this? Do you?"

"Way she explained it, might be safer than doing it the other way, but it's up to you." The Agent gave a shrug.

Lance shook his head and kept his eyes on the screen. In front of him, instead of the Docker, he saw two extremely large blob like objects that were serving as some kind of defensive satellite. Harvey had warned him about them, but seeing was a different thing altogether. Beyond them, he could see two ships, each roughly one eighth the size of a Docker, coming in fast to push past the blobs. It would be at least twenty minutes or so before they made it anywhere close to Lance's position, which he thought more coincidence than intention. He hadn't been in orbit long enough for them to be aiming at him.

He gave the comms console a glance and frown, looked at where he was in space, then sighed loudly. He leaned over and thumped the comms button.

"Fine," he said. "But I have to warn you, I am not sure I can actually do anything from up here. I might have to come down to the surface and do it from there. And if we end up with some kind of mega storm or something, that's on you guys. You're the ones who asked me to do this, so I am blaming you."

"Are you done, Viatri?" Weiz queried.

"Yes, Commander."

"Good. Doctor Ward has a few more things to say since you cut her off so rudely."

"You'd have done the same," he mumbled to himself. Estard gave a light chuckle behind him.

"Lance, thank you for taking this on, I know it's a burden," Deidra said on the other end. "There are a few things you perhaps don't know, and I am here to talk you through what we need you to do."

"You heard what I said to Weiz, though, right?"

"I did. You shouldn't have any issue changing the ionospheric conditions while you are in the ionosphere. Or above it."

Lance felt at the back of his head, reminding himself of why he was up there in the first place. He relaxed his grip on the control stick and forced himself to breathe normally.

"Which layer?" he asked.

"Ideally, you'd want a small buffer zone," she replied. "So, the one before the final outer layer. I just need you to charge the particles, the way you did at the mountain to give me an electrical storm. But, also, give them a polarized magnetic element, so it's less ESD and more EMI."

He took a breath before he responded. "You'll want to explain that to the laymen you've conscripted here. I know Electromagnetic interference, but what is ESD?"

"Electrostatic Discharge. It's basically lightning at that scale," Deidra let him know.

"I see." He didn't, but he said it anyway. "Let me concentrate. Wouldn't mind you sending Harvey up here so we can get a smooth landing, if you don't mind."

"Why didn't we think of that before?" Estard asked. "He carries us just about everywhere else, doesn't he?"

Lance gave a shrug. "I don't know. But I don't fancy dying, even if we do end up coming back relatively unharmed. I don't know how this level of power use will affect me. I might not be able to land at all."

Estard grunted but didn't respond to that. He had died once, and it had taken a while before his body had disappeared. Lance wondered if it meant he remembered being dead in a way the others didn't. If there was something that came after, or between, as it were. But it was not something he wanted to contemplate too much.

"Harvey wants your relative position," Weiz said, "he can't see you and he doesn't want to shift directly into space." She sounded annoyed.

"I thought he could just use me or Estard for reference?" he mumbled, but gave the co-ordinates.

"I told you it won't work like that, Viatri," he heard Harvey say faintly. Then moments later, the man was in the cabin with them, mere inches from his face.

"Good aim," Estard murmured.

"Alright," Lance told them. "He's here. Now I am going to do my thing, and you lot can just keep quiet and watch. If it doesn't work, don't blame me. I have two witnesses here." He turned to look at said witnesses. Estard looked slightly amused, with a tinge of concern. Harvey looked ready to rip someone's face off. Lance didn't think he'd ever seen the Captain that angry before, and it gave him pause.

"What is it?" Harvey asked him.

"You alright there, sir?"

Harvey gave himself a shake and the muscles around his face relaxed into a more impatient and annoyed look. "I'm fine, Viatri. Just tense from the shift."

"Well, no time like the present, let's get this done, shall we?" He wasn't really asking their opinion so much as he was preparing himself for what he had to do.

The proposition itself was immense. The whole of the ionosphere? How was he supposed to charge the whole thing? And how predictable could that possibly be?

He was momentarily distracted by two ships exchanging shots with the blobs.

With a breath, he refocused himself. He wasn't entirely sure how he was supposed to go about it, but he started with the thought of charging the particles in the second last ionospheric layer, as instructed. He imagined it travelling along the rim of the layer until it traversed the whole planet and rejoined where he started. Then he imagined the line thickening, taking in more of the layer. One kilometre at a time. And he imagine all that while pulling as much energy into himself as he could hold, because he thought it would take that much. Probably more. He might even have to do it in stages.

He didn't look to the others. In that moment, he was completely alone, outside the ship, creating a cosmic situation, nine hundred kilometres above the surface of the planet. When he finally released the energy, there was a very loud *wooomf* sound, and the instruments in his ship blinked on and off.

Lance tried not to panic, and he saw Estard and Harvey do the same. Harvey was reaching his arms out, preparing to remove them from the situation, while Estard said, "If it goes wrong, I'll keep taking us back 'til it goes right."

While Harvey looked aghast at the comment, Lance laughed. It was hard for him to see what the energy he had directed was doing, exactly. Truthfully, it was possible that visually, nothing would change. But he should be able to feel it in some manner.

"How long?" Harvey wanted to know.

"Give it five more minutes," Estard said.

Lance looked at him with suspicion. "How many times?"

"Just twice."

"Were you going to tell me?"

"Right in the moment we need to move," he advised. "Which will be in —" he looked at his wrist as if something should be there. "— three, two, one, MOVE!"

Lance jerked at the controls, confused at where he was meant to move to, or what he was getting away from, but the strength of the word had him in action before he could question anything.

Heart pumping, he asked, "What did we miss?"

Harvey also looked interested in the answer, as the Agent shrugged and replied, "Where the arc connected. You sent the energy all the way around, as you explained it before. We got obliterated that first time. Ship — in — pieces."

Lance shuddered. He didn't understand why they waited until the last moment, unless the Agent enjoyed flirting with death.

"How far back did you come?" Harvey was curious.

"First time? Twenty-one minutes. Last time, about six minutes, because I didn't have to wait for the problem to be explained."

"So, this is going to work?" Lanced wanted to know. "Except for the problem we just dodged, I mean."

"The EMP effect?" Estard made a face and moved his head from side to side. "I guess. I think so." Then he shrugged. "I wasn't paying attention to that part, exactly. There was something about us getting in the way, and a bunch of stuff I wasn't paying a lot of attention to."

"You didn't think that might be important?" Lance asked. "I mean, as much as I appreciate you preventing us from dying, we clearly made it back to the ground, so if it worked, we should have just stayed."

"Alright, alright, let me think." And he did, for longer than Lance would have liked. "Deidra said something about you only did the first bit. You have to do the next."

Lance didn't know exactly what that meant, so he decided it was best to put a call back in to the scientist.

"Is it done?" Weiz asked before he could even finish what he was saying.

"If it was, I don't think the comms would work. I need Deidra. Put her on please." He didn't have to wait long.

"What do you need?" the Scientist wanted to know.

"I did the fist part, but apparently there is a second part that I am not understanding. I need it explained."

They went back and forth for a few minutes to make sure they understood what the other was saying, and then when he was certain he had it right, he shut off the comms again. He took a deep breath and prepared himself. He had a feeling this would end in him causing another severe weather anomaly, but Deidra said that if he let it happen while they were in the upper ionosphere, then the planet itself shouldn't suffer too much, and it may even add to the density of the EMP field. He couldn't say that he was happy about any of it, but the others looked to him with anticipation. Harvey, ready to take them out of danger as soon as it was obvious the ship would no longer work, and Estard to take them back in time, if things went too far wrong. He didn't envy their jobs either. Even as he realised, he was contemplating their jobs so he wouldn't have to do his.

With an effort, he centred himself. He imagined what he needed to do as he gathered the energy inside him as he had done the first time, but this time it was like a rush rather than a trickle, and he began to feel ill. It distracted him with the thought of what had happened when he released the superstorm and he almost forgot what he was doing. He kept it building, though, to create the opposing charge. He hoped the woman knew what she was talking about, because to him, it sounded like a mad man's plan. Not that he liked her other one much better, but at least he wouldn't be the one doing it.

He had to hold the energy inside himself for a moment while he refocused on the task instead of trying to work through panicked and anxious thoughts.

Once the charge had built enough, he let it flow out into the ionosphere and directed it to charge the particles. He imagined it unfolding much the same way as he had the first time.

Sickness overcame him, and he knew that he was about to blow more energy, even though he didn't know where it came from. It might have been pieces of him, that the superstorm would come from. It might have been drawn directly from the space around him.

Breath heavy, he levered himself out of the pilot's chair and lay down on the floor. He barely fit, though he wasn't tall, but the cabin really wasn't designed to fit very many people. With just four regular crew on deck, it could feel crowded at times.

He was trying to put his head in a better space, to see if he could get it to dissipate harmlessly. A skill he felt he might need in the future, if it happened again. Instead, he felt a burp gurgling up, and it was sharp. He wanted to warn the others, who were looking at him as if he'd grown a new head, but he couldn't speak.

It felt quicker than the last time, and he didn't know what the consequences of it would be, if anything, but when he released the energy, it blew right through the hull of the ship. He imagined that from the outside it looked like a whale venting.

Harvey and Estard were holding tight to each other, and the cabin itself, though the atmosphere melted away quickly, along with the gravity. As Lance began to move upward, Harvey grabbed him, and they were suddenly on the ground.

Lance continued to vent the energy inside him, though the brunt of it had already gone. What ended up in the sky when he was done, were a few small storm clouds, a little rain, and a lot of lightning.

When he finally pulled himself into a sitting position, he saw that he was surrounded by the usual suspects. Weiz, Deidra, Kristin. Though the latter looked as if she were more interested in Estard than him.

"You did it?" Deidra wanted to know.

"I should hope so," he replied. "The last working ship is gone. The Docker is gone. You got a couple of —" He was cut off by the sound of a loud boom from far away.

He looked up to the sky and saw a streak of flame, falling oddly slow. Then another boom, and another streak of flame. He looked to Deidra for confirmation.

"Not my field of expertise," Deidra told him. "I seem to be saying that a lot these days. But, in answer to your question, just eyeing it, I would say they should land between one and two hundred kilometres away. Possibly in the ocean, which could be bad."

"You don't think they'll break up in the atmosphere?" Harvey queried.

"You might want to hope they do, because if they don't, even that far away, they are going to cause some very very big problems."

"Is it my..." Weiz searched for a word but couldn't seem to find it.

"Blobs?" Harvey filled in for her.

"Blobs," she continued looking at Harvey in a way that indicated she didn't like the name. "Or are they enemy ships?"

"I don't have all the answers," Deidra said through clenched teeth. "Much as I would love to, even if I had lost my memory and given in to the *god of knowledge*," she invested a great deal of scorn into those words and paused for effect. "Even then, I wouldn't know *that*!" She turned and moved away.

Lance looked up to the sky to follow the trails of what fell, to see yet another, smaller streak of flame. And another. He hoped nothing else fell.

"Well, that's your answer," he told Weiz as he tried to stand. "Those first two were your blobs."

Weiz gave him a glance that said she didn't appreciate his use of the word but said nothing.

Kristin had pulled Estard off to the side and they were talking in hushed voices, close together. It was easy to see something had changed between them, and a part of him was happy for them, while another part wished he'd had the courage to let Kristin know he'd been more serious than he'd appeared in his flirting with her. He knew that they were merely fledgling feelings, probably naught more than a schoolyard crush, but it was time to let it go.

Just as he turned, Ellis bounded up, and he took an involuntary step back. The woman was decent enough company, when he felt like it, but sometimes she would just stand around quiet. He had never been good at quiet company, and it made him nervous and uncomfortable.

"So, you did it," she stated. "We're all safe for a little while."

"Well, I certainly did something," he agreed, though he wasn't so sure it was what Deidra had in mind. He'd never seen an EMP in action, but he didn't think it resulted in what happened to those ships. Then he really gave it some thought. The boom, the flames, could just have been uncontrolled atmospheric entry. He shook his head and shrugged at himself.

"So, what do you think we'll be doing for the next few months, while the scientists work out how to rid us of our burdens?" she asked as she led him away from the others.

"Sleep?" he offered, though he wasn't serious. She gave him a smile, and he continued. "Probably start building that outpost we started on a couple of weeks ago but never got around to finishing, distracted as we were by the Bahana men."

"They are a strange lot, aren't they?"

"No stranger than us, I'd think," he replied.

"But you hate them for what they did to you?" She seemed indignant at his nonchalance on the subject.

He stopped moving and stared at her until he was sure he had her full attention. "What are you trying to get at?" He wanted to know. "I am not a fan of the way I was treated, obviously. But can you truly tell me, that were the right kind of Earth scientist here, they might not have done exactly the same thing? A Doctor Faets, but of a bio variety? I think you know the answer to that."

While she seemed a little chastened at his response, she firmly defended her position. "But they weren't. And they didn't. The Bahana men did."

"You want me to be angry? Is that it? Because I am."

"No," she raised a single hand. "I don't really know what I am getting at, I suppose. Just..."

He waited, but she didn't finish. "Just... what?"

"Trying to connect." She shrugged, blushed, and turned away.

He'd known, on some level, that she'd been doing it for some time, he'd just been ignoring it. Not that he didn't appreciate it. It just wasn't something he was really looking for, while they were in the back end of nowhere. It was partially the reason he had never spoken to Kristin. He didn't know how to let Ellis down gently, though, so he stood there like a lump, just staring.

"Should I just go?" she asked after a while, bravely facing him once again.

Lance took a deep breath and shook his head. "No, don't go. I'm just, slow to process some things, you know? We can take a walk."

He didn't know what he was doing now. Whatever happened next, was up to the scientists.

~

Greenway watched the small gathering break apart from his place at the foot of the mountain made by his hubris. No one was particularly happy about the situation they'd found themselves in, and the mood was sombre.

It was a struggle not to go off by himself and just leave them behind. Partially, the guilt of what he had done, was getting to him, along with the embarrassment and general feeling of not belonging.

Harvey turned his eyes toward him, said a few words to Weiz, gave her a kiss on the head and headed over.

"Aiden," Harvey said.

"John," Greenway replied.

"I cannot speak for the others, but I want you to know, for all that has happened here, I forgive you."

It was like a gut punch. He felt winded, and a lump formed in his throat. This man, who he had considered a friend, who he had betrayed more than anyone, forgave him. But every time he tried to form the words, he choked up, and nothing came out but a squeak, adding to his embarrassment.

He didn't want to seem ungrateful, so he managed to keep himself still, even as he turned his face away.

Harvey looked away awkwardly, even as he said, "I wish I could have done more for you, before it all happened the way it did, but we were all caught up in our own minds, you know. Doing our own things. What we thought was right, at the time."

Tears fell, and it was as if it freed his voice. He jerked his head back toward the Captain and snapped. "Don't you blame yourself for my actions, man. Not ever."

"I don't blame myself. I know it was all you. Or your consequence. I just..." He shook himself. "Wish I'd understood your mindset better, is all."

Through the tears, Greenway couldn't help but let out a low chuckle. "I wouldn't have minded knowing, myself. Some of it is so distant and hazy, like a dream, or another life. And some of it, I would pay to forget."

The scene that he played most often through his mind was the death of the villagers when they refused to build the temple. How he had so callously enveloped them into the soil beneath their feet. When he slept, he dreamed it. When awake, it was never far from his mind.

"What got me most," Harvey said after a while. "Was that you, before everything happened, thought we were dead. In purgatory. I hope you'll forgive me saying this, but you seemed a little bit insane, even then."

"I was," Greenway admitted. "Though in a different way, I guess. I had been searching for purpose in my life, which had become so empty outside my work. I didn't know what I was living for anymore. I was convinced that I was playing a game with God. And then I was one."

Harvey gave a grunt. "And what do you think now?"

"They were an experiment gone wrong. Their minds somewhat skewed by unfathomable lifespans. And I truly believe some of what they were rubbed off on us. The *consequence* of using our powers."

"I seem to have gotten away with little of that."

They both stood for a while in silence, contemplating their current existence, until Harvey was called away by Weiz and he disappeared.

Greenway didn't know what had driven the man to say the things he had, but in his heart, it helped. More than forgiveness from anyone else might have. Even Weiz. Because he couldn't get forgiveness from the dead, and that was who he most desired it from.

He didn't know how long he'd been just standing around, when Harvey finally returned, Estard and Viatri in tow. Not long after that, booms and flames in the sky.

Greenway closed his eyes and breathed deep, thankful. He wasn't sure that had been going to work, he just didn't want to use his power again. He'd made a promise, to himself and to Rochelle, and he intended to keep it, even if he died for it.

When everyone had calmed, and it was clear that Lance's work had had the desired effect, they took the rest of the day to congratulate themselves on a job well done. He was mostly happy to be left out of it and watch on from the sidelines. But a part of him thought if he wanted to change, then he would have to involve himself, no matter how uncomfortable.

So, he pressed forward, joined a conversation or two. He couldn't remember what they talked about, but he was surprised that they didn't just tell him to go or turn their backs on him. He didn't have much to say or to add to anything, but a few times he did find himself backing away from a private moment before they realised he was there.

By the time they lay themselves down for the night, Greenway felt more a part of the crew than he ever had. Despite all he'd done, and how he had treated them, they'd welcomed him back. Except Gordon, of course.

Just as he closed his eyes, he heard a shuffle beside him and saw a figure descend from the darkness to put a knee on his chest. He was about to push it off aggressively, when the face came close enough for him to see. Rochelle.

"What did you do?" she asked in a hot whisper.

CHAPTER TWENTY-SIX

They were alert and on top of her the moment she spoke to Greenway, though the way she behaved as if they weren't, it was hard to tell if she didn't notice or didn't care. Greenway had his hands above his head as he lay on the ground, her knee on his chest.

If Kristin hadn't recognised the woman and held him back, Harvey would have immediately deposited her with the other Bahana men. But Kristin held firm to his sleeve and said, "Let her speak."

"What do you mean?" Greenway asked.

"I told you to leave," the girl said through clenched teeth. "I wanted to avoid a war, not help you in yours!"

Greenway sighed and looked around at them as they waited. The girl seemed to notice the movement of his eyes and actually pay attention to those around her for the first time. She closed her eyes, bit at her bottom lip, then got up, gun dangling from her left hand.

Harvey looked between Greenway and the girl, and saw the man had some kind of feelings for her, so decided to stay out of it. Unless things got out of hand. It was Weiz who stepped forward and took the gun with an absent, "thank you," and Gordon patted her down from behind, emptying her pockets.

"Now you can talk," Weiz said firmly.

"Rochelle," Greenway started as he got up. "None here will harm you unless you make the first move."

"I'm supposed to believe you now, after what you did?" She kept her eyes on those in front of her, though she must have known there were more behind. Harvey thought everyone was up and looking on, even the scientists. He could just make out Dane and Deidra a little further off to the side.

"What are you talking about?" Greenway asked.

"The ships!" she yelled. "Falling out of the sky. Ring a bell? Do you know what you've done?"

"Why don't you explain it to us?" Weiz offered in what Harvey considered to be her motherly voice.

Rochelle eyed her sideways. "The others will come now. Those ships were there to pick us up. Us and you, if we'd caught you, but I let you all out! I made sure none of you were in the cells! And the deal was for you to leave."

"We can't leave," Harvey said. "Didn't Greenway tell you that?"

"Of course you can. You have the ships. You clearly have the men."

"We're bound to the world, child," Weiz said in a tired voice that made her sound much older than she was. "We're working on ridding ourselves of the curse, but you and yours just keep getting in the way."

"Because you don't belong here," she spat. "I don't believe in what my father is... was doing. But he was on one of those ships, and now he's dead."

Harvey had to admire the way she stood, back straight, in the midst of a group of strangers and announced her sorrow. Tears fell in rivers down her cheeks, though those not looking at her face would not have known from the sound of her voice. He would have been proud to have someone like her on his crew.

"Do you want to go home?" he asked.

"The others will come now," she said softly. "And I won't try to stop them from taking you. Leave or die. Or, I should say, you might wish you did. They will capture you, and they will torture you, though that is not how they see it. And you know it." She directed that last firmly at Greenway.

"They come too close, and they will be the next to fall," Deidra said as she took a step forward, one hand still holding to Dane's sleeve. "There is no way for them to capture us. Have you tried to use your tech?"

Harvey hadn't thought of that. They'd celebrated, but they hadn't tested if it worked on the ground, only that the ships had fallen.

Deidra held her hand out and waited until Gordon handed her something that looked testable. "The null field, how appropriate." She offered it to the girl. "Try it, see if it works."

Rochelle eyed them all suspiciously as she reached out a slow hand to take the object. Once in hand, she did something to turn it on, and lunged immediately at Weiz, who had her gun. She was stopped in midair by Ellis, who stepped forward and admired her own work, before redepositing the young woman where she'd been.

"Doesn't seem to work," she stated, seemingly pleased with herself.

A frustrated growl escaped the lips of their prisoner when it was clear she could not move of her own accord.

"Let her go," Weiz commanded. "In a way, she has been an ally, and she merely feels betrayed." She looked Rochelle dead in the eyes. "Am I wrong?"

The girl squirmed a little in her invisible bonds, and it was obvious when Ellis let go, by the way she turned almost a hundred and eighty degrees. She fell into a heap on the ground as she over balanced, but everyone kept their distance and allowed her to get up on her own. It ruined the moment, and Harvey heard at least two people trying to hold in a laugh.

Once she was back on her feet and glaring at Weiz and Ellis, Greenway came forward. "Rochelle," he said softly, hands raised. "Rochelle, please."

She moved her head in his direction but kept her eyes where they were. "Please what?"

"Please don't let it be like this. We sent Ensign Brioli yesterday," he said, and Rochelle's head swung around.

"You sent who?"

"Ensign Brioli," Greenway replied slowly.

"What did you tell him to say?" Rochelle's jaw was set, her face a mask of anger.

"To let your people know they had one more day before their ships started falling out of the sky," Harvey told her simply. "We gave them fair warning in an effort to minimise the loss of life. It's what you do."

"He never gave it," Rochelle responded, eyes turning distant. "He told us that your ships were no longer on the ground, and where to find you. Said there wouldn't be a better opportunity. I stayed, thinking I'd free you from the cells if they did catch you. But the men never came back, and the Guardian would allow no more to go."

So, the man had lied, no great surprise. Harvey said as much, and she stared daggers at him before lowering her head and admitting in a small voice, that the man had always had more anger than sense.

"I can take you home," Harvey offered again. "Or we can leave you in Greenway's custody until we're done here. But I hope you believe me when I say, we'll not stay longer than we must. And, if we fail in our mission, we will move to another world."

There was some murmuring from the others at his announcement, but no one contradicted him or argued. He kept his focus on Rochelle's eyes, even if she refused to look at him. The girl was thinking, and he couldn't blame her for that. If she went home, since she was not supposed to be on Eridu in the first place, she could pretend she had always been there, but it meant she wouldn't be able to warn anyone or say anything unless she wanted to reveal her part in it. Or she stayed, with Greenway as her guard, and life would not be much better.

"I'll go home," she breathed eventually. "Just, please, don't let yourself be caught. If they see you with me, we'll both be done for."

Harvey gave a nod. "Simple enough, in and out. I do it all the time. We've only got one problem."

She waited for him to finish, and he waited for her to ask. The moment was strangely awkward. "What?"

"I don't know which one is your home world, so…" he put his hands in the air with a shrug.

"You need me to tell you?"

"If you could, that would be great so I can avoid it altogether in the future."

The girl shook her head at him, and held out her hand. He took it and gave her a look that asked if she was ready, and she asked, "Do I just describe it to you…?"

Harvey barked a laugh. "I was just going to take you through the worlds until we saw something you recognised, but your way is probably better."

Rochelle gave a description of the forest outside the base where her family stayed while her father worked with The Hunt. It was brief, but it gave him enough landmarks to work with that he believed he'd be accurate.

"Before I do this," Harvey said, "I am curious. What would your army have done, if we hadn't left and done what we did?"

She raised her brows at him. "You mean that warning I gave you to try and get you all to leave?"

"Yeah, that."

"We have incinerators. We generally wouldn't use them on people, but they'd decided it might be best. 'Remove the scourge', as they put it. I don't know exactly what would have happened, but I can tell you it would have been near instant, and your shields couldn't stop it."

"In essence, giant heat ray?" Harvey wanted to know.

"In essence," she agreed.

"But they know that wouldn't kill us," he asserted.

Rochelle raised her shoulders. "Killing you was never the point."

"So why do it, then?"

"Balance. If you can, then so can we? You have a Firestarter, we have flamethrowers. You have a teleporter, we have transporters. You have a Creator, we have a nullifier — which incidentally works on almost all of your talents. For everything that you are capable of, we have created a similar or opposing force. How? My guess is the scientists who kidnapped and tortured your companions. As much as they say what they do is to help you, I think they actually use it all for their tech."

Harvey nodded. It made sense. Too much sense. And sounded an awful lot like certain governments back on Earth. "You don't think it was to protect yourselves?"

"I doubt it," she told him. "It started as a forgotten ancient mission to return the Shadowmen to their humanity, but it seemed to quickly become about something else."

"As most things do," he empathised. "Alright, let's do this, shall we?"

"About as ready as I can be. But I want a promise, before you go. Promise that you will leave. No matter what else happens, just go. As long as you're around, my people will keep coming back."

"You're not wrong," Harvey breathed as he took hold of her hand once more. "I promise. In as much as one man can speak for everyone. Now, let's hope you're right about your directions, or you may be a little stuck. I plan to bow out as soon as your feet touch the ground on the other side of this jump. Are you prepared for that? Come what may?"

A slow nod. "Come what may," she repeated.

He took a step, let go of her hand and took another before he could even catch a glimpse of what was happening around them. If he had even gotten the place right. He didn't know where he took her, didn't even have time to see the reaction on her face. But she had said the words and he had to take her word for it. He could always go back and check.

Back in the crowd of Giants, he shook himself of the urge. The girl was on her own, and there was nothing more that he could do for her.

Weiz took him by the arm. "Welcome back," she said.

"Thank you," he replied absently. "Is there a plan yet? Do we have a place to go? Or something to do? Or are we going to wait around twiddling our thumbs while the scientists work out whatever it is they have to work out?" It came out harsher than he intended, but there was a part of him that still blamed the scientists for all that had already gone wrong, and he couldn't escape the feeling that there would be more of that.

"Deidra suggested we could go back to the mountain city and settle in there for a while," Weiz told him. "She thinks it an unlikely place for any remaining Bahanians to come find us."

"Even if they did, we proved that their tech won't work," Harvey put in.

"Maybe so, but that could change. We don't know how long the effect will last. It's not supposed to last."

"How long?"

"You know as much as I do. Three or four months."

"For the core," he said. "Not for what Lance did. What was the projection for that?"

Weiz let go of him with a heavy sigh. "Let's go find out," she replied, and moved off in the direction of the scientists, expecting him to follow.

"Commander," Deidra acknowledged her approach, and the other scientists turned to see her. "What can I do for you?"

"Harvey wants to know how long you expect the EMP effect to last?"

The Scientist opened and closed her mouth a few times, looked to her companions, frowned, then said, "Ah, three or four months. I don't imagine it should be much longer than that."

The other three scientists shared a look that said they weren't so sure, but they were deferring to Deidra.

"Look," he said, thought only half formed. "We don't know how long that field will last, or if, by some miracle, the Bahanians have some tech here that wasn't affected by the first wave. You have to admit, we have ways of protecting our tech from that kind of thing, and intentionally or inadvertently, they may have the same."

They were beginning to shuffle uncomfortably and look to Deidra for an answer. Always Deidra. In a way, Harvey felt bad for her.

"What are you suggesting?" Deidra asked.

"Let's just move to another world while you work on whatever it is you need to work on. The EMP waves won't interfere with whatever it is, and if you need things from here, I can be your ferry. The Bahanians will have no way to know where we've gone. I don't really see a downside."

"Unless those other worlds are populated," Weiz said.

He looked at her with a frown that asked whose side she was on but, acknowledged the statement. "I know at least three are populated, including Bahana, but either of the other two should be suitable. But, even if they do prove to be populated, how would it be any different from here?"

"I think this is a decision for the whole group," Deidra said. "For myself, I find the idea favourable, because the field may interfere with what I need to do."

Weiz raised her voice and gathered everyone in. When she was sure they had everyone's attention, she gave the floor to Deidra.

"Captain Harvey has suggested that we should take up temporary residence on a new world," she told them. "But I think, perhaps, some of you would rather not."

"Does it matter what we think?" asked Hadley. "We just follow orders. If Weiz says we go, then we go." There were some murmurs of agreement in the small crowd. Even Greenway was nodding in the back.

"If it's that simple," Deidra said, "Then find what you need and get packing, we'll be moving as soon as you're done."

The crowd shuffled off to do as bid, even as Weiz turned and said in a whisper. "I have not given an order, nor agreed to anything yet."

"But you will, or you would not be speaking in whispers," Harvey told her.

He enfolded her in an embrace, and she let him. "When will this be over?" she asked.

"When we're home," he said and gave her a kiss on the forehead.

"That might never happen," she replied.

He refrained from pushing her away just to see the look on her face. He knew what she meant. That maybe, whatever Deidra was trying to do, was as much a coping mechanism for her, as it was a genuine attempt to actually rid them of what connected them to Eridu. And he had no answer, because she was right. It might not work, and they may never be separated from the place. But he had to believe. They had to try.

~

Estard felt exhausted, though he knew he shouldn't. The past few days had been more than a little hectic and had left him with quite a lot to think about. Whether he wanted to stay or go, be with Kristin or not, keep his power or not. And he had to admit that his power had been very useful in the past couple of days. Even if they did have to hang out in a cell for a while because he didn't think to use it before the null field got them.

Truth was, he was terrified of Kristin, even though he wanted her around all the time. Words were difficult, deeds were harder, because he constantly wondered whether or not it would disappoint the woman. It was just nerves, he knew, but he wished to push past them already, into the realm of familiar.

The idea of going to another world and exploring it together, appealed greatly to him, but it was hard for him to get a gauge on how Kristin felt about anything. At times, she could be quite a bit more forward than the women he was accustomed to, and sometimes, in other ways, far more reserved.

"Looking deep in thought, there, Agent man," Lance said as he dropped into a squat beside him. "I think we got it right this time."

Estard gave the pilot a nod. "Yes, we did. And only the third time in."

"What's on your mind? Do I want to know?"

He couldn't stop his eyes from locating Kristin, who was speaking softly with Gordon some distance off. "I don't know if you want to know."

"I know it's none of my business," the man started, then seemed to wait for Estard to indicate whether it was or not. Estard obliged, and Lance continued. "But, Kristin, she's going to be a hard fish to catch. She may never be as still as you wish, and you may just have to ride the currents with her. I've only known her since she joined the crew not a year gone, but she's a good sort. And I have her back."

A big brother talk. He didn't know that he blamed the man for it. No one else had performed those duties, though he had thought Harvey might.

"Truth of it is, she might chew me up and spit me out, and I'd come back for more. More often than is good for me," Estard replied. "But there is something about her, that has fascinated me since the day we met, and I still couldn't tell you what it is. I think I may spend the rest of my life looking for it."

"I wish you luck with that," Lance said with a smile.

"So, quite aside from my personal feelings, what has you popping a squat by me?"

"*My* personal feelings," the man answered honestly, though he didn't look at Estard.

"Ellis?"

Lance gave a slow nod. "Not sure what to think there," he said.

"Women are a maze, my father said. If you can't enjoy the twists and turns, pitfalls and surprises, you'll never find a woman worth your time." Though he wasn't entirely sure what that even meant, he would remember it for the rest of his life.

"Or maybe you just have to find one you can endure those things from, because you think the end is worth it. Perhaps enjoying it is just a bonus."

Estard shrugged. "You might be right," he sighed.

They sat in companionable silence for a while, each in their own minds, waiting for everyone to be ready to move to a new world. He didn't know what they could possibly be gathering, since all they had was in the large packs that the ground troops had left them, and Estard could see them all from where he sat. In his mind, they were all just making excuses for delay.

He stood and moved toward Weiz who said something to Harvey before she shooed him away. "Commander," he said to get her attention.

"Agent, what can I do for you?" She sounded annoyed.

"I don't think anyone has anything in particular to do, so you have to gather them up, or they won't get gathered," he told her. "I think you'll find most will procrastinate when faced with the unfamiliar."

"We'll give them a few minutes, Agent. I don't think any of us truly wants to leave unless it's to go back to Earth. We're merely doing this for the scientists. So they can do whatever it is they need to do."

Estard looked to the sky, the feeling that something was coming building in his chest. He'd never had premonitory feelings before, but he knew Kristin might help him. And it *was* a might, because she hated her power.

The moment he looked at Kristin he wondered if it was a real feeling, or one manufactured by his mind to give him a reason to speak to her. He stalled, half a step into moving in her direction, suddenly unsure. Another glance at the sky and he steeled himself against the stupidity of his nerves. The indecisiveness was unusual for him, and he didn't like it.

"Kristin," he said as he approached. She looked at him, did an up and down with her eyes, then said something to Gordon, who moved off.

"You know, if we're going to make a go of it, Agent man, you should probably start calling me Ana," she told him.

His brow furrowed. "And you should probably start calling me Julian, Ana," he returned with a little sass. For a moment his concern was forgotten as she let herself be enfolded by his arms.

"So, Julian, what brings you over? The look on your face says it's something serious."

He took a deep breath. "I have a feeling," he started, but didn't know where to go with it.

Kristin disengaged and took a few steps back to look him up and down with a frown. "A feeling about what?"

"Something's coming, and we should either move now, or do something about it."

"And I guess you want me to have a look?"

He shook his head. "I know how much you hate that," he said softly. "But I was hoping you might take me seriously. I don't know what it is, but my eyes keep drifting to the sky."

"There shouldn't be any ill effects with what Lance did," Kristin assured. "Unless that's not what you meant."

"I don't know what I mean, only that something is coming, and I desperately feel the need to move."

"How long?"

"Soon."

"Worst case scenario, you can always come back and tell us what happened, then we can avoid it." He didn't know whether she was trying to be funny. Her expression remained serious.

He was about to turn and leave, go back to the Commander, try and convince her to move faster, when Kristin grabbed him by the hand.

"Wait," she said softly. "I'm sorry. I'm not good at this."

He turned to look at her and replied, "Neither am I, but I am trying here."

"I'll look," she hesitated a little before she took a seat on the ground and indicated that he should sit across from her. He couldn't say that he blamed her, either. Though her consequence was immediate and obvious compared to some of the others, it didn't look like fun.

She closed her eyes and took a deep breath. He held her hands, palm down between them, and waited. He wasn't sure what to expect. What if she didn't have a vision? What if the vision she had was unrelated to the feeling he could not shake.

He opened his mouth to tell her it didn't matter, not to worry about it, he didn't want her to go through the pain of it for nothing, when the world turned white-purple around him. It took less than a second, but that light was followed quickly by white-blue and white-green, and a heat so intense, it was like he only felt it in periphery. While the people around him, melted like wax candles put in a fire place, and the grass and trees turned to ash in a heartbeat. But the one thought he had as he watched, stunned, was — *how am I not dead yet?*

He realised, almost too late, that he had used his ability to slow down time. To witness what was happening, so that he could better articulate it next time around. Even as he, himself, burned away.

There was no way for him to know how long it took to rouse in the field, unclothed, in a row of completely naked people. The odd thought he had, rather than being angry at having been killed and reborn, was that the packs would also have been burnt and they now had no clothes.

But rather than dwell on that, he concentrated and moved back. It wasn't like a rewind: that might have been more convenient. He had to guess, and hope it was right.

When he landed back in the past, he was standing in front of Weiz, his eyes on Kristin. "Heat ray, incinerator, firestorm, whatever." He almost tripped over his own words trying to get them out for the Commander.

"Excuse me?" she asked.

"Less than five minutes, we all need to be gone, or we're all going to be dead."

The Commander looked at him strangely for a moment, and then seemed to remember what his power was. "Harvey! We have to get going!" He didn't respond straight away, and she started searching with her eyes. "*Sheiße! Wo bist du?*"

Strangely, Estard could have sworn that Harvey had been with

Weiz the last time around. And perhaps he had been, but he'd moved off when Estard approached. Being the man he was, Harvey could have gone anywhere, and he'd have no reason to think twice about it. They were supposed to be safe now. Only they weren't.

The time seemed to pass far too quickly. Quicker than they could possibly get anything done, and before he knew it, he was facing that same white-purple light, looking over at Kristin with horror on her face. He thought, in that moment, that she might have seen something, but he could not ask, because she'd be dead before he got to her.

Rather than fight the inevitable, he let himself die quickly with the rest. When he awoke in the field, he shook himself, took a deep breath and forced himself back in time again. He pushed as far as he could make himself go. He had to give himself the time to convince the Commander that they needed to do something.

When he reappeared in the past, he was standing in front of the Commander, just as he had been the last time. His mind panicked. He couldn't understand why he could not take it back further. Why the time was so arbitrary. As disassociated from it as he felt, he still didn't want to have to burn to death, all over again.

He grabbed the Commander by the shoulders. "We gotta get outta here!" he shouted at her.

She looked taken aback, but didn't question, she just turned her head and screamed, "We need to get moving, now. Drop everything, run!"

And everyone did, except the scientists, who looked around, confused. Weiz gave Deidra a meaningful look and she got them moving. Once the Commander was satisfied, and she saw that Estard was too, they started running in the same direction as the rest of them.

There was no dignity in it. They didn't know where they were going, or what they were running from. They had been commanded and they followed. And Estard wasn't sure it would even make a difference. Though they were soon about to find out. It was like the futile run from the meteor shower all over again, and the loop he'd made in his attempt to save Kristin. With the same frustrating limitation on how far he could travel back.

It felt too quick. It always felt too quick. He went back, again and again, and found he was stalled talking to the Commander, giving him roughly two or three minutes to get them all out of the line of fire. And every time, Harvey was absent. Where was the man? What was he doing? When had they all begun to so heavily rely on him?

But he never quite managed to get them out of danger. Harvey might have, had he been there. Whisked them all away to another place, another planet. But Estard had to rely on who was there, and he could think of no one who might counter an attack like that. He didn't even know where that attack had come from, though he had to assume the sky.

As he sat up from his death, this time, he looked to the sky and scanned the horizon, searching for a sign of something they might be able to fight. Quite aside from the indignity of having no clothes for the foreseeable future, Estard just did not want to admit defeat. He wanted to find a way to push himself back further than where he had stalled at. Or find the right person to stop the attack altogether in the tiny amount of time allotted.

He looked along the line of naked bodies, reminding himself who was with them, and what power they had. Bridges the Firestarter, Zim the Healer, Weiz the Creator, Kristin the Seer, Hadley the Empath, Greenway the Mountain Maker, Gordon the Mind Reader. He turned the other way to see the rest. Fyord the Illusionist, Lance the Weatherman, Deidra the Encyclopedia, Ellis the Mover, and — the scientists were dead. Just plain dead. If he couldn't get this right, Deidra might never forgive him.

The sky was still empty. No sign of what had caused the

incineration, and he was about to give up and go back, when he heard someone say, "Is that a ship?"

He followed the pointed hand to a position in the sky. It was so far away he had to squint to make it out, but there was definitely something falling in flames. He had to assume it was a ship, because a bird would be too small to see. He said as much.

Which then begged the question, how had they managed to do it, if they still fell from the sky like the others had? Had the effect that Deidra intended been intermittent? Was she aware of the flaw? Was there something they would be able to do about it within his allotted three-minute window?

With a deep breath, he prepared himself for another trip back, but found he could not move time. Couldn't even slow it. His eyes searched the area, but he could see no one. He knew they had to be there, though, as he let out his breath in a puff, saying, "Null field." Those nearest him started searching as well.

Intermittent, he had to remind himself. It may not have been a perfect solution, but it was a pretty good one, and soon enough, the null field wouldn't work, and he would be able to go back and try again. *Fruitlessly, for the fiftieth time*, he thought. But he had to try, didn't he?

Before the null field gave out, he saw hundreds of Bahana men on the ground, surrounding them. They all held weapons and bore grave looks. It was as though they knew they were giving something up to be there, and they thought it worth it, but mourned for what they lost.

"Gordon, if you're going to do something..." Weiz said.

The woman shook her head. "Not for that many. I can't."

The Bahana men continued to approach slow and cautious. Estard continued to try and move through time. He didn't know which would come first — capture, or another time leap. But in a strange way, the fear of what they might do to him kept him alert and ready to spring into action. His powers might not have been working, and he might be buck naked in a field surrounded by the enemy. But he still had his pride. And his fists. All they needed was one moment where their powers worked, and the Bahanian weapons didn't, and it could be over fairly quickly.

"Deidra," he said as he thought it. "If I go back in time and tell you what happened here, would you believe it?"

Deidra looked stricken, stunned. She was clearly in shock at the loss of her fiance. Of the scientists. But she managed to shake it off somewhat to answer, "Of course, but I don't have an answer for it. It's Greenway you'd have to convince to do something about it." Even as she said it, hope seemed to peek through her eyes.

Estard turned his attention to Greenway, just as a shot rang out, stunning Gordon into unconsciousness. Then another and another. Too quick for Estard to do, or say, anything. He just kept pushing at the point where his power should be and hoped he got there before they got him. There were enough Bahanians that they should have just popped them all at once. But they didn't. It was one that moved methodically down the line, taking careful aim. He wondered if they only had the one.

There was only Bridges and Zim before they got to him. He would have gotten up and run to give himself more time, but he was afraid that would just draw their attention to him, and he would be next. He looked at Deidra, hoping she would understand his thought. Draw attention. He didn't want to say it out loud in case the Bahanians understood.

Zim went down, and the shooter took careful aim at Bridges. How stupid the Bahanians must have thought they all were, just sitting around, waiting to be shot. Just as the shooter lined up Bridges, Kristin got up and started running. There was nowhere she could go for fast cover. Between the meteor shower and Lance's cleanup effort, there wasn't much left in the area. But she understood.

The shooter turned his attention to Kristin as quick as the woman moved, but when he pressed down on his trigger all he got was an empty click. And before he could get another click off, time slowed, and suddenly, Estard was back in front of Weiz.

He turned on his heel, looking for the man. "Greenway!" he shouted.

"What?" The man popped up out of nowhere.

"We have three minutes. At most. The Bahanians will get through," he told the man. "You have that long to make a choice between doing what you should have done in the first place, and spending a great deal more time with the people we have been trying so hard to avoid."

The man searched his eyes. "But," the man started.

"No if's or but's, man!" Estard yelled into his face. "Make your choice. Us or them?"

With a wordless growl of frustration, Greenway fell to his knees on the ground and did — something. Estard felt nothing from whatever Greenway was doing. And though some of the others were looking at them as if they'd grown two heads, no one else seemed to feel anything, either.

Whatever he did, it took less than two minutes. Then, as he got to his feet, anger writhing across his face, Estard felt something go through him. Like the aftermath of an electrical storm, when static hit the air.

The hate and tightly controlled anger that passed over Greenway was both visible and palpable.

Greenway and Weiz both watched him as he watched the sky and waited for the white-purple haze. If it came, he'd failed. If not, perhaps another ship would fall. He did wonder, however, if the Bahanians had abandoned ship before the heat ray.

As relief swept through him, at the apparent success of what

Greenway had done, Estard looked to Weiz and said, "There's something that has been bugging me since the first time I came back."

"Oh? Just one thing?"

"Where's Harvey?"

CHAPTER TWENTY-SEVEN

For the first time since he'd gotten his powers, he felt helpless. Afraid of what might come next. To the outside observer, it had probably looked like he had just shifted the way he normally would, but he hadn't. It was unlikely they even knew he was trapped.

He was aboard a ship, he was sure of that much, but he couldn't shift. No matter how hard he tried. No matter the place he visualised. And he did try, every second.

Now he understood how the others must have felt every time the Bahanians had shown up. It had never felt entirely real to him. Because they couldn't catch him. There wasn't a whole lot he could do to stop them from getting other people, and doing things he'd rather they didn't, but he'd known *he* would always be free.

It was like being back on Earth again. Only then he wasn't so desperate to get away. Well, not really. If he could be back on Earth, he would gladly give up his power. But he'd have to make sure the others could be there too. They'd been through too much together to just leave them behind.

He shook himself hard out of the daydream. He didn't understand why it was becoming so hard for him to concentrate.

The room he was in looked like the inside of the brig. Four uniform walls, and darkness.

They must have come up with something new, to trap him the way they had. He hadn't seen any Bahanians on the ground, so he had to assume they'd picked him up with the same tech they'd used on Deidra, though he'd thought that wouldn't reach the surface. And after they'd been so certain that tech wouldn't work anymore. That they were safe. How many of the others had been picked up?

With a frustrated yell, he snapped his arm out in a punch at the wall. It connected with a dull thwack, and his hand came away bruised. He didn't think he'd ever felt so helpless in his life. Except for maybe when his wife had been dying.

Apart from Lance and Greenway, whom the Bahanians had begun work on immediately, everyone had mentioned having to wait long periods before and between seeing the Bahana men.

"Just calm down," he told himself in a whisper. "Wait and be patient. You will find your moment. Find how they are keeping you here and do something about it. You were an airman, long before any of this. Use your head."

It was like a prayer sent and answered as a door opened and a man dressed in all white walked in, the door closing behind him. He stopped just inside, scratched at his chin, and looked at Harvey as if assessing what he was and what he was doing there.

Harvey stared at the man without words. What could he have said? Should he have asked all the usual questions? Waited for the usual responses? Let them know that he was in every way an average man?

They stood facing each other for longer than would normally have been comfortable, but in the game of it, didn't seem too long at all. The man even quirked a tiny smile, before re-schooling his face to stillness.

"So, you're stuck, then?" the man asked finally.

"Nah," Harvey responded in an exaggerated fashion. "Just don't have anywhere better to be."

The man took a step forward and looked him up and down, tilting his head first to the left and then the right. "I don't believe that," he said after a while. "Though I appreciate the sarcasm. Days aboard a ship can be quite dull."

"Guess you weren't aboard one of the ships I had a better time on, then," Harvey replied.

The man quirked another smile. "No. No, I wasn't."

"Are you going to let me go?"

"It's possible. Though, not any time soon."

"I see."

"Do you?" He scratched at his chin again, and Harvey felt an itch building on his jaw that he tried hard to ignore. "I'm not sure even I do."

Harvey raised his brows. "It's your work, isn't it?"

"Yes, yes. We've tamed the Walker. But what do we do with you? Cut you open like the rest? Assess whatever it is that makes you the way you are? We've had very little success so far in that arena."

"And yet you continue."

"In Greenway we found some minor physiological differences. But, nothing that would indicate where the power lies. Much like your predecessors. So, we have to assume it lies somewhere in the neurons of your brain. We did try to look into that other man's mind, you'll have to provide me with his name."

"Lance Viatri."

"Lance Viatri, thank you." He gave a nod. "We attempted to see what was ticking in there, but it's a very difficult thing to do. One minor slip, we kill you, and you end up in that place where you revive. It's a curious thing. In some ways, you're all just as vulnerable as we are."

"So, what's the alternative?" Harvey wanted to know.

The man blinked at him a few times, a frown forming. "Ask, I suppose. What is it, that makes you capable of such feats? How is it, that your power alone works when others do not?"

"Through your null field?"

"Just so."

Harvey barked a laugh. "You're joking?"

"I fail to see the humour in it."

"Even if I could tell you what you wanted to know, you really think I would give away my one advantage against you? I mean, you've clearly worked out a way around it." He spun a circle, arms wide, indicating the room he was held in. "You must know that, or I wouldn't be here."

"That's just the thing, though. Why are you here?"

On the last word, the man began to stretch tall and become distant. The room flashed bright, and then dulled. His face was too close to Harvey, while the feet too far away. It was like suddenly looking through a fish-eye lens.

Harvey was so taken aback by the sudden change, he felt sick, and tried to take a step back. He wanted to vomit so bad, his stomach contracted, even as his throat tried to choke it down. The feeling stemmed from his forehead and travelled down his oesophagus, then settled right on top of his solar plexus. He couldn't remember the last time he had felt so suddenly and violently ill.

Hunched over with one hand pressed to the wall, keeping him propped up, and one hand cradling his stomach, he emptied its contents. Over and over, his stomach contracted and vomited a stream of what seemed to be thickened water.

The man was saying something to him, but it made no sense to his ears. Either he was losing, or had temporarily lost his ability to understand Bahanian, or something was very, very wrong.

Another stream of water escaped his mouth, while at the same time he felt he was drowning in it, breathing it deep. There was pressure on his shoulder, his chest, his back. A light, so bright in his eyes that he thought he had a migraine coming in. It came and dulled, effectively keeping him blind.

He could hear more people, though he didn't hear the door open. He tried to make his way blindly, even as he doubled over with another stream of water vomit. He pushed out with his free arm in a vain effort to push any obstacles from his way. Even if he had no idea where he was going, if he could just get to the door, maybe he would be able to shift.

Before he could make it, he felt a sharp sting on his left cheek. Repeated three times. And there was a foul smell beneath his nose, that he tried to struggle away from. It was then he realised, he was on the floor. He had at least three people around him, one of which, straddled his torso. He still couldn't see, everything was much too bright, but he was starting to make out the voices.

"... in the stasis tank, we won't be able to keep him. Work something out." It sounded like a woman, and from further away. Perhaps through a radio.

"We keep him in there, and he's liable to kill himself. You know what happens if he does that." It was the man to his left.

"Find a way," was all the woman said.

He could tell from the discontent grumbles that none of those surrounding him felt like the woman was being reasonable. Also, she was gone.

"Any ideas?" asked the man on top of him.

Even as they tried to find an alternative for him, he wondered if he would be able to shift, now. Clearly, he was not where he had thought he was in the beginning. If the prison they'd made for him was not real, there would be nowhere real for him to shift, and so he couldn't. But it sounded to him as if he were back in the real world now. And his stomach had settled. He listened intently to his captors.

"Locklear is a moron," a female voice from the back of the room. "We all know she wouldn't be in charge here if her father wasn't the General Director."

"What difference does that make?" asked the man on his right. Or *a* man, he supposed, there could be more than one. It was one of the reasons he hadn't yet tried to shift. He couldn't see.

"She means we won't be the ones faulted if he gets away," put in the man on top of him. "She's in charge, she takes the fall. Because her father installed her the way he did, she has to be better and more capable than anyone else who might have taken the position, and he will be under scrutiny if she fails."

"And so he should be," the woman grumbled.

"Either way, he has to go back into stasis if we're going back to Bahana. There is no way we can just leave him in a cell for that trip. If he wakes up, he won't stay long, you know it."

He felt the man on top of him shudder. "Could you imagine being awake for that?"

Harvey could now tell that he had some kind of mask on, or perhaps just goggles. He could feel the pressure of it on his cheeks and across the bridge of his nose, though he had felt nothing with his lashes. If he shifted, he could pull it off easily enough, though he didn't know what to do about the man straddling him.

He once again ignored the conversation as he concentrated on a place he could take them to get way. It really didn't matter where, but he wanted to be close to the others, so he had some help. He didn't want to give away just how awake he was, either. Which was difficult. He wanted to test his arms, but the men to either side were holding tight, which meant, even once he'd shifted, there was going to be a struggle to free himself from their grip. The question was if he did it here, or if he left them stranded wherever he landed.

"...awake." Harvey let the conversation soak back in on him, suddenly aware.

The men who held him were as still as a person could be. They barely even breathed, and Harvey kicked himself for not paying attention. They hadn't seemed to be talking about anything important. He had heard them, hadn't completely cut them out, but he hadn't been paying attention. And now he was pushing back in his recent memory for a clue as to what had been said.

"What do we do?" whispered the one on his left.

He felt a single hand remove itself from his right shoulder, and he didn't hesitate even for a second. He completely wrenched his right arm around, and as soon as the man lost his grip on it, he shifted with the other two.

The man straddling him was already falling sideways to the ground even as he used the momentum in his right arm to punch the man on his left. The man let go before the punch even connected, and Harvey shifted again. Two down. Once the one who had been straddling him finished his fall, he would be free of them. And they would have a hard time finding one another, because he put them on different worlds. Perhaps it was cruel, but it would be new lives for them.

Finally free of his captors, Harvey took the mask from his eyes and looked around. He was where he had meant to be, so his ability was working as it should. They hadn't used some kind of new null field on him, it had definitely been the stasis that had him unable to shift. For that he was grateful. He did wonder if they would come after him, or if they'd just leave.

After taking a moment to calm himself, he looked down at his half-dressed form and found himself once again thanking Major Preston for leaving the kits. Walking around barefoot in his underwear for the next three months or so did not appeal.

Though he was where he'd meant to be, none of the others were around, and for the first time he had to question how long he'd been gone. Not too long, or they wouldn't have still been in orbit. He was certain of it.

He was about to shift again, when he heard a voice behind him.

"How fascinating," said the man from the cell, walking toward him slowly and looking around as if he'd never seen wilderness before. "That of all the places you could have gone, you chose here."

Harvey shook his head and tried to shift, but nothing happened. He tried again, and nothing. His eyes found the man again and he launched himself at him, all the anger and frustration of the moment channelled into a tackle that should take the man to the ground. But it didn't. Harvey, instead, went straight through him, landing hard on the ground.

"I think you'll find that kind of thing doesn't work on me," the man informed him.

"Who are you?" Harvey wanted to know. Was he a Giant? Did he have some sort of power of his own? Was it tech? He had many questions.

"You can call me Liam," he said as he dropped into a squat over him.

"What do you want from me?"

"Exactly as I've said, we want to know what makes you able to do the things you do."

"Are you real?"

The man laughed. "Depends on what you mean by real. I am here, in front of you. I have my own thoughts with which to speak to you. I simply do not possess a real body."

Harvey sat up and wrapped his arms around his knees, clenching his left wrist with his right hand. The next question he doubted would be answered honestly, and he might be left confused.

"Did I really escape?"

The man sat down beside him and emulated the way he sat.

"No," he admitted. "You're still in a pod. On your way to Bahana, in fact."

"I can't work it out," Harvey grumbled. "How did you get me? I was with the rest of them. If you took me, you should have taken them all, but you haven't."

"What makes you say that?"

"You have them?"

"No. But I wonder what made you so sure we didn't."

With a finger, Harvey gestured all around him at the world, though at nothing in particular. "All this is a computer program?"

"Yes," Liam agreed. "Though possibly not in the same way that you understand it to be."

"So, we'll agree on that. But, assuming that your tech works anything at all like ours does — and I assume this knowing very little about our own — you would require a person to create an avatar of them. You could get close approximations, very close even, but any kind of scrutiny might pick it apart. You didn't think you could fool me with what you were capable of creating on your own, so you simply didn't do it."

Liam nodded along to the whole thought. "For someone who seems quite a simple man, you do know how to think. You are correct in your assumptions. Though, only partially. I could not make an avatar convincing enough."

"So how did you get me?" Harvey really wanted to know. He couldn't work that one out in his own mind.

"Your memory in imperfect. But, if you must know, we still have people on the ground. Someone sent you up, unconscious, though why only you, I couldn't say. Perhaps you were the only opportune target. Perhaps you went off alone to relieve yourself or take a moment. Or you were left behind momentarily for some task."

"In other words, you don't know."

"Just so," Liam agreed.

"Are you the program?"

"No," the man shook his head and looked into the distance. "I am, however, the only being who can move through the scenarios with a person."

"Some kind of AI?" Harvey was more curious than scared at this point. He didn't believe that he would be hurt in this place.

Again, Liam shook his head. "I am what is left of the Enatwa. After we ran from the Giants, as you call them. Greenway's short stint among us was illuminating, but we still don't know much about you."

"And what did you call them?"

"Our friends." The smile he gave was tight and full of pain. "We found a world, somehow connected to ours, though we hadn't known it at the time. Thirty-eight ships, four different directions, and I can't say what happened to the rest. Not everyone knew about them. Us Enatwa were as suspicious of each other as we were of outsiders. And, it turns out, we were right to be."

"Why are you telling me these things?" Harvey asked, head spinning. "A moment ago you were interrogating me for the Bahanians, whatever you might call yourself."

Liam tilted his head a little to look at Harvey. "Partly, because we have never told it. Partly, because we wish you to understand how things turned out the way they did. And I wasn't asking for the Bahanians. I was asking for the others."

"Then I am all ears, my friend," Harvey assured. "I have nowhere else to be until you allow me to leave."

"I appreciate that," Liam said, as if he truly meant it. "That you would give it freely, and I would not have to take it. Most of the others in this place don't understand at all. They are our descendants, and they have no clue. I tried to teach them, for a while. But they all seemed to leave believing I was just a program. An AI, as you put it, with a pretty story to tell."

"But if you were once a person — or people? — with feelings and flaws, that changes things considerably."

"Only to me, I suppose. Where was I?"

"You were as wary of each other as outsiders," Harvey provided.

"Ah yes, we were. And for good reason. I can tell you know of our mountain home. It was all that some of our people were aware of. Despite what she believes, the *Goddess of knowledge* does not know half as much as she thinks she does, because prior to the incident, she was a mere civilian, passing through a testing area that she had no idea existed. And while her power allowed her knowledgeable access to all she was aware of, it did not include secrets she did not know existed. At least, that's how I believe it works.

"Anyway, I digress, mostly because I had a relationship with the woman before it happened. Tatiana was her name, and she was a wonderful, lighthearted woman whom I regret to have lost."

"You found your own kind of immortality, though," Harvey noted.

"I suppose I did, at that. But it's less immortality, more a memory. Anyway, after the incident, that we were unaware of for some time, because the techs in charge had not known that anyone was in the vicinity when the malfunction occurred, we went looking for the affected people. They had started grouping up. Though she clearly didn't know how she knew these things, Tatiana had started gathering them, and teaching them about who and what they were, becoming a kind of de facto leader. And I, her spouse, and member of a secret faction working on new things, found out, quite by accident. I struggled with it, as I am sure you can understand, before I came to the conclusion that we had to do something about them."

"Why? Why do something about them? Why not just leave them alone?"

"Because some of them were already displaying such tendencies as you may have witnessed in Greenway." He shook his head. "I hope you know it was not entirely on him, what he became."

"Yes, I know it. The question is how do you?"

"I know everything that every person who has passed through one of these pods knows. Though I choose to discard a great deal of it. All the personal stuff, usually. Knowledge won't hurt, I have plenty of space for that, but feelings? They're too easy to get confused with one's own."

The man paused for a moment, and Harvey let him. It all sounded rather convoluted, to him. But if he was going to be stuck in this place for the foreseeable future, then listening to him was about as good as watching a movie, he supposed. It didn't have to be good, it just needed to fill the time.

Then it occurred to him. If they'd got him, they were probably never going to let him out of stasis. If they didn't let him out, then he would have no chance to escape. He was going to have to rely completely on the others to find him and set him free. Only, how would they be able to do that? If the EMP field was still in effect, and the last MM ship had been irreparably damaged when Viatri had done whatever it was he'd done to the ionosphere, they would have no way to get to him.

But there must, in the very least, be breaks in the EMP effect, else they would not have been able to trap me here in the first place. As much as the thought angered him, it also soothed him. If the Bahana men had caught him, then his people would be able to find him. That simple.

"Now that you've worked that out for yourself, I might continue," Liam told him.

"I guess so," Harvey agreed, a little annoyed at having been so easily read.

"We bombed the gathering." He said it so bluntly that it took a moment to really grasp what he meant. "There was death and destruction everywhere. Many thought that it had been the anti-tech

Uragoans, who had been setting fires to our farms and attempting entry into the mountain. They had the means, for they'd stolen it. So why not them? I think even Tatiana believed so. Though, by the time we got around to it, there was not much of her left. Certainly not much in the way of emotions. It was how I had found her out in the first place. Too logical by half for the woman I knew her to be. The woman I'd married." He smiled in memory of a woman who had disappeared thousands of years ago.

"We thought that would be the end of it. The damage done would prevent those who survived from gathering again. Of something close to eighty people, only twelve survived unscathed, a further seven badly injured. But, that's when we all discovered, they could not die. And as you can imagine, there was a great deal of discussion around that.

"Portuswain, my immediate superior, was convinced that we'd found the answer to immortality. It was something that many people of our time yearned for. Without a belief that something came after, what else could you strive for but a furtherance of your own life? And in that vain, they tried as best they could to recreate the experiment, meanwhile, leaving the *Giants* to their own business. Though we monitored them. Especially those who displayed egomaniacal tendencies.

"The experiment, as was accidentally released on those civilians, could never be repeated. Because it had been a malfunction. We had never noted what the malfunction was, and guessing and grasping at straws, got us nowhere. Meantime, some of the *Giants* had gone out into the world, where we could not easily follow, and they had convinced the Uragoans that they were their gods. That they could look after them and remove the scourge that was the Enatwa."

"What was the original experiment?" Harvey stretched and stood. Though he knew they were in some kind of simulation, for some reason, he could still feel stiff. Liam stayed seated.

"Something to do with micro blasting stone, as far as I am aware. I knew the project existed, but not how it worked. I wasn't a scientist, I just represented the people."

"A politician?"

"As you understand the word, I suppose so. Though we didn't have a government."

Harvey's mind stretched to understand how a society could have representatives, but not a government. Small tribes within a greater alliance, perhaps? Each his own little chieftain. He shook his head and sighed at himself. "Continue," he told Liam absently. "I wish to know how this ends."

Liam bowed his head and did as bid. "We had hunting parties sent out to deal with them. At the time, we were unaware of their Giant form, or their more innate abilities. A lot of good people never came home from that. Those who did, told stories of horror and fear. We decided it was time to break away. It had become too dangerous for us to exist as we were. Between the Uragoans being cheered on by their *Gods* and those who had become the *Giants*, we were outmatched. We had weapons, of course, but nothing compared to what is available now. If we didn't leave, we were going to be crushed.

"There were more than a few starship projects. As there was more than one mountain, though the *Giants* never knew of them. Or so we thought. We considered just moving to another continent and starting over. Or joining with another mountain. But, we found much too late, that the *Giants* had already made light work of such places. I don't know how they'd found out, though I'd have to assume the Uragoans close by might have had something to do with it. And I should have known better. I was losing the faith of my people."

"No disrespect here," Harvey broke in. "As much as I am curious to understand the origins of this little war, I've just had a thought."

"What is it?"

"I thought you could read my mind."

"I can, but I'd rather you just tell me," the man said.

"Why did you allow me to escape? I mean, I know I didn't really, but... I deviated away from the program designed for this place, did I not?"

Liam gave a shrug. "Not really. I didn't influence it in any way except to try and question you. I should not have been there. Perhaps it was my presence that triggered the Response Protocol."

"Care to explain what that is?"

"There are others like you in this place. You know that, right?" Harvey gave a quick nod of the head. He had known, he just hadn't thought about it.

"Well, the mind must remain active in stasis," Liam informed. "If it doesn't, the body will die. It's brain death, in its simplest form. So, if we skipped to the end of my tale, I tell you that I, among many others, developed the stasis programs. I was one of the test subjects. I got stuck in here, while my body died."

Harvey almost laughed, though he understood it was a tragedy. Perhaps an irony. Another who had found some kind of immortality. "I see. But this Response Protocol, what is it?"

"A simulation to see how you would react coming out of stasis. It takes into account your status — Prisoner, Passenger, or Crew — and whatever input the program derived from you already. Some of which includes a kind of mind reading, though that's not really what it is."

"Alright. I am here, I did what I did. I escaped to other worlds, and dropped off my would be guards before coming here. What does the computer do with that information?"

"It just tells the technician the risk of allowing you out of stasis long enough to transport to another facility. They can either come up with a plan that will counteract you, or they will leave you where you are."

Harvey threw up his hands. "Wonderful," he told the sky. That probably meant they were unlikely to move him, and he would not have a chance to free himself. He'd gathered as much already, but having it confirmed was another blow to the guts.

"Do you wish me to finish my little history lesson?" Liam asked, a brow raised.

"Sure," Harvey replied with a wave of his hand. "Go right ahead. I have nothing else to do, do I?"

"The Uragoans might have known about the mountain homes, but they didn't know about the Projects, which were never conducted within the cities. Some small ones that came close, perhaps, might eventually become integrated, but most were not. We'd already built and tested several ships that would make it to orbit and stay there for as long as we had food and water to continue. If we had somewhere else to go, then there we would go.

"We took all the ships, leaving none behind. We wanted no chance that any of the *Giants* would follow us. We spent years in orbit, testing new systems, creating this." He put his arms out and spun first one way and then the other, as far as he could while sitting. "We had a few destinations in mind. As much as we'd wanted to explore our own system first, we knew that it wasn't habitable. Of thirty-eight ships, nineteen came to Bahana. I do not know where the others went. Where they ended up. Perhaps they're still out there somewhere, in stasis, waiting to be woken. Though I doubt it."

"Sounds like a fun time," Harvey said sarcastically. "Let me finish the tale for you, though. The crew and everyone else on board were eager to start a new life and leave the old world behind. But there were some who believed it was beholden to you to fix what had been broken. Those who would go back, again and again, to Eridu —"

"Urago," Liam corrected.

"Urago. And hunt down and collect the Giants, in an attempt to cure them. I don't suppose you had anything to do with that?"

"No, absolutely not," Liam defended. "If I could have, I would have influenced them in the opposite direction."

"But either way, the war continued. At least until the generation that made the move, died out."

"Yes, I would say that's accurate." Liam confirmed.

Harvey sat back down next to the man. "So, what happened to your people? How did they become the Bahanians? How did they just move on?"

He shrugged. "I don't know."

"So, you don't know what happened to them?"

"Not first hand. Only as a history fed to me by the sleepers."

"Are you only on this one ship? Or all of them? If it were destroyed, would you persist?"

Liam laughed for a moment before answering while trying to hold down a chuckle. "Me as I am here would cease to exist, but there are copies of the program, including me, the aberration that they don't know about."

Harvey felt at his chin as he gave a slow nod. "You've never shown yourself to one of these people before?" Liam shook his head. "Then why show yourself to me?"

"Nostalgia? Curiosity? My mind is stuck in an unreal world. I wanted to know how you had come into your power. Why it was different from the others."

"And you can't read my mind?"

"Not in the way that you imagine. More memories than explanations. I can see what happened, but I don't know the why of it."

Harvey nodded. "And what's your assessment?"

Liam looked to the sky and seemed to swallow before responding. "I knew Anselin," he said. "He was a good friend. Another representative. He knew as much as I did about the Projects. But he never told the others. Not a whisper, not a word. At least, none of those who ended up in this ship, which is where they store all those they do not wish to revive."

"If they store them here, and the mind must remain active, the ship would never be turned off. Not completely."

"Correct," Liam seemed to approve of the logic.

"So, since the first of them went into stasis, you have been 'awake'," he said using air quotes.

"As long as the ship remains on, I remain awake, yes."

Another reminder that it was unlikely he was ever going to be woken. "Do you speak to the others?"

"Some of them," Liam confirmed. "Some I don't know to speak to. Some prefer to remain in ignorance of their situation. Some are stuck somewhere between awareness of the outside, and the world in here."

"You don't know me."

"No, but you are an oddity. The traditional null field does not work on you. And Anselin gave you his power. No one knew that they could do that." He scratched at his chin in thought. "I have come to believe that the incident may have been set off by Anselin. That he knew, somehow, what might happen."

"I am not Anselin, though."

"No. But why did he choose you? Over ten thousand years as a Giant, and they give their powers to the first aliens to set foot on the planet." He looked genuinely confused. "They had ample opportunity, if they had wished it, to pass the power on to whoever they wanted."

"Apparently they tried," Harvey told him. "But, for the most part, it came down to a few things. First, they didn't know how to give up their power, and it was the first six who showed them how. They chose us, because they believed that we would eventually leave, taking the curse of it with us. They were wrong about that part."

"There's more," Liam insisted.

"They thought we'd be able to fight you. Though, at first, they thought we *were* you. It's a strange world your people made."

"That may be true."

"You have sated my curiosity," Harvey let him know. "Have I sated yours?"

"In as much as you can, I suppose," he replied

"Will you help me get out of here?"

Liam looked him up and down with a frown. "Why would I do that?"

"Look into my mind, I know you can," he instructed the man. "Tell me I am not a person worth saving. That my boy, Jason, is a child who deserves to grow up without his father. All for a mistake. For something none of us asked for. And you'll see, too, that we'll work on a way out of this. That we *want* to go home."

Harvey waited, eyes on the apparition of a man. Not trying to stare him down, just drill into him the desperation that he felt. His sincere desire to leave all this behind and go home, where he belonged.

"You really think she can do it?" Liam asked after a while.

"Who do what?" Harvey asked, confused.

"The scientist who has Tatiana's power. Deidra. Do you think she can really put all the powers back into the world. Remove the curse?" He actually sounded hopeful.

"I honestly don't know," Harvey admitted. "But she hasn't steered us wrong so far. As scientists go, she might be the only one that I trust."

"If she can do that, she can cure them all." There was something in the man's eyes now, that Harvey had not seen before. Hope, maybe.

Harvey shook his head a little and then stopped himself. "Them all?"

"Well, the ones I feel safe letting go, at least."

"And you have the power to do that? Let us go?"

Liam looked up to the fake sky of his made-up world. "I can wake you, but that is the extent of it. You will have to get them out. And I need to trust you to do that. Can I? That is the question I ask myself. Can I trust you?"

"How many?"

"Thirty-one."

Harvey swallowed and asked in a dry voice. "That's not all of them?"

"A little under half," Liam said, looking at him now.

With a deep breath, Harvey gave a nod. "Alright. I'll do it. In as much as it is possible for me to do so. I will keep transporting until I can transport no more."

Liam gave a nod. "I suppose that will have to do. I have waited a long time for this." He gave Harvey a last look. "Do it. Do what I could not and save my people."

And Harvey woke.

CHAPTER TWENTY-EIGHT

Weiz was beside herself, both angry and scared. It wasn't like the man to go off by himself, especially without saying anything to anyone, which could only mean one thing. But he was immune to their null field, and if it were possible to do so, he would have come back already. At least, Deidra thought so.

Despite any difficulties it may cause him, Harvey was not a man to run away from his responsibilities. She couldn't imagine that he'd just taken a time out. And after Estard's little adventure, that he'd relayed to them with animated sentences, Deidra believed it was possible that he'd been taken. Not just somewhere on the world, but up in one of the ships.

They had done a cursory sweep of their perimeter and had sent Fyord and Hadley to check out the field where they resurrected. So far, nothing had been found to indicate what Estard had told them. But the ship had fallen from the sky almost immediately, and Deidra had to agree that the field had stopped working.

It had been more than an hour since Greenway had done his

thing and taken off. Deidra did wonder if they'd see him again any time soon. If he was capable of suppressing the nature of the Giant inside him.

She felt a hand come down on her shoulder, and she knew without turning that Dane was trying to comfort her. "Nothing ever goes as planned, does it?" She sighed.

"Very rarely," he replied. "But with these people, in this place, I am tempted to say more often than usual."

Deidra put her hand on his and squeezed a little. "There's something I am missing," she told him. "And I don't even know where to start looking."

"Because Harvey's missing?"

"Partly. That makes me more wary. We can't just go off to some other location, hide ourselves away until it's done. We can walk wherever we please, but we'll be trackable to any Bahanians who missed the boat."

"How likely is it that we'll run into those remnants, do you think? And even if we do, their tech wont work. Or, at least it shouldn't." His soothing voice almost sounded as if he were asking the question of himself, rather than her.

"I think that any of them close by will come at us if they believe we have the means to get them home," she admitted with a heavy sigh. "If we had Harvey, that would be true, but without him..." She didn't know how to finish.

"If we have to leave him behind," Dane started, but Deidra would not let him finish,

"Given the group we're with, how likely is it, you think, they will just leave the man behind? We might not know where he is, but if it were Weiz alone, I would wager she'd find out and go after him, regardless of where he ended up."

"And if he was on that ship that came down?"

"Then he'd wake in the field as per normal," she responded. Then almost laughed at herself, with the absurdity of that sentence. When did resurrecting after death become so normal, that she was no longer worried if one of her friends died?

"And if he was on a ship that made it away?" Dane continued, ignoring her snippy retort.

"Then we have no means by which to get to him. Unless we repair and somehow, refuel, one of the MM ships, which I think highly unlikely. And even if we did, assuming the EMP field that Greenway made is more permanent than Viatri's, we wouldn't be able to get it up into the air before a pulse knocked it out. And even should all that be a breeze to bypass, no one would know where to aim that ship."

"You do have a lot going on in there," he said, and kissed the side of her head. "I suppose you always do."

Weiz was busy trying to maintain her calm while others attempted to ignore her struggle. Until they could work out the fate of Harvey, they were stuck. Of all of them, Kristin seemed the most stoic. She'd just announced she was going to find them something to eat, and if anyone wanted to join her, they could. As long as they weren't loud about it. Estard, who Deidra thought would follow, had stayed behind, though she couldn't guess at his reasons.

"Should we just start here, and hope he turns up?" she wondered aloud.

"Well, I don't know about you, but I'd prefer somewhere with a little more shelter. I don't relish the prospect of spending my days on the side of a mountain."

"You don't?" She turned to look at him, and he placed his hands on her waist.

"Not even a little bit," he said, staring into her eyes.

She pushed off his chest and moved a foot away before it could get more intimate. Not that she didn't want to. Just that she was all too aware of the people she was surrounded by. To her mind, those moments required privacy. And they were unlikely to get it in this place.

"Shelter," she breathed. "We can find shelter, or we can build some. It doesn't take much."

"So, you want to stay here?" He sounded worried.

"We could move back toward the battlefield that never was," she offered. "Or go to the field. The others built a hut there for a reason. We could build something better, more suited to us."

"With what, exactly?"

She eyed him sideways, half convinced he was playing it dumb deliberately, and he knew how much she hated that. "Look around you," she told him. "We have an entire world at our disposal, and a great many of us with powers to help utilise it. But we could start with the barricade fencing that the soldiers left behind. I heard Harvey mention that at some point."

He threw up his hands. "I suppose it's not up to us, anyway. You'll have to convince your ATF friends that we have to move."

Deidra gave a slow nod. So that was the problem. That she was friendly with them. While there had been a time, not too long ago, where she might have shared his prejudice, she no longer could. She'd spent too much time with these people. Weiz, despite all of their differences and the fact they were almost the same age, she saw as an older sibling. Lance as a younger brother, Kristin as some annoying cousin to be put up with, even though she was the most self sufficient and least in her face. She just couldn't like her. Perhaps she'd spent too much time with Weiz and that feeling had rubbed off.

Harvey was the protective boyfriend of the older sister, which meant he was protective of all that she cared about, and that included Deidra. It might be an odd way to see them all, she supposed. But in the absence of her own family, she had adopted them as such. And Dane would just have to live with that.

"Weiz," she said firmly, eyes still on Dane. "Come here."

Though she couldn't see the woman, she could feel her shuffle over. "What is it?" she asked.

"I was thinking we should move and start building a shelter. Not too far. Just to the field. We can use the barricades to get a start."

She let herself look at the Commander then. Her face showed clearly how forlorn she felt. The struggle, in the loss she felt, and the responsibility she knew she held. Possibly even a struggle against some lingering side effects from overuse of her power.

Weiz nodded slowly. "Yes. Yes, that sounds like a good idea. Harvey could find us there easily."

"Best tell your people, then. Get them moving. We'll all take some of the load, carrying the fencing."

The Commander turned away and walked toward the others, a look of purpose taking place on her face. Deidra watched as she gathered them and let them know what was happening. There were times she looked and sounded like a leader, but this was not one of them.

They each took a pack, including the scientists. Deidra was thankful for her inherent Giant strength, because were she to have attempted to carry it any distance before that occurrence, she likely would have fallen on her face inside a few hundred metres. As it was, it was a bulky inconvenience she'd rather have done without. But she did like the idea of a change of clothes and some soap.

Once they were standing in front of the fallen barricading, Weiz instructed her people on how they might carry it between them. She mumbled something about needing to come back for a second trip, because the fencing at three-by-three metres, was too large for a single person to carry. And, even if they could, there still weren't enough of them to carry every one.

A lot happened in the that ten minutes that Deidra had mostly ignored. She wasn't sure how it began, or whose idea it was, but by the time they started making their way to the field, Ellis was floating eight sections of the fencing a foot above the ground like a Baby Rover. She had a look of intense concentration on her face, and Deidra couldn't tell if she'd make it, but she internally applauded the effort.

There was some argument with Viatri about how he might blow them along, and no one would have to carry anything. Thankfully, it was soundly defeated by the wisdom of his peers, letting him know just how dangerous and unpredictable that was liable to be. Weiz thought she might be able to make a large overland vehicle they would simply be able to stack them all onto, but was promptly reminded of the EMP issue. And fuel.

Estard stepped forward and offered a description of how a truck from the 1950's was made. "Not hardly any electricity needed," he told them. "Mostly combustion. And what electrical parts there are shouldn't be too badly affected, I think. Obviously, I am no scientist, and I could be wrong. But maybe worth a shot, if you can bring it in with a full tank." He looked to Deidra as if asking for some kind of approval.

Deidra gave a shrug. *Yes, it's fine. Should work, until the fuel runs out.* She repeated what Tatiana said to everyone else. Though Weiz seemed a little put out by the attempt, she warmed into it as Estard gave her every detail he could think of, and they ended up with what Estard called a semi. Ellis loaded the barricading into the back while Estard took the drivers seat with a smile. Weiz went up front with him, while those few who wanted a ride jumped into the empty second trailer. Those who didn't mind the walk, placed their packs inside, and walked along side it as it moved. Slowly.

"I thought vehicles from your time moved faster then this!" Lance told Estard through the window.

The man leaned out and gave him a look that expressed how stupid he thought that statement was. "On the road, maybe. But you try driving this thing over damp unpaved ground with a few ton in back. She's finding every dip, and I don't want to drive us headlong into a sink."

"What will we do about the river? Will it get through via the ford?" Gordon asked.

Weiz grumbled something completely inaudible, and probably not in English. "I'll make a bridge," she responded.

Tangentially, Deidra wondered why she could understand the natives, and the Bahanians, but she couldn't understand languages from her own world. *You could if you wanted to,* Tatiana told her. *Just concentrate, know what you're looking for, and it will come.* Why then were the native languages like listening to English, to the point where she often couldn't tell which language was being spoken. *Because they're our native tongues, though granted the Bahanian's derivation has drifted far from where we began.* Deidra sighed at the voice in her head. She couldn't fault it — it had the answers. And it was better than having answers and forgetting who she was. But she wished there were another way. Something somewhere in the middle that didn't make her feel like a crazy person.

Dane gave her a sideways glance, and she knew that her struggle with the inner voice was showing. "You doing okay?" he asked.

"Just fine," she responded.

The look he gave said he didn't believe her, but he let the matter drop, because he knew better than to push. He really was a great man, and not for the first time, she reminded herself of how much she loved him and why. He was kind, strong and often stubborn. He was supportive, understanding and occasionally arrogant. He would follow her to the end of the Earth and back, but remind her every step of the way that she was still a human being who needed rest and company, just like everyone else. He wasn't perfect, but he was perfect for her. And she often wondered if she was half as perfect for him, or if she just took him for granted.

"What are you thinking?" he asked. "I can see it there, behind those beautiful brown eyes."

She quirked a smile. "How much I love you," she told him honestly.

He stopped and swept her up off her feet, and she gave a squeal of surprise. He landed a kiss on her, and she melted into it before she remembered how public the arena was and tried to pull away. He let her.

When she was back on the ground, she gave his arm a squeeze and took a step to the side.

"When we have privacy, you will be paid in full," she said softly.

He smiled at her, but didn't respond. He knew exactly what he was in for.

~

Despite the way everyone behaved, Kristin could not believe that Harvey would just disappear without telling anyone. Weiz was beside herself, and she couldn't blame the woman.

She had to admit that since the Docker had come, the woman had stepped up to the job she was meant to represent, and she was glad for that. The respect she'd lost in those first months was slowly coming back, though not yet fully restored. They still had their baggage, even if Weiz didn't want to admit it.

As per usual, when it came down to what was happening next, she put her hand up for a hunt. After Estard's little time hopping escapade, which he told her all about, and in which she played almost no part, she felt the need to get her hands dirty. And she was hungry for something better than the rations the soldiers had left for them. To her surprise, Zim came, silent and broody.

It took them the better part of a day to find something worth shooting. What looked like a boar, though with feathers in its rear end, and the nubs of what once might have been wings, but now served as an extra set of feelers.

The creatures of this planet did often make her question the origins of life. Here was an ungulate that in it's distant genetic past, might have been a bird. Were there others like it? Did some of the breeds resemble ancient Earth myths? Unicorns, Pegasus, Griffin? Things of that nature. Though possible, she doubted it. But it did make her wonder how connected Earth might be to this world. And on which did humanity originate? Or was it simply parallel evolution with slight variation? It wasn't the first time she'd considered the subject.

Why had Heinrich chosen this world? That was something that had never been answered to her satisfaction. The scientists had worked out the where and the how, but not the why. Not so far as she could tell. Had he expected there to be Giants here? Or Gods? Had he expected people? Or any kind of creature, really. Had he expected to find life? Was that why he'd wanted to come to this place? How had he even found it?

"Can't get answers from a dead man," she mumbled to herself as she leaned over the dead boar to examine it.

"What dead man did you want answers from?" Zim asked. She'd actually forgotten the man was there.

"Heinrich," she replied simply as she shifted the animal to find a good angle from which to pick it up.

Zim moved forward, and with an ease that belied his slight frame, hefted it across the back of his shoulders. "Lead the way," he said. "And tell me why you are thinking of this dead man now."

It was an odd request to her mind, but she obliged, leading the way back to camp, and talking along the way. About the connections between Earth and Eridu, and how Heinrich had chosen this place.

"I heard him once, talking to himself," Zim said after she finished. "I don't think he knew I was nearby, because he certainly had no love for me. But he spoke about cave paintings and myths. So perhaps, our forefathers, in some way are connected. Or perhaps we grew independently on Earth, as similar as we might be. There was a dozen or more variety of human before known history. Perhaps they were one of them?" He shrugged and the boar bounced on his shoulders. Kristin was impressed by the nonchalance of it.

"A lot of perhaps in there, mate," she replied.

"Who can know for sure?" was all he said, then they fell into comfortable silence once again.

It was nearing night when they returned to where they had slept the previous night. Only Bridges remained, staring up at the sky.

"Where is everyone?" he asked. "No sign of Harvey?"

The man shook his head. "He could be with the others," he offered. "I don't know how his thing works."

"How long are you supposed to stay here?"

"Three days."

She looked at Zim then Bridges, then around at the sparsely placed trees until she found one that looked suitable. "We'll bleed and gut it here, stay overnight with Bridges," she told Zim, who gave a nod in response.

They spent the night in as near a silence as they had the hunt. Kristin didn't mind. It left her to her own thoughts. Like how was she going to deal with the Estard situation? She definitely had feelings for him, but he was a good fifteen years older than her, and five-hundred years behind the times. She found him attractive, and a little mysterious. But was that enough?

And did he really want her? Or just some idea of her that he had in his head? Some damsel that needed rescuing? Or a strong woman who needed a hand? Who was he looking at? Wondering on that question was part of her hesitation in committing to anything serious, despite her feelings. She knew it was a failing on her part, to concern herself so much with what he thought of her, instead of just taking it moment by moment.

The boar bled and gutted, her thoughts swirling too fast to keep up with, Kristin lay down for an early night, while the boys spoke quietly around a small fire. Her eyes on the sky, she wondered what had happened to Harvey. How he could possibly have disappeared, where he could possibly be. Might he be in the cells where she and the others had been kept? Why hadn't they thought of that earlier? *Because if he had been in one of those cells, there is nothing on this world that would prevent him from travelling wherever he pleased.*

"I hope you're well, Harvey," she said to the sky. "Come back to us soon."

~

Days passed by both slow and quick. Kristin, Zim and Bridges joined them at the field three days after they'd set up the barricades, so that they became a start to a small building with no roof. Nine, three-by-three rooms with three walls and no doors. It didn't give them much privacy, but it was a start, and it kept a few of them occupied with trying to find something suitable for the roofing and privacy screens.

Lance looked over at where Weiz stood next to the field. She'd been standing there so long, he had to wonder if she had even slept. He thought everyone had come to the same conclusion except her. Harvey was somewhere he couldn't come back from, or he would have been there already. Instead of standing vigil over an empty field, she should have been planning how they were going to get the man back from Bahana. Whatever they'd done to him, Lance was sure that was where they'd taken him. He just didn't know what to do about it. Yet.

Since the Bahana men were gone, and the scientists were doing their thing, the rest of them had found some strange ways to occupy themselves. Ellis was making piles of twigs and logs. She said it was kindling for fires, and that she used to do it when they'd first landed, though no one had noticed then. It perplexed him that she did it slowly by hand when she could have used her power, but he didn't judge it, or try to take it away from her.

Gordon and Estard had gone to find whatever useful things might be found, in the Bahanian cells, or the abandoned camps. What tech they found, they dumped at Deidra's feet, and she looked less than impressed with their offerings, but she always thanked them.

Fyord and Hadley, as strange a pair as they made, were always walking off somewhere, doing something they never cared to announce to anyone else. Lance didn't think they were romantic, more like best friends, though he could be wrong. And he struggled against the urge to follow them and find out what they were up to, sometimes. If he *was* wrong, there were some things he just didn't need to see.

Greenway hadn't come back since he'd done whatever he'd done to the core. He might well have been with Harvey. He might have been the one to take the man. Lance stood straight at the thought. It was the first time it had occurred to him that Harvey might not in fact be with the Bahanians. Then he sank. It was highly unlikely. The only reason that Harvey would not return to them was if he couldn't. And the only reason he wouldn't be able to, was if he was unconscious in some way shape or form. So, despite Greenway's abilities, Lance doubted he had him.

With a sigh, Lance took a step toward the woods in the distance. If he knocked a few over and left them to dry, they'd be fine enough to use as a roofing frame. He didn't know much about building, or wood, but he knew it started with drying some out.

"Where you going?" he heard Kristin ask from behind him. He turned to see her as she approached.

He explained, she listened. "I don't really have anything else to do," he finished with a shrug.

"The Commander is AWOL once again," Kristin said drily. "When the Captain returns, so will she."

"I don't know that she will," Lance returned. "Harvey is her life now. I don't know if she even cares about anything else. Or if she'd even try to pretend, now the Docker is gone."

Once they reached the trees, Kristin started looking around with purpose, tapping at trunks and pointing out trees she thought would be good. He wasn't going to argue, so he just marked them with a scratch at eye level.

"How many do you want?" Kristin asked.

"However many you think we might need to get us a good shelter going," he replied.

They spent the next few days knocking them down, dragging them out and stripping them bare. They elevated them and let the dry out. Though neither of them were too sure how long that might take, one of the scientists came around on the fourth day and said they were doing a good job. He was taking a break from what he thought was pure mathematical nonsense that theoretically shouldn't work. But here they all stood with their powers, and it made no sense at all. Lance shrugged and told the man he was just a pilot and couldn't help.

"I know that," he replied. "I just needed to get it off my chest. And that's a lot harder to do with your boss." Then he promptly turned and went somewhere else.

Lance and Kristin just frowned at each other, then shrugged, before getting back to their work.

Within two weeks they were staring at Weiz, who stared at the field, and dared each other to ask the woman to make them some tools for the wood. They played best out of three for Rock Paper Scissors, and Lance won.

The scientists weren't monopolising the Commander yet, but Lance had no doubt it would happen soon enough. Whether or not the wood was dry enough, they needed to get started.

A small crowd gathered behind them, and someone was taking bets. It sounded like Gordon. Estard stood beside Kristin, a protective arm around her shoulder. "You don't have to do it," he told her. "We can find another way to get this done."

She looked at him with pursed lips and both eyes wide. "Since when have I ever let her mood sway me?"

"Never," he answered.

"That's right," she said. "So why would I change that now, just cause she's having a sulk? Could be, maybe she needs the distraction, and no one has bothered giving her that 'cause she's the Commander and you're all too shit scared of her."

Hadley seemed to arch up at that. "Oi," she said from behind. "Not shit scared, *mate*, just don't care."

A few of the others laughed at that. Even Kristin barked a short one. But Lance thought Kristin was brave as hell. Not because he thought Weiz would do anything, but putting up with her in a foul mood like that was a courage all of its own.

Kristin took a deep breath and let it out fast, then turned to Lance with a smile. "Time to get her done," she said, and started moving.

"Good luck," he breathed in response, and watched as she stopped beside Weiz and started talking.

To no one's surprise, the Commander refused. Didn't even turn to look at Kristin. Then Kristin said something so low, that even with their somewhat super powered hearing, they couldn't understand, and Weiz turned to her, face enraged. She replied with something equally as low, and Lance had to fight against the desire to get closer just to know what was being said. But whatever Weiz said ended with Kristin slapping her hard across the face. He heard more than one stunned gasp behind him.

It took a moment, but then Weiz slapped her back, and it was on. Two women rolling in the mud, wrestling and slapping. Under different circumstances he might have enjoyed the show, but between these two, it just disturbed him. It looked close a few times, and the whole thing didn't last longer than three or four minutes. Eventually it was Weiz who came out on top, making Kristin tap out with an arm bar. If they'd taken bets on who'd win, Lance would have lost.

When she got up, she offered Kristin a hand and the woman took it. To his surprise, Weiz was smiling, and so was Kristin. They started making their way over to Lance, and he heard the people behind him scatter. He wasn't sure what they thought was going to happen. Weiz looked happier now than she had since they'd got there.

"Show me your logs Viatri, and we'll work out what we need to get them all cut up and cured." Weiz said as she approached.

Oddly, he began to feel wary of her. "Yes, Ma'am."

They spent the next few days cutting and curing the wood. Weiz made a walk-in kiln that sped the process up, but even then, it was as boring a process as Lance had ever taken part in. And it didn't improve Weiz's mood.

From time to time, Deidra stopped by and spoke to Weiz. For reasons that Lance would never understand, the two of them seemed fairly close. Though he would have bet his life that Harvey would make Weiz forget Deidra even existed, if he turned up.

Lance shot a guilty look at the field. They hadn't even bothered trying to find the man. They'd all decided that if he could get back, he would, and he had a greater chance of success than they would in finding him and getting him out of wherever he was. But even so, Lance remembered when the man had come for him, and helped him, yet he had done nothing to return the favour.

He felt Ellis beside him as she gently touched his hand. He turned to look at her.

"Don't feel too bad about it," she told him. "None of us did anything. Not because we don't want to. But because there is nothing we can do, right now."

He grunted at her. He hadn't realised he'd spoken. He knew it was the truth, though that didn't stop the feeling of guilt from building.

When the last load of wood was drying out in the kiln, Lance went to Deidra and asked the question that had been on his mind since she'd asked him to charge the ionosphere. How were they supposed to divest their powers in order to go back home. She had offered an estimated amount of time, but she had never explained the how. But he had an idea. Though he didn't know if it was viable.

"What are we doing?" Deidra responded. "Math, for the most part. But I don't really know how to apply it in this circumstance. It's not even clear where we start." She seemed genuinely puzzled.

"Why are you starting with math at all?" He wanted to know. "When, in any of this, have we ever used an ounce of math or science? Why don't we just play by the rules of the powers? Give them back?"

She raised her brows at him. Surprise? Or did she think he was a moron? It took her a moment to answer.

"What do you mean by 'give them back'?"

"If we can choose to give them away, why can't we just choose to put them back into the world instead?"

"We would have to —" she started, but he cut her off.

"No," he said firmly. "We won't. They only did it because they wanted to be done. It probably never even occurred to them that they could just give the powers to the world. Why would it? The world didn't give them their powers, men did."

"And if it doesn't work? What then? Back to the math and science you seem to scorn so much?"

Lance held up both hands in supplication. "If it doesn't work, then it doesn't work. Nothing changes. But if it does? It'll save you an awful lot of time. And I have to tell you, the other scientists don't know how to make it work, either. They've expressed what they think of your 'science' to us."

"Oh?" Her interest was piqued. "Do tell."

"They think it's nonsense. And there is no way to make it work."

"Just because they don't understand it yet, doesn't mean it won't work," she responded defensively.

"Do *you* understand how it works?"

She bit at her bottom lip and Lance could see her trying to formulate a response. Something that would make sense to him, not just her. Then he realised, she did understand, even if she couldn't articulate it. That, though she didn't yet know how to use it, the tools were there.

"I'm sorry," he said before she found the words she was looking for.

She waved a hand "No, you're probably right. The question is who wants to try first? Before the Docker comes back? Time was I would have done it in a heartbeat. But now..."

"Now you're afraid to live without it on this world," he finished for her.

"Maybe. Or maybe, I don't want to live without it at all," she admitted. "I just don't want to be attached to this place. But if the knowledge available through Tatiana allows me to keep them while removing that attachment? Do you think it's not worth it?"

"To take the powers home with us?"

"Yes."

"So, you're trying to remove the attachment, not the powers?" He felt at the back of his head.

"Yes," she repeated.

"But what if we want to get rid of the powers? Like Greenway. I am certain he'd rather live without them."

Deidra did a slow look around at the people they shared the camp with. "Have you seen him? He left us. Again. I know I should be more forgiving. That a great deal of the issue is his power. But he could have stuck around. Let us help him through it."

Lance couldn't help but nod in agreement. His own

consequences were new to him, but the potential for devastation was great. "I tell you what," he said after a moment. "I will volunteer to attempt to put the powers into the world. And if I can make that happen, then others will have a choice."

"You don't want to keep them?" Deidra seemed honestly surprised.

He shook his head. "What use are they in an ordinary life?" he asked. "If any of us go back to Earth with the powers still in us, and someone finds out? Likely we'll be treated no better than we were by the Bahanians."

The look on her face told him she'd never considered that. "You really believe that?"

"You're a scientist. You should know best."

Whatever she was thinking seemed to disturb her a great deal. Her eyes turned distant, her face took on a look of disgust, and the next words she uttered sounded as desperate and hopeful as any he'd ever heard. "No one would tell, though, would they?"

Lance shrugged and shook his head. "I wouldn't," he replied. "But I can't speak for everyone."

Whatever she was about to say next was lost in a look of surprise, and the Scientist stared behind him for a moment before she pushed past, and he turned to see what she was looking at. Two by two, half naked people were appearing next to the field. All looking dazed and confused. Men and women of differing heights and colours. He counted as they came and started with ten. He knew no more were coming when Harvey appeared beside them, panting like he'd run a marathon.

Everyone was staring, wary. Everyone gave them space and waited for Harvey to come to them. The man looked exhausted.

Until Weiz saw him. Then she came running, pushing past everyone to get to her man. He thought it would probably be some tender and embarrassing moment that he'd rather not witness, but instead, the Commander stopped in front of him, planted her hands on her hips and demanded, "John Harvey, where have you been?"

CHAPTER TWENTY-NINE

Harvey looked at Weiz with a deep tiredness that he felt in his bones after transporting so many people. He didn't know how long he'd been gone. The way she stared him down now, he wondered how many days in a row she'd been using her powers. She looked slightly unbalanced, and he wasn't sure he wanted to have that kind of conversation with her.

"Well?" The word was a barked demand. "Did you hear me? Where have you been?"

"I heard you," he breathed out as a sigh. "Don't want to let me get my bearings first?"

"Who are all these people? Where did they come from? Why were you with them?"

Harvey shook his head, raised his hands, and turned his back on her. He wasn't in the mood to deal with it, and he knew that those he'd brought with him would be very confused. They'd been let out of stasis by Liam, and they were familiar with the man, but they didn't know him. They had no obligation to stick around, and they may not want to, but he had given his word. He wondered how many of them were likely to cause problems for them, and how many would want to help.

With a will, he ignored Weiz as she continued some kind of tirade behind him, and someone else coaxed her into moving away. He was grateful to whomever was willing to suffer the woman's wrath.

He looked at all those he'd brought with him, and they all looked to him. Liam had filled them in, and they had probably known Anselin. They'd want to know why and how he had the man's power.

"Liam told you all what we're going to try and do here," he said after a moment. "But truthfully, I cannot make you stay. I don't know what your powers are, I don't know whether you want to keep them. I don't know how much time has truly passed for you as it did for those who were left here." He looked them all over, and it seemed every one of them desired to hear him out before staying or taking their leave.

"I don't know your names, your stories, your life before. None of us here knows anything about you, and you know nothing about us. So that means, trust without earning it. We trust you to stay. You need to trust us to get this done."

No one said anything, moved or asked a question. It was a little eerie. Like they were still in stasis, unable to move. He was running out of anything useful to say.

"If any of you are scientists, look for Deidra, she may be able to use your help." He shrugged. But as he turned to move away, and finally deal with Weiz, one of the women from the front spoke up.

"Do you have clothes?" she asked, looking around at the bare wilderness. "I mean no disrespect, I am very grateful to be out of that tube. But I, uh, I don't relish the thought of being half naked in public for any length of time."

Seemed the woman was a spokesperson for the rest, as the others turned and looked at each other with murmurs of agreement. They looked to him expectantly.

"We might have some," he replied. "But not enough for all of you, unfortunately."

"Women first," said one of the men, stepping forward. "Do you have enough for all the women?"

Harvey counted out the women with his eyes. They were not a fifty-fifty split, the women numbering only eleven. He gave a nod. "We should," he said.

"We'll wait," the man replied.

Harvey supposed that at some point he should ask for their names. He was fairly terrible at that.

The first person he saw who'd kept a respectful distance was Deidra. In a way, he supposed it was fitting. Directly behind her was Lance. "I think a few people are going to have to sacrifice their change of clothing," he told Lance. "Go find me some volunteers, will you?"

Lance gave him a look, but didn't argue, just turned and made his way toward the others, clustered about each other and looking on.

Harvey turned his attention to Deidra. "Who are these people?" she asked in a quiet voice.

"Giants kept in stasis for thousands of years," he told her. "I don't know how well put together they might be." He tapped the side of his head meaningfully.

She seemed to listen to something in her head, to which she nodded, then she indicated the crowd behind him and asked, "May I?"

He moved aside and gave a sweeping gesture. "Be my guest," he replied. "I think I should probably go get things sorted with Catherine. If I don't tell her the whole story first, then I fear bad things may come."

"Try not to be too hard on her," Deidra defended. "She just cares, that's all."

He nodded but didn't respond. He didn't know what to say to that.

The place was a little different to the last time he'd been there, but he did recognise it as the field. They'd used the barricades for shelter like he'd suggested, and a little off to the side he saw logs and wooden slats. Weiz was with Gordon over by the latter, and he steeled himself as he made his way over.

When Gordon saw him coming, she said something to Weiz and moved away before Harvey could so much as say hello. He didn't blame her.

He stopped two feet away and looked down on where she sat, as she stubbornly kept her eyes from him.

"Give it up Catherine, you aren't a child," he said. He felt bad, but he also knew it was the sort of thing to get her attention.

She looked up at him with fire in her eyes and replied between clenched teeth. "I thought you didn't want to talk to me."

He shook his head. So, it was going to be one of those talks. She'd been using her power too much, and he needed to be a little less abrasive than usual.

"Get up please, so we can talk face to face."

Weiz shook her head, and he breathed a sigh. "Why don't you just sit?" she asked in turn.

"Fine," he replied and let himself fall into a cross-legged position in front of her.

He stared at her. Without a word, without much of a thought in mind. He just stared, until she shifted in place and said, "Where were you?"

"I was in stasis on one of their ships," he responded.

"How did you get there? How did they get you?"

Harvey shrugged uncomfortably and squinted at the sky. "I don't know," was his honest answer. "I took Rochelle home, left her there, came back and spoke to you. Everything after that and before conscious stasis... I suspect that however they managed to get me, involved a hefty whack to the back of the head."

"You've been gone for weeks," she told him through tears of anger and relief. "I thought I was never going to see you again."

"But here I am." He spread his arms wide, and she looked at him with some consideration.

"Here is where standing would have been better," she said drily.

He shrugged and stood. "I didn't want to say I told you so," he started. But before he could finish, she was up and in his arms, sobbing like a child. This was the part that he had to deal with while she held her powers. If they were all lucky, Deidra would know what to do, and have them all out of their soon.

~

Deidra stood watching the new arrivals talk quietly amongst themselves. She tried to keep a respectful distance but didn't hide the fact that she was curious. There was a part of her that knew these people. And she was not being quiet about it, no matter how much Deidra tried to shove her down.

Why are you trying to shove me down? I can help with this, and you know it, Tatiana said.

It doesn't feel fair, Deidra replied inside her own mind. *It's not really for me to know without their permission.*

Nonsense, Tatiana asserted. *If you have my power, which of course you do, they are going to expect you to know. And they understand the journey I went through in my own mind first to lose myself and then find myself with knowledge inside.*

And that is how you help me from losing myself?

Without it, I fear it may have taken you at least another three or four hundred years.

Fine then, Deidra acceded.

So go talk to them! Tatiana demanded. *I can't control your body, much as I would like to at times.*

Deidra shook her off and started moving, feeling very glad that the woman *couldn't* control her. She'd never even considered the possibility before.

She saw Lance just ahead of her, a few others trailing him, all carrying piles of clothing. Maybe she should wait? *No,* she growled at herself. *You are not an easy person to live with,* she told the voice in her head.

Neither are you, Tatiana returned. *Just do it. Speak to them. They won't mind.*

Deidra watched as the clothes were delivered to some grateful women who started donning them immediately. While the men looked on longingly, they didn't ask for any. Once Lance and the others started moving away, Deidra stepped forward to address the man who had acted as their leader.

"Madresson," she said as she approached, and he snapped around to give her his full attention, eyes wary.

"Do I know you?" he asked.

"Tatiana," she replied simply with a tap on the head.

The man gave a nod of understanding, looked at the others, then seemed to decide something and took her off to the side.

They spent some time discussing what had happened since Deidra had come onto the scene. She filled him in on all she knew regarding the Bahanians, who were their own people now and no longer some derivation of the Enatwa. She told him all Tatiana told her to say about what had happened since he was captured. All of which was news to her as well.

When she was done, Madresson told her of what it was like in stasis. Of Liam and how he had helped them to stay as sane as possible, by speaking to them and helping them create worlds in which they could live. Tatiana had such deep feelings upon hearing his name that Deidra almost burst into tears, though she didn't say why. Deidra told Madresson, and he filled her in. Liam had been her life mate, though her memory loss prevented them from carrying on after she'd become infected.

All filled in for the moment, they stood staring at each other trying to find something else that was relevant.

"So, what next for you?" she asked at last.

"Liam told us you'd take our powers away," he said.

"And you're fine with that?"

"I spent a long time in a world that wasn't real. If staying in this one means never using my powers again, and dying in the normal span of things, then I am all in."

Deidra gave a slow nod. "Well, I am working on it, I am not there, yet. Lance is going to try and do it a more direct way, but I have a feeling it's not going to work."

"I don't know who Lance is," Madresson said, looking off toward the crew. "But give him a chance. Sometimes answers come from strange places."

"Well, I'll let you and yours talk among yourselves and decide on what you want to do, where you want to stay," Deidra said. "If any among you are scientists, please come see me. Or if you want to try Lance's method go see him."

Madresson gave a short sharp single nod. "And if any decide to leave, I'll let you know personally."

Deidra moved away feeling no better about the situation than she had when they'd first arrived. They were like a portent of something larger. Something she felt the need to be afraid of.

Don't be ridiculous. We'll work this out, and everyone will be fine, Tatiana tried to assure her.

"You're in my head but you don't know that I am worried who might be chasing that lot," she mumbled under her breath.

It wouldn't matter if anyone was, since we made it so they can't land. Can't even get close.

Deidra ceded the point without argument and returned to her scientists. After what Lance had said about them not understanding the math, she thought perhaps a different approach was going to be necessary.

After only six months, that felt like several lifetimes to her, they were finally all on the same side and ready to go home. She thought of everything they had been through, and everything they'd done. It had all been in an effort to reach that one goal — go home. Alive.

And now their powers were tamed. The natives largely left them alone, and the Bahanians could not get to them. It was close to over, and the last part was up to her. She even had faith that Greenway would return at some point. The optimism that was building felt almost alien.

They were going home.

Epilogue

Lance looked out through the same window he'd looked out every morning for the last few hundred years, at a sunrise that came over a mountain and painted the horizon orange and red. He'd stopped counting the years decades ago, and it was difficult for him to remember what life had been like as a pilot back on Earth. What had happened all those years ago, that had trapped them in a life of Magic and boredom.

He had tried and failed, several times, to simply give his power back to the world. Even tried to kill himself to get it done. A sacrifice to see if it was even an option. But it hadn't worked. Obviously.

Deidra spent years trying to reverse their 'condition', to give the powers back into the world, to the atmosphere, to whatever it was that had done it to the original Giants. But nothing worked, and even though she'd learned how to channel her knowledge and remain herself — for the most part — she'd run out of ideas within a few decades, and decided to spend what remaining time she could with Dane before he died of old age. One of her experiments had some interesting consequences, though. A development he liked to keep an eye on from time to time, in case something came of it. Somehow they seemed to spread the powers in a way that meant the natives would occasionally be born with some measure of it, even if it wasn't to the same degree. And they didn't share the immortality. Maybe there was a clue there, and they just had to be patient.

Weiz and Harvey got married, as if anyone was ever in any doubt of that. Though they had a rocky start while Harvey came to terms with the fact he would never see his son again, and Weiz tried to manage the emotional consequence of her power, they made it work. After a few years they started their own family, two sons and a daughter. It was obvious, after thirty years or so, that those children did not inherit their immortality. Their second son, Miles, died after being thrown from his horse and headbutting a jagged boulder. They waited for days at the field, but he never arrived. They buried him after two weeks, still hoping, but they knew. A few years later, Thomas, their older son, started to show signs of age. He had a wife, from one of the villages, and they lived there without interference from his parents. He had six children of his own, and seventeen grandchildren. He died at the age of eighty-six. Their daughter, Veronika, stayed with them in their little God Conclave, and had an on again off again relationship with Nadia, the daughter of Emosette and Dionun, two of the original Giants that had been aboard the ships in stasis. She died at seventy-two with no family except her parents, and those who stayed.

Kristin and Estard got married. It seemed an odd match from the outside, but they came to know each other as if each were a mere extension of the other, and any who interacted with them could see it. Though Lance had been a little jealous at first, he came to realise it was for the best, when he ended up with Ellis. It took them years to finally give into it, but they made a strong go of it before Ellis decided that she wanted to give her power up to their son, Charlie, and he was willing to take it. It had been a hard time for Lance, and he'd withdrawn some, but his son understood and let him take the time. It wasn't that he wouldn't have done anything for his son, indeed, he would have given up his own power to keep him around. But after more than a hundred years, Ellis had simply had enough, and wanted an end, one way or another. If they'd not had Charlie, Lance thought she would have found someone else's child to give it to.

Some of the Originals took a page from Ellis' book, and arrangements were made to pass on their power, either to their own children, or someone else's.

And Greenway never came back. They often speculated about what had happened to him, and sometimes Harvey and a few others would go looking, if only to be sure his early madness was never repeated. But the day he engaged the core was the last anyone heard from him.

After about a hundred years living near the mountain Greenway had made, which they dubbed the ship graveyard, they realised that the pulse they'd created effectively prevented the emergence of tech on the planet, which was both a blessing and a curse. It meant that the Bahanians could not return, but it also made it nearly impossible for Deidra to design anything that could actually be useful to them. Though she did manage, with the assistance of Weiz and Harvey, to create a system of portals that could be used by anyone, which moved through all six worlds — including Bahana. Lance had not seen the sense in it, but the rest seemed to enjoy the freedom it gave them. Several even tried to infiltrate Bahana, but though they found civilian life there to be interesting, they never came close to the organisation responsible for sending the ships. There were several countries, with different languages and cultures, much like earth, and people enjoyed their time there as a vacation. But no one was ever game enough to stay long, in case those who knew what they were, tried something. With the exception of Harvey, none of their powers worked on that planet, and they would have been sitting ducks.

They all finally agreed to move to a planet they called The Emptiness. It was the only uninhabited planet, they knew after Harvey had done a thorough survey of them all. It was semi desolate. There were signs of a previous civilisation all over the place, and Deidra, after several years of travelling and testing, told them it was something they'd done to themselves, though she never said exactly what. Lance wasn't sure she knew.

Gordon wrote a holy text, of sorts, to be left on Eridu, to instruct the inhabitants on the Giants. What they were, how they functioned, the lineage of some of their children who had stayed. She didn't give it to them, just left it somewhere it might one day be found by an enquiring mind. Lance wasn't sure anyone had ever found it, because he'd refused to go back. Refused to leave The Emptiness. He didn't want to meet anyone else that he knew was going to die before he could blink.

With a heavy sigh, Lance turned back to look at those seated around the kitchen table. All the people he'd left Earth with, minus Xavier — a name he hadn't thought of in so long, its presence in his mind jolted him a moment. None of them had aged a day, and despite their unusually long lives, they all appeared happy and at peace with their situation. But they were there for a reason.

Kristin squeezed Estard's hand atop the table and gave Lance a sad look as he came to join them.

"How sure are you?" Weiz asked Kristin. Strange as it seemed, they'd actually managed to become friends.

"As sure as I always am when I have these visions," she told the woman.

"Do we try to do something about it? Or..." Harvey lifted his hands, seeming to search for alternatives.

Estard and Kristin exchanged glances with Gordon, who nodded and spoke. "I've been compiling a book of these visions. The ones about Eridu. We plan to make a few copies and take them to some of the larger towns. Give them a fighting chance."

Lance breathed a sigh. "So we stay out of it, essentially." He was both relieved and concerned. If the Bahanians were once again becoming a bane on the lives of people with powers, even if the circumstances were very different, then he felt some obligation to do something. Though what that something might be, he couldn't say.

"They'll come to us," Kristin told him.

Harvey shook his head. "In all the years we've had the portals running, they've never once used them. And the ones who have a power like mine? They've never come here. At least, not anywhere in our vicinity. How will they even know how to find us?"

Kristin shrugged at him, and Estard put an arm around her shoulder. "It's part of the vision," the former Agent informed them. "We have to let them come to us."

"Do you have a timeline, at least?" Lance wanted to know.

Kristin made a gesture with her hand. "A few hundred years, maybe. The feeling is distant, but inevitable."

Weiz started to nod slowly. "Our part is largely over, but there are still consequences for what we left behind."

Harvey put a hand over hers on the table, and they shared an intimate look. "It's someone else's story, now," he told them. "Let them have it."

Deidra, who had said nothing until that moment, got up from the table. "I motion that we distribute the warning as proposed by Gordon, and remain faceless in the scheme of things. Those who agree, raise your hands."

It was unanimous, and quick. They didn't even need to look at each other. Seven people, seven hands. Harvey, Weiz, Kristin, Estard, Gordon, Deidra and Lance.

They stayed out of any planetary politics. Tried to stay out of view, for the most part. Some of them travelled the other planets from time to time, for a new experience, a change of scenery. But they did it as if they were normal people. Never drew any kind of attention to themselves. Not even on Eridu, where they could use some of their powers without anyone asking questions.

Lance swung his feet onto the spare chair by Kristin, and nodded along to a conversation he wasn't really listening to. They hadn't gotten home, but after a hundred years or so, it didn't matter any more. Life had moved on without them, and they'd made a new home with each other.

ABOUT THE AUTHOR

Lee was born and raised in Sydney Australia. Prefers cats over dogs, coffee over tea, and cars over bikes. She also thinks the biography section of the book is a little strange.